MW00532743

the alternatives

ALSO BY CAOILINN HUGHES

Orchid & the Wasp

The Wild Laughter

the alternatives

caoilinn hughes

RIVERHEAD BOOKS • NEW YORK • 2024

RIVERHEAD BOOKS
An imprint of Penguin Random House LLC
penguinrandomhouse.com

Library of Congress Cataloging-in-Publication Data

Names: Hughes, Caoilinn, 1985- author.
Title: The alternatives / Caoilinn Hughes.
Description: New York : Riverhead Books, 2024.
Identifiers: LCCN 2023028166 (print) | LCCN 2023028167 (ebook) |
ISBN 9780593545003 (hardcover) | ISBN 9780593545027 (ebook)
Subjects: LCSH: Sisters—Fiction. | LCGFT: Novels.
Classification: LCC PR6108.U3885 A79 2024 (print) |
LCC PR6108.U3885 (ebook) | DDC 823/.92—dc23/eng/20231016
LC record available at https://lccn.loc.gov/2023028166
LC ebook record available at https://lccn.loc.gov/2023028167

Printed in the United States of America
1st Printing

Book design by Alexis Farabaugh

part one

1.

The air is mild for October. Nothing shivers. Nothing smokes. A gentle westerly whistles at the panes of the lab windows like an unwelcome uncle, determined to raise the hairs on some young neck. Twenty necks bend to observe the experiment: a Perspex prism known as the "squeeze-box"—the size of a narrow aquarium—is filled with thin layers of colored sand. The ends of the box are movable, so that its contents can be compressed to demonstrate the effects of tectonic convergence.

Thrusts. Faults. Folds. Belts. Excuse me. Olwen presses a fist to her mouth to stifle a burp, and a few students snicker. Lo and behold: geologic processes for the puny human attention span.

There is something very bodily about Olwen Flattery that the undergraduates find wildly amusing. Moments earlier, she'd used a shard of slate to scratch her inner elbow psoriasis, and a puff of dead skin particles danced visibly in the ventilation. She placed the shard back in its tray and, with her chalky fingers, lifted out a teeny-tiny sanitized kidney stone for the undergraduates' scrutiny. *Moving* this kidney stone involved a person's hospitalization, she tells them. *Just imagine* the force it would take to move a mountain! And we're not talking about violent, sudden processes, like an earthquake shouldering up a mountain range. No. These forces are so incremental and immense, so imperceivable and unstoppable, that there's no halting their progress.

They're underway right now, as we stand here, on the shifting foundations of this institute.

The students scan their pals for clues as to how to feel. They have learned to take what levity they can from these light and flaky moments, as Olwen's lectures so far have been something of a shock wave.

We're a wreck, she says. Ireland is one big crash site, where the ancient continents Laurentia and Gondwana collided like two humungous cruise liners . . . long before the nouveau riche were evolved to populate them. The wreckage cuts stupendously across this island, from Dingle in the west to Clogherhead in the east. The island was underwater back then, so that story didn't make itself known for millions of years. And here we stand, sifting through the evidence of that collision in our desk organizers, all of us above sea level . . . for another decade or two, anyways.

Several students begin to agitate in the pause that follows. It's hard to read the undergraduates—to know what's getting through, what with the scarves cobra'd around their mouths and their minimal eye contact. They all seem hungover, or stoned, or just returned from a silent monastery meditation retreat in Bali they spent their loans on. But they also seem deeply unnerved, and it's not paranoia.

How information is delivered seems to be more consequential than the information itself, Olwen thinks. She is losing her strength to hand it over gently. But a teacherly muscle memory prompts her now—having pushed—to pull:

Have any of ye seen it?

She makes eye contact with each student in turn, in case—as first-years—they need drawing out. Shawna, an exchange student with the gall of a parking enforcement officer, asks:

Is it here in Galway? Because car rental in this country is a joke.

It's not in the immediate vicinity, Shawna, but—

I saw the Rock of Gibraltar, Eric offers out of nowhere—a very tall student, with asteroidal confidence.

Olwen hears the clock on the wall tick forward a cluster of seconds all in one go, like heart palpitations: harmless, but horrible. If you tell me you *flew* down to see the Rock of Gibraltar, Eric, when you haven't taken a *bus* to Dingle to ogle our own monumental bodies of rock . . .

In the pause that follows, Eric takes a seat and runs his fingers through his gelled hair, leaving striations that seem almost infrastructural, as if water might collect in them. Olwen is grateful when Fionnuala—not technically a mature student, but she has a lot of cop-on—cuts in with something likely to be relevant:

I went to Edinburgh during the summer—

For the festival? Geraldine clenches with envy.

Yeah, says Fionnuala, but we took a day trip to Siccar Point. She glances at Olwen.

You did not! Olwen replaces a chunk of granite she'd been using as a stress ball back in the specimen tray, readying herself to shake Fionnuala's hand.

Fionnuala smiles. It was a little tricky . . . to get out onto the rock. But it was worth it.

Olwen looks around the group. Does anyone know what historic expedition Fionnuala was honoring, trekking out to Siccar Point on Scotland's weather-battered coast, when she could've stayed in Edinburgh town to watch Shit-faced Shakespeare?

Everyone laughs a bit, releasing some pressure.

Do you want to say, Fionnuala, what you saw there? And who saw it first!

Fionnuala pulls at a mini harmonica pendant, traveling it back and forth along the necklace chain. By the end of year one, Olwen will count herself a failure if she hasn't replaced that pendant with a hand lens.

Fionnuala acts a touch more flustered than she is: Em . . . so, James Hutton, I guess back in the seventeen hundreds? Found these rock formations. These really crazy layered rocks, kind of like pastry . . . or maybe I just associate Scotland with pastry!

Sedimentary rock, like the strata of colored sands—Olwen gestures—in our squeeze-box experiment.

Exactly, yeah. There were horizontal layers like that, and vertical sections too . . . side by side, or on top of one another, at right angles. And the vertical rocks and the horizontal formed in totally different ways, in different time periods. And Hutton basically looked at them and instantly understood plate tectonics. Or a theory that led to it? Or . . . was it just that he knew that the center of the earth was molten rock, and that that was how new land was made? Instead of, you know, God making it. Fionnuala keeps glancing to Olwen for confirmation. Because before that, she presses on, he could see erosion happening and couldn't understand how all land hadn't been just . . . washed away by the weather. Like, how was there anything left? And the only explanation anyone knew for new land was God. But when Hutton saw those rocks, he knew they were evidence that the earth was *billions* of years old, instead of thousands. Because the formations would've taken . . . yeah, a really, *really* long time!

At Fionnuala's unsure expression, Olwen nods with the restrained pride of a surgeon confirming that they got it all, that the patient has plenty of life ahead. She points to a laminated poster on the wall labeled Geologic Time Scale, which breaks the history of the planet into units of time, from lengthiest to briefest. The unit of time you're talking about, she says, for a really, *really* long time, is an *eon*.

Geraldine, with a cynicism out of sync with the affirmative badges on her backpack, says: What's the bet Hutton didn't publish his theories 'cause he was afraid of the pope?

He did one better than publish his theory, Olwen says levelly. He published *findings*. First, he went cantering up the highlands to find irrefutable evidence to bear the theory out. Physiological manifestations. Brute facts. He found his proof at the meeting point of two rivers, where pink granite—igneous rock, intrusive rock, spewed up as magma and cooled slowly—was mingled like cream in a soup of gray sandstone, sedimentary rock, accumulated over time on an ancient seabed. *Thusly*—as last year's undergraduates loved to say—Hutton was able to throw the Judeo-Christian chronology of the earth out the lab window.

With a leery expression and a briny smell, Geraldine wafts the damp hooded towel she wears as a cape to help it dry from her morning sea swim. I'm pretty sure non-Western cultures knew the earth was billions of years old before some . . . equestrian Scot in a ruff.

That is a fabulous topic for a dissertation, Geraldine. I'm not the expert you want for that, but call in to me during office hours and we'll talk interdisciplinary options. Olwen waits until Geraldine nods. I'd take a guess, though, Olwen says then; I'd take a *guess* . . . that a few of them cultural theories, about cycles and eternity, involve higher powers. And Hutton's point was that no higher power was needed to create dramatic landscapes of deposition and compaction. An active fault is a great rejuvenator. The earth is in a continual geological process of destruction and repair, destruction and repair, as long as there's still heat at the heart of it. As long as we stay near enough the sun, which drives so much surface geology. But before ye go thinking the destruction around us is part of a natural process . . . Oil took *millions* of years to accrue, till we started boring holes in rocks and throwing in matches. And now, in under two hundred years, we've burned up *nearly all* of it. Europe's endemic forests took *millennia* to flourish. In five thousand years, we've destroyed ninety-nine percent of them. In Ireland, we went the full hundred. And soil! Ye know soil? That's been around for a while. Until we discovered the burger. We ruin a lot of soil to grow a burger. If we keep up our hijinks, we have fifty years of farming left.

A student at the back holds up his watch and calls time of death for the class. He is alternately shushed and supported by those around him. Had that been too much, too soon? A mood ring changes color on Fionnuala's finger as she tries to prize it past the knuckle, unsuccessfully. Olwen had one of those once, an eighteenth-birthday present from one of her sisters, along with the note: "This is a mood ring. If it's mostly blue on you, it's not broken. I stole it so you can't return it sorry.

Love you. Maeve." Olwen had heeded its warning—that she needed to do better at seeming buoyant to her sisters, whose guardian she had suddenly become. She wore the ring with the stone turned toward her palm.

She tries again:

Hutton showed us that we can read the landscape like a book, if we know the language. Its story begins a long, long time ago—or a really, *really* long time ago, she says, with a wink at Fionnuala. The girl is kind enough to smile, as at a rose seller, without buying the romance.

Let's fast-forward, so. Geraldine: take a firm hold of that handle and give a push at my signal, will you? Olwen stands ready at the other end of the squeeze-box. An Italian student called Luca asks if he can film the experiment. Olwen briefly delights in the idea—envisions the video being slow-mo'd and replayed repeatedly—but then, they're already so far removed from the earth, here on campus; another lens will only remove them further from physical reality. Isn't her job to minimize that distance? To solidify reality, with all its unendurable stresses?

Who can tell me what Luca is really looking at when he looks at that screen? she asks. And don't say anything smutty!

Luca's eyes dart leftward to his posse. Being first-years, their friendships are tentative. A few of them pull faces, implying an in-joke that probably doesn't exist. They shift back and forth like so many pairs of jeans being riffled on a clothes rack. Fionnuala, also bejeaned, troubles the wheels of her wheelchair and says, Electrons?

Olwen pouts at the vinyl floor to think about this for a moment. Actually, she says, that's not wrong. You're taking physics, Fionnuala? Don't let Dr. Brearton get spooked by the new safety regulations, and keep it all tidily on the page. If he's on form, he'll be injured by study week. She clicks her tongue. They'd have told Nikola Tesla to put manners on the sparks flying. Giddy murmuring spreads in response to this, but it seems to be prompted by the mention of study week, not about her call to pedagogical panache. The students do tend to focus on the wrong measurements—grades, likes, bits per second. Hours remaining. Olwen tries not to feel let down: they're the ones who have been let down, she knows too well, and yet she has to remind herself.

The answer I was after? About Luca and his phone? She pans the room for something glinty. The answer, young scholars, is rocks. (A few students sit up straighter at this new title: *scholars*.) Luca holds in his fist seventy-five of the one hundred and eighteen elements known to man, she says. There are more elements in that phone than there are in Luca's body. Fancy rocks. Rocks plus time. Carbon carbon carbon. And every text message involves more of it. Where would we be without it? We're Stone Age people still. We only have tooth whitening kits and Duolingo to mark us out as modern.

Ahh . . . it's okay? Luca asks, his brow scrunched. To make a film?

Olwen nods and turns to Geraldine, still grasping the handle of the squeeze-box with admirable fortitude. We have lights, we have a camera. We have the means to speed up geologic time. Let's observe how a seabed deforms under the pressure of a drifting continent. Let's close the ocean.

All twenty students crowd in, aggregating their odors like a chemistry experiment. As both ends are pushed, compressing the sand rainbow inside, someone whispers, *ASMR gold!* Olwen knows this has something to do with porn. She wouldn't object to a bit more gasping. Now. *See* how the folds are—

A scream rips into the room from the hallway. Olwen halts midsentence. Geraldine stops the compression. All twenty heads turn to the door. Another scream explodes right outside their lab. An awful, throat-shredding scream—not of panic or terror, exactly, or even bodily pain . . .

Stay where you are, Olwen says, and marches to the door.

What's she *doing*? Shawna says. She needs to *lock the door*! Help me block the entrance! Shawna directs a few classmates to lift a table by its ends.

Stop that! Olwen says, turning back to the class. It's not— You're not in danger. I mean, you *are* . . . but not from *this*. I know what this is. As she addresses them, another penetrating scream describes itself as plain, brutal torment. Do this poor lad a favor and stay put, she says, closing the door after her.

In the corridor, several doors are open, as teachers and students peer out to see what's going on. A few people crowd around a young man who is gurning on the floor, his hands knuckled at his chest like a city pigeon's claws. He is dry-eyed and ashen. He doesn't seem to register Olwen as she kneels beside him, removing her cardigan to tuck it beneath his head. All right, buddy, she says. His body is so clenched and rigid with the effort of screaming that his head is several inches off the ground, making it easy to slot the cardigan underneath. She tells him she's phoning his support person—she'd saved the number as Screamer Support—and while she's waiting for the call to connect, she urges people back to their classrooms. Some students have their fingers in their ears. He'll be fine, she says. It'll pass. The support person answers, and in no time she's hurrying down the hall, throwing her braids behind her shoulder in a gesture of sorry habitude. Thanking Olwen, she returns her cardigan and cradles the young man's skull with her palm. Olwen had seen her do that before and thought it was to stop his head from banging, but it must be for some other reason. Of course. It's not epilepsy. It can't be so easily relieved with material or chemical or logical cushioning: there is only the preverbal clutch; the hold; the exhausted, eventual submission. Olwen is still kneeling there as the support person speaks quietly and slowly—saying his name, then counting to ten, saying his name, counting to ten. Students from another class, having collected their belongings, file past him funereally.

Olwen had first witnessed this boy in the spring, and since then she's thought of him often. The involuntary screaming struck her as reasonable: a mind responding to its overwhelmed environment, like the atmosphere expressing its excess heat through storms, sea surges, torrents, pissy showers. Here he is screaming out a cyclone, bursting his young blood vessels. He's a second-year now. Fair dues to that perseverance.

No cause for panic, Olwen tells her class upon her return. He's in good hands. Try to block it out. Or imagine it's the drama students!

A lot of respiratory sounds come back at her in protest. Some confused questions. Is it Tourette's? Is he psychotic? In between the screams, Olwen insists: His distress is the same as yours or mine. Just, the vocalization is a nuisance for him. But he's used to it. It's not the first time. He has his support person with him now. It's better for him if we ignore it. The undergraduates are frowning, milling about like waiters at closing time, but Olwen powers through her own designated happy hour. She looks to the squeeze-box, but it can't be reset. The damage has been done. Now, she says, will we watch the experiment back on Luca's phone? Ye were distracted. When you see one of these grand structures in real life, I want ye to be able to knock yerselves sideways with your powers of identification, to have no doubt in your minds as to whether—

The screaming redoubles, and the whole group flinches.

I'm leaving! Shawna pageants her satchel strap over her head and across her torso.

Ah, Shawna. Stay. It's temporary. All this is fleeting! That's the point! We have to—

Another scream tears through their exchange. Without waiting for it to end, Shawna utters a strained laugh as she exits. A pal of hers retrieves her backpack and apologetically sidles doorward. Someone suggests they switch rooms. No, Olwen says, we need the lab. The lab is where it's real. Where it's tactile and comprehensible. This is where we can test and observe what we learn in lectures and seminars. If I tried to book a new lab, we'd lose half an hour. We don't have that time to lose. The lad outside? *He* knows that.

Eric leans dangerously against a table of polarizing microscopes. Eh, Olwen? To be fair, we're not going to learn anything with someone spazzing out in the hall.

Don't use that word! a mature student called Anushka berates him. She glances unconsciously at Fionnuala, then blushes furiously.

Eric! Olwen plants her fists onto her hips. She's right. Don't say *spaz.* And more important: don't underestimate the value of your being here, whether you're learning or screaming or clenching yer sphincters. This may be the last time in your lives when your intentions are good and unambiguous. Your intentions here are to learn: to come to some degree of understanding and wisdom about the earth, how it got this way, where it's going. You cannot afford to lose a minute's worth of that intention. Do you get me, Eric?

Eric rolls out his lower lip in purplish consideration.

They should call an ambulance, someone says.

Luca watches the door as a bowler might watch a bowling ball course the gutter.

The undergraduates are a strange assembly. They are neither blameworthy nor are they culpable. They are neither capable nor are they rubbish. They do not put their confidence in anyone outside their own earthly realm or socioeconomic generation, nor do they have any general confidence in themselves. Already, Olwen likes them a lot. Their expressions of discomfort suggest that they cannot block out the screaming any more than Olwen can block out their discomfort. She sighs at them like a bus. One that had best take them somewhere.

An idea strikes her.

She sets her gaze on Fionnuala's wheelchair. What's the battery like on that thing? Would it take you five k and back?

Fionnuala tucks her chin to her chest. What . . . ten kilometers? Yeah. Unless I'm carrying groceries or collecting boulders or something. Why?

And it can manage earth? Not this manufactured stuff? She stamps her foot on the vinyl floor.

Fionnuala shrugs. It got me to Siccar Point.

Ah, you're going far! The rest of you: Do ye know the city bikes at the hospital? The Coca-Cola greenwashing bicycles? Thirty seconds' walk from here. Ye know them? We'll depart from there at—she checks her watch—ten past twelve sharp. We're going to use this next hour to put the notion of an hour in context.

We're going on a field trip? Geraldine asks.

One last shrill scream from the hall, timed like a bell. The class jolts into action. Coats are shrugged on. Bags are flung over shoulders. *Natura non constristatur*, lads! Olwen says, encouraged. Nobody asks where the field trip is to, she's glad to notice, or how long it'll take. They just pack up and make for the road.

. . .

Having retrieved her own bicycle from her office, Olwen is the first to arrive at the bike station. I've spare inner tubes, tire levers, Allen keys, and a pump, she tells Eric when he arrives, thinking he'll be the sort to go in for technical talk. Squinting, he points to his ear to indicate he's on the phone. She'd missed his earpods—like the ones her sister Rhona goes around in, so none of the world can get into her head, unless she permits it. A minute or two passes before anybody else turns up, so Olwen becomes invested in Eric's sales pitch. He works for a call-center startup that lets him clock in in five-minute increments via an app, which records calls while the app is in use. He offers to do some research and call the customer back, but his offer must be turned down, because the conversation ends with a note of defeat.

Were they stingy? Olwen asks.

No, Eric says. She actually had some valid concerns about our nuclear policy, and—

Who's *our*?

Greenpeace, he says, returning the earpods to their case.

Eric, you're full of surprises. Good on you, working for Greenpeace.

Nah, the client changes every week. Next week's Christian Aid. Last week was the AA Motoring Trust.

Olwen lets a loud lorry pass and tries not to exude as much gloom as it does. With that business head on you, why are you doing earth science?

Eric looks into the middle distance and spots a couple of classmates arriving. Olwen senses something alter in his demeanor, as if he's swapping out whatever he wants to say for an easier script.

It's like doing an arts degree, he says. Kind of a non-choice, but good for the soul. Or something?

Olwen thinks of Nell, her philosopher sister—sick, single, arts-degreed, adjuncting her thirties away, shuffleboarding between Connecticut campuses, without health insurance, if ostensibly happy—and she frowns at Eric. If it's apathy you're selling me, Eric, I'm not buying it. You're doing it for a reason, and you can't name the reason yet, and that's fine. At this, she sees a slight flush cross his face.

Fionnuala appears with a friend called Rachel: a sophisticated young one who likely plays the oboe or the French horn. Rachel's only exchanges with Olwen to date have been about humidity. Olwen glances at the sky—so low as to lend the outdoors a bunker quality—and hails the benefits of fresh air, particulate matter be damned. Olwen sizes up the piddling turnout: Fionnuala. Rachel. Eric. Geraldine. And an accident-prone lad called Berat, who could capably direct the rebuilding of a superconducting rock magnetometer, but who you wouldn't trust to catch the change handed to him at a till.

Berat, you know we're not insured for trips beyond the campus?

Berat nods. Once, when Olwen spotted him using the printer's industrial-grade stapler to mend a rip in his trousers, he offered up the apologetic information that his mother and brother had both taken out life insurance on him.

Technically this isn't class at all, she tells them. It's extracurricular. Entirely nonmandatory.

Berat clutches the bike at arm's length, his body and the bicycle forming a precarious triangle.

So, this is us. We six voyagers! I won't keep ye long. We'll just sneak in a few million years before lunchtime. We're going down past Blackrock Beach. It's three miles. Twenty minutes or thereabouts. And we'll ride on the pavement wherever there's no bike lanes, since we're not . . . insured, she says, glaring at Berat.

Geraldine suggests to Eric that she'd rather buy him a pint than support Coca-Cola, if he'll let her ride sidesaddle. It's a single-speed, Eric says flatly, and it's vintage. Geraldine turns to Berat and suggests that he let her ride his bike, and he can perch on the crossbar. He can sit comfortably on her towel-cape, she says, lifting off the cape to reveal a spaghetti-strap vest. It's all Berat can do to close his eyes and back onto the crossbar.

What doesn't kill them, Olwen thinks. It seems wrong, though, to voyage out with so few youngsters in tow. She sends a text to her partner's two sons: I'm with a few of the undergraduates on bikes. We'll be passing St. Enda's. If ye fancy mitching, be at the school gate in 9 mins flat. Then she mounts her bike. She doesn't check for a response, and the rest fall into line behind her. As they approach St. Enda's school, the two boys glide in out of nowhere to join the troupe, glancing back at their school with the giddy mortification of culprits.

This is Cian and Tommy, Olwen shouts. Now we'll have a job to keep up with them.

Cian is eight, and he wears the expression of someone who has just laid down a winning gin rummy hand. Tommy, ten, has the crestfallen posture of having overlooked a lot of cheating. They resemble their father in their freckles—a darker brown than their hair—and in their strappy physiques. Tommy has had a growth spurt, so his backpack looks reasonable, whereas Cian's is Sisyphean, and it's hard for Olwen not to try to relieve him of it, despite his mettle. They have their mother's amber eyes, so Olwen can't look at them without seeing their loss. Cian still has several baby teeth with cavities from the fizzy drinks relatives poured in ridiculous quantities while his father didn't have the heart to stop them. Despite their experience, they are both still children, and the undergraduates are wary of what their presence means for the ambitions of this outing, but they nod sociably.

As they descend Threadneedle Road, the ocean silvers up to them like a platter licked clean of hors d'oeuvres. The wind of an hour ago has died off completely, and to Olwen it feels as though they are moving through nothing. No weather. No atmospheric mass. No dark matter. The boys, she notices, are moving easily through the world, moving of their own accord. When did this happen? When did their grief change into something travelable? She no longer needs to lay her hands on their backs to push them through it.

At the end of the promenade, Olwen leads them onto a narrow path past Blackrock's diving board, populated by fluffy-lipped lads in threadbare boxers who lob one another into the water like scraps of bread. She leads her troupe along the coastal path, past a caravan park, and across a sandy inlet to a cliff. On the way, Fionnuala had insisted that they go right down to the base of the cliff instead of viewing it from afar. If Berat is willing to lose his fertility for the sake of this field trip, she said, being lifted a few meters is the least I can tolerate.

. . .

The bikes are now jetsam'd about the sand and shingle. Dry rotted seaweed exudes its pungent smell. The students sit and stand and hunker variously, their backs to the ocean. They crane their necks to scan the cliff for something field-trip-worthy. The cliff is barely more than a mound of compacted dirt, with none of the structural formations they'd been expecting. Cian has busied himself extracting tools from Olwen's field trip daypack: a geology compass, a rock chisel, an all-weather notebook, and pencils. He hands Tommy the compass charitably and keeps the hammer. Olwen plonks herself onto a limestone boulder and leans on her knees. She inhales deeply, rasping as if the air is full of grit she must strenuously filter. This is for effect, to put the younger people in a state of concern and care. Once she senses their attention fixed upon her, she collects a mop of seaweed, tears off an arm, and begins to pop its air bladders.

These make one new air bladder per year, she says. Like the rings of a tree. There's . . . seven, eight, nine, ten, *eleven* here. So this yoke is older than Cian and Tommy. Now. I'm going to ask a question. Don't say the answer, you two, okay? Only nod if ye can answer the following: Do ye know what *that* is, and how it got here?

The boys follow Olwen's gaze to the cliff and back again. Tommy nods. When Cian begins to say *It's*—, Tommy grunts at his brother, wide-eyed, and shakes his head exaggeratedly.

Of course ye do! Ye've a firm grasp of the world around ye. Olwen winks at Cian and then says, My dear University of Galway bachelor of earth science undergraduates: What is this landform, and how did it come to be?

A lot of frowns are exchanged. Geraldine mouths to Eric: It's a cliff, like!

Coastal erosion? Rachel says.

At least she didn't say humidity. Think bigger, Olwen says. Not the last spring tide, but the last geological epoch. Bear in mind, she tells them, Cian and Tommy know the answer, and they're younger than this seaweed.

Yeah, but come on, Eric says. Their mum's a scientist!

Well, actually, their mum was a florist, Olwen says. She ran her own business. Without needing to look, she can feel the boys' ease with these stated truths.

When she'd first met them four years ago, Jasper's sons had seemed like ruptured tires for which she could only offer a paltry repair kit; she had to be careful what terrain she steered them onto. When their handsome father caught Olwen staring at him in a Starbucks, she had blurted out: Nice plans for the day? We're going to Mass, Jasper said, gathering the boys into his shadow. To *Mass* . . . on a Tuesday? Olwen asked. You believe in something *all week long*? No, Jasper said, not at all, actually . . . but we thought we'd try sitting beside people who do. See if . . . And he'd trailed off. Their drinks were ready simultaneously, so Olwen pretended to be walking in the same direction. Passing the Spanish Arch, she showed the boys fossil evidence in its walls. This limestone is three hundred and fifty million years old, she said, running her palm along its flank as though it were roadkill, still warm.

Limestone's composed of organic remains. Amphibians, reptiles . . . human bodies! She flashed spooky eyes at the boys, but it was she who was spooked, by their wounded, haunted expressions.

But okay, Olwen says to the undergraduates, I won't pit the generations against each other. The conundrum we have before us is called a drumlin. A landform Ireland is famous for. From the Irish *droimnín*. Little hump. It's a record of a series of glaciations in Earth's history. An epoch called the Pleistocene. Right above our heads was ice heavier than you can fathom. Heavier than all the data centers on the planet, and all the freshwater we're ruining to cool them. Fionnuala: Would ice be lighter or heavier than water, if we're talking the same volume? Lighter. Thank you. Fionnuala is our resident physicist, she tells the boys in a whisper. Like Olwen, the boys haven't taken off their helmets; they are a team within a team. And no harm to be helmeted, as long as Berat keeps stacking stones into what might be a cairn—a landmark for someone who has lost their way. So! she continues. Twenty thousand years ago, the ice above our heads would have been home to woolly mammoths and giant beavers . . . until the planet warmed and the glaciations ended. When the last ice sheet was in melt phase, retreating northward, it sculpted this. She gestures to the drumlin. A hard boulder—likely granite—would've lain at the glacier's base, just *there*, and as the ice slid across the boulder, bits of debris fell off behind it. What was left was this kind of . . . boob shape. You see all that stuff—pebbles, cobbles, sediments held together in a matrix of sand and mud? All that fell off the glacier. To see it now is to be reminded that our balmy atmosphere is temporary. It would've been temporary *anyways*, mind, because ecosystems are dynamic. But nature would have let us have a few millennia yet, if we'd been chill and sound and reasonable. Instead, we've been needy, grabby, arsony narcissists.

The boys smirk at Olwen's curse adjacency—they know how she is when she gets into the swing of it, goes off on one—but the undergraduates are unsmiling. Why? Possibly because of that *we*.

We've fast-forwarded through the habitable-Earth episode, you see.

We're nearly at the closing credits. Processes that should take *millions* of years are playing out over centuries. Decades. We flush nitrogen-phosphate topsoil into the sea and strain the remaining soil for minerals like it's a teabag. We impound rivers and change the sediment flux. We push glaciers up and out of existence and acidify the oceans. We sign the depositional record as if it's a guest book at an Airbnb . . . after we've trashed the place. The drumlins *we'll* leave behind will be made of Lego astronauts and Kalashnikovs and radioactive chicken bones and Jesus-in-a-manger figurines. Olwen tosses the bladder wrack she'd been holding onto the smooth, weathered stones. What use are our powers of identification, I wonder, if a drumlin—overnight—becomes a slag heap? No wonder we overdo it on the afternoon gins.

A pair of gulls scream past, their radish eyes seeking out a sandwich. The boys trail them, but the undergraduates' attention is trained on Olwen. What can she feed them but the truth? Going by their vigilant expressions, they suspect it is spiked.

Rachel, the meteorologist in the making, clears her throat. Dr. Flattery?

Olwen.

Rachel clears her throat again. It feels like you're saying that we're—after glancing at the boys, she edits the adjective—a powerful species.

You don't need to say it *feels* that way, Olwen says. You know it. That's a well-observed and peer-reviewed fact. We're geomorphic agents, changing the earth more than all natural processes combined. More than *weather*! More—

And if we made all that destruction happen, Rachel says, doesn't that mean we can make a different sort of change happen?

Chatter breaks out among the students, about reforesting and de-growing and eating plants and electrifying. Olwen might have added *greased lightning!* to their chorus, but instead she looks to the sky, where those herring gulls are doing their darndest to make up for the invertebrate shortfall. Thirty years ago, when her baby sister Nell was a toddler and already obsessed with the sea and everything that lived by

it, there were ten such gulls for every one there is now. Once, they were
a force to be reckoned with.

Who remembers the Geologic Time Scale from the lab? Olwen asks.
What was the unit of time Fionnuala wanted for "really, *really* long"?

An *eon*, Fionnuala says, without missing a beat. The liquid crystals
in her mood ring have shifted with the temperature to an unsettled
orange.

That's the ticket, Olwen says. An eon. That's the biggie. Billions of
years long. One size down from an eon is an *era*. Hundreds of millions
of years. The Paleozoic Era lasted two hundred and ninety million
years, for example. Shorter than an era is a *period*. A period is tens of
millions of years. Last and least, the smallest unit of geologic time is an
epoch. Not tens of millions of years, but only a few million. The Pleistocene, also known as the Great Ice Age, was an epoch. And what we're
looking at, she says, nodding to the drumlin, is proof that it happened.

And now's the Anthropocene, Eric says, popping the calcium in his
knuckles for a small applause.

Berat mutters, What?

Eric says, It's a new period of time—

Epoch, Fionnuala interjects, and then covers her mouth. Sorry!

Geraldine cackles. Cian and Tommy skitter, too, at Eric's popcorn
knuckles.

Eric lifts his chin at Fionnuala. Cheers. It's a new epoch, brought
on by old people. Eric rolls out his lower lip again, this time more resigned than curious.

Go on, Olwen says. What else do you know about the Anthropocene?

Anthro means human, Eric says. Or Anthropo.

It's Greek, Geraldine says. It means *man*. And *cene* means *new*.

If Geraldine has ever seemed like a humanities scholar who'd had a
spliff and got lost in the corridor, she does now.

A tumbling sound draws everyone's attention to Berat, who'd been
engineering his hapless cairn and is now furtively nursing his shin.

We tipped the system, Eric says, standing up when his phone rings. His height makes the act of standing seem confrontational.

She's actually calling back, he says, looking to Olwen. Do you mind if I—

By all means! Olwen says, amazed. She shakes her fist in the air feebly. *Always be closing.*

The phone call saves her from challenging Eric with the fact that the Anthropocene hasn't yet been formally ratified by the International Commission on Stratigraphy; that some of her colleagues would insist that crediting humans with effecting an epoch is tantamount to gaslighting. Where do we get off, thinking we're so grand? Yes, we might be the agent of change between epochs, but we do not *constitute* an epoch. All we are is a boundary event. Olwen can feel the muscles around her mouth straining, like coastal infrastructure that won't hold much longer. For now, she doesn't situate this moment in deep time for them. She doesn't tell them how soon the drumlin they're studying will be underwater. How long before the ancient story written there will be lost.

Instead, she hears herself ask a ridiculous set of questions: Will we be a line in the rock, do ye think? A band of pandemonium in the squeeze-box? A chapter in the landscape for future earth science undergraduates to study . . . in the next era?

In the silence that follows, Olwen spies teenagerly expressions on Cian's and Tommy's faces. Had she used the wrong tone, for something that was meant to be an encouragement? Olwen pulls at her clothes to let in a bit of air, and says truthfully: A geology education from the nineties didn't prepare me for the fact I'd be taking my students to the beach in October, in spaghetti strap vests. If I'd known, I'd be on the floor in some hallway screaming too.

Rachel pivots to the boys, anxious at the doomy lessons. Her throat makes a popping sound, like a jar of pickles being opened, but Olwen gets her words out first. The ozone levels were stabilizing, she says, when I was a fresher. We were awful naïve.

Olwen scans her students to try to glean what's compacting their brows in this unfamiliar way. She had meant to expand them. To show them that death has always been part of life on this earth. Everything changes and dies. Their time might be brief, but that's all the more reason to be in it: this real, definite, reliable, incompressible, unquenchable Earth.

Cian has retrieved his lunch box from his pack. Olwen watches as he peels the tinfoil deftly from his sandwich so that it forms a tray beneath the fluffy white bread, then tucks his thumbs under the bread to lift it to his mouth. Absolutely everyone's eyes are on him, on the complex structural process. When a slice of pale orange cheese flops out of the ascending sandwich, Cian snaps his gaze skyward for gulls. Breathing heavily through his button nose, he lowers the sandwich back onto its foil. He collects the cheese from the ground, showers it clean with his squeezy water bottle, pats it dry on his jumper, then sets it back in the sandwich.

Tommy, who has been watching everyone watch his brother as if their grades depend on it, says: Can we go back to school now?

. . .

They do. Olwen's class disperses upon their return, and her afternoon is dizzy with pointless meetings. Disputes about the faculty's strategic plan to do this and that. Tension between the such-and-such subcommittee and the student advisory board. Collective mourning over a research grant whose rejection means the loss of several PhDs—a rejection that will return each researcher to their private, sheltered, performance-review-sufficient caves; a rejection that will moot further collaboration. Inertia is go! Olwen crows to her colleagues, summarizing the proceedings; they chortle but don't include it in the minutes.

The final meeting of the day begins as Olwen is switching off her office light to go home.

Do you have a minute?

It's her colleague Markus, whose shirt, gridded blue like graph paper, is untucked, indicating a major crisis. Olwen has the urge to take hold of his shirttail and play Xs and Os on it.

For you, Markus, I have a "hot minute," as my sister Nell tells me is a unit of time in America. Olwen recrosses the heat threshold of her office. The heat comes on automatically from the first of October, which was two days ago, and the college hasn't adjusted this for global warming, for fear of sparking fury among the fury opportunists. Speaking of which, she says, I was—

The comments are in from *Nature Geoscience*, Markus says.

Olwen scans his expression. Will you take a drink?

No, because I'll be pulling an all-nighter on the appeal. He hands her his phone.

Olwen reads the letter aloud in the Kent accent of the suspected editor:

> Thank you for submitting your manuscript to *Nature Geoscience*. Please accept my apologies for the delay in getting back to you, which was caused by recent staff changes. This delay is all the more regrettable as I am sorry to say that we cannot offer to publish your study.
>
> This manuscript, despite its quality, contains too much analytical work and scenario assessment to constitute a Comment or Perspective piece. It would be better considered as a research paper. The longitudinal data gathering is to be commended: such slow work can be systematically disincentivised, given the possibility of failing to arrive at statistical significance after two or three years, and the publishing outcomes often demanded by the academy.
>
> We do not doubt the significance of your findings on the reshaping and erosion of these three sites due to

climatic change. They certainly contribute to the Anthropocene and Great Acceleration debates. The scenarios analysed provide useful indications of potential trends.

However, we did view more sceptically your central argument, that erosion exacerbated by climatic change is disappearing the surficial geologic record. That while there is some regulation in the extractive industries to protect sites of geologic significance, there are no such measures or mitigation attempts to protect the geologic record being erased by the effects of climate change. While you provide indisputable evidence for this erasure, I am sorry to say that, in our view, this is not a problem in need of address. Rather, it is simply the creation of a new geologic record.

The material dispersal, drift, and dissolution of Quaternary landforms you cite as case studies are creating the record for future geologists. Yes, it will be a record that displaces previous records. But a flood-induced mudslide cannot be compared to the excavation of a quarry, as the former is a natural process. At the risk of oversimplification, the movement of earth surface materials is a straightforward matter of geology. What is happening to these materials—coastal decay, wetland extension, river basin spread, mountain range erosion, the extinction of lifeforms, and so on—will evidence the conditions of this geologic period/epoch.

For these reasons, we are unable to conclude that the paper provides the sort of significant conceptual advance in our understanding of geological processes that would be of immediate interest to a broad readership of researchers in the community. We feel that the manuscript would be better suited to a more specialised journal, whose readership would benefit from the detailed case studies and the novel methodology and modelling employed therein.

I hope you will understand that our decision in no way reflects any doubts about the quality of the work reported. I hope you will rapidly receive a more favourable response elsewhere.

Olwen opens a filing cabinet and takes out a couple of gin miniatures. She throws one to Markus, so that he can't refuse, and uncaps her own.

I love this stuff, she says after draining it. Beara Ocean Gin. It's almost saline. Marine science's finest.

Do you have time to talk through how to adapt it now? Sorry, but I won't sleep tonight otherwise.

No, she says after a pause. We won't be bothering with that.

I'm sorry?

Markus watches Olwen put on her helmet, clip the chinstrap, then tighten it. His own jaw hangs loose.

Try a lower-tier journal if you like, she says. Or rejig it to fit into parameters someone will like. By all means. Different set of reviewers. Softer terrain.

Markus shakes his head rapidly, as if to make the apple fall from it. I can't go a rung down! I need a top-tier publication this year. For tenure track. It's one of the criteria in my performance review. Not just a paper in submission, but *accepted*.

Glancing morosely at the light switch, Olwen sucks at her teeth.

We can protect the integrity of our research, she says, or you can play the game. You can duck and dive in whatever direction is beneficial. I'll have to leave you to it. I'm not feeling sporty.

• • •

Olwen now relays the events of the day to her partner, Jasper, the pair of them spinning slow circles on his office chair while rain hisses at the window in the navy blue evening. Jasper is a video editor and producer; his home office is an amphitheater of monitors and stage-lit glow.

Electro house music intz-gnnnnnz from the headphones around his neck. Olwen isn't one to sit on laps, but she'd spotted a flirty comment on one of his videos and teased him: OBSESSED. *Jasper you're an alchemist. I wish I could—* He'd wrestled her onto his lap and spun the two of them around so fast she couldn't finish reading the comment. There was no need to be coy about his admirers, she told him. He should avail himself of every chlamydia-free opportunity. Monogamy is an onomatopoeic word, she said—it's as boring as it sounds! But he'd shut her up with beardy, hungry kisses until both their heads spun. It had been easy for him to laugh off such suggestions four years ago, when they were first together, because he knew it was her way of telling him she wasn't trying to replace his dead wife. There could be no such thing. The last time she'd brought it up, he thanked her for the free pass but said he'd like to continue trusting his instinct—which was to love the fuck out of her exclusively, if that was okay—and that, no matter what, she should feel free to trust hers.

Now, with each slow rotation of the chair, they see each other in their window reflection. Olwen feels older than she is. Jasper looks older than he is. But he is so well recovered from when she met him, from when she first moved in. She can't but marvel at the absence of bruising on every inch of his skin, and in the vast majority of his anecdotes.

Tommy reckons your students are scared of you, Jasper says. He thinks it's the hammer you carry around. One of them nearly called social services—

Ah here!

—by the sounds of it—

You're the one who's making them cook dinner! Olwen slaps Jasper's face, quite hard, then kisses the bristly cheek. It feels of lichen.

Jasper presses his face into her neck. I hope we're stocked up on Gaviscon.

Guess what they're making? Olwen bites her lower lip.

What?

Baked beans and sausages with the packet potato farls. Jasper glances at one of his screens. Yum!

They've nearly stopped spinning when Jasper pushes off the ground again, and they swirl like a planet and its addict moon. He's happy with their trajectory. He is amazed every morning that the day seems like a possible project, that the turn of it proves fulfilling; he is amazed every evening when Olwen completes her steady orbital course only to be there again, drawn back to them, still. He doesn't feel the atmospheric drag, as Olwen does, or dwell on all the debris falling. She has tried to talk to him . . . but she doesn't want to undo the work they've done here. What would be the point, for her to see them through to this safety, only to declare it unlivable? She hears herself speaking, as if she's watching them from the threshold:

And I said to them: Would you not think of a vegetable? And Cian said: The sausages are made of vegetables! They're just brown 'cause it's all mixed together! *God* he's awful cute. And then Tommy got in a tizzy, saying *potatoes* are vegetables and beans are *too* he's pretty sure and they're in *tomato* sauce and it's *tomato* ketchup so basically *all* they're *cooking* is *vegetables*! Now . . . the fact is, he's less cute, but he's accurate.

Oof. The wrath of Tommy is the worst kind of wrath.

Don't I know, Olwen says. She breathes in deeply, considers their rate of deceleration on the chair. The wrath of Tommy belongs to the boy she'd heard about—the boy he'd been before she'd met him, before he was bereaved. It makes him sort of a stranger to Olwen now, but one she is very glad to have cooking her dinner.

The fire alarm hasn't gone off yet. Olwen sighs.

Jasper sniffs and rubs his nose. Well, I don't blame you having a drink after that day, he says. If I heard a screamer in the hall, I'd be with that American student, barricading the door.

Olwen thumps his arm. You would not.

I would! You're the first responder in this house. I'd push you through the door, then barricade it.

The room seems to bounce; Olwen realizes it's because she's laughing. She feels the warmth of Jasper's body as he reaches around her to respond to a producer's message on his screen. You won't bother with adapting the paper, then? he asks. Is it because they said it's just a research paper? Haven't you and Markus been at that one for months? You should appeal.

Freeing her arm from behind Jasper's head, Olwen turns to watch what he's typing. She sees a window full of tabulations; another, larger one, of steady work coming in, which he has the will to do; and more, she sees Jasper, sees that he is well. Her vision softens at this long-awaited scene. She moves around it, to capture its buttermilk glow. Then she turns her gaze to the real, rain-drizzled window, where their bodies are reflected as a Venn diagram.

It's not an adaptation they want, she mutters. It's concessions. As if we're politicians. She presses her brow, which feels mulchy. Quick-tempoed snare-heavy music bickers from his Bluetooth headphones. Jasper is thinking it's not like her not to retaliate. She can feel him think this. They've done all the hard graft! It was such a lot of work! They'd been meticulous. The findings are substantive. They should challenge it. How about an even bigger journal? *Science. PNAS.* As if to contradict him, she says: What's another research paper? What's another ten research papers, bent over backward? She hears the rattle of cutlery from the kitchen. Or is it the music? A sensation slides up her back, like a tide that slips in while you nap and wets your towel. When she gets to her feet, the feeling travels in the opposite direction. It had been his hands on her body, she realizes, wanting her to stay . . . wanting to make them eclipse one another. A lovely, obstructive phenomenon. Black flecks glint across her vision. Obsidian rapidly cooled.

She frowns. Do I smell burning?

• • •

Deep in the night, the whitewater noise of a sound machine keeps Jasper sleeping. Normally Olwen thinks it a shame to null the howly west coast weather, but tonight she's glad for the barrier the sound machine puts between her partner's peace and her own tossing wakefulness. She gets out of bed, pulls on layers of fresh, wrinkly clothes from the laundry, and pads around the house, getting the feel of the darkness. She won't turn on the lights. She wants neither to reignite the day that has been nor to start the new one. She does, though, want a drink. On the rocks! she says to the lamp, smacking its shade like a shoulder. She catches it before it falls. On the rocks, she says.

One freezer drawer is dedicated to chopped homegrown rhubarb. That had been Maeve, the chef, taught her that. She scoops into the rhubarb with a crystal tumbler and jiggles the glass for the dull, dulcifying *thuck*. Groping from the kitchen to the lounge drinks cabinet, she enjoys the hug of her woolen socks. There is nothing like a pair of snug-fitting, finely woven socks. Shoes, next. Nothing like having a pair of shoes on, and going somewhere in them. She was a little late in learning that herself. On account of having to keep her sisters alive. Ah, she'd done well. She'd done wonders. And it's been a while now, really. Long enough.

Her throat contracts at the cold gin as she pours it. Frozen rhubarb cracks and thickens in the glass. What with the sound machine, it's hard to know if the rain has stopped.

It hasn't.

Standing at the back door, she watches the suburban florescence make ash of the droplets. Rain comes down on everything, and everyone on the street has a vague sense of how it will go up again and down, up again and down, describing the guttering as gin describes a gullet. As to how it stays clean . . . we'd all confess ignorance. Ah, they're all fine without knowing. Aren't they? Olwen knocks back her drink and chews on it. The batch of rhubarb she'd planted had been a sour one. Those plants do better higher up. At altitude. Olwen browses the night for its pinnacle. Trees regulated to neighborly heights nod and shift around, perfectly spaced, perfectly orderly, their branches tucked in like guests who regret coming to the party. Olwen salutes them. She's brought the bottle to the threshold, she notices, so she re-fills and thinks of a toast. To ten more papers? she whimpers. She is panting, but she cannot see her breath.

Can we go back to school now? Tommy had asked. What presence of mind. What a gut! That boy has some knack for gauging when to step back from a patch of land . . . when a subsurface fault could cause it to subside.

En route through the bewildering house, a splash of gin into the glass to wash it of vegetable fibers. Before swallowing, she thinks to transfer it into a Thermos, then adds just a finger's worth or two, for the journey through the house to the garage, where she shuts herself in before flipping the light switch.

In the jumble of belongings and equipment, amid the suburban freight and affluence, slow as the lights are to illuminate what's there, Olwen sees almost at once what she's come for. Where to, now.

2.

Just in, Maeve—

See attached scanned letter direct from Sir Jeremy Charles!!!

We know asking for another event is above and beyond, but the team here feels it's so important to keep up the momentum with this relationship. I know you were concerned that the last event didn't do much for book sales but, at this stage, we feel it's more important to consider that relationships with such influential supporters could have a significant impact down the line, should book 3 go ahead. We really hope you're up for it, Maeve?! I don't want you to feel pressured but we do need to confirm with them by late afternoon. The party is for 13 people (2 gluten free, 1 pescatarian, 1 vegetarian, 1 pomegranate allergy (probably just an aversion tbh)) and the fee would match the last, all costs covered. So they've given you the go-ahead to really see what you can get your hands on in terms of produce.

What a treat!

Look forward to hearing.

Claire.

To Whom It May Concern,

It was my great pleasure to meet your Irish culinary star at
Lord Names's luncheon last month. Your author proved to
be just as charming as I'd been led to expect, and her crab
soufflé will surely have made it into the diaries of any dia-
rists in attendance. Never in my life did I suppose I would
eat jellied European eel—wrestled from the waters of
Suffolk Stour or otherwise—without having lost some
dreadful wager, and, yet, I did; without regret.

  We would be glad to further support Ms. Flattery, and
the thought struck me that some introductions could be
made at another such event—preferably supper. She was
understandably busy at the luncheon, but it would be no
great stretch to lend her an aide this time so that she
might join us, for a course. I know the company would
love to hear her speak on the inspiration behind the *Gourmet Cooking in Brexit Britain* series. Undoubtedly, a rous-
ing story lies behind the books, and hearing it told from
an Irish immigrant of whose skills Great Britain is the
beneficiary would prove particularly interesting, if not
important, to those invited.

  I propose my Notting Hill town house on the tenth of
December, to dine at 8.30 p.m. Should Ms. Flattery like a
tour of the facilities in advance, and to confirm her avail-
ability, please telephone the number given.

Yours faithfully, Jeremy Charles

The afternoon has already begun to darken. The bare trees lining
Studland Street are bone and knuckle. All day, cirrus cloud has blocked

the sun, and tonight it will block the moon, so they are on their own inside its ice curtain.

Maeve can't run to catch the black taxi passing the junction up ahead, as she's carrying a pantry's worth of foodstuffs—the balance of her current account, give or take a wasabi root. She could have had everything delivered to the Charleses', but they'd already sounded put out by the fishmonger's delivery arriving separate to the poultry farmer's. They'd rather not be apprised of the sources of their food; only to know it in sum: best-in-class British food, unpretentiously presented on good china.

When she reaches the crossroads, she finds the taxi waiting. The driver calls from the window, All right, love? Maeve heaves two large cooler boxes into the cab before climbing in. In place of a handbag she's wearing a case of knives. A basket of herbs and edible weeds hangs anachronistically from her elbow—a *My Fair Lady* prop on the set of *Taxi Driver*. When she gives the Notting Hill address, the cabbie sniffs and rubs his nose with his sleeve. Maeve inventories the contents of the boxes for allergens or for the offensive article. She can't place it. They drive silently along Paddenswick Road and Goldhawk Road, which are deserted save for the odd double-decker bus and a clique of schoolchildren headed for the underground. Sweat prickles at Maeve's hairline and lower back from carrying all that tackle. Maeve lives on a houseboat, and she hadn't wanted to order a car directly to her mooring because, while she's usually not alone on the boat, she's still a single woman. She leans away from the seat and pinches her shirt from her damp skin. Having taken her cue from the blazers and cravats of the luncheon, she'd donned her very poshest clothes: a vintage blue velvet blazer, a clean black silk shirt, navy cigarette trousers, and brogues. The atmosphere in the cab changes now, as if a light bulb has gone out in a room, morphing the room's shadows. Maeve feels the frown on her mouth before identifying its source: the driver's gaze on her in the rearview mirror. When she catches his eye, he says:

It's not all that bad, is it?

He'd been wanting to talk. Oh, she says. She smiles and picks one leaf of hairy bittercress off its rosette. No, it's just work.

The cabbie squints at her and sort of trembles his head. I thought I recognized you, yeah . . . that accent . . . Yeah. You're that chef. From Instagram.

Maeve pops the bittercress leaf in her mouth and looks out the window. Ah no, I'm from Ireland.

The cabbie sniggers. Yeah! I knew it. I'm good with faces, me.

A refectory table of faces, skin gaunt and delicate as garlic casings, floats into Maeve's mind. At last month's head-spinning luncheon, she had only heard their whimsical titles. She'd wondered at the rankings: which of the lords, baronesses, viscounts, dames, earls, knights, counts, barons, dukes, marquesses represented the root, bulb, stalk, feathery frond? Hopefully the sous-chef will remind her of their names tonight. The scene changes out the windows as they approach Shepherd's Bush Green and they pass a strip of competitively glaring shopfronts, restaurants, tanning salons, pharmacies, Chinese medical centers, tattoo parlors, barbers, kebab shops, phone repair factories, pound worlds, off-licenses, fabric emporiums—each and every one with a sale on, besides the restaurants.

Then the low-ceilinged colorful shops peter out, replaced with white plastic and scaffolding-wrapped buildings and terraced red-bricks. The driver is saying that he saw her on *Piers Morgan*. Yeah, you was flogging a book, wasn't it? On about British grub. What's lovely. What's not. What *can't* grow in Britain. Pineapples, papaya, avocado, mangoes, none of that lot. Greenhouses don't cut it for that lot, wasn't it? What else? Coconuts. Rice.

Cripes, Maeve says. You remember more than faces, then. You remember more of that interview than me! To be fair, it was Piers Morgan, so, I had to prep with a bit of dissociation meditation—

Melons! The driver announces this to himself, glancing out his window at a lady in a burqa pushing a double pram. He hits the M so hard, his lips go white. A Deliveroo moped weaves dangerously in front of them.

Are you a fan of, eh . . . Are you a fan of cooking, then?

Nah, not much, he says. I find it monotonous. Not how *you* do it, I'm sure, but I don't have the time.

The GPS puts them nearly at Notting Hill, and the housing changes to four-story white Victorian town houses, mostly terraced, some semidetached. Parked cars have the gleam of being freshly waxed or freshly purchased. There was a time when Maeve thought it mad that anyone would have a car in London, until she'd started catering. She'd bought a van. It had not gone well.

As they wind through side streets, pastel shades begin to interrupt the white-and-red brick patterns. Oh wow, she says when they pull up to the address—an end-of-terrace four-story with a double car park and stairs leading up to its grand portico entrance. Those are some Tory Tuscan pillars! She raises her brows at the driver, who just sniffs and presses buttons on the meter. Rummaging for her credit card, she notices a New Car Scent air freshener dangling from the mirror. She'd wondered at the smell that had been undercutting the herb bouquet. Behind the air freshener tree hangs a white plastic badge with red lettering: LEAVE. A bit of nostalgia for the recent past, for its crusade. On the meter, red lettering reads twenty-one pounds seventy-four.

Limes, the driver declares with satisfaction, and takes her card. That's the other fruit won't grow on home soil. He purses his mouth and hands back the card machine, as if imagining tequila with just the salt. No harm, he adds. We've still got the Commonwealth for that.

. . .

Two Cavalier King Charles spaniels are first to greet Maeve at the entrance—both losing their wits at this goodie-smelling stranger. One barks and one growls. Their tails twitch like white quills scribbling rapid fine print. A whistle from the back garden sends them scraping and slipping along the stone-floored reception through the living room out to the patio garden. A housekeeper had opened the door to Maeve, introducing herself as Beverly as she hastened to collect the cooler boxes, apologizing—she should be gone by now to collect her kids, but guessing which extra chairs might be allowed outdoors was tricky. They'd be dining outdoors this December evening, Beverly said, in such a way as to indicate that the words belonged to someone else. (Except *December*—that was hers.) A new glass-box wood burner had been acquired for the occasion. Maeve gave a slow, information-received nod, problem-solving the courses in this new context and deciding that the lobster ravioli—which will pass through a stretch of winter evening before reaching the guests' teeth—had better not be deconstructed after all. The pleasure of that dish comes from the stack slipping apart gloriously at the touch of a fork; the contrast of silken pasta sheets with the firm sweet fibers of lobster meat. Given the conditions, however, she would have no choice but to take the ravioli and seal it.

Just as the front door closes behind Maeve, the "aide" mentioned in the invite—not a first-timer at the Charleses'—arrives. Oh *fab*, Lettie, Beverly says, thanks ever so much for coming early. I'm rushing to get the kids from school—every second they're at the gate's an opportunity for some thuggery. Your lobsters arrived an hour ago, and I've moved what was in that fridge to the basement, so the kitchen's all yours. There's just whatever came delivered and a few bits in the pantry. Can I leave you, Lettie, to show Ms. Flattery around, and just text me if anything's missing? I'll be back later. I set the table outside as best I could—it can't be the right cutlery, because I didn't know the menu, but Mrs. Charles will set you right. Good luck, Ms. Fl— sorry, Dr. Flattery.

Oh Jesus, no! Just Maeve!

They *were* wondering, actually . . . for the introduction. Mrs. Charles won't go by Lady neither. Right, I'm off!

Go! Please! And thank you! Maeve says.

Please, thank you, nice to meet you, Lettie says, and curtsies at Maeve.

As they put their things in the cloakroom, Maeve scans her conspirator, dressed in a black chiffon top, black trousers with a white stripe down the sides, a white silk headscarf covering the front of her hair (coiled in thin dreads on her crown), and gold hoop earrings with a big pearl dangling from each. The hoops kiss her cheeks when she smiles.

You've worked here before, then?

Once, Lettie says. But they know me from the Corner House. I'm a host there. It's my night off. Lettie widens her eyes briefly. But I'm on scholarship at Chef Academy, too, so I'll be helpful. I wore my toque!

Maeve glances at the white headscarf. Nice! So. Show me all the sticky pans and booby traps.

· · ·

The kitchen is on the second floor. Its balcony has stairs down to the patio garden, where tables have been put together. Stone tabletop fireplaces are as yet unlit. The patio is multileveled: at the rear, alongside a terraced flower garden, steps lead to a pergola on the second deck, with sofas and stools around propane heaters.

Maeve is relieved that the kitchen is on a separate floor. She doesn't love being watched while cooking, which is surprising for someone whose career took off thanks to Instagram videos of her cooking. But those videos had begun as love letters to her sister Nell in America, during a year when Nell—a brilliant, broke philosopher—was homesick. Maeve had offered to bring her over for a week, but Nell said she didn't want a spring break visit; what she wanted was the luxury of spending an open-ended amount of time with her sisters, a continuous present. The closest thing Maeve could give her was to make Nell her rapt audience on the other end of a camera, as she whisperingly prepared meals at 5 a.m. in a shared apartment (before she bought the houseboat), often re-creating favorite dishes from their childhood. Re-cording the videos via Instagram Live had originally just been con-venient: they used the app to message each other; Maeve could see if Nell was still awake; they only needed their phones. (Maeve had a tripod; Nell kept her video off, recorded audio only.) To Nell, the ses-sions had not only been a balm for homesickness but had given her a new, stimulating, disembodied space to think . . . to test out unformed, informal ideas fit for midnight vol-au-vents. Nell found that new ideas dizzied into being amid the willed hypnosis of watching her sister cook, as jumbled memories of the thousands of meals Maeve had cooked for them bumped up against the fertile *nowness* of cooking and of livestreaming. (Maeve had wanted Nell's image in the videos—with her unpindownable, waistcoat-wearing Edwardian suffragist beauty—but Nell wasn't one bit interested in that.) Later—having met Jasper and having been inspired by his video production skills—Maeve hired a producer to split and crop and adapt the content to various platforms: YouTube, Insta Reels, TikTok. Her minimal, murmured culinary di-rections were interspersed with Nell's voiced meditations. The produ-cer introduced additional cameras, lighting, expectations. He toyed with adding beats, but the crackling of Nell's shoddy microphone proved to be well-pitched. People liked to watch fish being expertly filleted while having the miracle of the loaves and the fishes picked apart for its secular ethics: the phenomenon of humans flexing their morality when they're being observed (whereby five loaves and two fish make five thousand morsels); shared experience as a resource for meaning-making; myth as more persuasive than argument. In the hours between one person's supper and another's breakfast, Meals and Meditations gained a following.

Maeve lays everything out on the kitchen island's marble surfaces, whose veins her very best knife won't cut. She and Lettie had to move a human-size arrangement of flowers to make space for prepping—sourcing measuring cups and mixing bowls, grouping ingredients and utensils for each course, task-listing; washing and peeling, trimming and weighing, pestling and marinating, kneading and rolling. Maeve is designating the dinner table as the fish workstation when she hears clicking coming up the balcony stairs. Oh *do* pipe down, Ruth, a woman's voice reprimands the howly dog below. Alighting in the kitchen, Mrs. Charles speaks smilingly to Lettie and Maeve: They're afraid of those floating stairs, so at least they won't be under your feet if you have the door open. Hel-*lo*, Lettie! Thank you for coming, at such short notice. We're *so* delighted that you could. And . . . Mrs. Charles eyes the pasta sheets drying on racks, pausing at the darker gluten-free sheet, before extending her hands to Maeve in a gesture demanding that they be cupped. But Maeve's hands are full, so Mrs. Charles presses her own to her chest. Maeve, if I may? We're thrilled. Just thrilled. You'll make more magic in this kitchen in one evening than in its hundred-and-forty-year history.

Maeve laughs, having halted in her work, a measuring cup now buried in a bag of flour. The key is to make *enough* magic, I find!

People must say this to you all the time, but I feel I *know* you. The *cook*books. Mrs. Charles gasps. Food photography is all in the food, but the *portraiture*! It's just so *warm*. The summer light scintillating off the water. What was his name, the photographer?

Thank you! Well . . . it's different photographers. But those were taken by my friend Halim. A mime artist who lives in a tent on the deck of my houseboat. Maeve smiles, knowing how feral this sounds and taking joy in that. She could have just said "friend" or "roomie," but her deck-dwelling artist-in-residence won't be collapsed into a noun as neatly as his mini canopy tent. (In fact, for financial reasons, it had been Maeve who'd taken the portraits, with the help of a production designer pal; she'd simply positioned Halim by the mounted camera to press the shutter release.)

Maeve waits for Mrs. Charles to respond, but her lips press together as ravioli edges and she blinks, as if these bizarre particulars might unblur. Finally, she declares: How *novel*. She then noses about for a moment, saying she knows they have so much to do and she shan't interrupt them, but she must steal Maeve away for a jiffy. Tapping her phone on the countertop to check the time, Maeve sees a notification from Nell: "Spoke to the last of Ol's colleagues. No one's heard from her. Her classes are all reassigned for next sem—" Maeve doesn't click to read the full message: she can't think about that tonight. Washing her hands, she gives Lettie a few quick instructions, then follows Mrs. Charles down the stairs of this wing and up another set to the third floor. En route, Mrs. Charles asks:

Which course will you join us for?

Maeve says: The sixth.

On the landing, Mrs. Charles halts and turns to her. Of?

Maeve has to concentrate to understand. Oh, the last course, she says. Cheese and port.

At the very end? Mrs. Charles puts on a sulky face and goes to the study. You see, you'd rather convinced me on your mantra of food and fellowship, Maeve. Cheese is an afterthought. Unless we do it the French way, and have cheese *before* pudding, and *then* we'd have your company sooner! And should anyone call it unpatriotic, I'll take the blame!

Though she barely weighs enough to bend the fibers in the Queen Anne wing chair, when Mrs. Charles sits at her desk, the furniture yields to her. Various materials drape from her stick limbs, their patterns rendered all to pleats. Maeve sits on the Chesterfield sofa, facing a floor-to-ceiling library, and says she can't join them before all the hobs are off. But she'll be far more relaxed when she does.

Quite, Mrs. Charles says, levering her whole body into this syllable by her elbow on the leather-topped desk. I expect we shall *all* be *quite* relaxed, if we're on to *port*. She blows air out her nostrils, as if port is notoriously bigoted. Jeremy and I do make *every* effort for our guests to feel relaxed. It's just so important to us to have our cherished friends feel at ease under this roof. They must be free to joke . . . with impunity, as it were. Unquotably. Do you know Howard is *quite* the raconteur! Lord Howard Gillies? He looks forward to these occasions when he can rollick a little, for a brief moment. He's on the Basingstoke

Committee, and his brother-in-law has keen ties to Ireland, so I know he'll love to meet you. Framed by Burberry curtains, Mrs. Charles shuffles around in a drawer now and extracts a checkbook. She unfolds the reading glasses that hang from a gold chain on her chest and slips them on. Do you know, I can't tell one dog from the other after one glass of wine. Poor Ruth took such offense last weekend, she nearly went to live with the neighbors! Now, Maeve, when we introduce you, I'd like to get it right. She hovers the pen over the payee box. Do we say Doctor?

Oh god no! That's just honorary.

Yes, I had seen that, but one—

For my achievements and influence in the culinary arts and broadcast industry, don't you know! Maeve mock-flicks her hair off her shoulders, though it's tied up. If I went around calling myself doctor, I'd get an almighty slagging from my sisters. None of their doctorates are honorary. Nell's took her eight years!

None of their doctorates? How many doctorates do they *have*?

Maeve glances to the hallway, thinking of the vichyssoise that will need to be chilled over an ice bath before going in the fridge. Three. I have three sisters. They all have PhDs. Olwen says it's Bayesian statistics, is all.

Mrs. Charles is incredulous. *Four* Irish sisters . . . *all* with PhDs?

And *none* with husbands! Maeve says this tongue-in-cheek but immediately regrets it. It is both too rude a parody of Mrs. Charles's intonation and ambitions for women other than herself . . . and a nauseating, friendly-rapscallion bit of self-sacrifice that will only intensify Mrs. Charles's endearment toward the heretical Irish.

Truly, husbands can be done without, says Mrs. Charles, laughing sympathetically. And yet . . . one keeps going back for more of them! She folds the check in half and hands it to Maeve. And do your sisters live in Ireland?

Oh, em . . . just one, that I can say for sure. Rhona. Yeah, she's in Dublin. And Olwen . . .

Possibly because she has already given too much of herself to this evening, she feels like giving more for the hell of it. She feels like telling the truth: That their oldest sister is gone. That she'd lived in Galway until three months ago, when she went out to the garden to get rhubarb for her gin and kept walking. That she left her job and family, and now no one knows where she is, and it's all they can do to send undelivered responses to the solitary text she'd sent them at the start of October, saying: "Had to take off. Sorry. I'm as safe as I ever was. Don't come looking for me." Well. It's not *all* they can do . . .

Maeve rises from the sofa, makes excuses about leeks. Of course, Mrs. Charles says. Don't let me keep you. Ah, it would be a great help if you have receipts for this evening's produce? We can be under such scrutiny, you understand. And do please sign here.

. . .

By eight, the guests are all on the second deck, clinging to their drinks as to the edge of a swimming pool after a long day of laps. The men have established themselves about the place.

In the kitchen Lettie had encouraged Maeve to boss her around, but Maeve said that was precisely why she left the restaurant business. Its brutal intensity. Its sadistic efficiency. It's like with cows, she told Lettie—you can taste the pre-slaughter adrenaline in the food if it's come from a stressy, stratified kitchen. Maeve had no real authority figure growing up, so she could never get used to having one in her workspace, let alone being one. Besides, in the rest of her life, she's impulsive and a bit frantic . . . but she's chill at the chopping board. The trickier the dish, the more it centers her. Nah, Lettie'd said, stress is the pressure I make diamonds from. No pressure, no diamonds. Her teeth had shone. She's adapting to the lack of pressure now, though, telling Maeve about her daughter while rapidly laying out the miniature bowls and plates for the first courses. Her sense of humor is *legit*! she says.

Like, last night I asked her: What's your favorite dish? And there was this epic pause, and then she shouts: Bowl!

Lettie laughs at her own story, and Maeve is spellbound. What a gorgeous, precious thing you have.

She's ace.

Don't ever let her leave, Maeve says.

Lettie catches her own pride in the silver serving platter she's wiping the edge of. Love her. The *dirty* little prick.

Oh, they're gross, aren't they? Maeve says. The Q-tips! The tampons! Toothpaste spit in the sink! Towels covered in bronzer! And that . . . sharp fart smell of singed hair.

With mild disavowal, Lettie says, Thank God Ella loves her skin. And her 'fro.

Maeve's eyes go to Lettie's never-idle hands. Wow. What a brilliant thing to be able to say. Go her.

You have daughters?

No, I . . .

You want one?

Maeve squints. I thought you said you liked her?

Lettie laughs and glances at the clock. I mean kids.

'Cause I, too, have commitment issues . . . but that was pretty quick to offer her up! Like: Take her!

So you want one, or what?

Ah, Maeve says. Maybe. Yeah. I'm . . . I have sisters. She fiddles with the appetizers, which are already spaced perfectly and ready to go. They always licked their plates, so I could never tell which ones were clean . . .

You mean—

. . . or if it hadn't been enough.

—*little* sisters?

Not anymore. We're all adults, we keep telling each other. But I'm not sure I'm responsible enough to have—

Oh my days! Lettie is peering out to the patio. Mrs. Charles just put out *nuts*.

What? Maeve goes to the window, to situate herself in the moment. To remind herself of the participants, that a meal is something communal. It's not a one-way tender. But the kitchen is lit up like a showroom, blinding her to anything outside of it. She points to the appetizers, tells Lettie, These can go down now, and—*if* you *can*—collect the nuts. Or don't bother. It's their party. This is red mullet with anchovy-rosemary sauce on a cabbage leaf—a fancy fish taco. Gluten-free. This is Welsh rabbit terrine on prune and cardamom sourdough from Bristol. And for the vegetarians: kale and cauliflower tots made with almond flour; and the pastry is English mushroom and dark ale from Staffordshire Brewery.

Yes, Chef! The gold hoop earrings brush off Lettie's cheeks.

After another twenty minutes of preparation—minutes that are squeezed for every second—Maeve makes her appearance at the long table to announce the menu. Even as she addresses the company, she is rehearsing for the cutting, piercing, brushing, layering, reducing, resetting, pouring, piping, grating, turning, drizzling, shaving, dusting, whipping, enrobing, adjusting, placing, plating choreography of her hands, which will commence the second she's back upstairs. They all pay her their full attention, with a sort of bovine curiosity and gastrological suspense.

We'll open, she says, with an amuse-bouche: a celeriac medallion with a puree of Swiss chard and truffles from Dorset. We'll follow with a classic vichyssoise. Our primo will be native lobster from the Cornish waters, in ravioli with saffron and pinot blanc foam, and sturgeon caviar . . . in place of salmon roe, which would have had to come from Alaska . . . For our vegetarians, we'll have canal-side nettle and ground elder ravioli in butter and sherry. Our main plate will be roast Nottingham partridge in a chestnut and cassava nest, with a cider and caramelized onion gravy, served with a smoked beetroot and tarragon salad. For the vegetarians, the same chestnut-cassava nest will be full of Brussels sprout "eggs" with runny Red Leicester yolks! At this, the party breaks into chatter—amused to the hilt with this egg proxy; relieved to have moved on from the non-native roe. Maeve continues over the din as Lettie arrives with the celeriac dish, on a tray borrowed from the restaurant. *Pudding*, Maeve says, glancing at Lettie, who'd instructed her not to say *dessert*, will be a mascarpone semifreddo with a fig and crab apple compote with flaked Kentish cobnuts! Finally, I look forward to taking all your complaints over cheese and sweet wine also from Kent. Enjoy, folks.

A smattering of gemstone-protective applause, a few knee slaps, a wager won on the absence of chocolate (cocoa beans don't grow in Britain), and a factless spat about the origins of cassava. There's no music, Maeve notes, but then it's not her party.

In the kitchen, her eyes never leave the food except to give instructions when Lettie can't sense what to do next: when to turn something; when to dress it. Maeve works surgically, intent on livening the food at a precise point in the future: it must revivify the moment it meets the palate, not a second sooner. She moves along each plate, tapping a strict cluster of sturgeon roe on each, reminding herself perversely of rationing; there was a cherry tomato pasta she'd make as a teen, but she could only use two tomatoes per sister, because the punnet contained a dozen and the next day's lunch could use the spare four.

Lettie trails her with lobster leg garnishes. This is *extra*, Lettie says. Next time I read Ella "Hansel and Gretel" . . . them bread crumbs is getting upgraded.

Temperature control being a challenge, Maeve removes her apron and they both serve. All it takes is the costume alteration for her to become invisible at the party: the conversation doesn't pause to receive them. One man barely leans aside to make way for his plate as he bitches about his friend's son. (And he *marches* to the wine bucket, *extracts* the bottle like . . . King Arthur's sword, and cries: *That bottle* was *not* to be *opened*; it was for *studying*!) At the dietary-restriction end of the table, Tony Blair is the subject of conversation. These ladies do

make way for the plates, smiling graciously. Tony's one big mistake was
going into property too soon, a lady says. You must always wait a
significant amount of time, because—she hushes—the people don't
like it.

I blame the wife! declares an elderly lady with a baritone voice; not
a vegetarian. Maeve keeps her eyes down so as not to invite interaction. I blame the wife, because she's greedy!

En route back to the kitchen, Mrs. Charles catches Maeve by the
aura and whisperingly suggests she get Lettie to call Beverly. If she
turns up quickly, it would relieve you *both*.

I think she's already on her way, Maeve lies, doubting that Beverly
can afford to skip whatever she's busy with.

Oh *good*. In the meantime—Mrs. Charles still has Maeve by the
air—perhaps Lettie could fetch more wine from the cellar. I'm afraid
to step away and let this go chilly.

. . .

Night has foregrounded itself by the time Maeve is seated. The firelight
gives the winter air a formaldehyde quality—pointed incisors and pocket
squares and ivory brooches float around in the glow. Wood burns neat
orange in a glass cube at the table's end. A six-foot flue carries the fumes
beyond them. The tabletop firestones are set to maximum. Set between
the flames are cheese platters, each with three cheeses; a tiny jar and
spoon; a block of pale jelly; a dish of oat-thyme thins; and lightly candied
walnuts.

Joining the party at last, Maeve feels herself subject to the eerie
glow too. A placid Irish specimen. Relieved not to be at the head of the
table, she is congratulated on all sides: What a performance! Well
done! Mrs. Charles, seated beside her, pivots her body to Maeve to
prompt some sort of speech. A man at the other end of the table asks
her to stand if she intends to speak, he's hard of hearing. Oh, Henry!
the hostess responds, she's been on her feet for hours. Do let's be con-

siderate. Maeve demurs and stands, feeling a crackling ache already where her cheeks meet her ears.

Thank you, everyone . . . for sending nothing back to the kitchen! And to the Charleses for inviting me, and to Lettie, without whose help the meal would have ended with soup. She's a Michelin star in the making. Lettie smiles sweeter than the wine she's pouring. The pearls on her earrings hang over the flames as snowflakes that won't melt.

Now. If I told you that one of these cheeses is vegan, Maeve says, could you guess which?

An elderly man pats his breast for spectacles, and a few people exclaim, *Oh my! Goodness, really? What? I missed that.* Some lean in for a closer look. Some cut tidy corners and enact scrutiny on their forks. Watch your cuff, Benjamin, you'll singe it!

What does that mean, *vegan cheese?* asks a lady who'd had no query about *amuse-bouche.* Her neighbor privately explains the concept of food that isn't animals.

I . . . I . . . I know what this is! says a shiny-faced man with a peeled-plum mouth. One cheese is . . . one of the cheeses is not in fact cheese but cake. When you cut it!

It'll be the Wensleydale, Sir Charles announces from the other end of the table, having tried the other two and now balancing the Wensleydale on his knife as plainly inedible. What is it, then? Tofu?

Ghastly! A lady seated beyond the rampart of men now scowls at the Wensleydale.

No. Maeve shakes her head. No tofu anywhere, I promise. Fermented cashews, yes. If you'd like to try them, the pear jelly should go with the Roquefort, nothing with the Wensleydale, and there's a Tydeman's Late Orange apple mostarda for the hard cheese.

Lord Howard Gillies, the alleged raconteur—seated opposite Sir Charles and exchanging beleaguered glances with him—addresses the company: I've never heard the word *vegan* uttered from anywhere other than a high horse. You're not about to make us all feel miserable, Ms. Flattery, are you?

Maeve, who has her eyes closed to savor the blue-blooded Roque-fort, opens them and turns to Lord Gillies. He doesn't face her. He doesn't need anyone to reply, only to receive his assertions. I'm not a vegan chef, Maeve says, but London has some fabulous ones. There's a place in Bethnal Green called—

What I cannot fathom—Lord Gillies says in lieu of *shut up!*—is why one would eschew the real thing for an imitation. We don't have cocoa trees in Britain, I'll grant you. But we *do* have plenitudinous heifers.

Quite right.

We bloody well do!

—a few million in commission still, I hope?

In my experience, Maeve says, all or nothing doesn't make for great cooking. And it's my job to expand people's—

Your cooking is fine, Ms. Flattery. But *cheese* isn't cooking. Cheese is cheese. And if it isn't, it isn't. It's a compromise.

Now, now, Jeremy, Mrs. Charles says lightly.

The French melt it and call *that* cooking, a lady says.

I hope it's okay to point out, Maeve says in one go, that it doesn't come out of the udders as cheese! Cheese is made. If we food makers don't challenge ourselves to improve and perfect new alternatives, *ex-cellent* alternatives won't exist. They'll be just compromises, as you say.

Whereas what we've got here is *excellent* compromise.

Maeve's head ducks back, as if to avoid a tomato thrown at her. She scans her end of the table, but it's a lot of ladies' wrists and people staring into their crystal port glasses, waiting for the queen's face to ghost forth and reassert the food chain. Maeve asks the party lightly: Does my food taste of compromise?

The I-blame-the-wife elderly lady declares boomingly: *There* you have it, Ms. Flattery! The proof is in the pudding, which is capital. To Mrs. Charles, she says: Petulance shan't sour it. (Her expression reads: try lending your husband the other side of the bed to get out of on the morrow.) *What of it* if our Wensleydalean friends have been pooh-poohed this evening? Even *Turner* saw fit to denude North Yorkshire of its cow pats.

The Roquefort's also vegan, Maeve says gamely. It took me eight weeks to make it, on my boat. But the hard cheese is goat.

Gasps and gollys meet this information. Someone by the name of Clement, as the proprietor of five thousand acres of idyllic North Yorkshire moorland, takes offense. Another man's eyes dart to Maeve's breast for a sign of plumpness, as if she might have nursed the Roquefort into existence herself. The dominant expression is one of bamboozlement.

Well, you had *me* fooled, says one of Mrs. Charles's friends seated nearby. It's delectable, and just right with the pear.

Mrs. Charles uses this positive beat to inform the guests that Maeve and her three sisters are *all doctors*! Maeve's degree is honorary, so she's coy about it, but the others are de jure and I just think, how wondrous—four female doctors in one Irish family. I mean, it's highly unusual! Your parents must be so proud!

Maeve bites into a cracker so she won't be expected to hold forth. Various conversations rouse along the table: *honor* being an indefatigable subject. Though he speaks at a moderate volume now, Maeve can make out Lord Howard Gillies telling his audience that it's like his new neighbor in Suffolk, a certain Jay *Lee*. (The monosyllables are given as if they are not phonetic.) The Baron of Cowdenknowes or some such Scottish purlieu. He bought his feudal title at an auction!

No matter how she tries to steer away from personal questions, the ladies surrounding Maeve want to know her *story*. They must expect it's very different from theirs, and seemingly it doesn't end badly, so they're inclined to hear it. When did she first know herself to be a chef; what are her aspirations; is she aware that she has an admirer in the MP Sir David Anderson? Though she doesn't really want to, Maeve is tired, so it's easier just to tell them:

When their parents died, she explains, she was thirteen years old.

Her younger sister, Nell, was nearly twelve; her older sisters, Rhona
and Olwen, were fifteen and seventeen. Various relatives moved in and
out, looking after them in shifts. This angered and confused the girls,
who resisted management, who preferred unsupervised sadness. Their
parents hadn't been typically parental. So when Olwen turned eighteen, she became their legal guardian. Funereal lasagna and shepherd's
pies and gooey casseroles arrived by the bucketload for the deep freeze,
but Nell was already a vegetarian and Maeve said the microwave made
everything taste of cabbage. They made a pact: if Maeve would agree
to be her sisters' dinner-lady, she would never have to strip a bedsheet
or clean a toilet bowl again. (She would also become the grocery shop-
per, which came with the dilemma of what to spend when her older
sisters weren't being open about how much they had. Envelopes would
drop from extended family like overripe fruit with no predictable season. To eat this one, or hold on to it?) The four of them got along best
when each did her own thing, then came together for intense, dizzy
judgments of one another, of their various lives. Well, the three others
liked it that way, and Maeve put up with that fact.

Most days, to prolong their being hysterically, bickeringly together,
Maeve made them all three-course meals. It had seemed like magic,
sprinkling grated ginger and chili onto honey-roasted squash for the
first time, prompting Olwen to go droopy in pleasure and Rhona to
clasp her raging throat and hiss words like *public liability insurance*.
Olwen had got special dispensation to do the first year of her degree
part-time, so she could stay with them, while she drove back and forth
to Galway once or twice a week. By the time Olwen had earned an
MA scholarship, Nell was nearly seventeen. She assured her older sisters that she was ready to move, to let the house be sold, as Rhona—
ever mercenary—had proposed. So Maeve had known very early on
that she'd work with food. But after culinary school, she learned that
restaurant kitchens—with their aversion to the chaos and happen-
stance she so enjoyed—wouldn't suit her. Several years in enough
Dublin and London kitchens to count as a sample settled that. The

very last restaurant where she'd been head chef was run by such unin-spired, micromanaging pedants that, when she arranged for a leftovers charity pickup after a particularly wasteful New Year's banquet, she was fired. They'd cited food safety standards, to which she'd replied that, as far as she knew, *food* was safer than *no food*.

Despite its relative precariousness—she tells the Ladies now—she doesn't mind her freelancing setup. The catering keeps her learning. Her subscribers keep her passionate; they're a sort of family. Besides occasional bursts of income, her followers also gifted her the oppor-tunity to write books. Which is a really amazing thing, she says. And then, she hears herself revealing: And maybe the reason it's going wrong now is because the opportunity came to *me*, rather than *me* seeking it out . . . which means the relationship with the publisher to begin with had a totally different kind of . . . love, and power dynamic. But . . . well, now we're struggling to agree on a direction. And it seems *I'm* not the one who gets to lay down the bread crumbs.

The women are, ever so subtly, swaying; traveling in some sort of carriage, separate to Maeve's train entirely. They observe her across the tracks, through several windows. One lady holds her head, dizzied by this disturbing sequence of images. Another reasserts her cashmere shawl, a shade of blue she has had lamentably described to her as *baby*.

When the first verbal response to Maeve's outpouring is an ap-palled inquiry into the nature of her parents' tragic deaths, Maeve dabs her mouth with the wrong side of a napkin and excuses herself to help Lettie with the coffee.

The only hot drinks requested are a few Irish whiskeys, so Mrs. Charles suggests they move indoors and warm up over a nightcap. Beverly and Lettie arrive to clear the table.

A grand piano is a corner feature in the living room, but still no music is played. There is a six-piece suite, a wall-shelving treillage with a TV, some decorative books, backlit plants, and a selection of hound-themed ornaments. There is a prosperity of lamps. The inlaid rose-wood flaps of an Edwardian envelope card table are sealed to a close, its four chairs regularly dusted. On a mahogany cellarette, decanters are lined up with specific glasses. The guests are trusted to know which decanter contains port, sherry, brandy or cognac, whiskey or bourbon based on the shape of the glasses set before each. Maeve takes a snifter of something amber and goes outside to help her colleagues clear up. When they won't let her, she shifts around in the dark, feeling the heated environment's clutch. She senses what it must be like to have social skills and expectations that delimit interactions to such a tiny club. She troubles a moth bite in the velvet of her pocket. Sir Charles and chums are stood around the wood burner holding tumblers to their breasts as bridal bouquets. Occasionally they take a wistful sniff. A man whose lips barely wrap over his teeth, even though the lips are full and the teeth are straight, says: One does feel oneself being pulled in a great many directions.

No, no, Edmund. That won't do. You should have said so in Winchester.

I feel as though I'm being stripped for parts.

No, no. Forget all that. What?

I'll have Aurelia arrange the papers for a syndicate.

That's a *hassle*, Jeremy.

Nonsense. It's nothing more than a signature.

It occurs to Maeve now that it wasn't Sir Jeremy Charles at all who'd generated the invite. The enthusiasm had been *Mrs.* Charles's. They fall silent, sensing a foreign body. Edmund tucks his thumb between waistcoat buttons, his posture conveying an imaginary cummerbund.

Baron de Ramsey, Lord Gillies, Sir Charles. Maeve smiles and lifts her glass an inch toward each man—she's noticed they don't cheers.

The baron really puts the air into Hello, before adding: Dear, there being no such titles in your republic, I must inform you: the title *Sir* is accompanied with a first name, not a surname. Sir Jeremy, for example.

Oh, Maeve says, smacking herself on the forehead. Of course, it's not like Doctor!

His brow raises infinitesimally, as if waiting for her to revise her toast. Maeve has the strange urge to mimic the blunt manner of these men (or their equivocation styled as frankness) . . . to put them at ease? She likes people: she wants them to feel comfortable and welcome . . . but he hadn't put her at ease. He endows himself with the space around him such that, almost at once in the province of his body, rent is overdue. It's a privilege she wants to elbow. She forgets the baron's first name, and he doesn't offer it.

Sir Jeremy Charles, she says. Am I right in thinking you have an estate in Newbury?

Sir Jeremy regards her lapels, as if for a recording device. Hungerford, yes, he mutters. He'd spoken to his wife about the importance of initialed, paginated boundaries: a robust nondisclosure signature. Had she not put her foot down? Damn woman. Damn goodwill contracts.

It's a stunning countryside, Maeve says. Lovely forestry around there. What's it called . . . Savernake?

He wets his lips. Yes. We quite enjoy it, at Easter. He glances to the gentlemen. The muntjac give good sport.

I wonder . . . Maeve hears herself get so far, only to hesitate. She steels herself. Why shouldn't she ask him for a favor that costs him nothing to grant, except a brief moment of realism? Why shouldn't *he* be the good sport? I wonder, she continues, if I could moor my boat for a while on the canal that goes through your territory? It doesn't need any supply, it's solar-powered. It's for this third book, you know, I'd love to include—

What's it *called?* The baron says this in the same intonation Maeve had used a moment ago, only louder.

Sorry? Maeve turns to him. Her heart races.

The first was *Gourmet Cooking in Brexit Britain,* if I recall? The second, *Haute Cuisine Remains?* The third book: What's it called?

The baron, it appears, is somehow an intimate of the publishing house. He must have heard tell of the dispute. Of what she'd presumed to call it: *Feasting on Scarcity.*

I haven't decided on the title yet.

Then, what's the thesis?

Em . . . Maeve tries to laugh but can't. She glances at the telescope-proof sky. *Do* try this at home? Now she manages a laugh. I mean . . . it's a cookbook. Cookbooks don't tend to have a thesis—

Of course they do.

—beyond what goes with what . . .

All books have theses.

. . . but even that's not prescriptive.

With so *many* siblings in the academy, says Sir Jeremy, joining the baron, you must know that books are bound by more than glue.

Having done without his eye contact all evening, Maeve now wishes Sir Jeremy would crack his binocular stare. Okay, she says. Well . . . the recipes work from a pantry of food bank basics. Pasta, rice, tinned veg-etables, cereals, legumes, beans, and pulses and so on, as well as produce that can be foraged or grown from shared community facilities like al-lotments and chicken coops. It promotes bringing people together to—

And there you have it! The baron cuts her off. No surprise your publishers find it unacceptable. They're a business. They work with markets. Not milk and honey. His eyes are half-closed, his chin lifted, as though he is basking in midmorning sun.

She's a communist! Lord Gillies says, and storms off to the loo.

No, Maeve says. I just know what's coming, in terms of food short-ages. What's already here.

Shorter chips in the pub do no harm—

Jesus. I'm not talking about short chips! I talk to food producers every day—

Then, a baritone voice: I *invented* communism!

So pronounces the wife-blaming elderly lady, her plangent voice-over relegating all other noises and details to mise-en-scène. She tries abortively to trap a burp with her lips before continuing. I was nine years of age! Which is a long time ago—in case you thought I was sporting a veil, it is cobwebs. My brother and I were engaged in a picnic lunch when I noticed the Heskworth children had twice as many sandwiches as we did: theirs were triangular; ours were soldiers. Their nurse was a large lady called Carol, and Carol made sandwiches with so much stuffing they could have been upholstered. I suggested we pool the sandwiches and divide them equally so that we might arrange them into various shapes and make a game of it. Call it collective ownership. *That* was the day Lionel accepted that *I* should be the one to sit in the House of Lords, and I set to work on a consortium for the admission of female peers, and five years later, they were let in. It proved to be another sort of House work, of course, and quite dull for the most part. What do you think of that for an ism? she asks Maeve.

I think it warrants a top-up—

Absolutely not. I came to say goodnight. She wags the paternal handle of her walking stick at them and departs.

Maeve follows her swiftly through the living room toward the cloakroom, but Mrs. Charles catches her with such a look of need, she can't ignore it. The hostess felines her shoulders around her ears when Maeve agrees to sit by her on the two-seater. To Maeve, she appears tucked together like a heap of campfire twigs, romantic and primed in fire starter. She confesses how *moved* she was to hear about Maeve's orphaned sisters; how they looked after one another so bravely and practically; what they managed in the face of tragedy. I find it just . . . What I would have *given* to have a daughter . . . such as you, she says. She tilts her head to Maeve without a glint of armament and puffs out mausoleumic air. Maeve feigns interest in the shelving unit to turn away from the smell. She imagines the trophies and graduation photos that might have lined the shelves instead of candelabras, bronze dogs, Regency mirrors, and urns. On the bottom shelf are stacks of Maeve's books. The publisher must have sent them over to be displayed, for the guests to take as party favors. But the Charleses must have deemed it uncouth.

Mrs. Charles, Maeve ventures. I was chatting with your husband, but we got cut off. We'd been discussing the possibility of mooring my houseboat on the canal running through your Newbury estate for a while?

Mrs. Charles tries to clear the fog from her eyes. Oh?

No one would know I'm there. The thing is, I'm trying to get out of this book contract, because the publishers hate the latest manuscript. They want a totally different book, I'm afraid. I mean, I gave them blue and they want red. But it's the best book so far, it's the first one that's really my own. I toed the line too much on the second. I let it be steered. But this one could have an impact. I want to put it out myself and hire a publicist, and profits will go to food banks. I bought the houseboat with the advance from the three-book deal . . . to have fewer costs. But I'll have to pay some of it back. A few months off mooring fees would give me some flexibility. And I'd be invisible. I'd even leave the watercress.

Mrs. Charles receives this request as something curdling within her lovely, clear evening. Oh no, that's not . . . there's the question of insurance . . . is very complicated . . . and tax . . . discretionary trust . . . could really be . . . *very* difficult I just, I can't see Jeremy being . . . he's fiercely protective of the estate . . . its privacy and so on and it . . . But then she pauses. No, she says finally. I'll tell you what. There's something else. A *suitable* way to support you. All right? I do *so* support you, Maeve, and this struck me earlier, in fact. I chair a literacy trust and there's a gala. We're having a benefit gala in January, the whole thing. There's the catering, and I could get you the wine and champagne contracts, which are lucrative and . . . well, less labor-intensive than your—she hiccups—intricate cassava nests!

Maeve lets an unsmiling Polaroid develop between them. Yes, she thinks, the wine and champagne contracts *are* lucrative—high markup, low labor—and she hadn't been given tonight's drinks contract. Perhaps it wasn't stinginess, though; perhaps Mrs. Charles wanted to gloss over quite how much wine would be needed.

It's cheap to moor outside London, Maeve presses on, so it's not that big a deal. It's just everything coming at once, with the license and insurance, the commercial kitchen space I lease, paying back the advance, and my sister . . . my sister needs these medical tests? Because she's on a work visa she can't afford insurance, even with Obamacare . . . my youngest sister, Nell.

At this, Mrs. Charles presses the knuckles of her one hand against her mouth. The other arm is punching her necklace-spectacles into her elbow, scraping them with a reef of alexandrite and diamond.

She's . . . Seeing that the other reasons hadn't mattered one whit to Mrs. Charles, Maeve says: Nell was always really self-contained. You'd never know if something was wrong. When our folks died, she barely cried, but she changed her hairstyle to cover the alopecia. I was the one who knew how she was because we shared a room. She's really sick. She has to lecture sitting down. She has three jobs, and she's driving between campuses without feeling in her feet. If she hits another car, I mean . . . Rhona's the one with cash, but she won't take responsibility for stuff she has no say in. She's not ungenerous, but, if she wants to make a charity donation, she forms a charity. And Olwen might need a search committee, but Nell is not a charity.

Into her fist, Mrs. Charles says: Follow me. She stares at Maeve, unmoving; her eyeballs becoming increasingly transparent, like egg white slowly un-poaching. She then glances across the room to clock her husband. She gives him a reassuring frown and gets up without using her arms. With Maeve standing behind her, she makes a scribbling gesture at her husband to indicate vague aims at nondisclosure contracts and signatures and leave-it-to-me. The flush in her cheeks could be anything—the Bollinger, the pinot noir, the pinot blanc foam, the cider gravy, the stuff from Kent, the brandy. Like an umbrella swinging in some gentleman's hand, she is a thing gratuitous . . . moving through the coterie and the reception. She ascends the stairs and closes the study door behind them. Maeve isn't quite sure what led her here or what she's waiting for. After rooting around in a desk drawer with veterinarian courage, Mrs. Charles extracts a map. She sets it on the table and proceeds to don her spectacles. She unfolds the map as though Beverly has called in sick and there's nothing for it but to figure out this bedsheet business once and for all. Orphans have come a-knocking.

Here! She hits at a spot on the map with a satisfying timpani crack. There's a mooring. Willow trees will obscure you, your boat. It's the site of an historic confrontation with his father, and Jeremy won't go within a league of it for the rest of his life. Mrs. Charles looks Maeve up and down, delirious with purpose. This is a recourse to which she had given some thought. You have a jester to keep you cheery, I recall. You have a goblet, no doubt, to stave off thirst. Now. All you need, for the brutes, is a gun.

A hot iron might have been run across the night, such is its composure. Nell's bedsheets are starched with sea air. Her ash-brown hair, cut into a bob with a general-purpose scissors, silvers the pillow. Though she's the youngest of her siblings, Nell was the first to gray at the edges. She is thirty-three. Her frown line deepens as she sleeps. A neon earplug has fallen loose and is kissing her chest, rolling back and forth with her breath like shoreline debris. The sleep is uneasy. As she often does, Nell is dreaming of the watery horizon by which her parents died.

After supper one night, when the girls had retreated to their bedrooms, their parents had gone out into the weather. Nell remembers hearing them rushing, shouting, howling like wolves through their estate. They had gone to the cliff path in a gale, and a gust of wind had blown them into the horizon. Well, it blew the lighter one, and the heavier one reached out to grasp her—reached too far; grasped too well. Nell has pieced together their ending frame by frame, down to the moment her mother's watch-face cracked on a rock, freeing the hour hand. Making their final minutes indivisible as the first time they met.

Paul Wallis had owned a wineshop so narrow that a handbag once took out all the Spanish reds. Leonora Flattery had been teaching evening classes in honors maths for leaving certificate students while doing a part-time master's in applied maths. Defying probability, it wasn't she who walked into Paul's wineshop but he who enrolled in her evening class, a thirtysomething vintner among spirit-and-mixer teenagers. Paul had been a foster child who moved out at sixteen before finishing school and moved countries continually, toward cheaper bars, more sociable backpackers, guesswork labor and languages. After living as much of his life away as he had in Ireland, he returned for his foster sister's wedding and—true to his spontaneous tendencies— found himself leaseholder of a nine-square-meter shop front in Wicklow town. At first it was an experiment, to master the place inside-out, from its floor mop to its accounts. Taking leaving cert maths would help, the bank informed him. He and Leonora counted the ten-minute break of that first arithmetic class as their first date.

The time between one and ten minutes was infinitely divisible, Leonora said soppily when she told the girls this story. To this Maeve reacted swooningly, Rhona sarcastically, Olwen warily, knowing the low that was sure to follow her mother's high. Nell, transfixed by the idea of a moment's divisibility, had questions: How can you divide a moment without reducing it? Why do sums have only one answer? Who can confirm if an answer is final? Leonora replied that it was good to question the teacher, because there were many ways to arrive at the right answer, and even though an answer was either right or wrong, there wasn't only one right answer, nor was there only one wrong one! There were all the surprising, elegant, conniving, evading, tortuous solutions her brilliant daughters could thrash out, Leonora said. Nell protested.

Now, in the dream, Leonora offers her daughter a warning:

So engrossed with the stars was Thales of Miletus that he fell into a well, and all the village people laughed, because a great, lofty-minded philosopher had been so foolish as to take the ground for granted—

. . . but here the dream breaks, because this is Nell's knowledge to share. Not her mother's. Had Leonora known about Thales of Miletus, she would have torn her gaze from the horizon—that dividing line—lest she fall into it. Nell cannot get back into the dream, to make the words ring true in it. A pinging sound from beyond the dream echoes down through its tunnel, and Nell wakes. She cranes her neck toward the bedside table, where her phone glows with texts. Her sister Maeve:

Hi love. Any word from OI?

I spoke with another of her colleagues, no real clues but let's swap notes anyway

Also, hi, how are you? Did you get the pillzz??!?

Oh shit. It's your middle of the night . . .

Really hope your phone's turned off!

The sheets crackle as Nell turns the phone face-down and pulls her arm back into the duvet warmth. Her upstairs neighbors, postgraduates at Connecticut College, fell quiet sometime around 3 a.m. Now it's 5. The quietest integer of night. Beyond, in New London's dock, the ferries are huge, still metal bergs in the water. None will ripple Long Island Sound before sunup.

Trying to get back to sleep, she rolls onto her belly and feels how her body would fall were it not for the bed and the floor and the bedrock. It's easy to forget the act of resistance involved in simply standing. Toilet basins refilling upstairs is a soundtrack to the building. She rolls onto her back and swings herself to a perch on the mattress edge. A path of anti-slip shower mats leads from her bed to the bathroom. Over the past couple of years, Nell has slowly lost all sensation in her feet. As she explained to the one GP she could afford to pay out of pocket (a work visa means sky-high premiums, so she can't afford insurance), it began as a *percentage* of sensationlessness, rather than a case of total numbness in a small area that had spread. No, it was a general loss of sensation in the whole region of the foot up to the shin, which became more and more total. The feeling might have already been 20 percent lost before she really noticed it. Now, she could saw off her toes without feeling a thing. If she concentrates on her connection to the ground, she falls over. So she has to focus on where she wants to go and to will herself in that direction. She sits on the toilet; the room spins. She is exhausted. She reaches for an empty seltzer bottle on the shower floor, fills it with warm water, and squirts liquid soap into it. She holds her palm over the opening and shakes it. Then she steps into the shower and pours the soapy water over her body. She clings to the shower bar she installed a few months back, which will possibly lose her her deposit.

Today will involve flitting between campuses. A lot of getting herself from A to B. Before that, though, she'll swim. It'll be pitch-black, but no boats to worry about, and swimming is her only means of regaining equilibrium. A swim or a tenure-track position. There's almost never time for a proper swim on a weekday morning—she needs at least an hour in the water. She grabs her wetsuit from the towel rack. The soap helps her slip into it. The neoprene is still coldly damp from the last swim and her teeth chatter. By the front door, a plastic bag contains her fins, snorkel, booties, and an underwater headtorch. She throws on a thrift-store trench coat and inserts a fish-gutting knife into the holster on her thigh like the garter of a mobster widow.

. . .

Face-down, there is no horizon. There is only dark gray element, the tunnel of torchlight through it, and plankton snowing horizontal. She gives herself over to this enormous physical body, of which she can see only a well's length. A snorkel is threaded through her goggles so there's no need to turn her head to breathe. The movement of her long fins comes from her quadriceps, hamstrings, hip flexors, buttocks, obliques, lower back. She feels her spine by way of all the voluntary muscles holding it. Her legs are strong in the bracing February water, but they feel hollow. She is steadier here than on land. Her inner ear is calmer. Meter by meter, the shocking water that had bled through the worn-out neoprene warms now by her skin and scalp. The follicles of her hair pulsate inside the wetsuit hood. She pees a little. Heat travels up the cleft of her bum and spreads around her groin, arousing her momentarily. The physical world: her flesh in it. Fishers Island is four kilometers away. She's swum there and back many times. It takes her two hours in fins. Two hours in her mind, the body in balance. Not today, though. Today, she is swimming under the fading moon and wants to be out by sunup. Moonlight clarifies the normally murky water. She wants to take this clarity with her.

Perhaps this is the night-sky clarity Olwen had wanted when she took off on her bicycle. Months ago now. When she'd taken off in the night, in bad weather, was it to prove she could do it herself, without reaching out to clasp another person's wrist? But that had been proven long ago: it was everyone else who'd needed Olwen. Her own needs had always been minimal. A natural Stoic, she sought no praise. She harnessed resilience and readied herself for all outcomes. She understood the earth's processes, its critical transitions, and focused on what she could control. Nell had learned from Olwen that happiness could come from how well you use your rationality. But it had rained and rained, Jasper said, the night she left. A weird, warm October downpour. She'd failed to close the door on her way out, leaving a river to flow into the garage. You really have to shoulder that door shut, he said, and it makes a racket. She hadn't wanted to wake us.

The good waterproofs Olwen kept in the garage were gone, too, Jasper reported. Pragmatism was characteristic of Olwen. Also generosity. In a bolt of inspiration, Nell had tried to exploit that: she'd emailed her missing sister, confessing a rapidly worsening physical state, telling her she needed a drug that was unavailable over the counter in North America but could be sourced in Ireland. Olwen, she knew, would never ignore a call for help. True to form, the pills soon arrived in her mailbox, unbranded, direct from a factory in India, without so much as the lick of Olwen's tongue on a stamp. If all else failed, she told herself, she could resort to asking for a substance only family could provide: bone marrow. That would work, she was sure of it. They'd be in the same ward. They'd have to be. Only, Olwen might take a notion and give all of it. Some processes, once begun—she might say—are almost impossible to bring to a halt.

Nell grins in the ocean so that water leaks into the badly chewed mouthpiece of her snorkel. She halts her inhalation and, with the air left in her lungs, blows the lid off.

. . .

Do I need to be worried?

Nell frowns at Ron's question. He is the dean, but he is her friend and knows better.

You sure? The dean angles his head as if checking the cut in a bar-ber's mirror. His beige suit looks as though it's still on the rail. He forgets to eat. His desk drawer is full of snacks Nell has gifted him over the years. Honeyed seeds promising nonperishability. Eternal pretzels. Platonic dates. Ron's husband has terrifying food allergies, so he never takes the offerings home.

Ron Jeong is a forty-one-year-old full professor and adoptive father of two. He cares about everyone below his rank at the university. All the hardy turtles.

So . . . it's not fatal?

Nell presses her fingers to her neck and after a moment reports: No.

Because normally a staff member falling over in the parking lot is cause for concern. Not to mention paperwork.

She'd just let her concentration slip, in a moment of relief, after driving the hour's commute from New London to Quinnipiac Univer-sity in Hamden. The car is an automatic, so she manages by pressing her right knee to accelerate, her left to brake. But then, walking across the campus parking lot, she'd missed the ground.

Your feet again? And you drove here? You *still* won't take the train?

It's two and a half hours, Ron! Plus a bus between here and Southern. I'm lecturing on Happiness down there in an hour. Parting her fringe, Nell massages the furrow between her brows. There, she says, disappearing her frown line. That's my prep work done.

Ron examines the contents of several folders before locating the one he's looking for. Bangs were a good choice for you, he says. He stands to hand her the folio so she doesn't have to.

Thanks.

So how are you teaching happiness? he asks.

I'm not teaching it. It's the ancient Greeks subbing in for me today. Eudaimonia, etcetera.

Ron says: I love it how you're always gunning to impress me. Surely it's the *physics* of happiness you're teaching, with all that *magnetism*.

Oh, you want a compelling narrative arc? Okay. Coming out the cave used to be happiness, till Salvation was happiness, till the discovery of aspirin, and then it got awkward.

Why, Nell, can't you write that way? Throw in a little . . . universal appeal?

Now Nell sits forward. Because I'm trying to fit out the young in the intellectual virtues! I'm trying to sell them on the philosophical life—in as wide a sense as Aristotle meant it—as a life of happiness and privilege. An alternative to the political life, which you're leading. Also good.

Aristotle had a rich wife, Ron says, uncapping a jar of chewable vitamins. That's the only reason he was able to sidestep the obligations of an ordinary citizen! Ron throws the dusty orange chewable into his mouth and turns the open jar to Nell.

No, thank you. I prefer my nutrition in the long-winded form. Nell opens the folio Ron had given her to find the updated course reader for

Ancient Philosophy: From the Pre-Socratics to the Fall of Rome, which has
been rebranded as *Age-Old Thinking, Today: Hedonism, Cynicism, Self-
Help, Growth*. The content is now broader and shallower, to accommodate the widest possible array of students: law students getting to grips
with alternative facts; chemistry students developing moral elasticity
for careers in big pharma; misanthropic literature majors; philosophy
students who haven't done the reading. Taking it in, Nell says:

Practical virtues trump intellectual virtues every day of the week.
Suck it, Aristotle.

I'm glad you think it sounds practical, Ron says.

It sounds . . . commercial!

Yeah, well, in antiquity, they didn't have enrollment quotas. A
notification chimes in Ron's Outlook calendar, lending that topic its
closing jingle. And if you wanna divest yourself of banal daily commitments, quit commuting. New Haven would make a lot more sense
for you as a base.

Oh my god.

Especially since Connecticut College dropped your Philosophy of
Mind class—

Oh my god, Ron! Do you want to see how many tabs I have open,
trying to find a cheap studio?

Good. And see a proper doctor already.

I can't, and you know that.

We need to make time to talk about your situation—

Anyway, it's nothing.

—because in the long run, it's unmanageable. But in the short term,
I'd like to help you cover what I can, if you'll let me. But I need you to
let me, as a friend. Not as your colleague. And it's not nothing.

Nell waits to make sure he has said his piece. She glances at a clock
on the wall beside them. The second hand moves continuously. It's not
one test, Nell says. It's dozens. It's a bankruptcy of specialists. That's
the collective noun, right? It's a nonstarter. But thank you.

It's not—

But thank you.

Ron's breathing betrays his impatience. If you won't let me help you, Nell, then please, *please* help yourself. Meet with the grant advisor like you promised. For the love of God, write a publishable book. You know? Try a little pop nihilism. I don't know, get your sister to set you up with your own YouTube channel. You're aware Bethanne is gunning for tenure track, and she's been loud and clear about her capacity to take on your groups.

Nell draws brackets around the word *Growth* on the folio cover. She adopts the position of the Skeptics who, when controversy arises, practice noninvolvement . . . in order to protect peace of mind. A practice known as *epochē*, which is translated as either *suspension of judgment* or *withholding of assent*, depending on the judgment or assent of the translator. She might work this into the lecture later. Nell imagines herself being phased out, for failing to bring enough product-demo to the Happiness lecture. She imagines Bethanne stepping directly into her life, bounding across the path of anti-slip mats between Nell's bed and bathroom, just another obstacle course to be tackled with positivity. She imagines Bethanne in a trench coat made of grant applications. Bethanne with a two-book deal in her fish knife holster. If one day she ventured to just *ask* Bethanne if an adjunct can go on sabbatical, Bethanne would probably book her a transatlantic flight, or a CT scan.

Ron sighs so that his suit seems to hollow out.

Oh, stop sighing! Nell says. And stop pointing your concern at me. It's rude. She flicks through the folio. The course reader is full of bolded words that make it sound like a CrossFit manual: strength, courage, joy, love, interest, motivation, internal discipline, truth identification, transformation, aspiration, social healing, growth. What is this anyway, she says, the *fifth* module that's been redesigned in two semesters?

The dean looks to the ceiling, exposing his Adam's apple, which is so pronounced it seems as if the skin will pierce. It's just branding, he says. Words. The ideas are the same, however they're packaged.

And what are *words* but *world-disclosing functions*?

I'm glad you think so highly of them, Nell. That's easy to forget, when you publish in journals so obscure the Special Collections can't even order them. And those librarians once ordered in a handkerchief with a love haiku written in lip-liner that Susan Sontag used to clean her nose.

I agree that philosophy should be accessible, Nell says. But writing's not the same as teaching. And anyway, I'm an immigrant. One of the many functions of an esoteric writing style is to protect myself from the retribution of the regime.

Which one? There's more than one regime to worry about.

Nell tries to get Ron's attention, to share a look of disdain at the cheapening academic standards they are both subject to, but he is surveying a spreadsheet. She says with some caution:

Accessible can't mean unserious?

Ron's gaze travels to the wet patches on Nell's shoulders. I hear your concerns. Then, meeting her gaze, he says: But as your friend, in the interest of your job and your health, I'm telling you, *cool it*.

A knock on the door behind her makes Nell start, but Ron doesn't bat an eyelid.

Nell fusses to fit the folio into her laptop bag, full of Meta-Ethics papers that need running through software to check for swaths of cut-and-pasted internet.

Eat something, she says on her way out. Next time I'm here that drawer had better be half empty.

• • •

Nell hums tunelessly in her car en route to Southern Connecticut State University. The wide roads are quiet this time of day, and the sunshine gives the tarmac a freshly mopped look. Black cherry trees and CVS pharmacies line Dixwell Avenue. She'd discovered the benefits of humming online, somewhere between doing lecture prep research, googling recent landslides that might have trapped Olwen in a cornucopia of fossils, and stepping through a medical-diagnostic looking glass. The Mayo Clinic says that humming stimulates the vagus nerve, negating the fight-or-flight impulse by triggering the parasympathetic rest-and-digest response. Omming at the traffic lights, Nell decides to weave this into next week's lecture on Hindu philosophies of happiness. She knows of at least two premed students taking the class who'll appreciate it. One of them has been emailing for reading recommendations on the ethics of euthanasia and genetic engineering and witnessed suicide. That last email she has flagged.

A Home Depot billboard commands Nell's attention, and she signals left. She should be able to nip in and still get to class in time to set up the PowerPoint with a few minutes to spare. She takes a hand off the steering wheel to push her knee down at the light.

The store smells of tangy plastic, varnished pine, and, weirdly, cinnamon buns. Nell finds the AstroTurf section. There are twelve varieties of it on huge horizontal rolls. She runs her palm along them and checks the prices: $34.98 per linear foot. Damn. The cheapest is $6.21 per foot. Holding on to a demonstration faucet for balance, she spots someone in an orange polo shirt and waves them down for assistance, something she really, really hates doing. The young man's eyes go to Nell's hand, wrapped around the metal spigot such that she might tear it off. Can I help you, ma'am? She asks for a length of AstroTurf. The man excuses himself and returns with a measuring tape, a stick of blue chalk, and an insurance-friendly cutting device. How much you need?

Em . . . Nell looks at her feet. She only needs a width's worth . . . Just about ten centimeters, she says.

He takes a docket from a plastic bucket beside the rolls of material. He fills in the product ID and looks to Nell, hovering the pencil over the quantity box. You mean ten feet, ma'am?

No. Nell tugs at the AstroTurf too hard and it barfs out two meters' worth. She rolls it backward, like too much unfurled toilet paper. Just that much, she says, indicating with her free hand. That strip.

The clerk's eyelids seem to tilt like blinds, but he is obliged to keep them technically open. You want four inches of AstroTurf?

Exactly.

His nostrils flare, as he marks out the length of a Barbie garden on the AstroTurf's underside in blue chalk and tugs it to the floor so he can cut it from end to end.

It occurs to Nell that she's been in North America for too long. If you made this demand in Wicklow town, the shopkeeper would fill the kettle and tell you to hold on till the next customer wants Astro-Turf and see will they donate you a scrap of it; meanwhile, you'd be asked in a tone of profound concern: What lamb a the lord jaysus situation has you needing four inches of fake grass?

Can I borrow that knife? Nell asks the sales assistant.

No, ma'am. His center of gravity shifts. We got a staff safety policy.

Oh . . . kay. Can I borrow your chalk, then?

If the clerk says anything in reply, Nell misses it, as it takes all her concentration to work her shoes off. She steps onto the AstroTurf, trying to sense its prickle. She takes the piece of chalk and traces the outline of her left foot, then her right.

Sorry to be a diva, she says, but could you cut out these shapes for me?

The clerk stares at the blue footprint outlines. To himself, he says: I mean . . . But he gets onto his knees and obliges. You'll be charged for the whole section that was cut. Not just these dimensions specifically.

Buy one foot, get one free? Nell says with a smile when he turns to hand her one AstroTurf footprint. She feeds it into her shoe as an insole, then puts the shoe on.

The man studiously ignores what she's doing, then—with some hesitation—stands up and extends the second piece to her, like a slice of pizza dropped on the floor that someone's fixing to eat.

It's just something I'm trying. Nell lifts one shoulder, feeling a bit preposterous. It's nothing deviant, she says. I have a condition—

That's your business, ma'am. Here's your docket. Thank you for choosing Home Depot. You have a good day.

. . .

Okay, she tells the students, today I'm going to try a different approach. I want to paint you a picture. When some of them shift their gaze toward the whiteboard, she adds: A *mental* picture, with words. Bear with me. No need to take notes.

Nell always stands while lecturing. Pacing around usually keeps her focused, though she's been pacing less of late. She sets a lyre down on her desk, then turns to face the hall. She braces herself with her fingertips on the tabletop behind her. She tries to perch on the lip, but quickly discovers that won't work and scoots herself fully onto the desk. Feeling weirdly girlish, she hums, then masks it by clearing her throat.

Picture two gardens, side by side, she says to the eighty-some mixed-discipline sophomores tiered before her.

Gardens, like, backyards? a student in the front row asks, with her hand up.

Yes, Nell says. Two adjacent gardens: two conceptions of how to live. The differences are *subtle*, mind, but you'll see that they lead to *very* different realities.

Right in Nell's eyeline is a Danish student called Mikkel. After eight weeks, Mikkel hasn't yet spoken a word in class. He had, however, shown up for her first office hour, asking curtly why Kierkegaard wasn't on the reading list. Nell had made the mistake of admitting, with a touch of shade, that the course design was not her own. Now, Mikkel chews his bright pink knuckles, looking down at Nell with the concentration of a junior doctor in the theater, ready to step in should the consulting surgeon show signs of hesitation.

Garden one, Nell says levelly . . . belongs to someone we'll call Alex.

What Alex wants . . . is for his garden to be flourishing and product-
ive. So he brings in benches and stools for sitting and thinking. Nothing too comfortable. No cushions. No recliners. He installs a pond
with fish in it, and a sundial. Tools to investigate nature and behold
the night sky. The garden is Alex's attempt to create a blessed life.
Right-thinking people will admire and want his garden—his happy
life—for themselves.

"Right-thinking!" someone scoffs from the back of the lecture hall.

According to Alex! Nell adds, leaning back a little, to see everyone,
and to encourage getting perspective on the picture. Contentment?
Cheerfulness? Relaxation? she says. He thinks they're overvalued. He
believes that everything in the universe has a purpose and is goal-
oriented. From the universe itself to every animal and plant and human
in it. A chicken coop in his garden serves to remind him that his role on
this earth is different to that of a chicken. His inherent purpose, as he
understands it, is to exercise *reason*. Reason is a function particular to
humans, and it's how *well* we use our rationality that determines our
happiness. Through reason, we can attain good. So says Alex.

Keep in mind: happiness isn't the *goal* of his garden, or of life. In his
view, a life guided by reason is a good life, and happiness is a byproduct
of that. The more our life is filled with virtuous action, is spent developing our intellectual and physical potential to the max, the more we'll
find it brings pleasure. But pleasure should be avoided if it comes from
an activity that's inherently bad or not worthy. And a noisy rooster
among the chickens will do nicely to keep Alex from lying in and missing his phenomenology lecture. The rooster won't run out of battery!

Alex invites all his like-minded friends to join him in the garden.
They all look like Alex, but that's beside the point. The point is, you
need some *externalities*—such as roosters, such as interlocutors—in order to be virtuous. And sure, this can seem self-serving. Using your
friends and roosters to make you virtuous. Then again, it's hard to be
loyal if you have no friends. It's hard to be generous if you have nothing
to spare. It's hard to be a good teacher if your students cut class. (Nell

glares at the few empty seats, hears a few groans.) It's hard to be courageous if you're never in battle.

Every so often, even though he doesn't feel like it, Alex takes a walk outside his garden. His bubble. Because bad experiences, in moderation, are indispensable to a healthy psyche and happy life. He doesn't actually hold himself to any external obligations; he feels no responsibility to society or other people or gods. So he has to trust his peers to hold him to account, to ensure that he tackles each situation as it comes and responds to it correctly.

And who decides what's *correct?* a student asks. Is it just Alex?

The corner of Nell's mouth lifts. It's a question she put to her mother, in variations, many times.

Alex has posted no rules for ethical conduct in his garden, Nell says. No commandments or moral imperatives, no sign reading DON'T POUR YOUR DREGS IN THE POND. You have to train your reason to lead you down the right course of action, every single time. If you're properly trained in rationality, you'll be virtuous by instinct. You'll respond just as correctly to the wineglass as you will to the rooster—that is, with temperance.

The *best* life—so says Alex—is the life of theoretical inquiry. But he also recognizes that he'd be failing in his virtues if he neglected to act on behalf of his fellow citizens beyond the garden wall. Because you can do wrong *simply by failing to act.* So Alex gives away his immoderate wealth. And he spends much of his time working through societal problems to see if he can solve them. He builds dioramas in his garden. He invites his peers to participate, supporting and challenging them and expecting them to do the same. If a university dean were to visit his garden, Alex would welcome his contribution as a political theorist: a person responsible for working out what would make the whole community happy. How did you create this thriving environment? the dean might ask. Did you follow a blueprint? Ah, but Alex would reply: you should be asking how to foster *virtue*—since virtuous citizens will be prepared to live in harmony and to contribute to their communities.

A metal water bottle clanks to the floor. Several students turn to Mikkel, whose juddering knee is shaking the whole bench.

One day—Nell continues—at the far end of his garden, Alex marks out a site for his own burial plot. Why? Because he believes that a person's happiness can be diminished *after death*. If, for example, his friends decide that one of his beliefs was flawed, and they feel they must debunk that belief as a myth, then the happiness of Alex's life will retroactively be diminished. Needing to think on the matter, Alex excuses himself, takes a shovel to the end of his garden, and begins to dig.

Meanwhile, in garden two, someone we'll call Evan is constructing her own model of the good life. She sees Alex digging, and she hopes he's turning the burial site into a spa pool, as she's advised him it's a mistake to let a reminder of death and loss loom over your life. Live in the moment! she says.

Evan has invited lots of like-minded, attractive friends to brighten her garden. She's bought them recliner chairs and sunshades, a swing and a hammock. Evan isn't interested in torturous conversation or torment in the soul; she feels no obligation to relieve anyone of their wrong opinions. She won't admit pain into her garden. The citronella of mosquito candles imbues the breeze. A talented musician friend lounges on the grass strumming a lyre, a symbol of wisdom and moderation since ancient Egypt. Happily, Evan's friends are just as bent on achieving inner tranquility, so she can trust that no tin-eared chancer will ever "have a go" at the lyre!

Nell meets eyes with a student in the front row now, and the student takes a chance:

Professor?

Yes . . . Dakota?

You said this analogy shows how subtle ethical differences lead to totally different realities? But they're both private garden parties. Right? He cocks his shoulder. So, it's like shades of white. Call it *eggshell*, call it *oatmeal*, call it *oyster* all you like.

That's very well put, Dakota . . . Nell takes a moment to think. Do you remember Obama's metaphor—that you can redirect an ocean liner by a meager two degrees, but after a few years you'll wind up in a very different country? . . . I want us to be able to trace back to those slight shifts in ethics that might have happened in the past, that we're complicit in now, to understand how we arrived at our conception of a good, happy life. If we have one. Nell judges from Dakota's pout that this has earned her another thirty seconds of garden talk.

Evan pins it on *pleasure*. Pleasure is an intrinsic value. Pain comes from doing evil or from excess. She happens to be a brilliant cook and she makes plenty of delicious food and wine available, but her company avoids overindulging in love, wine, or religion. Annoyance or pain are too likely to follow. She and her friends don't rely on luxuries: expensive clothes, big houses, power . . . Happiness is more achievable if you *reduce* your needs and wants to what's necessary and natural: health, shelter, food, security, friendship. Once these natural desires are met, she holds, you can achieve a mental, physical, and emotional stability that's supremely pleasurable. A state free of fear and frustration, since pain feeds on fear and uncertainty.

For Evan, religion is a means of instilling fear in people and should be avoided. The gods need no appeasing. They don't get involved in daily human affairs. Humans, she feels confident, won't be punished after death. Death ends all experience. At the end of Evan's garden, there's no burial plot but a simple urn: a good container for atoms. For her, atoms *are* the whole universe—even the gods are made of atoms— and they are eternal and largely random and pointless. Yes, atoms can be swerved, through free will and voluntary action. But the universe is largely mechanistic and purposeless. Nature has no purpose, nor do animals. Humans aren't substantially different from animals. Evan is reminded of this now, as the rooster crows next door.

Then there's a sudden racket—the learned men are shouting in Alex's garden. Evan and her guests gather their robes and hurry to the wall to see what's going on.

Turns out Alex has dug up a chest of gold in his garden! There he

stands, in a trough of cash, weeping. For once, he seems unable to reason out what to do next. Seeing Evan, he gathers an armful of the loot
and carries it over to her; perhaps she'd have a use for it? But Evan
won't touch it. She knows that disruptive politics and dishonest, power-
hungry people are sure to enter the scene with this money. Power only
makes you want more of it, she warns him. Power makes people syco-
phants. But you like nice things! Alex argues. You could go on a pleasure bender! Evan says that no, she wouldn't do that, as such a spree
would make her less happy than if she'd been moderate all along. Re-
specting her position—they both consider moderation a virtue—Alex
withdraws to reason the dilemma out with his peers. Finally they decide they'll put the money toward a political campaign—not for Alex,
who's too busy with contemplation, but for anyone who matches him
in virtue and who feels it's their purpose to rule.

A couple months later, after Alex's garden has turned into a bust-
ling campaign headquarters and the continual politicking starts to
grate on Evan, she sends him a note that says: Justice is an agreement
between people not to harm one another. I know you believe that all
these macho meetings have a purpose, but my pleasure garden is wilt-
ing. How about we go halves on a higher wall? And I'll throw in my
recipe for rooster pie.

Nell skims her pupils' faces from her position on the desk, her legs
hanging numbly. House lights on! she says, miming pulling a light
switch to stir them. So who are Alex and Evan? And what are the two
distinct philosophies of happiness they expound?

Is that a lyre? someone asks, pointing to the instrument on Nell's
desk.

Nell twists to look at it. It is, she says. This one's a Kiganda bowl
lyre. A master's student brought it back from a trip home to Uganda.
I'm surprised she got it through customs.

Can you play it?

Nell points at her head and says: Tin ears. I won't torment you.

When the student gave her the instrument, Nell had felt a rush of pride—and with it a fresh surge of ambition for the tenure-track position she craved, for just such meaningful connections with serious and inspiring supervisees. Adjuncting mostly means teaching undergrad survey courses, but still she wants to teach well, to help the students tap into a different mode of thinking. While hunting for traces of Olwen online, Nell had found a Zoom lecture her sister had given during Covid. Even though the students were all just faces on a screen, Olwen had delivered the lecture from a big auditorium, setting her webcam up in the stalls so that she had room to move around, to throw her energy at it. Nell could see the curiosity and captivation caught on the faces of the students' feeds. Since then, Nell had been trying a more narrative approach with her own students—attempting to engage their imaginations with stories before moving on to the kinds of clarifying arguments that would help them withstand epistemic scrutiny.

The analogy of the gardens had occurred to Nell while she was attempting to understand Olwen's mindset when she left. She'd been trying to follow the stepping stones of truth Olwen had balanced her life on, to discover which direction she might have struck out in. Olwen, she knew, had always been closer to the Stoics than to the philosophers she'd just described. She sought no praise, braved up to mortality, focused on what she could control: her own thoughts and actions. But Nell had always felt there was something provisional—something temporary or contingent—in Olwen's approach to control. "The mind in itself has no needs, except for those it creates itself," said Marcus Aurelius. "Is undisturbed, except for its own disturbances. Knows no obstructions, except those from within." But Olwen's mind knew plenty of obstructions and disturbances beyond itself. In all gardens, she saw the uneaten birdfeed, the folly of cut grass.

A voice calls out: What's that story *from*?

It's a fable, another student says.

A fable has animals, says another. It's a parable.

It's not in the reading material, someone gripes, flipping through the coursebook.

It's not in the Bible either, the student who'd called it a fable tells the student who called it a parable.

I made it up! Nell says. In the hope it'll help you get your bearings in the philosophies we'll be considering, to see how each new model for a good life relates to those that came before it, and to track how it led to those that follow. These are just two of many—and the differences between just these two are significant. If a real body of citizens followed them, they'd lead to two very different societies.

Massive differences, one student says . . . between two ancient Greek men!

Nell looks at the young woman. They are such a force of resistance, her students. Of course that *is* what they're training in: an argumentative approach. A philosophy degree does nothing if not teach students to constantly anticipate objection. Greeks, yes! she says. Is it . . . eh, I'm so sorry, Laura?

Lauren.

Lauren. Nell nods. Fear not: there'll be massiver differences coming up. We've got the Chinese traditions of Confucius, Laozi, Zhuangzi; the Hindu Bhagavad Gītā; then the Japanese Buddhist traditions of well-being. Western religious traditions, from Augustine through nineteenth-century transcendentalism to the Harlem Renaissance. The Persian Sufi Conference of the Birds, if anyone's got ahead on the reading. Then contemporary mindfulness, which I suspect you'll all have some knowledge of, and creative practice approaches to happiness. But today we've got the ancient Greeks. Can anyone identify which ones?

A slouched guy in a brimmed cap sits upright, gearing up to speak, but Mikkel beats him to it:

"Happiness is the greatest hiding place for despair." He gives Nell a look of shared culpability.

Nell tightens her grip on the table edge. The room won't quite stay still for her. She hears herself say: I'm afraid Kierkegaard is too late for this garden party, Mikkel.

In what sense? Mikkel asks.

In the sense that he's not an ancient Greek.

Is Evan *Epicurus*? Lauren asks.

The *hedonist*? a student beside Lauren says.

Nell is so relieved, she sends a double thumbs-up in Lauren's direction.

Alex is clearly Aristotle, Lauren adds, now backing herself. So it's Aristotle and Epicurus.

Denmark is the second happiest country in the world, says Mikkel, louder now. Do you want to know how we do it?

No one responds, but Nell notices several students craning forward a little, to hear from this figure who never speaks.

In Denmark, he goes on, nobody says: You can be anything you want! Make the ten-year plan of your dreams and it will come true. You deserve happiness! Mikkel looks at Nell like they've both scanned a menu and found nothing meaty. What we do . . . we lower our expectations.

For just a moment, Nell wonders if this could be a cri de cœur . . . rather than an accusation.

Hey Prof? someone shouts. You got mail.

Nell holds her breath for several seconds, then hears herself gasp. Now the students are all looking at the projector screen, where a mail notification has obscured the top corner of her PowerPoint slide. It reads: *YOUR QUOTE from New Hampshire MRI.* Heat races up from her chest to her cheeks. In a rush to get the lecture started on time, she'd forgot to turn off the Wi-Fi on her laptop. She shimmies her bum forward on the desk to stand up . . . but her feet on the floor might as well be sinking into a pond, so she stays put.

Ah! Bodily pain. I'm not sure Evan would let me into her garden, she says, and a few students laugh kindly. Mikkel: we *will* come back to the World Happiness Report, have no doubt. Meanwhile, I hope your low expectations will be exceeded. And Lauren: I wonder what gave Alex away as Aristotle?

While Lauren holds forth, Nell considers what else might pop up on the screen. News of Olwen, returned from circling the globe with a backpack full of samples? News of Olwen's body, found in some lake with a backpack full of rocks? How could Nell have let so much time pass without realizing that reason alone might not be enough to lead her to her sister; how could she still have faith in words when they had utterly failed to elicit a response?

As the students are filing out after the lecture, an improbably joyful woman approaches her. For what it's worth, she says, the gardens were really beautiful. You did a really good job. Nell waits, open to what might follow. She would be grateful to be called out for unsound reasoning, truly. To be vivisected while she's still alive, while there's a chance she can be treated and sewn up neatly and plopped back into the murky water she loves.

The woman glances behind her, in case there's a line she might be holding up.

Just . . . she says through a huge smile now, but hesitates, her teeth catching on her lower lip.

Go on, Nell says encouragingly.

Do you . . . The woman leans in, gesturing vaguely toward Nell's midsection. Do you need a hand?

Oh, Nell says, and shakes her head, dislodging a bit of trapped seawater in her ear. She is so taken aback by the offer, and at the same time relieved that it's not a come-on, that she nearly jokes that no, she can get herself off pretty well. Instead she just thanks the student and says: I'm waiting for the hall to empty out, so I can . . . annoy the gods with my lyre.

• • •

On the drive back up to Quinnipiac for her phenomenology class, Nell stops for gas. Though there's an attendant to fill the tank, she can't afford the tip, and she's embarrassed to ask for just five dollars' worth of gas, so she manages by herself. At the till, a marked-down protein bar promises to be a FULL MEAL REPLACEMENT. It comes in a double-pack. She buys one to bring to Ron.

I need to keep you alive, she says, handing him the bar as she drops into his guest chair. You're the only one who I know won't use this as an excuse to end my contract.

Use what? he says, confused. What happened?

Nothing. No. It's just . . . It's what I have to do. And I can't see Southern having me back after. So I need to know I'll be able to come back here.

What do you mean? After what?

How ready would you say Bethanne is to take over my classes?

Ron stands up. For a moment, he just stands there. Then his chin suddenly dimples and his eyes flood, as a man just emerged from a cave. Did you just come from the doctor?

Nell shakes her head. It's not that. But I need to go on sabbatical. As soon as possible.

Is it a tumor? On your spine?

No, Ron.

I *knew* it. It's a barnacle.

No, it's not me at all. Nell looks at him with apology. It's my sister. I need to go find her.

Ron lowers his spectacles past the bridge of his nose. He pauses. Nell, I hear you. But . . . have you tried Facebook? Because taking on a whole cross-continental sibling search mission is . . . You remember Cadmus?

Nell says nothing.

When Cadmus went on a quest to find *his* lost sister, the Delphic oracle told him it was useless. Told him to give up already, follow a cow, and build a town on the spot where she lay down. That's how Thebes got built.

Are you telling me not to try, Ron? I don't follow your cow.

Point is, we'd be lost without you. *We'd* be lost. Ron takes off his glasses, rubs his eyes. Free of glasses, his cheekbones have a varnished look. He spins around to face his bookcase and, after a moment, full-circles toward Nell again. How would you even start? You can barely make it up the stairs to my office, but you're going to lead a search party all over Europe?

I have to, Ron.

How do you even know she's in Europe? he says rapidly.

Olwen stopped flying *years* ago, after COP21. And the Trans-Siberian Railway is on her bucket list, but it's not the best time in history for that.

If you're talking rail, can't you get to, like, Tehran by train?

From Ireland? Tricky.

She might not want to be found, Ron says. She could be living her best life.

She could be. And then we'll know.

She could be *going through* something, your sister. A change. Maybe she's . . . maybe they're coming into their own, in some way. And maybe they need to do that alone.

Olwen's been menopausal since she was, like, twenty-five. She was fanning her graduation gown and wafting us all with her hot flash funk. And there's no way she'd concede the female condition. She finds it too funny.

Ron isn't hearing this through his armor of disappointment. Hunched shoulders. Crossed arms. Low brow. It'll be hell convincing management, he says. I can't set a precedent that adjuncts can go on sabbatical. We'll have to call it sick leave, Nell. You caught scarlet fever on campus and the college board should be glad you can't afford a lawyer and we should be counting the days before you're back with us, onto the tenure-track treadmill.

Nell looks up at him. My lease ends soon.

Ron meets her gaze and chews the inside corner of his mouth.

When I come back, she says, I might need your couch for a bit.

At that, he loosens his mouth and brow. I'll kick a couple fish out of the aquarium.

Nell laughs. Okay.

Don't put your snorkel on eBay.

I won't.

He uncrosses his arms and lets something go. We should all be so lucky to have a Nell.

Nell takes one of the protein bars from his desk and rips at its plastic. Save it for the board, she says. She sniffs the protein bar and winces. It smells like cocoa butter foot cream!

The dean returns his glasses to the bridge of his nose and sits down. Take it out of my office, please. I have a *lot* of work to do.

He seems almost gleeful saying this, Nell notes, as if being confronted by a creature with an explicit goal has reminded him of his own purpose.

4.

At the kitchen island, Rhona and her son listen to the *Intelligence Squared* podcast over breakfast. An old colleague, from her stint as a research fellow at Oxford, is arguing against the use of citizens' assemblies as a way of increasing popular participation in government. Specifically, he is arguing that these assemblies foster governmental cowardice. *Wow.* He really is threading the donut there, don't you think, Leo?

Leo's chair is set to its maximum height because he likes to be eye-to-eye with his mother. He inventories the objects on his tray, probably calculating how many whole blueberries there would be hadn't they been halved. Named after his dead granny Leonora, red-haired, brown-eyed Leo hasn't much of the Flattery about him, apart from being early to teethe. At eleven months, he has the bite of a coyote. He dips his zucchini-carrot pancake soldiers into the tomato relish with the precision of an artist painting a red nose on a clown. What's that, darling? Was that *nom* . . . or did you say *mum*? Rhona hurries the French press along. Hmm? Did you say *mummy*?

As far as her sisters know, Leo came into Rhona's life in more or less the same way as her black walnut floors: a catalog, a felling, and a pricey installation procedure. In fact, Leo was the result of two missed contraceptive pills, a night of MDMA, and a moonlit sea, after a beach party at an electoral reform conference in Lisbon. The man must have been ginger. Wet, his hair had looked black. High, his eyes had looked infrared. Hard, he had felt meritorious. Rhona hadn't ascertained his conversational skills, or if he spoke English for that matter, but she can already tell that Leo—once he's ready to break out with that long-awaited first word—will speak volumes, and not just to fill the silence. It's there in the way he squints at anyone who tries to use gobbledy-gook to engage him instead of saying something substantive. He's squinting now at the podcast, and Rhona couldn't agree more.

It's shocking, she says, hearing him speak for a motion *against* letting people speak! Even more shocking, he's wasting half his argument on a *quibble*. Yes, fine, if recommendations from assemblies get taken up by government and put to referendum, the *referendum* arguably lets politicians off the hook. But when would that ever happen, except on hot potato issues the government's consistently refused to catch? It's a quibble. Not a counterargument.

Leo picks up a pancake soldier and smacks it around.

Exactly, Rhona says. It's a straw man. Anyway, if a politician wants to let himself off the hook, he doesn't need the permission of his underlings. Some people are well able to unhook themselves. I've seen it.

Getting to the wobbly-voice stage of the debate, her ex-colleague is saying: That *traditionally elected* politicians would cede the national agenda to *random* members of the public amounts to an abdication of their primary responsibility as the figureheads of our democracy! However corruptible local councilors might be—

Rhona switches off the podcast. That's embarrassing, she says. And irritating. That was meant to be a favor I'd done him, recommending him for that show. But now I've thrown his credibility under the bus by letting him speak for himself.

Leo drops the bloodied soldier to the floor.

Oops!

Rhona is an expert in citizens' assemblies, a subject of increasing interest internationally, and it was she who'd originally been invited to appear on the podcast. More precisely, to participate in an Oxford-style debate before a live audience at Conway Hall in London. But she's been trying to travel less this spring, in advance of a period of upheaval: a turbulent front that's been looming, sure to make land before long.

What have we here? she says now, extracting an envelope from the morning's newspapers. Don't tell me it's the *council*—Rhona gasps at Leo as she breaks the seal—committing to a *start date*?

The shorefront residents of Burrow Road and Claremont Road in Sutton, Rhona's well-heeled enclave on Dublin's north coast, have been lobbying the council and the Office of Public Works to invest in seawall defenses. Their gardens have taken a hammering in three extreme tidal events in the past decade, depleting the dunes between their rear gardens and the sea. When one of the homeowners tried to file an insurance claim for patio and landscaping damage (including damage to "architectural foliage" and "fine art in the garden shed") after one storm surge, the insurers threatened to rescind coverage of the whole strip on the basis that the sea-sprayed Victorian terraces of Burrow Road were increasingly exposed and drastically overinsured. The Sutton homeowners petitioned for a new breakwater, but the county council waved them off—they had far more pressing work in Sandymount and Clontarf, where constant road repairs were draining the region's wallet, and giant sandbags have become permanent installations—and besides, an infrastructure project that costly would have to be approved and paid for at a national level.

So Rhona and the other residents—with the support of the local golf club—lined up their solicitors, impermeable as sandbags, and suggested that a robust seawall to replace the futile palisade between their rear gardens and the dunes would suffice in the short term. In addition to improving their properties, they maintained, it would help protect regional rail lines that were also at risk. Much like a mini citizens' assembly—albeit not deliberately *representative*—a group of extremely busy citizens had come together in a room over a series of weekends to confront a structural problem, to hear from experts on its extent, and to receive quotes and plans to have it mitigated. On its own newly minted letterhead, it wrote to the council lamenting the long-term effects to future investment in the area should the big insurance companies withdraw coverage. To hurry things along, the residents proposed to make their own generous contribution, totaling €1.3 million, to the project—on the condition that the work be underway by summer 2023.

Please be advised, Rhona reads to Leo, construction work to commence on May twelfth! *Ooh.* That's *soon.* She widens her eyes and glances toward the hallway. Road access will be temporarily obstructed between Lauder's Lane and the church tower . . . la la la . . . Please find enclosed a noise and vibration impact assessment for the early construction period . . . Wow. Five pages of vibration frequency stats. We've talked about civil servants, haven't we, Leo, and losing the will to live? Rhona swills the remainder of her coffee and drains it. So we might do an Airbnb while that's going on, somewhere nice. Beatriz can look after the place, can't she? Rhona listens for sounds down the hall again and whispers: Do you think she'd finally seem comfortable, if she had a chance to make the place her own? Without us? Or I could leave you with her? Leo follows his mother's fingers as if she might have foraged something from his person. Sorry, darling. That wasn't funny. I'm not your auntie. I won't take off.

Beatriz is a postdoctoral scholar from Peru. Rhona had hired her to do the work of a think tank research grant she'd won. After sending a delighted email about the job offer, Beatriz had Zoomed Rhona in a bit of a panic, saying she wouldn't be able to accept the role after all; she'd looked into Dublin's rental prices, and it was impossible, it was just not possible. Her brows had tented above the frames of her foggy glasses. This was a disappointment: Beatriz was not only hugely impressive academically, but Rhona *liked* her. She could see them getting along, perhaps becoming friends. So, on the spot, she'd offered her a room in her place, "rent free," in exchange for a little babysitting now and then. "The house is fully soundproofed," she concluded, sealing the matter for herself more than anyone. In a flood of relief, Beatriz blurted out that her brother was autistic, that he, too, was very sensitive to noise. When Rhona cocked her head at the response, like a crow considering a shoddy nest, Beatriz blushed and course-corrected: *Everybody* needs noise cancellation headphones sometimes. And she loved babies! Thus reassured, they set a move-in date. She had arrived at the end of last summer, ready for the academic year.

Lately, Beatriz has been waiting for Rhona to leave the house before emerging for breakfast. (Always "toasts.") She cycles to the university instead of taking a lift, even in the rain. Then again, Rhona isn't always driving to campus, and Beatriz is a creature of routine and head-to-toe waterproofs. Rhona cleans traces of relish from Leo's fists and relocates him to the playpen, then goes outside to unplug the car and throw a gym bag in the boot. She checks the bonnet for seagull droppings. The morning has a laundered calm about it, undercut with chemicals. Contrail creases in the brochure blue.

Up the reds! the neighbor, Jim O'Rourke, calls out, jogging toward her from the postbox at the end of his drive. We did it! His belly is so large that the dressing gown rides up his balding shins.

Running a victory lap? Rhona closes the charger port on her Tesla and returns the plug to its dock.

Come in for a celebratory Nespresso, will ya?

When Rhona glowers at Jim's scarred cleavage, he covers it with the torn envelope and adds: Half-caf and no biscuits. Full communist.

Rhona sniffs at his flower beds reprovingly. Please ask your wife to switch to chemical weed killers. Vinegar isn't as environmentally friendly as she thinks.

Jim shimmies the letter at her. A dispute! We're in business. Get in here till we litigate it.

Jim. I have a *job*.

He looks accosted. That's actually cruel.

Jim was the European Union's eminently sociable Commissioner

for Neighbourhood and Enlargement until a double-bypass knocked
him sideways a few years ago. Under the influence of heavy painkillers
and mandatory leave, he'd promised his wife he'd "stop going so hard."
Seeing through this half-hearted, plaque-bound promise, she said she
was sorry, she had no choice—in this moment while he was briefly in
the country—but to leave him. As much as she loved him, she knew as
a GP that she could no longer live with the constant stress about his
lifestyle. She was weary. He would kill them both. With the gallantry
boost of a few milligrams of oxycodone, Jim had committed to early
retirement, then and there.

I have a baby! Rhona protests. I can't leave him in the house!

Bring the boss man over. I'd change a nappy, so I would, just for a
whiff of chaos.

Rhona purses her lips. Sometimes Jim reminds her of Olwen: The
wide stance. The brutality.

Then she has an idea. I'll be two minutes, she says.

Back inside, at the base of the stairwell, the house seems quiet. A
bit of whining from the kitchen, but that's just Leo testing his range:
tenor and baritone are both within his gamut. Rhona takes out her
phone and sees that Beatriz has been online for an hour. Without having come down for so much as a coffee! Rhona phones her. Good
morning, Bea! I didn't know if you were up or if you're working from
home today, or . . . ? Oh? Okay. I'm just popping over to Jim's to discuss the council letter. We have a start date for the seawall construction! May twelfth. Soon, yeah. It's brilliant. We might have to find
another place for a few weeks, but we'll talk when I'm back from next
door. Leo's fed and in his playpen. Could you keep an eye on him
while you're having breakfast, Beatriz?

• • •

Jim's kitchen on the second floor has a wall of sea-facing windows.
They'd need sunglasses weren't it for the smart glass: the windows

change their tint and opacity on command. Jim commands it now to turn off opaque mode. Give the paparazzi some fodder! he says. They'll be round on day one of construction, wait'll you see, sizing us up for who made the fattest donation. He smacks his own dressing-gowned ass, possibly to indicate money taken from his back pocket. Rhona doesn't ask Jim what he'd been doing this morning that had required the privacy of opaque windows; it was probably depraved.

Jim has all the gadgets. It started out innocently enough, as a decoy when he'd been struggling to find topics of conversation with his teenage son during Covid lockdowns. Though the lad has since absconded to dorms, Jim is loath to quit the habit of ordering gadgetry online. He has barely anything left to quit. At this stage, he's at the diagnostic bidet end of the what-to-buy-a-man-who-has-everything-but-a-purpose spectrum.

He sets a coffee down before Rhona, who is seated at the bay window's half-moon table.

Jim, why am I in your ridiculous kitchen? At . . . She glances at a clock on the wall, its time segments depressed and raised like an Escher staircase. Unable to read it, she awakens her phone on the table. At ten past eight in the morning?

Where would you be that's *less* ridiculous?

Rhona huffs, but she is glad for Jim's friendship. He is admittedly desperate, but she knows that he finds her interesting. Feigning interest was the one aspect of his job that he willingly dropped. He is staring at her phone now like he's just made a prank call and is hoping for retaliation.

What's all that?

The Olwen Search Party WhatsApp group is flooding messages onto her screen, Maeve and Nell trading long-shot ideas to catch Olwen's attention. Currently pouring in are links to straggly rescue animals in need of Olwen's resurrectory powers; they might also serve as sniffer dogs for the hunt. The sisters haven't yet asked Rhona for a place to stay; they'll probably wait till the last second. Rhona slides the messages away, tells Jim absently: They've put me forward for the vice presidency of the EPSA.

Vice, did you say?

I'm already on the executive committee with IPSA, and I'm chairing a research group for them, so it's—

Who are we on about?

You know. The European Political Science Association. And the International.

Jim selects a rock sugar with a tiny pair of wooden tongs and drops it eucharistically on his tongue. The committee position wouldn't be in my top five, he says with an air of closure. He sucks ponderously. The chair, though . . .

It's more *international* collaborations and networking, she says, ignoring him. Which I was all about five or six years ago, but now . . . Now I think I need to double down on this island.

Don't let Leo restrict your playing the field! Jim takes a second rock sugar.

Leo's not a constraint. That has nothing to do with it.

She knew he wouldn't understand. Jim *lived* for international schmoozing. He thrived at it. He could get anyone to undig their heels, or clogs, as the case may be. He could bridge any language gap. He rolls the rock sugar around in his mouth. Rhona's shoulders are up by her ears at the rattling of the sugar against his teeth. Can you not?

Jim chomps the sugar obligingly, then says: They're giving you the time of day, Rhona. All the bigwigs. Why would you go small? You're positioned to have serious international sway, and you're obviously equipped for it. Why limit yourself to this wet island?

You're projecting, Jim. It's not about constraints or limitations. It's that . . . the more sway I have internationally, the more dubiously I'm seen here.

What?

I mean it. I spent years on citizens' assemblies here, doing grunt work to get people on board. But now I'm treated like I had another *agenda* all along—that it was all an excuse to create some kind of exploitable product. Including my own career.

Says who? When Rhona doesn't answer, Jim lowers his chin to his chest so that his chin cleft and sternotomy scar line up. That's madness, he says. That's in your head.

The thing was, it *had* been in her head, until just now, when she'd come out with it. But Jim is out of practice at encouraging people when they're approaching some sort of concession. He's fixated on the wrong things. The pulsing screen of her phone, for one.

Sweet Lord, what I'd give for a double-booked lunch hour, he says. For a high-pitched call from a sweaty PA. He massages his jaw.

Do you want me to drop a hint to your wife about the value-add of part-time de-retirees?

He shakes his head brusquely. No, just . . . Read me your inbox. Slowly. Tell me who you've got back-to-back.

Rhona sips her espresso, then swills a bit of water to keep her teeth from staining. The gym, she says, for one thing. (Jim groans with displeasure.) I've to drop Leo off to his minder. Beatriz is showing promise at her *actual* job, so I should let her get to it. I've a PhD student to pull back off a bridge, an editorial meeting for the EPSA journal, a UN online panel thing, oh, and I've a bunch of Northern Ireland stuff; you know the deal. All the usual bread and butter.

Do you know what I have on? Jim says huskily.

Don't, Rhona says. I'll never be able to unhear—

I have *banana*, Jim persists. I have *flaxseed*. I have spinach, mango, frozen yogurt, an Xtreme Hi-Power blender. He gets up to hunt for the various constituents.

Rhona picks up her phone. With all the drama her sisters are fabricating, it's hard to know if it's a comedy or tragedy or what. If Olwen wants to be left alone, that's her prerogative. Nell shouldn't be jeopardizing her job. Jobs. However many she has. They're being childish, talking about Odysseying across the Irish Sea in Maeve's canal boat. (Olwen gave up flying years ago "because Planetary Boundaries," she'd told Maeve the last time they were all together, for Nell's thirtieth more than three years ago, and Maeve fears Olwen will hold it against them if they fly across the ocean in pursuit of her.) Thankfully, somebody noticed that direct flights from Boston to Dublin were considerably cheaper than to London, and the fiasco of putting a canal boat in the Irish Sea was forestalled. Now Maeve and Nell are planning to meet at Dublin Airport to begin the expedition. In which direction, they don't yet know.

To give her credit, Maeve had thought to phone up all the Irish polytunnel companies to see if any kind of greenhouse had been sold to an Olwen Flattery in the past six months. At Christmas two years ago, when Maeve spent the holidays with her and Jasper and the boys, Olwen was harping on about them. If she'd gone off the grid somewhere, Maeve reckons, a polytunnel would have been on her shopping list.

Will I give you something to do? Rhona asks her neighbor, who immediately steps away from the blender.

Sliding back onto the bay window bench, Jim flares his nostrils. Don't toy with me.

It's painful, she says, watching my sisters at this . . . reality TV orienteering. I can see exactly how it'll play out.

Reality TV lands differently when you're forced into early retirement, Jim says sorely.

They both have enough of our dad's DNA to have pent-up backpacking energy in their systems to get out. Skinny-dipping in glacial lakes. Spewing ayahuasca tea. Rhona drains her water. I'd like to arrange it so they can just—she splays the fingers of her hands—skip that whole episode.

Go on, Jim says.

I made some calls to see if anything popped up on the land and property registry.

And?

They needn't bother backpacking to Galway. Olwen sold her one-bed on the docks. Where she lived before moving into Jasper's. So she has *cash*. It won't have gone under a mattress. If I know Olwen, she'll have put it in the soil. In land. Matheson, the firm who handled our parents' wills, is the obvious choice for her, but if not them she'd use someone comparable. If you could drop a line to your pals at Lavelle or Matheson, maybe Felton McKnight. Have them check for a cash-deal contract in her name late last year?

Jim claps his hands and the ceiling lights come on. Consider it done! This'll carry me over from the smoothie till elevenses.

With Olwen's voice in her ear, Rhona stands and claps to turn the lights off again. Will you stick around for the construction? she asks Jim.

It's the only action I'll see all month.

It'll be noisy, Rhona says.

Hang on. I thought your house was soundproofed? I've been absolutely banking on it.

Rhona squints at the glimmering sea: the best white noise machine on the market. She envisions the band of concrete that will soon silence it, that will shield them from erosion and make their salty gardens green.

. . .

Back at the house, Beatriz, already in her bike helmet, is loading the dishwasher. Leo is on her hip, using her helmet as a bongo. The kitchen smells of toast. Rhona offers her a ride to campus, suggesting they discuss some new reviewers' comments to a paper in the car, but Beatriz claims she needs the exercise.

Oh come off it! Rhona says. Then Beatriz turns to her and there is a moment of discomfort when Rhona can't find anything appropriate to add—"I can tell you're avoiding me" or "You don't need the exercise; you're in great shape" won't work—so she says nothing. She goes to take Leo, but Beatriz holds him like a vendor refusing a too-low offer.

I watched your TED Talk, Beatriz says. The women in leadership?

I really liked the part about setting quantifiable goals, about *balance*. I made a list of goals for myself, to separate work from life. But I keep blowing them.

Oh. Rhona steps forward. Let me separate this sticky guy from you. She frowns at Leo. Were you putting Bea to work before she's digested her breakfast, Mr. Flattery? Did you dive right into geopolitics instead of making small talk, asking how she slept? How'd you sleep, Beatriz?

Good, thank you. And you?

Leo isn't done with his drum solo yet, and Rhona has to tuck her head back to keep her French twist in place. She gets a baby wipe for the stubborn relish on his lovely chubby cheek. Rhona got her full four hours' sleep, but she doesn't say as much, so as not to be intimidating.

Any plans for tonight?

Tonight? Beatriz collects a brown paper bag from the counter and folds it closed. Tonight I have to catch up on a double episode of *Casualty*. The season finale, so if you hear a crying tantrum, it's not Leonardo.

We won't hear a peep. That reminds me: the construction work. Do you have a moment?

Beatriz takes her phone from her windbreaker pocket to check the time. Not really, I—

I've just had an idea! Give me *one* sec. Rhona carries Leo to a play area by the window, switches on his digital music mat (a gift from Jim), and fits on the accompanying headphones so he can have that noisy fun just for himself. In her five-inch heels, she jogs back to the coffee machine, fills the portafilter with ground beans, tamps it, and places two espresso cups under the spout. Let's have our two o'clock meeting now. Free up your afternoon.

Beatriz unclips the chin strap of her helmet and declines the coffee: I just cleaned my teeth. She pulls a copybook and pen from her backpack and sits at the island—helmet still on—sure that this will end up being in addition to their standing two o'clock, not a replacement.

How's the family? Rhona asks.

Eh . . . Beatriz flashes the bottom row of her teeth. Good.

I bet your brother misses you?

Why, you want to employ him? Beatriz smiles reproachfully. Is this work, Rhona, or—she puts on an Irish accent—*having the chats*?

Rhona takes one of the cups and rests it on her palm. You remember I mentioned the construction work planned? It turns out, that starts on May twelfth! But I just checked my calendar and I'm due to fly to Chile that week to deliver the CERG report to their congress. And it occurred to me . . . *you* could deliver the report, Bea. You're perfectly capable of commanding a presentation.

Beatriz sits blank and powerful as a page.

We can flatter your seniority, Rhona continues. We can print new business cards, push your expertise on mixed-member proportional representation. Plus, you wouldn't need a translator. You know the analysis, and Alexandra and I can get you up to speed on the rest.

Beatriz is not taking notes. She shouldn't be stunned. By now she's used to her boss's perennial spring tide of ideas: as soon as a destination is arrived at, it becomes the setting-off point for another, more extreme destination.

Meeting with these groups could be very important for you, Beatriz. It could create opportunities for when your contract here is up. It makes so much sense, now that I think of it. And I never stipulated to the public official that it would be me delivering the report. All we stipulated was an in-person appearance from "a delegate from Trinity." The construction work here will be messy—this whole road will be cut off temporarily, to get all the equipment in. If you can handle this for me, you could tack on a visit home to Peru. There must be a train from Valparaíso to Lima, all along the coast?

Beatriz rests her pen on the unopened notebook, removes her glasses to clean them with the hem of her shirt. While she's cleaning the lenses she squints and says, No.

No? You don't want to go?

No, there is no train. A bus, yes. Forty-two, forty-four hours. The bone shaker.

Rhona knocks the espresso back and then swaps the empty cup for the full one, airing the whites of her eyes in the hopes of waking everybody up. Tricky terrain, is it?

That sort of thing. The Andes, the Atacama—Beatriz scans the open council letter on the countertop—and a union of truck drivers stronger than a border wall.

And there you are, Rhona says. *Just* the doctor the country ordered.

Well . . . that's flattering, and generous. It's certainly interesting . . .

It's a step up.

The report is going to annoy people, no? Beatriz looks through clear lenses at Rhona now. It isn't like your crowd-pleasing citizens' assembly work.

I wouldn't call—

We are telling elected officials, Beatriz cuts in, to reform their electoral process—even though it will surely make it harder for some of them to get reelected?

It's a report they commissioned! Rhona says. As one of many great strides Chile is making as a progressive democracy. And it's a *free* democracy . . . unlike Peru. Which I say just because there's no doubt regarding its usefulness. It'll get serious consideration—

I'm not so close to it as you said.

I wouldn't put it in your hands weren't you capable of catching up.

Beatriz looks across to Leo's small fists, hammering their muted music. With government agencies . . . I'd be nervous about saying the wrong thing, provoking problems.

Being able to switch to Spanish if something's not landing . . . that's gold. It means you can *repeat* yourself, which buys them time to hear the facts and to accept them. You'll be nimbler than I could be.

Beatriz frowns at Leo, who's lifting the music mat and slapping it against the floor.

Rhona finishes the second espresso and rinses the cups. We're basically there to smack of scholarship, to float the idea that hard evidence can actually inform policy-making. Come along now, Leo. You'll be late for your nine o'clock. You don't want Ms. O'Hare to start doubting your commitment to cardboard tube communication.

Warily but steadily, Beatriz seems to be stepping around some blockade in her mind. I brushed his teeth, she says.

Thank you.

He has so many of them.

I know. Rhona looks genuinely dismayed. And not a single word for me, out of that packed mouth. Not two complimentary syllables has he strung together for his mother.

Well . . . without any words, he can say a lot of diplomatic things.

Rhona looks from Beatriz to her son. She walks over to him, crouches down before him, and removes his headphones. Is that true? My small tactician? Hmm? Do you think I need handling?

. . .

Having freed up that hour at 2 p.m., Rhona considers how to use the gap in her schedule. Much as she'd love to collect Leo from childcare for an hour's mutual worship, the last time she stole him away in the middle of the day, Ms. O'Hare from childcare gave her a talking-to about routines and expectations and boundaries. With so many women in her life demanding boundaries, it's enough to make Rhona feel transgressive.

Another woman keeping her distance is a member of Parliament from the Department of Public Expenditure and Reform who Rhona's been trying to pin down for a face-to-face. The TD is scheduled to address a select committee at Leinster House during a 1–3 p.m. session, so she might just catch her.

Rhona has a media pass, thanks to the occasional op-ed and not-infrequent TV and radio commentary, especially during election cycles and referendums. She slips into the media gallery of Committee Room 3. Though it's not a huge room, the layout of tiered varnished pine tables, shaped as a shoehorn within a shoehorn, facing the front bench—with computer monitors at every station—makes it hard to immediately see who's present. Busy scanning the room for the TD, Rhona hadn't noticed who she'd taken a seat beside: Vince Grealish, chief political editor of the *Irish Times*, for whom she's written many articles, and who—as Jim would put it—she'd give the time of day. Vince is pretending to inspect some lint on his lapel as Rhona settles and whispers hello.

O Rhona How Are You, Vince mouths. Then flushes. His pen and paper suddenly come into their own. All the clicking ballpoints in the room sound of crickets stridulating. Someone from the Central Statistics Office is speaking, making short shrift of the post-lunch attention span.

God, he's tedious, Rhona says.

Vince groans in agreement . . . or possibly in amusement at Professor Flattery's contempt for dry oratory when she herself thinks the public is dying for another three thousand words on referendum structure. If she could learn to tell a story without quite so much emphasis on *procedure*, he's told her before. But Rhona does have good ideas, now and then, and she has the conviction of a tennis ball launcher; he can't pretend he doesn't admire her work ethic or her resilience.

The thing is, Vince has openly—if awkwardly—*criticized* Rhona, but he also wants to work with her. And that is one of the better compliments she's had. So it's probably just *in her head*—as Jim said—that he seems to be leaning away from her now, tucking his elbow tight to his side, as if she might link his arm and steal him into a corner. His note-taking must have taken an inspired turn, because he opens a speech-to-text app on his phone to auto-transcribe the address while he scribbles furiously in the notepad on his knee.

Has Ellen McSharry spoken yet?

Vince shakes his head. She had to go.

What?

He stops writing. She'll be back, but she'll be up last.

They flipped the order?

Vince looks at his phone, where the text of the address is now interspersed with their exchanges, then pauses the auto-transcription. Over the thick rims of his glasses, he tells Rhona: She left the tap on.

Is that a metaphor?

Vince lowers his head to hide a smile, flashing the shine of scalp on his crown. She got a call from her downstairs neighbors, he says. Who had water streaming down their wall. Vince glances at her conclusively and turns his transcription back on.

Rhona stops herself from saying what comes to mind about that TD—something about things falling through the cracks and things being pushed through them—which might make Vince feel implicated in gossip. By the time she thinks of what to say, it sounds contrived and she drops it.

Vince removes his glasses, shakes them like a sugar packet, and puts them back on with renewed studiousness. On another neighbor's laptop, Rhona notices what's really happening: a message from Leinster House Cyber Security. Temporary suspension of service. A security operation is underway. The session must adjourn for ten minutes.

It's all go today, Vince says, and shakes his head.

Rhona collects her bag and feels a hand on her shoulder. Someone is standing behind her: a columnist called Yvonne or Yvette or Evie.

Rhona Flattery! You must have one of them time turners, like Hermione Granger. You're *here. There. Everywhere.*

Oh! Rhona reluctantly shifts her knees to let Vince squeeze past with his briefcase. Oh, em . . . good seeing you, Vince.

There's me perusing the *FT* over me fry-up—the woman says loudly—and there's your mug: a two-page spread, no less. (She pulls a scandalized face.) Next thing, over me lunch I'm catching up on the

UN symposium on Parliament elections, the Zoom recording, and it's yourself . . . with your two cents. Which you never run out of. Rumor has it you're doing *major* spadework in the North, finding sponsors for this, that, and the other. *How* do you do it?

Oh, Rhona says, trying whatever she thinks will end the conversation quickly: It's less than it seems.

Why do you do it? the woman adds.

Rhona gives her the puzzled-yet-flattered look the woman seems to want. She clearly hasn't watched her TED Talk, so Rhona does a bit of self-plagiarizing: Well . . . as Frances Willard said, you *have* to. "Do everything." Campaign on all fronts. And, despite all the racism, she got us the eight-hour workday. So it can be done without witchcraft. Though . . . Rhona pauses here . . . it did cause a rift among the women of the nineteenth century.

It's hardly a part-time gig, your professor at Trinity! the woman says with a sort of lewd expression, as if describing a horse.

Yvonne.

Rhona takes a chance on the name and, when it's met with acceptance, she considers taking a punt on the surname too. Rhona realizes that the thing to do would be to say something in response—to offer some humble explanation—but there's nothing she wants to answer or ask of this hostile person, now gazing at the brightly colored set of toy keys attached to the Tesla fob Rhona's taken from her handbag. Leo likes to have his own set of keys to rattle, to assert a meeting concluded.

You'll not be accused of staying in your ivory tower anyhow, Yvonne says. Fair play. Are you due to speak?

No.

Are you in here to get used to the view, then? Yvonne is clutching the back of the chair Rhona'd arisen from.

Rhona doesn't like it when serious questions are posed flippantly. She doesn't like it when people don't say what they're saying. Especially when there's no threat of negative repercussions. If you're asking if I want to work in government, Rhona says, absolutely not. She takes her earpod case from her handbag. It's just history I'm eyeing up, she says. Not a bad belvedere, the media gallery. Good luck with your write-up.

As she shuffles out, inserting an earpod to catch the end of a staff meeting on the way back to campus, Rhona hears the woman say to her back: Good luck to you, or Fair fucks to you, or something of that order.

This sort of unparsable interaction can throw Rhona off for a whole day. She's read about "negging," and surely that's what that was? But it can't be unless Rhona craves Yvonne's approval, which she doesn't.

Her relief must be apparent to Vince when she bumps into him outside the revolving door, on his way back in. She stops and removes her earpods. Vince blows out a lungful of smoke with the words, That's my fresh air for the day, then nods and tries to step inside.

Rhona doesn't get out of the way. They're not started up yet, she says.

No? Vince says, pinching some imaginary tobacco from the tip of his tongue. By the time we get back in, the dust bunnies will have the run of the place.

Rhona's mind goes straight to the empty chamber of Northern Ireland's long-suspended government. You should see Stormont! she says. She feels herself making exaggerated expressions, a strenuous effort to establish casual rapport. The white elephants have gone into hibernation, waiting for the assembly to reconvene!

Still going strong, the old elephants? Vince says. You've been spending time in the North?

Yeah.

Vince smiles a little and looks almost at ease. Good memories, isn't it, with elephants? They never forget. Even if they should.

If things were easy to forget, there'd be no trauma.

Vince looks at Rhona with a new focus, and, feeling her heart thrum, she has the urge to tell him: that was something she'd heard from a pharmacist at a Boots in Armagh, after listing side effects, when she'd bought a morning-after pill.

Someone scoots out past them, and Vince leans to the right to peer inside.

Oh, before *I* forget, Rhona says, one of my early-career researchers has done some work on the reforms proposed for the European Parliament, on how the policy reorientation towards the EU Project could spell trouble for Ireland. She has a study coming in the *European Journal of Political Economy* in a fortnight . . . and I think the timing would make it a great article. What with the goal to enact reforms ahead of the European elections. In case it's of interest? She'd gladly draft something for you.

He doesn't need to know that "early-career researcher" means over-achieving undergraduate, Rhona thinks.

She notices a shift in Vince's expression, like mercury lifting in a barometer, and his guard seems to go up. Send it through, Rhona, I'll take a look.

A light rain begins to freckle Vince's tan coat. His glasses are now dappled in rain, and they've fogged up, so she can't read his level of discomfort, which is never nil. This is what makes him so effective. He makes politicians nervous, because he's not swanky or glib or good at buying people drinks. He's upright and responsible. He's sharp. He spots structural flaws in an article and in a character with CT-scan precision. He's simultaneously utterly present with you—a sort of presence that Rhona usually feels with people only in the middle of the night—and far away, too. Perhaps what she really likes is the fact he doesn't have an in-between. Rhona becomes aware of her own appearance, that her hair will frizz in the rain . . . but she doesn't want to give him reason to go. A ten-minute meeting reminder pings on her phone. She takes out a folder from her handbag and holds it above her head.

A security guard steps toward them and says, If we can keep the access area clear, folks. Vince almost bows, he nods so humbly.

We could get dinner? she blurts out. My lunches are booked for a week, she says. But I could do dinner. Tonight?

The morning's four coffees percolate through her rib cage. Or maybe it's adrenaline. Tomorrow night? she adds.

Vince makes a strange hawing sound, as if spinning a mental Rolodex to find his own card.

The hesitation might have to do with expense, so she adds, My shout.

He clears his throat dryly and jerks his head toward Leinster House. Assuming it'll take them another few minutes to pay the ransom, he says, and retake their own security system . . . I can stretch my legs in the direction of Trinity, if that's where you're walking. He casts a glance at the folder above her head and adds: If it's a pitch you have for me?

I have my car, Rhona says bluntly. So I have to move my car. She thinks: What does he mean, a pitch? She *has* pitched him. The pitch was dinner.

You *drove*? Vince looks toward Trinity, which is barely six hundred meters away.

I'm thirty-seven, she says. I don't need the steps.

He laughs at that. Though Rhona isn't smiling. God help us if you start exercising! Now he coughs his real cough. He points in the direction of a smoking shelter. We could duck out of the rain for a minute? He starts walking in that direction while speaking, so Rhona follows, still holding the folder above her head. I presume you got wind we're losing a columnist? he says. Is it the column you're after?

Rhona stops walking and shivers the drizzle off her blazer. I'm sorry to hear about your staff turnover, she says. But I'm not angling for a column. I'm not angling for anything. I couldn't fit a column in my schedule if it was the fall of Rome.

Vince takes off his fogged glasses to try to lower a barrier: Had he offended her? I put that badly, he says. I didn't mean to be presumptuous—

I'm late for a meeting.

In the car, Rhona suddenly catches on her body the burnt-match smell that she used to pick up when her father collected her from post-school study, after closing up the wineshop. That smell . . . Reminding him to change gears. Rolling down the window to keep him inside the lines. Pulling the handbrake, once, when they kissed the bumper ahead. Keeping tabs on his license and registration. Going at long last to her mother's study to find it locked.

Don't you dare run that light! she shouts at the car in front. When she beeps, the car accelerates through the red light, and a child in its back seat twists to take her in.

. . .

The flower vases in Rhona's house are all full. She has a subscription of gladioli and hellebores delivered fortnightly.

It is a glorious paradigm of a house. It's the third one she's owned, and the rungs she'd cleared between her second property and this one make it a contender to be her last. It certainly feels like home. Though sometimes she envisions its high-ceilinged rooms to be full of people. She envisions her sisters opening her cabinetry for whatever they need, craning their necks at the two-tone horizon swathing each easterly window; she sees them turning up at her beach garden door in the night like tidewrack. She has hosted people here, but mostly for work events, and for one mistaken postnatal demonstration of how a circle of people can have nothing in common but stretch marks and innie belly button prejudice. No strangers have been admitted to this house. No handsome council donation can protect a single mother in her four-bedroom semi-D if its doors don't have strict terms of admittance.

It's approaching midnight when Rhona puts on her activewear. She slots her phone into the waistband holder and tucks in a credit card. A Fendi zip-up jacket is reversible for entering the club suitably and taxiing home safely. From a bathroom drawer she takes a hair clip of dark horn, with a hollow locket center that Rhona now opens. She licks her fingertip and dips it into the ecstasy powder. Her reflection, rubbing the powder into her gums, arouses her. I cleaned my teeth, she says, and sucks them. Next, her knuckles move inside the navy-black metallic fabric of her leggings like an animal slinking beneath the surface of a moonlit pond. She lifts a knee onto the marble basin and watches her forearm steal farther below her waistband, until the baby monitor crackles and complains. A look of nuisance crosses her face in the mirror, then a flush of disgust. Her saliva has the bitterness of over-extracted coffee. She washes her hands and clips her hair back tightly.

Leo's dream must have turned a benign corner, because he's out for the count when Rhona checks on him. Then she pauses by Beatriz's room. She knocks but hears nothing. She knocks again and opens the door to see Beatriz asleep with her reading glasses on her chest, an e-reader by her side. She looks beautiful. She smells of resinous wood. Rhona lifts the reading glasses from her chest and places them on the bedside table. Why has she never thought to ask Bea what she reads? That would be a nonwork thing to chat about. Rhona turns on the Kindle to see what she's been reading: a PDF of the European Union Election Observation Mission Constituent Assembly Report for Ecuador, circa 2007. You *see!* Rhona whispers, though she'd only meant to think it. She feels a rush of fondness toward Beatriz for taking her work to bed with her. So *she knows* there's no separating work from life. You can put something between them, for decency, but it will be an ornamental room divider, not a load-bearing wall.

Beatriz stirs now. Rhona pulls back.

Beatriz? Bea? I'm so sorry . . .

Beatriz lurches suddenly and she pulls at her duvet. What is it?

. . . if I woke you. I'm so sorry if you were already asleep. Were you?

Beatriz squints at Rhona's workout leggings, the plum lipstick sharpening her cupid's bow, the baby monitor she's holding.

I'm just popping out and I wondered—

What time is it?

It's not late. Eleven something. Barely midnight. Leo's fast asleep and I'm *sure* he won't wake before I'm back, but *just in case just in case* . . . can I leave this here with you? Rhona places the monitor on the bedside table and turns up the volume. I'll turn off the other monitor as soon as I'm back so he won't wake you in the morning.

Beatriz mumbles, Fine. I suppose. You have your phone?

I do. You're a gem. Sleep tight. Rhona tiptoes out, whispering: Stay asleep.

• • •

The corporate cab is waiting outside the electric gates. How do you rate the Tesla? the driver says as they pull off. The drivers from this company don't make small talk. He must be new. He is scoping out her car and her house in the rearview mirror.

My *husband* finds it a bit tight for his frame, Rhona says. I regret that it's a Tesla. I'll buy something different soon.

What? The driver looks back long enough that she knows his eye color. Audi? Porsche?

A twenty-first-century rail service would be a nice alternative. She frees her phone from her waistband to dissuade conversation.

This is a hybrid, the driver says, sliding his hand along the dashboard.

Rhona glances at the steering wheel. Mercedes. An expensive hybrid. The weight of an engine plus a subpar battery for inefficiency, crap performance, and costly maintenance. Is it yours? she asks, and the driver says it is. She channels Leo and pulls an expression that could be a smile of approval or an anal contraction.

Her phone buzzes conveniently: a text from Jim. An Eircode, followed by a text:

THE COUNTY LEITRIM. If I was doubtful before, now I'm
convinced your sister needs a hard and fast rescue. Will I arrange a helicopter?

An Eircode—not a rumor, not a general vicinity, but an exact location. Rhona clicks the GPS link and gasps. I don't believe it. She's on
the border. Rhona barely hears the driver ask if she's all right. She
clicks on the message and selects Forward, but then pauses, imagining
how her sisters might respond. Congratulations? Thanks? No possible
response would lend her a feeling like knowing something, all alone.
That's what counts for her as nostalgia.

Another text from Jim pings, obscuring the map:

As the drone flies she's 162 kms from us. My baby only has a
10km range. Will I see if I can find us a mq1 predator on the
dark web? It can do 700 kms, loiter for 14 hours, then return
to base no bother.

The weapons manufacturers don't need your philanthropy, Jim, she
replies. I'll name a scholarship after you if you'll fund us a PhD student. Thanks for finding Olwen. I for one will sleep easier.

It's true, she thinks. And she feels . . . the sort of pressure release
that comes with switching from her left side to her right in the middle
of the night, in between REM cycles.

. . .

It's after 4 a.m. when Rhona tiptoes up the stairs and into Leo's bedroom, shoes in hand, soles clacky with other people's spilled cocktails.
Rhona doesn't drink when she's on MDMA. She dances. Tonight she
danced for four hours straight. My little man, she whispers, grinning
through the dark like a white-toothed Cheshire cat. My perfect, *perfect*

human! Hmm? Now that your reflux is under control, *perfect* barely cuts it. She turns the dial on his moon lamp to illume a thin crescent glow, enough to see him by. He sleeps on his belly. Crouching to peer through the bars of the cot, she sees him fast asleep: his eyes are creases that might not yet have ever opened. She lets down one wall of the cot; it's queen-size, but still she slides her palms beneath Leo's warm chest and knees to move him inward, to make room. *Oof.* You're quite the bicep curl, my darling. She takes off her jacket and frees her hair from the horn barrette. It's salted rigid. Her workout clothes glitter in the mock moonlight, silvered with dry sweat. She climbs into the cot and lies on her side, her arm as her pillow. Leo's back rises arrhythmically, and Rhona recalls having to come in here every night to turn him from his tummy to his back, until she noticed he could roll both ways at will. He could get himself out of many undesirable situations. It made her weep. Other sources of pride of late include his not pooing during the night, his survivalist appetite, and the rapid reflexes by which he slapped away an old lady's hand as it made for his cheek in the park. He had no idea where that hand had been, when it had last been rubbed with a disinfectant wipe.

Rhona badly wants to stroke his hair—its blazing copper coils— even if she'd be scalded, but she won't disrupt his sleep. If she wakes him now, he might have to sleep in in the morning, and she'd barely have any time with him at all. He'd barely have time to commune with her. I'm deeply, deeply impressed by you, Leonardo Flattery, she says quietly. You are *such* an impressive person. Did I ever tell you that? His top lip puffs out above the bottom one, as he sighs deeper into his dream. If Rhona believed in ghosts, she would swear that a ghost is clutching her throat now, challenging her breath, grasping after that brand-new life. But it's Maeve who believes in ghosts. It was Maeve who'd spent years chasing their parents' spirits through the house, making the meals their father used to make, trying to conjure their scents exactly, leaving fingers of whiskey and shortbread on the sill of their empty bedroom.

Rhona knows it's the child himself challenging her breath with the wild generosity of his need.

It is astonishing. This love. It is so ridiculously jeopardizing.

As she lifts her face from the mattress, sniveling, Rhona's gasps send wisps of Leo's hair aloft like the fleur-de-lis of a crown. If you can, darling, she says, and *only* if you can, will you tell me that you won't be okay?—yes, *won't* be okay? that you won't, for example, *thrive*—if one day I walk off a cliff?

Rhona holds her breath to catch any outbreath of reply from her son. He has no coherent sounds for her yet, and studies suggest that he should. He should have a word for his mother. A monosyllable. Hmm? The truth is, Rhona is afraid for the sounds he might have, when they come. What if she cannot bear them? She pulls loose a corner of the fitted sheet and rubs her face with it.

Leo?

Soon there is a sound, but Rhona misses it as she nurses a sudden cramp in her calf. It's the baby monitor clicking off at the other end, no longer searching for its sister signal. The live-in researcher, no longer listening or hearing. The ocean gaining on a soundproofed house.

part two

1.

On the first night, Olwen had wanted to carry herself across a threshold of tectonic scale. She'd wanted to make slow but undeniable headway through the landscape one inch on a paper map, minimum. She'd set off on her bicycle at midnight, moving swiftly out of the city into the space-black country roads, where her flashing lights had the conspicuousness of a comet, sure to snuff out before too long.

She hadn't anticipated that the roads from Corofin to Gurteen in the wee hours would be boy-racer country. When a yellow Nissan Skyline pulled a handbrake turn in front of her at 4 a.m. and proceeded to follow her in reverse for a full five minutes, matching her sixteen-kilometer-an-hour pace, she was not—as they say—game. The lads inside smacked the dashboard as if a woman cycling alone at night were a high-risk, high-odds sport they all had stakes in. Giddy up, ya feek! Give it welly, ya big *ride* ya, hup! She's fuckin' sweatin', lads! *Drippin'*! We've a rope in the boot. Will we hitch her? Give her an aul *tow*?

Squinting into their modified headlights, Olwen felt her pulse trip sickly as one of them leapt from the moving vehicle to sprint alongside her. He bore his furry teeth to the warm October night air, any threat he might have posed neutered by his effort to keep pace. Burning clutch and stale hash filled the air, as well as Garnier Fructis structuring gel, which Olwen recognized from the undergraduates. ("Someone has a rotting apple in their bag?" she'd asked in class one morning, and Eric ran his fingers through his hair and sniffed them.)

Suddenly she felt her bike tugged backward: the lad had grabbed her pannier bag, trying to keep up. The jolt nearly toppled her. When Olwen spoke, finally, she pitched her voice at a volume quiet enough that the car had to stop revving to hear her: I'm fleeing a murder scene, lads, she said. If I go any faster, t'would only be conspicuous. In this light, what the boys saw strapped to the top of her pannier bags—a saw, an axe, a collapsible-handled shovel swaddled in tarp—took on new significance. Her sprinting escort found an extra gear in his Reeboks, catching up to the car before it spun a screeching semicircle and tore off into the delirious dark.

No thanks to that encounter, nor to a pickup truck that passed her slowly, twice, in the space of half an hour, Olwen dismounted her bicycle long before she'd intended to. She heaved the bike and accoutrements over a stone wall and pitched her tent behind a copse of sycamores in an agricultural field, a whole county shy of her destination, with a trough to wake up to instead of a lake. She was barely eighty kilometers distant from her memory-foam California king, and Jasper, and the boys, and the godforsaken undergraduates.

. . .

On the second night, her sleeping arrangement was altogether perverse. She'd spotted Labby Rock, a megalithic tomb, a few hundred feet off the side of the road. She'd only meant to climb inside the stone structure for a nightcap, but dehydration must have got the better of her. A dolmen made a serviceable tent—cold, but then Olwen always welcomed a nip in the air. Inside the five-thousand-year-old tomb, having doused her torch and her sobriety, she tried to doze off to thoughts of the ancient monarch upon whose grave she was curled. Would you rather, she asked this mineral bedfellow, slurrily, be a *king* in Neolithic Sligo . . . or a *scientist* in neoliberal Sligo? By 2 a.m., she was asleep under the seventy-ton capstone.

She woke a few hours later to a memory: one of her touristy students had mentioned that a throne was up for grabs off the coast of Donegal. Tory Island, the country's remotest inhabited island, was in need of a new monarch. Perhaps she should make haste for Donegal's docks, throw her helmet in the ring. It might become her. An island from which she could heckle an Icelander; an island with a population counting down from 110; an island whose rough seas would delimit any weekend Tinder prospects, freeing its inhabitants from the tyranny of tourism and the delusion of choice; a treeless island with long, dark, howly nights. An island, moreover, with kings—a largely ceremonial office she might gladly accept, since the throne was newly vacant and doubtless commodious. And cushioning was on her mind.

All the more so when she got going on that third day. The sound she made mounting the saddle was close enough to yodeling that Jasper would've snuck out his recording gear to sample it. She was taking country roads, which were universally blind-cornered, dog-frantic, and happily unkempt around Ireland, but they were hillier now than in Galway, and they were testing her. (The Celtic-tiger rural mansion eejitry was mercifully subdued here; though, on the negative side, there were more derelicts.) Doing miles and miles on a bicycle had the effect of awakening the body and of lulling the mind. It didn't stupefy it, but it did simplify its concerns. The uncomplicated, meditative literalness of moving forward, feeling every change in road surface, avoiding potholes, flipping off BMWs . . . it was lovely. Probably the same effect that Nell felt while snorkeling. Unfortunately, unlike her little sister's, Olwen's legs were not benumbed. By midafternoon, saddle sores made pushing past the Leitrim border impractical, if not unhygienic. Salt crackled in the creases around her eyes, the third eye included. She put in at least two miles cycling in a public-toilet hovering position, which burned the common enemy out of her quadriceps. Finally accepting that she'd have to stay put for a day or two, she found a secluded spot and set about administering lubricant to the region until it looked less feral.

Petroleum jelly to the groin. Gin to the county Leitrim.

Sausages, butter, bananas, Edam cheese (since they had no Sheese), a large crusty loaf, berries for dessert gin, two Lindt Chilli bars, and one Lindt Intense Mint, in case she forgets to brush her teeth: she'd bought all that before remembering that Cian and Tommy's sausages were what she'd had the night she took off. Even her camping stove had their grubby fingerprints all over it. A soup-can stove she'd built with them to pacify the arson curiosity the boys hadn't shaken since their mother's cremation. It ran on white spirits. For a brief optimistic moment, stove-building had seemed a survival skill worth teaching. Nelsonian knowledge would've been the better lesson: willful blindness. But she was failing to sustain it herself.

I like a hot meal, she announced. But I like a cold meal also.

She was speaking to her groceries, as she'd laid them out on the grass that evening. No one was convinced. Forgoing the sausages, she crawled into the tent with the bread and cheese and liquid fuel. The temperature had dropped; a fog was condensing in the valley. Fog formed on pollutants, and that was what Olwen saw in it. Chimney smoke, or a recent gorse fire. She kept the tent vestibule open to look out on the valley nonetheless. Where are we now, when we're at home? she asked the landscape. She'd swiftly grown bored with her paper maps, and she had to conserve her phone battery, so she let herself be guided by whim and misanthropy. One glimpse of cars, cut lawns, nest-less trees, concrete, litter, or any such indicator of human activity, and she'd take an abrupt left, right, or U-turn onto some smaller, craggier, backmost road, usually ascending. All of which meant that, by now, she wasn't quite sure where she was, except perched between the cleavage of two moderate mountains.

Leitrim, she had to admit, was a fine thing. A landscape of moss-ensconced stones and tree trunks and ice-sugared rocky hills. In the morning, everything would be spangled in frost. The fields on this upland plateau were cloddy and briary and unmanaged. The heather hadn't been cleared. It was in bloom, completing the postcard bogland color palette of burnt umber and sienna, blackish greens, rusty oranges, pale purple, and ashen yellow sedge—all darkening rapidly as Olwen lay on her side in the nude, looking out, charting the peat. The booze warmed her, but she was goosefleshed nonetheless. Dimly lit, with one knee cocked up to air the saddle sores, she was a French Romantic lady-in-recline portrait: erratically nude, framed by nylon drapery, bravely flouting both academic and social standards. She held the wedge of Edam cheese by its red wax skin and ate it like a sandwich.

It was twenty-one years ago, the first time she'd seen bog in this way. She'd been a first-year undergraduate, barely a year into orphanhood, an eighteen-year-old guardian to three lost girl-shaped articles. (Well, two. Rhona, somehow, had always remained her full self. She had always known where she was, where she was going.) The field trip was their first class outing of the year, to the "bog road" in Roundstone. A blue-sky January day. A new year that felt of nothing; no kiss or minute's silence gave it weight. Professor Ian Baxter, whom they called Professorian, came sporting a hammer—"for ore hunting, later"—and a spade. But he didn't need a spade to dig up peat. There were shelves of it on display all over, both where it had been cut for turf and at the natural edges of the blankets. We made such easy work of cutting it, Olwen thought. The bogland, he told them, was Ireland's rainforest. The most efficient carbon sink on the planet. Olwen was barely mentally present that year, as evidenced by the Cs on her transcript. Perhaps that was why the professor—a childless man with a mild phobia of young people—singled her out, leading her, with a hand on her back, to a wall of cut peat. You're, what, a hundred and sixty centimeters, or thereabouts? he said. Homo sapiens reach their maximum height at your age. It took you eighteen, nineteen years to reach this full stature? Well, this peat is about head height. And *it* forms at a rate of *one millimeter* a *year*. So . . . Olive, is it? (Olwen didn't correct him.) One Olive—he marked the peat above the crown of her head—is one thousand six hundred years of pounded peat. At this a rupture of jokes disrupted the lesson, as the one Pete in the class took a round of congratulatory thumps.

Hastening to reconvene their coarse imaginations, the professor held out the handle of his spade: There's another two or three meters beneath us, he said, should anyone care to dig down to the era of Caesar? Or a smidgeon deeper, to Homer perchance? Olwen would normally have had something outrageously funny to say, if only to stop herself from howling . . . but at that moment she found she couldn't catch her breath to speak. She was stunned, winded, by that back-to-the-wall measurement: what the peat was storing; how much had been cut out and burned, all for the comfort of a few cozy evenings, in the scheme of things. What decomposition. How blackly dense it was, the absence in every direction.

Feeling the cold, ancient record against her back, Olwen had thought of Nell. When Olwen asked Nell how she was tolerating all the twits telling her their parents were "in a better place," Nell had looked around the living room to see what sort of a place it was. She landed upon a photograph from her father's backpacking days, printed on a big canvas on the wall, and she said: If Mum and Dad's atoms travel on a riptide to Tahiti, maybe they *will* be in a better place.

Olwen had pushed down the tag sticking up at the nape of Nell's neck. Age 8–12. Her frame was stubbornly small.

Excellent point, she said.

But they won't have any consciousness, Nell went on.

Oh? said Olwen. Are there no consciousness atoms?

Nell pressed her pale lips together. Everything about her seemed tiny, but tiny amounted to plenty.

Just as well, Olwen said consolingly. You wouldn't want a consciousness atom . . . blowing into a urinal.

Nell had snorted then, and a riptide sucked all the blood up from Olwen's chest into her head.

What resilience.

Stepping away from the peat, Olwen turned to face up to it. Its slow

accumulation. Its sudden exhaustion. Its probable re-accrual, long after their life spans. Or something like it. Without humans, possibly.
Something like it would grow again. That's what Earth's surface
proved. It was thin gruel. But it was not nothing. She would reach for it.

For her sisters, she began a bid to fill the gaps. She made her voice
boomy. She made her person matronly. She wore her hair such that all
caps fit, including a square one. She let the others try it on and said:
Mum would've liked the sight of that tassel. Did ye know she always
wanted to do a doctorate? In these ways, Olwen administered such information. She ignored Rhona's narrow, knowing stare. From a catalog, she bought equipment for her own sudden tutelage: tools to bury
and tools to dig.

. . .

Twice in the night, Olwen was awakened by a nagging sound from
somewhere nearby. Not so near to her tent that she could identify its
direction, but the sound was a sort of screaming, so it was hard to tune
out. She let out a scream herself, lowering the chassis to urinate—
jaysus she'd done a number on her quads. A touch of delirium was in
the family history, so at first she figured the sound for a waking dream
of that poor lad screaming in the corridor. Feeling the cold soil between her toes, Olwen considered how much farther a scream would
travel in this unwalled environment. She'd drunk enough to sleep
through a full bladder, but this nagging, this scream, had penetrated
her consciousness. She rooted around in her bag for earplugs, and she
slept then—later into the morning than she might have. Even as she
was cooking her breakfast (the vegetarian sausages; she was less emotional in the mornings, and they would only spoil if she ignored them),
she could still hear a sort of mewl in the distance.

After breakfast, Olwen went looking for the source of the animal
noises. With the fog lifted, she could see the glacial glen below, where
hedgerows bounded the pastureland. Sections of wet heath and fens

too. Brambles with late-season blackberries she might trek down for later. All around, Sitka spruce forestry: some clear-felled, some coppicing, some verdant. Up here, the landscape was less structured. There were fewer discernible boundaries for all the scrub—whitethorn, blackthorn, ash, and holly—and sedges.

On her cross-country walks, Olwen would usually bring a square foot of carpet—handy for straddling barbed-wire fences. But the fences up here were few and far between, and the stone walls were half tumbled. Still, it wasn't easy going, trudging through boggy soil and stiff tufts and deadwood, losing a shoe to muck and roots and cushiony mosses. The grass was slippery but also spiky. But the rougher the landscape, the less resistance she felt within it. She had no plan. As she tried to get a fix on the whimpering—a sheep, almost certainly—a stream babbled forth out of nowhere. Before she saw it, she'd stepped into it and one shoe was penetrated with icy water. Gasping at the sensation, Olwen lowered her other foot into the water and indulged in the cold extravagance. Soon, very soon, to reach such cold water would be a pilgrimage. It was then she caught sight of the animal.

Well, you're not blackberries, she said.

Neither lamb nor sheep, it was something in between: a sort of sheep teenager. It had got itself tangled in a blackthorn shrub, scrounging for sloes, and the poor thing was worn out from the ridicule of life. Maeve is the forager in the family, Olwen said. However, *sloes* I'd make an exception for. She made her way toward the animal, talking calmly over its revivified bleating. D'you know what you can make with sloes . . . is sloe gin. Lovely, tart stuff. The old lamb or young sheep was getting more thorns latched to its wool as it tried to get away from Olwen. Sloes had stained its wool purple in places, like red wine spills on a fireside sheepskin. Olwen slid her arm in over the back of the emo creature's neck to wrestle its head beneath her armpit. Thorns pronged her fleece. When she had it in a headlock, she took her Leatherman from her pocket. You'd want a machete, really, but . . . knife, scissors, nail file, and pliers are our options. We'll have a go with a knife. And tell me, while I'm laboring over you: Are you a laggard, or did you try to make a solo job of it? I mean, did you fall off the back of your team . . . or were you making a solo sprint for it, to get up the luscious hill first? Are you a breakaway, is what I want to know?

Rank stress wafted off the animal. The talk wasn't helping. As soon as she'd cut it free from the last batch of thorns, it bucked into another layer of them. This creature might have a heart attack, she thought, if it hadn't already. Try that stunt again and I'll steep you in tikka masala, Olwen said. She had a headache, probably from lack of coffee. The sky was glary overhead, where a sparrow hawk flew mean orbits. Gray clouds clogged the horizon as if a mound of dust had been swept to the edge of the room. If rain was en route and those saddle sores were to have any chance of healing, Olwen was going to need a highly salacious novel to keep her in the tent. Alternatively, a pub with a pool table.

She loosed the woolen boulder from its tangle, wrapped her arms around its midsection, and carried it down the hill until she reached an empty stonewalled field and hesitated, knowing the creature would only destress once it could see more of its eejit kind. So she continued cradling the pongy thing for another half mile down the road, until she came upon a field of livestock. To be able to identify the sheep's whereabouts, in case it needed veterinary attention or had been reported stolen, she marked an oily X across its back in bright pink bike-bearing lube—the only colorant she had at her disposal. She wasn't a woman for the lipstick. When she lobbed the animal as gently as she could across the stone wall and electric fence, she wondered if the oil was flammable.

Some of the pink oil had come off on her fleece, so she felt moderately like a suicide bomber an hour's walk later as she entered the first pub of Kiltyclogher village, An Spa Sláinte: a thirsty suicide bomber, allegiant to the call of last rounds.

• • •

Fabulously refreshing about the Spa Sláinte was that nobody in it had any questions. They had answers only. Olwen learned this early, when she made the brazen move of seating herself at the bar and chanced upon their mode of communication. Sorry to crowd ye out, she said, but I can't sit down there among the churchgoers. I've been handling animals.

The barfly next to Olwen, twisting sideways to her without taking his eyes off his own pint, said: A great many of them comes in wouldn't mind it, and a more of them do be at it.

The young barman, Dan—rather than asking what she'd like—seemed to be hovering his hand over variously shaped glasses, waiting for Olwen to tell him "Bingo." He agreed that all manner of people were let in. Farmers, he said. Dog-walkers. Lion tamers.

No, a man two stools down protested. You wouldn't allow bring in it.

The lion? Dan asked, then swiftly clarified the thing for himself: I suppose it would be a sea lion, realistically. So no. I mightn't allow him in.

Oh, he be very cruel the odd time, the same man piped up. There was one day he threw a fella out on the roadside, on the *roadside*, and the poor fella only twelve year old with the thirst for a crispy pint.

Olwen laughed and said: A crispy G-and-T would do nicely.

For a while, as she settled herself, competitive frugality was the talking point. The man at the end boasted he hadn't met a barber in all his life. Some women do spend a week's wage in a hairdresser, he said. Some of them, he added in a gossipy tone.

Olwen tamped down her bicycle helmet hair and cocked her head at the balding barfly between them, whose remaining hair was black as an oil spill. Nothing wrong with a home dye job, she said, to save the pennies!

From behind the bar, Dan laughed. It's the Guinness did that! Without the Guinness, John would be blond.

Go on and pull me another, so. John petted his scanty black hair. I'm fading.

Vidal Sassoon would be cheaper, Dan said. He pulled the pint all the same. Dan was young—maybe Nell's age—and black-haired himself, but he didn't lord it over his loyal customers.

To spare John further slagging, but staying on topic, Olwen said that the only way to come at winter was in two pairs of socks.

I'm abstemious about the radiator . . . until Advent, John said. I don't *touch* it.

The feracity of various fields was discussed thereafter. There was only one farm owner among them that first night, but an intimate knowledge of land was a currency they were all rich in. Olwen held forth with the story of the sheep and a detailed description of the field where she'd deposited it. The rowan trees at its wayside. The fact that it was a teenager sheep. The fact of the greasy pink X.

When she dismounted the barstool to leave, she winced involuntarily. Her legs were spent.

You wonder how the sheep run so far on their little shticks, Dan said.

They manage! a man called Diarmuid piped up, surprising everyone that he was awake beneath his low cap.

Olwen wrestled some cash from her pocket, forgetting that she'd paid along the way, refusing the lure of a tab. She said: They can go as far as their hearts will let them, I suppose.

That's a fair distance? Dan said, affecting a north county lilt that inflected the end of the sentence. The lad had a way of shifting register so that one minute he was spouting risible client management banter; the next he was a medium, speaking vague, weighty proverbs in a tone of deep condolence.

Olwen took it as the first question posed, and waved goodnight.

. . .

No eyelid was batted when Olwen turned up on the second afternoon in a row, and on the third. Leitrim had the fastest-shrinking population in the country. They weren't about to scare off a blow-in who seemed to know her way around a volcanic belt. The sheep husband had been located without even the use of a phone book—a horrible nice man, according to the regulars—and on the third night he came in to buy Olwen a thank-you drink. Feidhlim was his name. He had one of those labor-dried faces that no lotion regimen could permeate. A teetotaler, but an absolute addict for a game of 25s. Cards. Ah, he was awful vulnerable, Olwen thought, deciding against it when the opportunity arose to clean him out. His jacket was worn to a shine; his car, parked outside when she arrived, was a rust repair pointillist painting. He'd ticked the forty-five to sixty-four age group on the latest census, surely, but that was as specific a bet as Olwen would make.

They were sat at the low tables. Dan got the deal, Feidhlim cut, and hearts were trumps. A box of matches was employed to keep track of tricks won. For four players, they were doing their best to make a tournament of it. Olwen quickly figured out how they managed to give and get answers about their lives without a single question being posed: they'd take a stab at a fact, and it would be affirmed or denied or ignored or revered or put right.

And the cocaine was disguised as hunks of coal, Dan was explaining, and it got past all the customs inspectors without a shniff.

This discussion arose after they'd pieced together that Olwen was some sort of rock specialist. The only other rock women Dan knew specialized in crystals. Perhaps Olwen was the same? he wondered. Was she here to reveal their futures? Dan flashed the palms of his hands her way, on the unlikely possibility that she'd spot a line of shocking significance. A clairvoyant crystal healer would be the type to travel by bicycle, he figured.

Cocaine dressed up as coal! Olwen said. You'd want to be on Santy's bad list around here, so.

After five nights in the tent and river showers only, she looked and smelled the part. Her biscuit-brown hair had the consistency of a baking experiment that hadn't risen. She laid down the ace of trumps to give Feidhlim a chance to get back in the running, fairly sure he had the five of trumps, the best card in the pack. Feidhlim *did* have the five of trumps, but he himself could afford to lose. Whereas a tenner, to this ramshackle woman—what value might it have? Was it a bridge to the next day? Would it put an extra hour's distance between herself and some fist-swinging Galway city crofter? He played the three of trumps, pinched out a matchstick from the box, and laid it upon Olwen's pile. Then, sleight-of-handing his last card, he threw the last round too.

The others wanted a smoke break. Talk of chemicals had made them twitchy. They drew premade rollies from a tobacco pocket, took the matchbox, and went outside.

No cute moves when ye return them matches, Olwen called out.

No cute moves yerselves, said Dan, the bartender, leaving his post unattended.

Gripping his blackcurrant water in the new silence, Feidhlim made a show of the gold claddagh ring on his wedding finger. He seemed possessed of some unfortunate knowledge.

Is it a he or a she? Olwen asked. Or a they?

You could almost hear the skin on Feidhlim's brow crinkle. The sheep you spared?

Olwen nods at his ring. The betrothed?

Oh! A she, a she! Sheila. Heh. Feidhlim bent his head, coy, and wished he hadn't removed his cap so he might tip it now to the mention of her. A horseshoe moustache concealed his smile, but his nesty eyes didn't.

She works on the farm as well?

She does that, and she does cleaning part-time down at the Health Centre in Manorhamilton. Dé Luain, Dé Céadaoin, Dé hAoine.

This was the first bit of Irish Olwen had heard in weeks, since watching Tommy watch a cartoon on TG4 for his Irish homework. She knew the words—the days of the week—from her own childhood schooling, and by assuming she'd know them, Feidhlim had as good as given her a gold star. Was that shiver in her belly inadequately boiled water, or was it a rush of pride? She'd spent her career checking the undergraduates' patriotism, pulling the nation out from under them with the sobering history of plate tectonics. God forbid she should be beset by patriotism for the first time in her thirty-nine years in An Spa Sláinte of the County Leitrim. All her Irish coming back to her suddenly, she realized that the pub's name didn't mean *Cheers, Spa* but rather *Health Spa*. They were satirists, not yobs.

I don't know how she does it, Feidhlim said. I have no idea how she does it. He fiddled with his pile of matchsticks, as if his wife might take the same materials and make them a castle. He said: For tea the night, she did lasagna, and better than a restaurant. I'm no use that way. I'm a disaster. I've one pot blackened to tar, and I only cooking soup from a can.

Olwen clicked her tongue. What took you down? Cream of mushroom?

Feidhlim turned his other cheek in reply. Leek.

Jesus Mary and the Saint of Jerusalem. Olwen swallowed the remainder of her drink and considered the return of Dan. I've some expertise in the area of canned soup myself, she said menacingly.

Feidhlim ran a knuckle across his moustache. He thought to ask was she an artist, but he didn't want to sound glib. He couldn't picture her with a paintbrush. Maybe with a long-handled roller. A lot of soup dinners was likelier what she'd meant. He said: You're cycling a long way.

Arragh. I dunno yet. I'd planned to. I hadn't planned on stopping, but. 'Twas my own foolishness to have a plan.

Oh, they're deadly things.

Deadly.

Deadly.

No radio played in the background; no TV was mounted in the corner. It impressed Olwen a great deal, that sort of commitment to the moment. What with Jasper's video work, and the fidgety sons, and the students using apps to rack up telemarketing gigs in five-minute increments, she wasn't used to such minimalism. The unadorned moment: the absolute basking in it. For all the cultural products "having a moment," very few quiet moments were up for grabs. Mindfulness was having a moment, and Nell had to gut her philosophy syllabus in response, to present all thought as ahistorical. Localness was having a moment—a preview to the Scarcity moment—and Maeve had to rehash her UK menu to flaunt its blue-and-red roots. Sustainability was having a moment, and Rhona had to dash off her op-eds explaining why the Green Party wasn't. (It was to do with the Localness moment, which meant that Sinn Féin was having the Sustainability moment.) After so many years of trying to dig into the moment—to put it in context, to know its makeup—Olwen had forgotten how it felt to take it for granted.

For a moment Olwen lost track of where she was, and when she returned, Feidhlim was speaking to her in a swift, quiet tongue—it was English, but the Queen would have made head nor tail of it—saying roughly the following: That the hillside where Olwen had pitched her tent was owned by a fierce article of a fellow—a right cur, between themselves—and she'd be as well to relocate herself out of there, even if it was only the night or two she planned on staying. A circus tent could be mounted in his own garden, Feidhlim offered, and she'd be welcome to do so, but if it was privacy and a vantage point she enjoyed—why wouldn't she, marvel at a bit of landscape—he had a few acres on the eastern lee of Sliabh Dúch. He asked for her phone to put a location pin in it.

Olwen hadn't turned on her phone in days. Even then, she'd kept it on airplane mode. Now she had to go into Settings and turn off data for everything but maps before turning off airplane mode, which Feidhlim no doubt found peculiar. If she was trying not to be discovered, though, he was happy to supply the canopy.

In fact in fact as a matther of fact . . . He cupped his two hands to receive the phone as a lesser oblation. Olwen passed it to him, wary of a man with such manners, who doesn't drink. She would set it charging behind the bar, after this.

If you take this road here—he indicated on the map—and then this one . . . it's a dirty road, mind, but tractors have gone up it . . . and you could manage a puncture? You could. On the right there, where I'm pointing, is the auld house, the bungalow my father grew up in, the roof gone in on it long ago. There's bags of meal and animal feed inside, but it's a lovely flat bit of land there, with tall oaks and a Lebanese cedar my great-granny got for her wedding. And water still spits from the tap from a well bored . . . I'd say . . . an eon ago, but I've a hunch you know what an eon is. And I don't and I don't want to! I've rings enough around my face. Now, the water'd be a bit orange, but it's only iron in it, so you could leave out the spinach. But I drunk it myself and 'twas lovely refreshing. The point is, there's land there you wouldn't be booted out of.

I'll say no more, he said, here's the team back. And I'm sorry to tell ye, I went ayzy the last game, in view of the rescued sheep. But now the thanks are said and I've a pack of Taytos in my budget and the odds are shtacked against ye.

When Dan brought over the Taytos and the next round of drinks, Feidhlim split open the foil crisp packet until it was flat on the table between them.

How's that for intimidation? Dan said gravely. When a man can break a mirror without a shiver.

Feidhlim ate a crisp and a half. Olwen humored his poorly disguised concern for her well-being by wolfing the rest of the pack. Once it was eaten clean and the salt-and-vinegar powder was fingered off the metallic inner surface of the packet, Olwen could have sworn that Dan inched the foil packet toward her and checked, with bated breath, for a reflection. Was she here to stay, as a new friend . . . or was she a washer at the ford, here to foreshadow some carnage?

2.

Sorry about this—Nell leans heavily on her borrowed suitcases—
but the lady beside me gave me a sleeping pill and I'm still . . .
I'm asleep. If we rent a car, can you drive? There's cash in the
glove . . . in the sock . . . I'm going half. It's in the bag. Don't do the
whole . . . None of that . . . I'm going half.

Maeve had found Nell in the Dublin Airport arrivals hall, sand-
wiched between two rolling suitcases tall enough to graze her ribs.
Maeve pounced on her, hugging her breathless, as if she were trying to
recouple two halves of a gigantic clamshell, but Nell just clung to the
suitcase handles. There she stood, cringing as Maeve thumbed the
corners of her puffy eyelids, pushing her fringe back to reveal her baby
grays. Minutes later, Maeve is still staring insatiably at her sister, trying to spy the three and a half missed years on her face, but Nell's pale
skin is so lovely and unlined as to give it a blurred-edge quality. Does
she exist in time and space? No grasp Maeve has of her sister feels firm
enough. Nell's clothes belong to no era and to several people before
her: trousers with pleats, a yellowed silk shirt buttoned to the top, a
tapestry waistcoat (depicting a forest scene, with moose and maple
leaves) covering up pink bleach marks on the shirt. A boxy jacket of no
discernible color or fabric is threaded through the handle of a suitcase.
It looks like she's wearing unflattering yellow-brown eye shadow, but
she isn't. The only thing clear-cut about Nell's appearance is her ashy

brown bob. And her undeniable beauty. Its sketch-like quality, as though she's stepped out of a John Lavery portrait.

Maeve tries to wrestle one of the suitcases from her, but Nell holds firm. These two bags are all my stuff, she says. I'm gunna be cagey about them.

Nell had a yard sale before leaving. She stored most of her books in Ron's office, then took what books his shelves couldn't hold and priced them for sale by the kilo . . . until some dad—pushing a pram, sucking in his belly—offered five bucks for the weighing scales. Without the scales, she felt unable to sell the remaining books—to assign them a value more nuanced than heft!—until she flagged down a former student cycling past and strapped those centuries of reason to his mudguard with bungee cords. Do you at least want a dollar for the cables, Prof? The cords? she'd said. You can't do without them, Sejad. They're holding the ideas together, just as your skull will, once you've read all the books! I'll look out for an email with your thoughts. I'm keen to hear what you make of the Mary Midgley . . . that's a good chaser to the Lakatos, oh, and the Frantz Fanon's unmissable. Sejad looked down at the books, rubbing his forehead, the cost dawning on him.

Nell tells Maeve all this, in sleepy, cursory disclosures, as Maeve steers them to the 740A bus outside the airport. When she asks where they're going, Maeve simply says: South. She lets Nell sleep on her shoulder, exuding transatlantic flight. Maeve loves it when a thing smells like what it is. Nell is journeyed. Searching. Ungratifiable. Hard to pair with anything. Despite her states of being—pansexual, nymph-faced—a mustiness undercuts her youth; now, at thirty-three, just as it had when she was eleven. She probably willfully keeps reincarnating, flipping off enlightenment: Nell has never seemed interested in an end state. That's probably the real reason she isn't in a relationship: she's opposed to finality. As her big sister, Maeve always wished she had good advice to give Nell. But she had none. Which was clearly Rhona and Olwen's fault.

There's nobody in the world Maeve loves more than Nell, even after

Nell broke her heart by leaving for the States. Her leaving hurt Maeve more than the death of their parents, because at least they'd been to-gether in that movement—and, as far as Maeve knows, her parents lack the capability of return . . . an option Nell possesses but resists, year after year.

The morning after they died, Olwen had stolen into Maeve and Nell's shared room at 5 a.m. The sound of the swollen door brushing against the carpet slipped into Maeve's dream, in the form of tide sucking away from a beach; she kept running out toward it, but it kept eluding her, until a cold hand landed on her forearm and squeezed her awake. *Shh*, love, Olwen said to Maeve, pausing to check that Nell was still asleep. Olwen offered Maeve their mother's bathrobe to put on: Come with me, will you, love?

In the darkness, leading Maeve down the hall, Olwen looked like an adult. In the kitchen they found Rhona, an off-duty constable tak-ing measure of the survivors, watching for their fight-or-flight re-sponses. Rhona and Olwen had agreed that Maeve would likely excel in a crisis, and she swiftly confirmed their prediction. She unplugged the landline and burned the address book. She took the long string of pearls that had been her mother's mother's (and were therefore likely haunted) and cut it into four lengths to make matching ankle bracelets. She mounted a crusade against the parasitic ivy that was strangling the ash trees their father had planted in the garden, pulling a hamstring as she kicked at their roots. She bought a first aid kit with extra space blankets, which she wrapped around her sisters and stapled at the neck, making cloaks. When Nell had a panic attack, Maeve helped her es-cape out the bedroom window, knowing that it would never have dis-persed going through the front door. When Rhona needed a nap but wouldn't take one, Maeve locked her in the bathroom, where she'd lain a pillow in the bath. When Olwen had to choose urns for her parents' remains, Maeve emptied a pot of its plant, saying: That thing was just as dead.

On the bus, with Nell sleeping on her shoulder, Maeve's phone pings suddenly. It's Rhona, making a rare appearance in the Olwen Search Party group:

You land today? What's your plan?

Trying not to shift too much, Maeve replies: Just landed—we hopped on a bus to Wicklow

Rhona is typing.

Maeve taps in: Ol did love it there. Before everything. I thought it's as good a starting place as any. She'd more likely head for the hills than the coast but we'll start in town and head up, ask around

Rhona is typing.

Maeve: When we're closer to Dub again I'll give you a bell

Rhona: Have you passed the quays yet?

Maeve: Nearly

Rhona: Get off at the next stop.

Rhona: Davenport Hotel Merrion Sq. Go in, have lunch. Be there in 30.

Maeve is typing.

Rhona is typing.

Maeve is typing.

Maeve is trying to convey to Rhona that she wants to take Nell to see their childhood house, to climb with her into their hiding spot in the hedge, to spy on the new owners . . . to walk the Glen Beach cliff . . . to swim. She wants to suggest that Nell needs it as much as she does. Nell seems more . . . shattered than Maeve had been prepared for.

Maeve: I just want to go and spend a moment in Wicklow before we meet, Rho. It's a sort of urgent rushing feeling I don't want to ignore. It's been years

A new message from Rhona pops up in another WhatsApp group, between the two of them.

Rhona: I know where O is.

Maeve stares at this message for a moment, without being able to grasp it. The space beneath the name, where it says if a person is typing, is blank. Rhona's closed the app. And the matter.

The bus swings around the customhouse, lurching to avoid a jaywalker. The river Liffey glares in the window, glum for being stapled to the city with so many bridges. There are no barges or catamarans. There are no river taxis or floating businesses like on the Thames, but still—even since she'd last been here—the Brexit exodus of banks from Canary Wharf have led dozens of them into Dublin's docklands, glassing it. She watches the river's surface, that smashed screen, its course steered with concrete. Ulster Bank George's Quay is coming up. Merrion Square will be next. What can she do? Pretend she hasn't seen the message; that her battery had died. She pictures Rhona turning up in the lobby, no one there to meet her. It would be cruel.

Maeve shifts her shoulder to wake Nell.

Nell is wildly disoriented. Where is she? When are we?

Always ask what a pill is before you swallow it, Maeve tells her. Always save half for me.

Nell's head slips off her shoulder as she shimmies out of the seat.

We're lunching at the Davenport Hotel. On Rhona's orders.

Nell looks groggily and warily at Maeve. She keeps waiting for some compensatory information.

Rhona's shout?

· · ·

Rhona's car is murderously clean and acquittingly silent. In the back, Leo sleeps in his baby seat, next to Nell. To his left, Nell tries not to stare at him as they drive. They've never met before, and it feels a bit rude to pore over his unconscious face. Plus, she hasn't seen Rhona for three and a half years, and even then for only a few hours. Concerned that her reactions to the child—which Rhona will be scrutinizing in the rearview mirror—might not be satisfactorily gushy, she fixates on his miniature high-tech shoes. A lot of feelings are not where they should be.

There are no toys in the car, so Nell frisks her coat pockets for something to show the child when he wakes. From a thesis on genetic epistemology she'd supervised, Nell knows that Leo is in the sensori-motor phase of development, when children benefit from abundant stimulation and objects. Finding nothing usable in her pockets, she'll have to make do with abstract objects: Numbers. Sets. Sounds. Concepts. Possible worlds.

What was his first word? Nell asks.

In the mirror, Rhona's face glitches at this question. He's a *very* light sleeper, she whispers, deflecting—he'll need another ten or fifteen minutes before I can risk waking him. *Then* we can talk.

Nell rolls out her lower lip and nestles herself against the door, to get out of Rhona's eyeshot and search Maeve's reflection in the side mirror, but Maeve seems to be elsewhere. When Nell closes her swollen eyelids again, her mind darkens. She thinks of the last day Olwen accompanied her home from school. Nell must have been thirteen. They were walking along the bank of the river Vartry, in thought-teeming silence, when suddenly Olwen pushed her in, uniform, backpack, and all. "To prepare you," she'd called out, "for a suddenly watery environment!" Nell had already seen her sisters grieve in far stranger ways, so she wasn't particularly angry. But she was perturbed. For all Olwen's sturdiness and gall, as she stood on the riverbank shouting her warnings, a thick shadow seemed to spill from her in two directions: into the past and into the future. It was not the river water but that shadow that had made Nell shudder and cough that afternoon. One day, Nell knew then, she would have to escape it.

There's no music in the car, but this is not her road trip. Maeve finds herself craving a joint, to bring this chaotic situation into better chakric alignment. She'll call for a toilet stop in some midlands town of artful reputation—Mullingar, she thinks, or Longford—to acquire some local calming agent. The gamified way Rhona negotiates the motorway lanes, they might be shaking off a stalker. Maeve considers suggesting that they slip into a truck's wake to spare the car's battery, but Rhona shows no signs of range anxiety.

When Nell's snoring resumes in the back—a soft *K* each time her tongue taps off her palate—Maeve twists round to admire her sleeping companions. The lapping-water sound Maeve finds familiar and reassuring. After their parents died, she'd needed to hear that metronome click into rhythm in their bedroom before she could so much as close her eyes. She shifts her body to study them more closely, clutching the flank of the seat, taking in the baby, the perfectly weighted calligraphy of his features . . . She wants to ask Rhona if she'd chosen a redheaded donor or if that had been a surprise. She wants to ask if she'd done the insemination at home or at a clinic—the procedure has to be done at a clinic if it's to be a donor baby and not automatically a legal guardian, she'd read, but that's expensive—and did she have to do IVF? What's Rhona now, thirty-seven? Maeve is thirty-five.

More and more, these days, Maeve is thinking of Halim, who's been living on her boat and who's looking after it now. As a mime artist, he prefers to speak as little as possible, so it had taken some time for him to communicate his name and his birthplace of Bosnia. When she asked how long he'd been in England, he looked around him in a burlesque of bewilderment. Maeve has never seen him out of character: even on the rare occasions when he speaks, he does so as a mime. He has no costume to take off. Or perhaps it had been taken for him, and those quiet gestures are what remain.

She'd first encountered Halim when she spotted his canopy tent on the towpath of an obscure canal as she was mooring there one afternoon. Its whimsical appearance had made her feel safe in an unfamiliar setting. She watched him cast out an imaginary fishing line, sit down, and wait—then, after several hours of astonishing patience, stand up and reel it in again, empty and brilliant. She heard nothing from him until five o'clock that morning, and the first sounds he made were extracted against his will: Cries at his ribs being kicked in. Pleas as his every coin was robbed. The guttural wrench of his stomach emptying out. When she'd tried to phone an ambulance, Halim held his two white palms flat in front of him—as if indicating a wall, or surrendering to a police officer—and said simply: No. No paper. His black-and-white clothes had become clownish with the purple and red that bloomed through his white face paint. The blood looked fake. His mouth was smudged to bubblegum pink. Only when she insisted did he allow her to carry his tent onto her deck to take them to a safer area.

Halim seems to want to move through the world as silently and lightly as possible, so even toying with the notion of entangling him further in her life is ungracious . . . possibly hostile. And yet here she is, auditioning him in her mind as a donor for a hypothetical baby. Maeve isn't *sure* she wants a child—she loves the moment and always wants to be in it; she is less good at thinking about the future—but she wants to host the idea on the deck of her mind for a while. And it is one small thing to admire about these times: that a penniless, passportless mime artist could gesture a baby into existence without touching another body, making a coin appear on her palm, if she chooses to open her hand.

The rain they have moved into sizzles and bursts on the roof of the Tesla, like eggs frying on too strong a flame. It's an all-glass roof, tinted in a way that reduces the sky to a high-resolution screen saver. On a sunny day, a tomato plant would thrive here. It's clean enough to cook food in. How does Rhona have time to keep her car this spotless? Or has she had it cleaned for the occasion? Maeve reclines her chair a little to watch the raindrops sperm back across the roof.

You have a car, don't you? Rhona asks very quietly.

Maeve jolts the chair up again. She shakes her head.

But you had one! A van? Rhona says, audibly frowning. After a moment she adds: But how do you manage without one?

I borrow. Maeve's tone is curt, so it sounds defensive when she says: Your kid's unreasonably gorgeous.

Rhona's shoulders relax, and she adjusts the rearview mirror to check on Leo, who looks even more like her today, now that he's temporarily on the brunet spectrum. Hmm. He has my bone structure.

Maeve blows air from her lips while rolling her eyes, a trick that leaves her sort of dizzy in the spacecraft surroundings. Why has she let herself and her little sister be abducted by this hermetic woman, in her sleek vehicle? Why would she ever trust someone who, after all these years, has never bared so much as a chink in her armor?

He has your features all right. Tweaked little CRISPR nose on him.

Rhona turns a scowl on Maeve.

Come on, Maeve presses. Don't tell me those perfect circle nostrils aren't edited! Maeve checks her own nostrils in the passenger-door mirror, glances back at Nell's. Look: Flattery nostrils are a one and a zero. Not zero-zero. Only the left sides of our brains get enough oxygen. We got that from Mum, all of us, so it's a dominant gene. Leo's nostrils can only have been recoded at the genome.

Rhona's attention lowers to her phone, ringing mutely in a slot beneath the huge navigation screen.

To herself, Maeve says: Probably to make his breathing quieter.

The phone glows with a +51 number. Rhona lets it ring for another few seconds before tapping her Bluetooth earpod. Leo's naptime no longer all that precious? She'd probably been listening to an audiobook the whole time—a how-to on gaslighting.

Bea. Is that you?

Rhona's whole body tenses in a way that makes Maeve wonder if the caller is a lover, and if she had it totally wrong in supposing Rhona to be the dominant one in the S&M scenarios that surely play out in her million-euro lair.

So nice to hear from you! Rhona beams, unabashedly earnest. ¿Qué tal?

Maybe it has to do with the rain muddling them together in the car, but the distance between them seems to keep shifting. On the phone with this person, Rhona emanates warmth and care. She is concerned and attentive—really listening, not just waiting for the other person to stop speaking. Maybe, with other people in her life, Rhona is the type to twirl an imaginary phone cord around her finger as she listens to their stories, urging them on, inviting extra detail. Maybe she only conducts herself horrendously with her siblings.

Or maybe . . . Maeve thinks, maybe forgetting is the nobler thing.

Beatriz's voice comes through the one earpod loudly, which is just as well given the strident rain. Rhona twigs that she's calling from her Peruvian number—and that's why it's a +51 and not +56, a detail that had momentarily thrown her.

It's one of the men! Beatriz says in such a panicked tone it sounds as though she's been mugged. He said they're from La Corporación, but what *is* that? The corporation! Just any corporation? I tried to ask them, but they were . . . evasive and cryptic—

Who, Bea?

The corporation men! They said they're here to support my presentation and to offer whatever assistance I would need. And I didn't know if . . . to pretend I was confused or to go along with it. But they were in my hotel, Rhona. In the *lobby*—

Bea? Rhona says.

Just sitting there, waiting . . . with polished shoes. Probably—

Beatriz?

—their briefcases were empty. Or maybe full of cash. I said I didn't need any assistance, but I . . . I wasn't thinking and I gave them my business card—the new cards you got me, Rhona—and they asked for one, so now they have my phone number, my email, probably my room number by now—

Beatriz?

They've already emailed, and now they're calling—

What do you call that breathing you do?

—saying we should meet to go through my presentation, the report, the recommendations, to make sure de que todo vaya bien. Like I don't know what that means! I'm afraid to go down for breakfast. And there was another weird guy at the airport—

What's that yoga breathing you do, Bea?

What?

The loud breathing.

Ujjayi?

Yes.

Why?

That.

What?

Do it now.

How do you know about that? Can you hear me in my room at home? I thought it's soundproof.

I went to a yoga class once, Rhona says. Pre-Covid . . . but even still it made me feel sick, all that wet breath. Rhona can hear the constriction in Beatriz's throat, but she presses on. If it's for anything, it's for moments like this. Do it now, will you? The ujjayi?

I should never have come here alone, Beatriz says.

Rhona stops herself from saying anything to the contrary. Is there a chance that Beatriz . . . won't actually be able to deliver the report this afternoon? What's the time difference . . . No, it's too late to fly over now herself, to take over or hold her hand. She wants Beatriz to excel, anyway. She's given her a *chance* to excel. This week, she has just one job. Yes, it's delicate. But Rhona, at any given time, has ten such fragile jobs balanced on the crown of her head. What exactly had these men done, anyway? Treated her to a little mild intimidation, standing there in their polished shoes? That's what it is to be a female academic, getting coverage, effecting policy change, making an impact: Being trolled. Doxxed. Being threatened with reprisal, or ruination, or rape, whenever a new article is published. It's not an easy field to traverse. Isn't she used to it by now? If Beatriz can't duck a few entry-level thugs in a hotel lobby . . .

But no, she corrects herself. All of that, maybe, is new to Beatriz. Yes. It must be.

Rhona looks back to smile at Leo, then passes the dregs of the smile on to Nell. How would Nell handle it, were Beatriz *her* postdoctoral candidate? What is it the Americans always say? *I'm sorry that happened to you.* Or, if you're in the middle of it: *I'm so sorry that's happening to you.* But Beatriz isn't the type to want placation. Back at home, she's always talking about trackable balance goals, about separating work from life. Rhona gives her six more months in academia, before she caves in and sells out to industry or throws in with some NGO.

In the meantime, though, Rhona has to do something, if only for Beatriz's peace of mind. She tells her she'll arrange for her to change rooms and talk to the hotelier about their lax security. She'll book her a driver for her whole stay in Valparaíso. She'll text her the driver's name, number, and registration. And then a stroke of inspiration: She remembers a local researcher she knows there, a man called Sergio from Valparaíso University. Surely he'll be thrilled to meet Beatriz someplace nice for an expensible lunch before going to Parliament; Beatriz could describe the situation to Sergio and get his savvy on-the-ground verdict and—very likely—his assurance that she is perfectly safe. His being tall and handsome won't hurt.

Remember, Rhona says somberly, in these situations there's always *Casualty.*

Maeve and Nell, already concerned, exchange wide-eyed looks.

How is Leo? Beatriz asks. Has he said his first word yet?

But Rhona is already in execution mode. Sergio will take care of you, she says. And I know you'll do brilliantly today. I'll go make those calls now.

Oh my god, Beatriz says, as a ringing comes over the line—Bea's hotel phone. Rhona presses her earpod closer to hear what's going on.

Hola? Es la habitación 402. Puede enviar seguridad? Hay alguien en mi puerta. Envíe a seguridad, por favor!

Beatriz? . . . Beatriz?

Beatriz is panting on the phone. Someone knocked on my door, she whispers. Oh my god.

Beatriz? Don't open the door. I'll call the hotel.

Rhona hears nothing for a moment. Then she hears a door creaking. Beatriz? Rhona looks at the map for the next junction to pull in at. But then Beatriz comes back on the line, her tone of voice calmer:

It's okay. It was next door. They had . . . it was room service next door.

Are you sure?

Beatriz says, Yeah. Sorry. I'm completely stressed. It was too late to call last night and I didn't sleep.

Say "No, Rhona," if you're not safe.

I'm fine. It was a mistake. Thank you.

I'll call you very shortly. Rhona presses the earpod to hang up.

The windscreen wipers speed up to an almost undanceable tempo as they drive west. At least the rain will keep the black car clean.

Everything okay? Maeve asks.

Hmm? Rhona says, trying to figure out if she should find a driveway to pull into. Just the road is so windy and narrow, and it's lashing rain, and the house isn't far now.

That sounded serious, Maeve says with bare concern.

Yeah, well, no. It was a false alarm.

Was it a colleague of yours?

Mmm, Rhona says, tapping the screen to recheck the route. Next exit onto the R299. She hadn't inserted the destination into the GPS but knows where she's going.

Nell leans in front of Leo to stare at the map. So . . . *not* Galway, then?

I'm afraid not, Rhona says. Looking at her son's reflection, she adds—trying to keep the wobble out of her voice, as that's the sort of thing he picks up on—Your aunty Olwen has abandoned all that song-worthy coast for a coast of *four* prodigal kilometers, in a county with roughly two sets of traffic lights for infrastructure. How's that for a midlife mishap, Leo?

Maeve is blathering about a couple she knows in Leitrim who run a tree nursery. Good soil.

Nell is sniffing. Leo must have done a sizable number. Who'd blame him? Show a city child such a vast dominion of cows' arses and something would be amiss if he failed to pull scatological rank. The road is windy. The palette for miles and miles is greens and grays. Every other field is dotted with puddly lakes—or floodwaters—all of them a sluggy gray. The houses are the brick gray of a future under contract but not yet fulfilled. The monotony is broken by an occasional fungus green. It's hard to see the white line on the road for the firmament dragging along it. But just now, a blackness comes into view in their lane, some distance ahead. It's a cat, grooming itself. Maeve gasps. Holding the steering wheel firm, Rhona says:

Look at the dead cat.

She gives the horn a light tap. Then a thump to the undercarriage, as if the car is being burped. The Model 3 is really too low to the ground, Rhona mutters; miss a speed bump and you'll scrape the metalwork. A silence—no, a kind of *off* feeling—in the car prompts her to scan her passengers in the mirror. Her sisters look as though they've just had their bottoms pinched by a teenager. They both speak at once:

Are you not gunna—

You didn't even brake!

—stop the car? Nell twists back to the rear window.

That's someone's pet!

It might not be dead—

It's dead.

That's just *brutal*, says Maeve.

—it could be . . .

I hit the horn! Rhona says.

Unused to raised voices, Leo's face puckers.

You didn't even *slow down* . . . or *swerve*, like, even *slightly*—

There was no one in the other lane! You could've—

I hit the horn! Rhona replies sternly. You saw me! What do you want me to do? Swerve my car in this lashing rain with a baby in the back and *hydroplane* it into Leitrim . . . all so some cat can keep rimming itself? She raises her brows at Leo's iffy reflection.

There is a brief lull in which Leo auditions a whinge. Now that the child is distressed, Nell is starting to get him.

Seriously, Rhona, Maeve says. You just made that calculation and said: Look at the dead cat?!

For a split second, Rhona lifts both hands innocently off the wheel. I beeped the horn!

She beeped! Maeve says, looking out the passenger window at the newly haunted day.

In the back, Nell and Leo are inspecting each other like tourists considering the admissions fee to a museum of lesser-known history. Nell offers the quiet assertion, as if he might contest it: She did beep.

One practical feature of the Tesla Model 3 is that hitting the horn automatically saves the next ten minutes of dashcam footage to the hard drive, in case it's needed for insurance or legal purposes. And so that cat will live on the drive for as long as it might take one of her sisters to relay this anecdote to Olwen, and perhaps to make a tedious Schrodinger's cat joke of which Rhona would be the butt. And what of it? None of them—not one—has a person in their lives that they'd level a cat for.

Nell is still trying to engage with Leo, who frowns intensely, suitably cautious.

You see, Nell speaks quietly . . . The nice thing about *abstract objects*—like numbers, Leo, your one-two-threes—is that they're *causally inert*. A number can't be hit by a car, can it? A set can't feel its square root, or smell poo, or be obliterated by gamma rays or terrorists. That's why your granny liked numbers so much. Nothing can get at them.

Nell plucks a fistful of air and places the abstract object carefully on Leo's lap.

Here you go, she says. See what you think.

act one

SCENE ONE

Three hundred meters up the northeast of Sliabh Dúch, a hundred-year-old farmhouse and barn. No other houses are visible in any direction for the dense forestry, farmland, and sister mountain, An Tor, to the east. The landscape eastward takes on the wintry colors of bogland. This side of the valley is verdant.

The small bungalow and barn are shrouded in trees, shrubs, and unkempt grasses. The stone barn hasn't been renovated besides a new roof of orange corrugated iron to carry a solar array, and the wooden double doors once used for livestock have been restored and painted green. Beyond the barn, backing into a section of forest, is a large, crude polytunnel and outhouse.

The farmhouse itself has been renovated impressively for a span of just eight months, though not to any catalog standard; mostly, to make it weather-proof. Its lumpy, lime-rendered walls have been insulated and white-washed. A restored slate roof is covered with solar panels. There's a heat pump to the rear. The traditional tiny, deep window hollows have new double-glazed windows painted the rich pine green of the barn doors. Where a porch once stood is a bay window, with the front door set to the right of it. There are high gable windows at both ends of the house. In front, where there are notions of a patio, a plastic garden chair rests on its side.

In the car's headlights, the steel cattle gate is scintillating with rain. One side is held open with a stone. The other half is shut, so there's no driving through without getting out and letting oneself in. There's no driveway, just a field with flattened moss, mud, leaves, sycamore seeds, and broken stone where building equipment trekked in and out. The branch of a willow tree, blown off in the morning's storm, is strewn on the ground.

In the car, they are all peering through the rain for signs of life, but the windows are dark and there are no vehicles. It's only when Maeve spots a ladder perched against the eastern gable of the farmhouse that she thinks to look up, to where the rain is coming from . . .

MAEVE: Oh my god!

NELL: What?

MAEVE: There she is!

NELL: Where?

Maeve leans so far forward that her breath fogs up the windscreen. Rhona ducks a little to make her out: Olwen, on her hands and knees, crawling across the roof's apex, above the solar panels. She's holding something.

RHONA: That's nowhere near high enough . . .

The deafening rain, and Nell's bending sideways in the back seat to fix Olwen in her gaze, is enough to mute the unspoken half of Rhona's sentence.

MAEVE: Should we—

NELL: Don't honk!

They don't. All eyes on Olwen, inching across the roof. She doesn't seem to notice them.

MAEVE: Are your headlights on?

NELL: Don't flash!

RHONA: We'll wait till she's down.

MAEVE: I don't think we should just . . . *watch* as she falls! . . . Or doesn't fall?

RHONA: We'll wait till she's down. Then can one of you open the gate? And move that tree.

Leo whines. Back on the roof, halfway across, Olwen lowers her torso to the tiles.

MAEVE: Oh my god.

Once she's in position, Olwen replaces what had come loose: the cowling from the extractor fan's chute. She braces one foot on the top edge of the solar panel, to sit her center of gravity on the front of the roof, then stretches over to the far side to reset the cowling.

RHONA: (*into her phone*) Sergio! It's Rhona Flattery. (*She audibly smiles.*) I hope this is still your number . . . or maybe you had to give up your identity after OLAF? God, it's been how long . . . Stockholm, right? We shouldn't've let that happen. Listen: Tell me you're in Valparaíso today? And that you have no plans for lunch? (*She lifts her thumb to send the message, steals another glance at Olwen, then scrolls to the top of her WhatsApp chat list and selects another name to leave a voice message for.*) Carolijn! I need you to book a driver for Beatriz in Valparaíso. A very secure corporate car service, okay? Could you cc me when you send her the driver's details, car reg, model? Get the driver's mobile, too, and the depot number. She needs him from basically now on, at Hotel Casa Higueras. And can you tell the hotel manager to give me a call ASAP? Thanks.

Leo mewls again. Rhona turns to cup his ankle, gives him a what's-going-on *expression.*

MAEVE: (*to Rhona*) I mean . . . if I'm ever on fire in the kitchen, do feel free to finish what's on your plate.

NELL: Okay.

RHONA: Olwen's the one who climbed onto a roof in the middle of a storm.

NELL: Well . . .

RHONA: Ah, she's seen us.

NELL: . . . since she sees us.

Nell opens the car door, swings one leg out slowly. Finally standing in the weather, Nell waves at Olwen, who is at the top of the ladder, staring at them, not waving. Maeve opens her door but hesitates before getting out.

RHONA: Are you in or out? The car's getting wet.

Maeve can barely hear through her heart in her ears and the rain, but she opens the squeaking gate and drags the branch out of the way. As Rhona drives in, Maeve hurries back to join Nell at the gate, now feeling the fact of their trespassing; that they are not invited. Maeve huddles into Nell, holding her at the waist, shivering. Nell seems unaffected by the stormy conditions.

NELL: Don't fight it.

MAEVE: What?

Nell is looking up at Olwen, wondering which of them is up on the river-bank this time. They watch the rhythmic notation of Olwen's huffy breaths as she takes in the fact of them, like a French horn player counting out a too-brief rest. No . . . No, she is not guided by any script. She is not taking a pause of any set duration. After some moments suspended in the weather, in simple refusal, she climbs down the ladder. Maeve and Nell stay at the gate. Olwen collapses the ladder, then carries it across to the barn. She says something that none of them can hear. Rhona, still in the car, turns to Leo.

RHONA: Here we go: the psychodrama as it curtains up. (*She gets out and opens the back to detach his car seat from the belt-clips.*) It'll be messy, Leo, but I'll do my best to limit your exposure to . . . *aware-ness,* let's say, rather than knowledge.

Olwen opens the front door and steps inside, closing it off to the elements but leaving it off the latch.

Linking elbows with Nell, Maeve tries to rush to the house, but Nell pulls her arm free.

NELL: Don't run at her.

Trusting Nell's instinct better than her own, Maeve slows. It dawns on Rhona that Nell isn't able to run. Holding Leo in his Turtle Air by Nuna car seat, she waits by the door so that they can all cross the threshold together.

Olwen is straight ahead of them in the kitchen, hunkering to get a bucket and sponge from beneath the sink. With her bristly hoary-brown hair, her gray fleece, and her glistening green waterproof trousers, she looks like a moss-covered boulder. When she stands, she processes their dull reflections in the kitchen window, which looks out onto an upward slope of a rough, clodden field and (beyond the polytunnel and outhouse) a sepulchral forest. Olwen gets on her hands and knees to mop up the ceiling leak, now only trickling down into the kitchen. Weather dribbles off her. She wrings the sponge into the bucket over and over.

Nell and Maeve exchange glances. Having never seen Olwen turn her back on them, they are thrown. Rhona scans the place for motivation and intent.

The kitchen is divided from the main room by a breakfast bar and a single thick beam from floor to vaulted ceiling. A rear door leads to the bungalow's only extension: a storage room where the battery inverter hums. To the left are a trestle table and mismatched chairs. To the front are a couch, armchair, coffee table. In the wall facing the barn, a set of French doors have been cut in. There is very little in the way of stuff. The salvaged timber floors are unswept.

To the right is a wall with three doors, none of them on the latch. Rhona ducks into the first, which is a cupboard-size study. The second is the bathroom, from which Rhona retrieves a limp towel (taking note of the solitary toothbrush). Though Leo is heavy in the car seat—and Rhona can feel the burn of this morning's Pilates planks and shoulder taps—she doesn't put him down. She towels her hair with her free hand, returning to her sisters. Olwen is now effectively polishing the floor.

RHONA: You're alive, by the looks of it.

Olwen levers herself off one knee to stand up. When she turns, her gaze goes straight to Leo. He was barely three months old when she last saw him; now he's nearly one. He discerns that his role is to be quietly magnificent. After some time, Rhona extends the towel to Olwen, who takes it but doesn't dry herself.

MAEVE: (*tearing up*) Ol, it's *so* good to see you! . . . Alive!

Olwen snaps her gaze from Leo to Maeve.

OLWEN: You knew I was alive.

Nell frowns for a moment at this, which catches Olwen's eye.

You flew all the way here.

NELL: Sorry. . . . And sorry that it took so long.

Maeve presses her palms against her sternum, as if struggling for breath.

Olwen looks at the floor.

OLWEN: I don't think I ever asked anything of ye.

When the truth of this sinks in, Maeve heaves with emotion.

MAEVE: But Olwen, we're so worried!

Maeve feels a sudden hand on her back. She knows it's Rhona's hand because it begins to pat her, as if to dislodge a chunk of meat.

OLWEN: So I have to allay your fears, have I?

MAEVE: No! Just . . . we *love* you and we want—

OLWEN: Ye're all grown up now.

RHONA: We are. We're not the demographic for running off in the night.

Rhona says this as she lowers Leo's car seat to the floor and unclips him from it.

Women pushing forty.

Leo whinges a little, and Rhona takes him up and rubs his back, showing that she's capable of maneuvers subtler than a Heimlich.

NELL: I'm thirty-three.

She says this in an effort to share in the runaway accusation as much as to deny pushing forty.

MAEVE: (*crying again*) Sorry, it's just . . . so amazing to see you all together. In real life.

Nell smiles at her. As does Rhona, the way a lactose intolerant person smiles at an offer of ice cream.

I mean . . . forgetting everything . . . it's still a really long time? (*Maeve turns to Rhona.*) It was Nell's thirtieth, wasn't it?

MAEVE: I half thought Leo might have a little cousin . . . (*She looks at Olwen, who is, in fact, larger.*) It's been, like, eight months . . . I mean . . .

Olwen folds the towel as if it requires concentration. Maeve once showed Jasper and the boys how to fold their napkins into turkeys, and Olwen had looked on from afar, aloof, until they looked around to see she'd made the tea towel into a lobster.

I have to say I was sort of excited but I'm also really, really glad you didn't cheat on Jasper—

OLWEN: Forgetting everything . . .

Olwen says this so loudly that the new rosacea in her cheeks intensifies.

While yer coats are still on.

She gestures to the door. Leo is whingeing again, and the rain on the vaulted roof is a crescendo without a climax. It's enough to conceal Rhona's mutterings.

NELL: You do deserve some space. If that's what you're asking for.

OLWEN: I deserve space?

NELL: If you need space. I get that.

Nell looks at Olwen, hoping she'll remember the emails they'd exchanged years ago when Nell was extending her studies in the U.S. again and again, and couldn't express why, but wanted Olwen's blessing.

We'll go, and come back later—

MAEVE: What? We're not going! We just got here! (*She is looking desperately between them.*) We can't go. (*to Olwen*) We don't know that you're okay!

NELL: Maeve. (*She clutches Maeve's forearm.*)

RHONA: (*to Maeve and Nell*) She's okay. (*to Olwen*) You're okay? (*Olwen doesn't deny it.*) You have food, you have water, you have shelter, you have heat? (*Olwen almost nods.*) What is that solar installation—six, seven kilowatts?

OLWEN: Eight.

RHONA: For one person?

Pause.

OLWEN: I count five of us now.

RHONA: Are you planning on hosting people?

Pause.

Jasper? And Tommy and Cian?

Olwen cranes her neck to inspect the ceiling: the exposed beams are giving off the smell of something long-barreled where the leak had run along them.

OLWEN: A vegan schnitzel in the toaster is what I'm planning. The toaster's an awful power suck.

RHONA: So you're still taking in nourishment.

Rhona looks around for a clock. Finding none, she moves Leo to her other hip and takes out her phone. The home screen is full of voice messages from Sergio and Beatriz.

Olwen sees that Rhona's attention is now elsewhere, and a hard curl appears in the corner of her mouth.

OLWEN: (*quietly, but not softly*) Ye're too early.

MAEVE: We can do better than that for nourishment! I can cook something?

NELL: (*whispers*) Go easy.

Nell is shivering a little.

You were saying, Ol?

MAEVE: Can I . . . get a glass of water, just?

Olwen dumps the towel on the breakfast bar. Anticipating all her drawers being opened and her circumstances charted—after all she'd done to wipe herself off the map—she goes to the kitchen and takes a tumbler from the drying rack. She retrieves a bottle of gin from the cupboard. Pours herself a triple and downs it.

OLWEN: Refresh yourselves however ye see fit. Then let yourselves out.

Leaving the tumbler on the counter, she makes her way to the rear door, then heads out to the barn.

Maeve and Nell stand there helplessly. Rhona holds Leo out to Maeve.

RHONA: Can you take him? He needs changing.

MAEVE: Oh!

RHONA: I need to get his day bag from the car.

MAEVE: Oh.

At the click of the front door, Maeve carries Leo by his armpits over to the couch and then stands him on her lap, facing her.

Hi.

She smiles at him for a while, but she's still sort of crying, so he's not smiling back. His arms bash around the place, but he's not trying to get away. He'll want independence soon—he'll want to get the lay of the land—but for now she's new enough and enough like his mum in the nose and cheekbone to hold his attention. After some time, Maeve can sense that Nell is watching them.

NELL: Suits you.

Pause.

MAEVE: (*to Leo*) I'm glad that's what the smell is. I thought it was Auntie Nell.

NELL: Hey! I've been traveling for eighteen hours.

MAEVE: She came straight from the eighteen hundreds. *At least.*

NELL: And I went to the airport right after class, so these clothes are two days in.

MAEVE: (*to Nell*) If this is part of your celibacy strategy, it's not going to work.

NELL: It's not a—

MAEVE: You're still irresistible. (*to Leo*) Isn't she a babe? (*Leo looks unmoved.*) No, *you're* a babe! No, *you're* a babe!

Leo reaches out for a white gold chain Maeve's wearing, and he pulls it off her neck.

Oh. Fuck.

Nell can't see, but Maeve is weeping again.

NELL: Did he break it?

MAEVE: He did, yeah.

NELL: Don't get too attached, eh? That the message?

MAEVE: That's actually a pretty strong necklace. (*She tries to control her breathing.*) Leo is fully ripped.

NELL: (*hearing Maeve's upset*) I'm sorry. Was it sentimental?

MAEVE: No. Not at all. I get sent these things, from businesses. I usually wear them a couple of times and do a post and sell them. (*Leo hands the necklace back to her, in a sharing gesture that normally earns him a huge smile.*) Thanks. (*Pause.*) Maybe Olwen can fix it. She has tools. (*Maeve twists round to Nell, who's still standing.*) What are you doing? Sit down. (*Nell stays where she is.*) Can you help me move this coffee table? Maybe we can find a rug or something for Leo to play on.

NELL: It's funny to come such a long distance. And then you find yourself in a space full of smaller distances.

SCENE TWO

Some time passes while Rhona is out in the car and Olwen is out in the barn. Nell sits on the cushioned ottoman that skirts the bay window. From the couch, Maeve is watching Leo, now playing with an egg tray, a ziplock bag, and the letter holders from a German edition of Scrabble they'd found in the ottoman. He is crinkling around on a stray piece of tarp.

On the breakfast bar is a jug of water with ice and ribbons of cucumber, and glasses left out for Rhona and Olwen.

MAEVE: I'd love to see Rhona being *influenced*, just once, or changing her mind or fucking up or taking a notion, you know? But she comes to every situation, every *conversation*, with her conclusion already formed. She's just . . . she has no tolerance for other people's choices.

Nell tips her head to the side, anticipating the fall of Leo's stacked letter trays. Maeve helps him collect them.

NELL: You mean for Olwen's choices?

MAEVE: Everyone's.

Pause.

NELL: Do *you* have tolerance for Olwen's choices?

MAEVE: Well, we don't know what they are yet!

NELL: One of them was to be left alone.

Nell pulls out the crown on her watch and starts winding herself into the right time zone.

Can I borrow your phone?

Maeve waits for Nell to be ready to catch her phone, which she does with reassuring coordination.

I'm gunna book someplace. I hope Leitrim's cheap.

MAEVE: There's always Tinder.

Nell frowns at her, but she doesn't see.

I just realized! Being bisexual must make it twice as hard to be celibate?

Maeve looks up to see Nell's displeasure.

NELL: Now who has no respect for other people's choices?

MAEVE: I'm pulling the piss.

NELL: I'm serious, though. About booking somewhere.

MAEVE: We're staying here!

NELL: Yes, we'll stay in the situation. I'm not about to fly home. But this feels way more . . . violatory than I anticipated. I'm not staying if I'm not welcome. And I get this feeling we might be . . . hurrying her through some process that needs time.

MAEVE: I don't want to rush her either! I'm with you. Let's take it really, really slowly. I'm fine with staying close by. Like in the poly-tunnel. (*She plucks an imaginary egg from the egg tray and passes it carefully to Leo.*) Halim might've lent me his tent, if I'd thought of it. Might've been a way to get him to go *inside* the boat, while it's empty.

Leo flings the empty egg tray across the room in protest at having been given nothing in the guise of something. His mood is turning. Hadn't his mother registered that he needed changing? Nell looks out the window to check on Rhona, on her phone in the car.

NELL: That sounded serious, with her colleague.

MAEVE: Conveniently. (*Quietly imitating Rhona*) These are stakes of my life!

NELL: Huh?

MAEVE: (*holding back*) To put our little crisis in perspective.

Maeve has been stroking Leo's hair, and now she seems to be inspecting it.

Is his hair *browner*?

NELL: I thought that.

MAEVE: It was more . . . heirloom carrot before, wasn't it? Now it's stick.

Maeve gets up to go and retrieve the egg tray, and then curiosity gets the better of her: she tests the sturdiness of a wooden ladder bolted into the wall in between the doors to the bedroom and bathroom. She climbs it up to a sort of open attic area above the rooms, being used for storage. The vaulted roof slopes so that there's not quite enough room to stand up there comfortably. But it would most certainly be tenanted as a room in London.

Her camping stuff's up here! There's a blow-up sleeping mat *and* a foam one! Come *on*. Maybe we should just camp out up here and be really quiet for a couple of days and then she'll resign herself to the fact that we're here.

Olwen can be heard reentering the house via the mudroom to the rear, and Maeve hurries down the ladder, just in time to look flushed for Olwen. Olwen stops and Maeve stops, as if they are two cars on a tiny country lane, and the local etiquette for reversal is unclear. Maeve pushes one of the egg-tray hollows inside out and says:

On the way here . . . there was a cat in the middle of the road.

OLWEN: I'm in no mood for omens.

MAEVE: No, there was an actual cat. Nell saw it. (*Maeve gestures to Nell to have her back.*)

NELL: There was a cat on the road.

OLWEN: (*to Nell*) I'm in no mood for thought experiments either.

MAEVE: It was black, but it was just a normal cat.

Olwen scans Leo's crying face, as Nell opens the ottoman for something else that might distract him.

So Rhona sees this cat, a good hundred meters ahead, in the middle of the road, and goes: Look at the dead cat!

Maeve's jaw drops at her own story.

OLWEN: It was dead?

MAEVE: No!

Long pause.

OLWEN: But it was soon to be?

MAEVE: Yeah!

NELL: To be fair, it *was* raining really hard. And her kid was in the back, and—

MAEVE: She saw it, and made that calculation, and announced it, and then . . . thud.

The rain has lightened to a drizzle outside—the darkness lifting somewhat—and Olwen switches off the overhead light. Maeve has laid the ground for Olwen to say something funny and cutting and timelessly true, but she says nothing.

NELL: We'll get out from under you, Ol. I'm just tryna book someplace.

Olwen takes the jug from the kitchen counter, carries it around the counter, around Maeve, to the sink. She sniffs the jug before holding her hand against the ice and cucumber inside it to pour out the water. Then she sets about filling the jug with gin and tonic.

OLWEN: Ye can stay for a drink, and to say whatever you simply must get off yer chests. There's another storm on the heels of this one. Ye should be gone before it lands.

Maeve had been wincing at the jug, hoping Olwen's hands were washed, but she's now extending her glass. Olwen gives her a sphinxlike stare as she fills it.

MAEVE: Thank you.

Olwén pours herself a glass. Then she leans on the kitchen counter, facing the French doors, but with her gaze unfocused. Rhona opens the front door.

OLWEN: Look at the dead cat. Look at the sealed fate. Shed a tear, if ye're well hydrated.

Rhona's holding the charging cable of her car, connected to a three-pin adapter.

Not her first time making that calculation.

From the doorway, Rhona looks at Maeve, who wears a guilty grimace.

MAEVE: (*to Rhona, with her shoulders lifted apologetically*) We're allowed to stay for a drink.

RHONA: We have no choice. The nearest charger's fifty kilometers away.

Rhona gurns at these folk networks. To Olwen:

Can I plug my car in?

Olwen nods. She goes to the bay window and opens one of the small upper windows. Rhona goes back outside to feed the cable through. Nell tries to get out of the way. Rhona returns a moment later with the day bag on her shoulder, wipes her feet, and takes Leo to the bathroom to change him. Olwen opens one of the ottomans, roots around, and takes out a piece of chalk. She finds herself face-to-face with Nell, who is standing with a degree of concentration.

OLWEN: You're looking chalky, Nellie. Are you well?

NELL: You look . . . (*with envy*) sturdy.

OLWEN: It's muscles. From the manual labor. (*Nell's expression goes a bit religious. Olwen looks down at herself.*) Underneath. I don't wear them on top, like the lads. Showy. (*Her gaze wanders but lands back on Nell, the way a fork of lightning would land upon the thing closest to it.*)

NELL: How do you feel?

Olwen contemplates the piece of chalk on her palm for a while. Her breathing is louder than it had been before she'd gone to the barn.

You abandoned your students?

OLWEN: You abandoned your students.

NELL: Not exactly. There's just a couple weeks left of term, but I got most classes covered. Except for Quinnipiac, but those students agreed to do the last few classes online. Thankfully.

Olwen drops her head into a deep nod, letting her gaze blur upon Nell's feet.

OLWEN: They're awful adaptable.

NELL: You think?

Olwen almost smirks to herself, but she doesn't share what she's thinking.

Nell glances at Maeve, who is behind Olwen, taking the tiniest sips from her drink.

MAEVE: Are you teaching this week?

NELL: I've got a two-hour phenomenology seminar tomorrow.

MAEVE: Really?

NELL: Who am I kidding? It's pop psych.

MAEVE: Holy shit. I get to attend my sister's lecture?

NELL: It's a seminar, not a lecture. You'd have to do the reading.

MAEVE: I will!

Olwen glances commiseratingly at Nell.

Yes I *will* do the reading! (*to Olwen*) How's your Wi-Fi?

The bathroom door opens. Rhona is disinfecting her own hands, having done Leo's.

OLWEN: It isn't.

Rhona notes the humming inverter in the mudroom. She settles at the dining table, with Leo on her lap. From her day bag she takes out a brown paper bag of organic snacks.

RHONA: (*to Leo*) Pear slices or chapati fingers?

MAEVE: Do both, Leo. Add a dollop of mascarpone. Sprinkle of cinnamon. Nutmeg. Star anise. Toasted almonds.

Olwen goes to the kitchen and pours a small G&T for Rhona. Extends it to her.

RHONA: No thanks.

OLWEN: (*imitating Rhona*) No, she says. *No.* See that? *I* can say *no* now too.

RHONA: (*correcting Olwen*) No thanks, she says. I don't drink-drive. It's a miracle we survived Dad's after-school pickups.

Olwen pours Rhona's measure into her own glass. She takes a slug from it.

MAEVE: I really like the house. Especially the ancient stove! Does it work? Do you cook with it?

OLWEN: It's full of mousetraps.

MAEVE: But there's no oven?

OLWEN: I have a microwave and a plug-in induction hob.

MAEVE: You have . . . *a* hob?

Olwen looks sternly at Maeve.

OLWEN: These are your questions? (*to Rhona, quickly*) You'll have to plug your car out in thirty minutes. I'd like a hot meal tonight.

RHONA: Half an hour? At, what, ten amps? That'll barely get me out of your gate.

OLWEN: Ah, you'll extract yourself right enough.

Rhona smilingly shakes her head, as at some vexing inevitability.

RHONA: You'll be forcing guests on yourself, which is a round-about way to do things. No?

OLWEN: It's unlike you not to have done your calculation, Rhona. (*Pause.*) I've done mine.

Maeve clutches at her neck for the necklace that Leo tore off.

RHONA: It sounds very rough, this calculation. Were you in a rush making it?

Maeve takes the necklace from her pocket and starts to try to reconnect the split links, thinking the sight of it might put Olwen in mind of her tools. Olwen watches Maeve put the link between her teeth to widen the gap.

NELL: (*looking around her*) This doesn't look like a rush job.

MAEVE: No. It's really nice. Except maybe it's a bit stark.

Olwen shakes her head a little, smiling at Maeve, resisting the lure to take the necklace.

OLWEN: Girls. Ye're years too early.

Olwen refills her drink and peers outside as if there's someone there.

This won't be how ye show up here.

NELL: But you expected us to come eventually?

OLWEN: I warned ye not to bother me.

NELL: You did. And sorry.

Pause.

And you don't owe us an explanation . . .

OLWEN: How many watts would do you?

NELL: But we'd have tried to respect your choice if you'd have given us *any* indication of what was going on. Your whole bailout—did something happen?

OLWEN: Time is it now?

RHONA: (*eyeing the jug*) Too early.

OLWEN: (*surprised, mistaking Rhona's comment as an echo of her own*) She's listening.

MAEVE: Not even close to half an hour. And sorry if I'm missing something, but don't you have a battery?

RHONA: Of course she does. You can hear the inverter.

OLWEN: By all means! Hold the wee fellow up over the roof, and if the sun shines out his arse, charge the car to your heart's content. But with this weather, my battery is holding my store for the week.

MAEVE: I guess it's a fuse thing? Like on my boat, you can't have too many things plugged in—

RHONA: Do you remember, Leo, I was telling you about the new Irish eco-Marxists? How they gaze out the triple-glazed windows of their modest country cottages, scowling at airplanes, boldly clinging to the means of production, distribution, and exchange.

OLWEN: Oh, clinging! (*raises her glass, turning her back to them to look out the kitchen window*)

Maeve directs the following question to Olwen in a childish voice, hoping to divert the attack toward a political theory rather than any person:

MAEVE: What's an eco-Marxist?

RHONA: Grazing on your polytunnel radishes!

MAEVE: I've heard of eco-socialists. Is it the same?

NELL: Uhm, I don't think it's particularly Marxist or socialist to live *off* the grid? The grid is a communal thing. If you're siloing your own land and property and water and power supply, that's not exactly—

RHONA: (*to Maeve*) They both want the same society in the end. It's how they get there that differs. The Marxists are willing to seize the state through a violent overthrow. They're willing to put people through a lot of pain.

MAEVE: Hang on. Who's the—

OLWEN: You think it's communist, the way we're going? I suppose we're moneyless (*she points at Maeve*), stateless (*she points at Nell*), classless (*she points at herself*). Is that communist? Or is it anarchist?

RHONA: So you left the academy to shun the elite class?

MAEVE: I actually do have some money, it's just that . . . I have to give it back.

NELL: Being off the grid is actually more . . .

RHONA: (*to Nell*) Libertarian.

NELL: . . . libertarian.

OLWEN: Go on, so. Anarchist. If you put a gun to my head, I'm anarchic.

RHONA: You're making it up as you go along. There's no plan.

Olwen wears an unfamiliar grimace.

OLWEN: We're way past planning.

MAEVE: I think we should sit down.

NELL: (*very quietly, to Maeve*) Can you see if there's a pen and paper in the ottoman?

RHONA: (*to Olwen*) Oh?

Olwen retrieves an unopened packet of paper and a clutch of pens from the study.

NELL: Olwen, do you mean that everything feels predetermined? Intractable?

Maeve gets up to add more tonic to her glass, her every motion exaggerated, as if to draw attention away from Olwen; convinced they need to be easy company to get to stay.

MAEVE: *I* don't believe that. Even after all Mum's belief in determinism. The hard sell she gave it. *I* think everything's either willed or random . . . and ninety percent of everything that's tragic is random, and ninety percent of everything that's romantic is willed.

Pause.

OLWEN: How many kilometers are you short?

RHONA: Forty.

MAEVE: (*to herself*) I thought that was profound.

OLWEN: What's the efficiency of a Tesla? And don't be smarmy.

Pause.

RHONA: A hundred and fifty watt-hours per kilometer.

While no one is looking, Nell finishes her drink so her hands are free, then pushes herself to her feet and propels herself to the dining table. There she sits opposite Leo, who is standing on the bit of chair between Rhona's legs, so he's the correct height for the table. Nell doles out paper and pens.

OLWEN: Point one five times forty . . . you need six kilowatt hours. Maeve! Take a stab at what she'll get in half an hour on that socket?

MAEVE: Fuck off.

RHONA: Don't swear near my son.

OLWEN: Try it.

MAEVE: Sorry.

OLWEN: If I'd a penny for every spoon you thrust at our gobs, saying *try it*—

MAEVE: Slag *anything* about me *except* my crap maths. Mum practically disowned me.

OLWEN: (*looks baffled, the booze effusing in her*) When did one of us ever laugh at you? And you short of breath for all the cackling at the rest of us. You remember that time I tried to give you a night off cooking, and I made that parsnip and carrot pasta thing? Which was perfectly edible—

MAEVE: It absolutely wasn't! You just boiled random things!

OLWEN: I used what we had in abundance.

MAEVE: Did you even salt the water? Adding cheese can't solve *every*thing!

OLWEN: How was I to know cooking has to involve tiny quantities of ingredients you're either out of or never heard of?

Rhona is mutteringly explaining the calculation to Leo:

RHONA: A socket puts out ten amps, even in Leitrim. That's two point three kilowatts.

OLWEN: I said you could have *half* an hour. So call it one kilowatt hour. Accounting for losses.

MAEVE: Ah, come on, guys. I really think we can take a minute.

Maeve beseeches Nell for support, but Nell knows when a force is unstoppable and when an object is immovable. She busies herself instead with Leo's line drawings, writing a philosophical question to accompany each one.

RHONA: (*putting her pencil down*) It'll take six hours.

MAEVE: To charge you up? Okay! Six hours is a perfect *minimum* amount of time to hang out and catch up and get used to one another's craggy faces over dinner. I can go pick up some bits. Maybe it's all the talk of Ottomans, but a veggie moussaka could be an option? And what a bonus—by then your literal battery will be fully charged.

RHONA: That's to charge it enough for forty kilometers. But Olwen hasn't got six hours to give me. If I deplete any more than thirty minutes of her reserve, how will she keep her gins chilled?

Maeve looks blankly at Rhona, wondering if Trinity professors get any de-escalation training at all.

MAEVE: We don't deplete one another. Us spending time together is . . . restorative.

After a pause—long enough to scroll through the terms and conditions—Nell reads out a couple of the questions she's written to accompany Leo's line drawings. They are collaborating on a picture book to do with counting:

NELL: "How come 1 and 2 have three letters, but 3 has four?"

She poses the question to Leo and waits. She shuffles the pages to read another, buying Olwen time.

"Can 4 ever just be itself, or must it be *of* something . . . like sisters, or horsemen?"

Olwen sucks in a lungful of air, as if to revivify herself, but it is unconvincing. Rhona surveys Olwen.

RHONA: You see, Leo? Auntie Maeve, who wants to satisfy everyone, is onto something. When she said it comes down to the fuse. The circuit breakers would go if more than two or three sockets are in use. It's why being on the grid is sensible, adult behavior. And it's why only *one* of us should have come to see if our big sister had lost her marbles. But she *hasn't* lost them. Look how she counts them.

Olwen has placed her chalk on the table and made her way to the bay window, leaving a trail of drips across the floor. The wet fabric of her trouser knees darkens the cushion. Rhona watches her, annoyed to be the one who made Olwen crash from roused to melancholy, as she is wont to do.

But at least with that inverter running, you'll get some heat for free?

Olwen sees that the rain has moved farther west. The sky has that oilish quality of colors that won't mix, despite so many of those colors being gray. A cartoonish yellow glares behind the clouds. It all sits upon a white canvas: no base layer of blue. The whole place is a white canvas, after all. That is the point.

Does it double as a heater? (*Pause.*) Just by being in use?

OLWEN: (*subdued*) The inverter's efficient . . . It doesn't lose much in heat.

RHONA: But if it's a four-kilowatt inverter, losing even tw~~~ ~~~rc~~
in heat, that's still . . . eighty watts of residual warmth? For nothing.

Pause.

MAEVE: (*to Olwen*) Is that a lot?

OLWEN: The heat of a body, is all that is. Full throttle, you get the
heat of a human body.

Rhona cuddles Leo, relishing his warmth. Without pen or paper, she tallies her sources of power. She can think of many more grounds to push Olwen. But it's ridiculous to push someone who is making to jump.

Nell—who's been getting the feeling of being partway through a lecture that isn't landing—decides they should start again. Return to a baseline, with no assumptions of shared understanding, and build from there. She gets to her feet—and, because this is such an act of intention, everyone looks at her.

NELL: (*to Rhona*) Is your trunk open? I'm shivering a bit.

RHONA: The boot?

NELL: I need a change of clothes.

MAEVE: (*sorely*) Hallelujah.

RHONA: It's open.

Olwen watches Nell make her way to the front door and remembers teaching her to ride a bicycle. The key was not to jog alongside her, not to hover a palm by her back. She was self-reliant. So it's uncanny to see her entertain any threat to that fact.

OLWEN: There's another storm on the way. I'm taking the calm
while I have it.

Thinking of sloes and other stabilizers, Olwen exits through the mudroom and—before anyone has a chance to shout after her—disappears on her bicycle.

SCENE THREE

Olwen hadn't warned them to be gone by the time she returns, if she plans to return, so they are still there more than an hour later. It's nearly 5 p.m. Nell is taking a cold shower. A meeting is underway on Rhona's laptop, tethered to the 4G on her phone. She's listening in through an earpod. Leo is strapped to her torso in an outward-facing carrier. He wields his two-handled mug as a trophy for successfully watering the herbs in a box on the kitchen sill.

RHONA: What next? Will we play Wiping Surfaces?

She squats down to get wipes from the bag and hands the pack to Leo, catching his dropped mug midair. Maeve appears with Olwen's camping stove, which she found while snooping around in the barn. Leo waves a baby wipe at her, desperate to bring this new territory up to spec.

MAEVE: You're moving up in the world, Leo. That looks comfy.

Rhona sits down, bringing the dining table within Leo's disinfecting reach.

RHONA: (*to her screen*) Precisely, Densua. Take a look at the Bolivian example, where "Democracy in Practice" is advising all sorts of institutions: schools, workplaces. (*Maeve pulls a face for having interrupted, but Rhona waves dismissively, listening to see if further elaboration is needed.*) It's fine. I'm back on mute.

MAEVE: (*in a whisper*) I can take him for a while.

RHONA: No, he's about to get cranky. We'll have to leave.

MAEVE: A nature walk's a great cure for the cranks.

She reaches out for Leo, awaiting consent. Rhona casts an eye over the meeting, hovering her hands over the carrier buckles.

RHONA: If you're sure . . . Just a short one. It's . . . I'd put your coat on first. (*Maeve does this.*) He's used to having milk with his afternoon snack, but I didn't bring any. It's fine, I mean, we're not staying here, but we're not driving home. He tends to fall asleep in the car, and he's *just* settling into a nap. We'd planned to book a place in any case, this week, while the sea defenses are being built—

MAEVE: What milk does he have?

RHONA: My whole street is—

MAEVE: Dairy, nondairy?

RHONA: —a building site. He has pea plant protein-enriched milk.

MAEVE: Nondairy. (*She goes to check the fridge while Rhona frees Leo.*) I'd be surprised if Ol has no soya . . . Plenty on the beverage front, though. (*She glances at Rhona, then closes the fridge and checks the cupboards.*) No need to resort to white Russians just yet, Leo. She has oats. I'll make oat milk.

She sets some sea salt and two bowls on the countertop, then fills one bowl with tap water and tips in oats to let them soak. She hums, rummaging through the cupboards, finding a hand blender. Olwen's always been partial to a soup. She can't find any honey or maple syrup, but there's a two-kilogram box of Medjool dates.

We can sub. And these will go with the blue cheese I made for her birthday. If I remembered to pack it. (*to Rhona*) You know it's her fortieth in a few days—next week, isn't it?

RHONA: (*tuned back in to the meeting*) They're copying the Sortition Foundation's method, which is to randomly select households from the Royal Mail's database and to send invitations by post. They stratify for gender, age, geography, ethnicity, and disability, and address any gaps: Say, if the citizens' assembly is on a topic that disproportionately affects a certain group, that group will be given a platform inside the assembly. For the final stage selection, they use an open-source algorithm, and they publish their methods in *Nature*.

Maeve takes the baby carrier from the dining table and figures out how to put it on with relative ease. She buckles up. With a little help from Rhona, she collects Leo and fits him into it. He is armed with baby wipes in each fist. They go to the kitchen, where Maeve makes exaggerated motions with the ingredients for Leo's sake while Rhona's speaking.

RHONA: Yes, exactly. The point is transparency. (*Pause.*) I'm afraid I'm going to have to leave it there. But thanks, everyone. And, Carolijn, could you share that PDF with the group? (*Pause.*) You're very welcome.

She leaves the meeting and goes immediately to get Leo's shoes from the threshold, beaming as she puts them on him.

You're going to try out your new shoes, Leo!

Maeve misses Rhona's pride and fear at the brand-new rubber-soled shoes on her one-year-old. At what they signify.

On the way back, you might see if he's up for a walk, holding both of his hands? He's walking well now, as long as he has something to hold on to every few steps.

MAEVE: Ooh. You up for that, Leo? Wobbly walkies, like your auntie.

RHONA: (*taking the dirty wipes*) Which one?

MAEVE: Are you still in a meeting, or can I . . . ? (*sinking the blender nozzle into the mixture*)

RHONA: Go ahead. (*returns to the laptop but remembers the fuse*) No! Wait!

As soon as the blender starts, it cuts out, as do the ceiling light, the fridge, and the car's charging cable.

MAEVE: Shit.

RHONA: I'll get it. Please don't swear while he's . . .

MAEVE: Sorry.

RHONA: Switch that off until Nell's out of the shower. (*Rhona carries a chair to the fuse box, finds the culprit flipped switch, and the ceiling light and fridge hum back on. She unplugs the car charging cable and returns the chair to the table.*) *Now* you can blend.

Maeve searches the drawers, placing certain items on the counter. At the sound of one open-shut drawer too many, Rhona, back at her screen, blurts out:

What are you looking for?

MAEVE: Clean tea towels . . . to strain the milk.

RHONA: We have muslin cloths. They're washed at sixty degrees in a non-bio powder.

She goes to the bag to retrieve one.

MAEVE: Well that hasn't changed—you still have all the solutions. (*Rhona hands her the muslin.*) Sorry. That came out passive-aggressive.

RHONA: Yes, it did.

MAEVE: Ugh. Sorry. I blame England. They're all about the hint. I'll watch you and learn how to be overtly aggressive. (*Maeve keeps a straight face for a moment, until Rhona makes to retrieve her son, and Maeve breaks into a smile, batting Rhona off. The smile lingers on her as she strains the milk. Rhona returns to work.*) I'd forgotten about Ol's carrot-and-parsnip pasta. I used to tell that story all the time. I added more and more details until I couldn't remember what was true. But it cracked people up. You'd see them thinking: well, *maybe* with a herb brown butter sauce or . . . if the carrots and parsnips were julienned . . . And then I'd top it off by mentioning how she'd served it: with a jar of Sicilian olive and caper tomato sauce. And this look would cross their faces, as all the worst meals they'd ever had *re-fluxed* in their minds. Don't splash, Leo. (*Cupping her hands around Leo's to help him squeeze the cloth, she sees that Rhona has gone back to reading emails.*) And then the shredded cheddar garnish. (*Maeve is silently laughing now such that tears trickle down her cheeks.*) Ol was so grumpy and bloated from eating so much of it. Just to prove a point.

Back on her phone, Rhona declines and blocks a LinkedIn connection request from a familiar redheaded man in Lisbon. Her pale face suggests a flashback to an overrich meal.

MAEVE: Everything okay?

RHONA: Who do you tell that story to?

MAEVE: Hey?

RHONA: Interviewers? Instagrammers?

MAEVE: Oh. Yeah, sure.

RHONA: That's your primary audience?

MAEVE: It's hard to know. My readers aren't the same as my followers. Why are you asking?

RHONA: Because I'm interested in your business. Not because I want to buy shares.

MAEVE: (*taken aback*) Sorry, it's just . . . I don't even think about it as a business. The *catering* maybe, but not the books, not the videos, not social media. My followers aren't clients. They're a sort of foster family. In fact . . . take a photo of me and my mess sergeant, will you?

Maeve takes her phone from her pocket and holds it out to Rhona, who doesn't take it. Rhona's lips tighten, to say I-don't-put-my-son-on-the-internet. Maeve puts her face alongside Leo's.

Oh come on. We're adorable.

When Rhona refuses to take the phone, Maeve retracts it and scans her notifications.

RHONA: It seems very haphazard. Are you financially stable?

Maeve pulls a face at her phone.

MAEVE: Tom Hiddleston just followed me!

RHONA: Who?

MAEVE: Loki. (*glancing up*) You know, the actor who plays Loki, the Norse god . . . (*her expression turns*) A shape-shifter.

Maeve puts her phone away and prizes the muslin from Leo's fists.

My followers definitely aren't the readers the publisher's steering me towards . . . standing around the rosebushes of their ancestral estates, debating the point of nationhood. I've stood there, feeding them croquettes.

RHONA: And here we are, in our family's country estate.

Maeve washes Leo's mug in the sink, fills it with oat milk.

I'm surprised you want to cater.

MAEVE: That's actually a very meta thing to put to me right now. There's an email in my drafts folder, ready to send. I could send it right now . . . About the third book I'm contracted to deliver. It's way past deadline. The publisher won't go near the draft I sent them. We tried to find a middle ground . . . to soften the more hard-hitting stuff, but (*groans*) it's so watered down, it's just . . . pointless. I knew I was pushing my luck, but I thought they'd let me take it a *little* further. We must have had twenty emails just on the title. I think I have to break the contract. It means giving back a third of my advance, which is—

RHONA: By pointless, you mean commercially unviable?

MAEVE: —the bones of thirty grand. No. I mean . . . (*She can't find the word.*)

RHONA: Isn't the point of a cookbook *dinner?*

MAEVE: Fuck's sake, Rhona. You can be . . . Do you even own my books?

Rhona looks blankly at Maeve. She spent a month's Trinity salary buying two hundred copies of each of Maeve's books and sent them as part of Christmas packages to her clients and colleagues. Not her only income, of course, but still.

Sorry, Leo.

RHONA: I know they open with a four- or five-page essay. How can four or five pages possibly be so contentious?

MAEVE: The series has been about cooking from British sources. So this one's about working around food shortages.

RHONA: Food shortages?

MAEVE: Yeah.

RHONA: It's not a cookbook about . . . import problems, is it?

MAEVE: No. Yeah. Exactly. Some of the shortages are in a round-about way because of Brexit—like fruit going to rot for lack of im-migrant labor. And obviously food costs have shot up since Brexit, and a hike in cost of living is a type of scarcity. But the book's really about changes to what's *producible* in screwy conditions. It's about trying to create a resilient cuisine when the whole food system's compromised.

RHONA: Are these generalized biblical warnings, or are you deal-ing with specific crops? Is this a cookbook with case studies?

MAEVE: There's a mixture. But it's not biblical. It's real.

RHONA: And these ideas, Maeve . . . where did you come by them?

It is so clear that Maeve didn't come up with this angle that Rhona feels like a parent cornering a child into confession. Leo demands another cupful of milk, which Maeve sets about fixing.

MAEVE: Ol's been sending me some research articles about it. There was this one paper . . . about dry soil and dying organic matter in southeast England and, yeah. (*Maeve pulls a spooked face.*) Basically that, and how water requirements will make certain crops unviable there in no time. And then in the southwest, it's going to be unbelievably costly to fix soil that's dying because of wetter winters, and . . . It's really complicated. I just want to get people thinking about the meaning of *cuisine* when nothing is really in season. Nothing is in . . . a normal season.

Rhona flicks her eyes up from her phone, without pausing her tapping.

RHONA: Olwen's been sending you research articles?

MAEVE: (*immediately blushing*) Not *lately.*

Rhona's gaze drops to her phone again.

RHONA: That article on southeast England's soil was published four months ago?

Maeve tightens the lid of Leo's mug as if it contains a radioactive substance.

MAEVE: It was barely two lines! She didn't tell me where she was or anything! She wouldn't answer any questions. I didn't—

RHONA: Do you need the money?

MAEVE: Yes! I mean . . . yes. But not *desperately.* I could get a kitchen job. But I've . . . had a lot of costs. (*The blushing expands like a spill.*) And I need money for Nell—

RHONA: But you won't get a job or have a boss.

MAEVE: I've had jobs!

RHONA: Or do a GoFundMe with your . . . Norse god followers.

MAEVE: You make it sound like I—

RHONA: How much does Nell need? I'll pay it.

MAEVE: She hasn't even paid enough to find out how much she'd need to pay. But she won't take your money. The only reason she might take mine is that she earned it by contributing to those videos, even though the whole fact of it makes her uncomfortable. I'm giving her half the Meals and Meditations income, just I have to defer it temporarily because of some stuff that's come up.

RHONA: So write the book your publisher wants. Fulfill the contract. Use a pseudonym if you want. Or put your agent to work finding a compromise you can both tolerate. Do the book, decline the book tour.

MAEVE: It doesn't work like that. And I don't have an agent.

RHONA: What? Why? *I* have an agent, and I barely consider myself an author!

MAEVE: Look, I didn't plan it this way. It all just happened . . . weirdly . . . casually. A producer friend said he could help me improve my video content in exchange for a cut, and I was like, well I *do* have ideas that are hard to pull off on my own, and it could be *fun*, as long as it doesn't get stressy and cynical. I was doing it out of joy, and for . . . yeah, my own reasons. And then I was approached by a commissioning editor—

RHONA: It just floated up to you, this life. You're just . . . riding the flotsam, wherever it goes.

MAEVE: Why does every chat with you feel like an audit?

Rhona looks at Leo, who's twisted round to see why Maeve's voice is less pleasant.

I *have* problems to be solved. *I* am not a problem to be solved.

RHONA: I'm simply pointing out that you didn't *set out* with something you needed to say. So what's made it all so important now? Can't you put it in an op-ed?

Leo loudly gulps the oat milk.

Maeve goes to the front door and slips into her Doc Martens, tucking the laces inside—it's too hard to tie them while Leo's strapped to her front.

MAEVE: People who read op-eds on the food crisis in *The Guardian* click their tongues, then click the Ottolenghi freekeh and burnt aubergine recipe in the margin. Anyway, it's not an op-ed.

RHONA: You want the Lifestyle editor at the *FT*, but I could put you in touch with—

MAEVE: It's not a think piece, Rhona! I'm not trying to be a talking head.

RHONA: Far be it from me to . . . (*She stops herself from saying "to guess what you're trying to be."*) . . . to play down the global food crisis. (*Pause.*) Listen. I spend a lot of time in the North . . . In fact, I'm there next week. You could come with me? Take photos, interview farmers . . . If not for this book, there's a story waiting to be told about how Britain's cheap food policy gutted Northern Irish agriculture—

MAEVE: Fuck it. I'm sending the email. I'll publish the book on my own. Somehow.

RHONA: If my child learns his first word from you, I'll sue that book advance right out of your—

As Maeve's phone emits the tiny fighter-jet sound of an email sending, Nell emerges from the bathroom, freshly clothed but barefoot, hair wrapped in a towel.

NELL: Where's Ol?

Preoccupied with their screens, no one answers. As Maeve watches Nell struggle to traverse the room, though, her wrist twitches, triggering her phone's Undo function and unsending the email.

Nell exits through the French doors. Outside, she unwinds the towel from her head and uses it to dry the patio furniture. Maeve heads outside, too, with Leo in tow. She heads past the polytunnel and through the trees and sloped fields behind it.

In the house, Rhona tries to phone the hotel but can only get through to their mobile number. Power is down in the whole valley, she learns. The hotel can't guarantee car charging. Through the window, she sees a man arriving on a Yamaha quad bike. It's Dan, the bartender from An Spa Sláinte, though of course she doesn't know him.

Tesla Roadside Assistance can arrange an on-the-spot charge for a fee, but when Rhona says, "I trust it's an electric *vehicle you'd be sending out as a knight in shining armor?" the lady replies: "That depends on which technician we can match you up with in the area. What's the address?"*

RHONA: I'll call you back.

Outside, Dan comes across barefooted Nell, who has fallen asleep on a chair in the garden. He kills the engine and straddle-walks his vehicle through the gate. He takes stock of the Tesla and of the visitor and of the inevitability of a person's past locating them no matter how they thwart and buck their life's course, trying to lose its tail.

Normally, Olwen comes out to him. He'll wait. He'll try not to stare at the barefoot sleeping woman. Through one sly, half-closed eye, Nell studies this black-haired, big-eyed man, who is contemplating the earth as if waiting for a fist to punch up through it. Stealing another glance at her, he finds himself meeting her stare.

NELL: Can I help you?

Dan clutches his chest.

Do you need me to sign for something, or . . . ?

DAN: You've the life frightened out of me, nearly.

NELL: Sorry?

DAN: No, I'm sorry.

NELL: I'd get up . . . if it was so easy.

DAN: Don't do that. (*He waits awhile before speaking again.*) It's Olwen I'm after.

NELL: She went off on her bike in a strop.

DAN: Oh. (*He looks down the road, mind racing.*)

NELL: I'm her sister Nell.

DAN: Dan. I'm Dan. Good to meet you. Nell. A sister, is it? She never said. I wouldn't ask, mind, but. Jeefers, you . . . ye're very different. You're lovely looking. Not that she isn't—sorry—she's gorgeous. She's a radiant woman. Just . . . ye're different. (*Pause.*) I'm a gobshite.

NELL: Take a seat, Dan. There's a towel to wipe it down.

Dan looks at the garden chair deferentially, as if he would be wiping some creature off it.

DAN: I won't interrupt your peace. Only to say the power's gone, I came to tell Olwen. See if she needs anything got. Candles or gas or what have you.

NELL: There's a blackout?

Dan looks skyward.

DAN: Not yet. But there will be. I was onto the fella, and the outage could be seven, eight hours. Minimum. It's more than one mast knocked. There's two big landslides as well, tell her, a hape of muck just past Glenfarne there, and a big slip down Sliabh an Iarainn. Another downpour on its way, and not long enough in between to send the lads up the ladders.

NELL: I won't tell Olwen that detail or she'll strap the ladder to her bicycle, to give it a go herself.

DAN: (*smiles*) Is that right?

NELL: She was on the roof when we got here.

DAN: (*the smile wavering*) Is that right? There's a crowd of ye? (*Realizing this is too direct a question for decency, he adds*) To catch her.

Nell watches Dan kick out the quad bike stand so he can sit without having to balance it.

NELL: And landslides, you said . . .

DAN: (*glances in the direction he'd come from*) It's muck that way past Glenfarne, where I'm based . . . just as well I resisted the white carpets in my bachelor pad . . . And it's worse past the Cavan border. Then south there's two unpassable spots this side of Benbo, Derryherk . . . But the serious slippage is on Sliabh an Iarainn, beyond Lough Allen. The walks'll be closed now to tourists half the season. But with that accent, you're not from here. Sure, what am I on about?

NELL: Once upon a time, a landslide for Olwen was like Six Flags.

DAN: What's that?

NELL: What? Six Flags? Oh. It's . . . roller coasters and stuff. A fun park.

DAN: Oh, got you. A fair.

NELL: I was just saying, landslides were like Olwen's version of that. She took me once to the cliffs right by where we grew up. Before our parents fell, I mean—obviously after that she wouldn't go near them. But before they died, she'd get this crazed excitement to go down after a storm, in case the cliffs had eroded. I guess she was sixteen-ish, this one time. I'd have been ten, but I remember it exactly: the dark, wet cliff-face freshly open. Like . . .

DAN: A slice of barmbrack?

NELL: What? . . . Oh, the Halloween cake? (*She laughs.*) I was gunna say it was like a sext, you know? You want to see it, sure, but not at length and not too close. Not, you know . . . (*She pinches open her fingers as if zooming in on a photo.*) But the way Ol looked at it, it was like that rubble was *packed* with information. A landslide was like a fortune cookie you had to know how to spot, and then how to collect and crack. No, that's a bad analogy. Fossils don't tell the future. They're all about the past. Back then, I think she felt you could only know the future if you knew the past. The present, she could take it or leave it.

DAN: And what sort of thing would she be after, from the past?

NELL: Good question, Dan. (*Dan almost gasps at his own blunt question, or perhaps at what she did with the A in Dan.*) You should ask her. But if I had to guess, and I one hundred percent should *not*, because . . . well, if I had to *guess* . . . she might've been after some understanding of scale. Not to be humbled; not *Ugggh*, show me your sublime enormity, bedrock. But . . . to know the moves the earth has in its back pocket. Gestures it's made before, and is *capable* of making again? To know a process that's more ancient than any social or animal processes. To know a body that doesn't have to fight for its continuation? (*She pauses, frowns.*) It wasn't for consolation. I know that. She was into it early, before our parents died. Landslides were her fireworks. If she even found consolation in it—in the durability of bedrock—that's long gone. With landslides so frequent, and in populated places. (*Pause.*) But as a kid I think it gave her a way of being in the world, being able to know such a huge story. It's an unavailable story. To most people. We can read *about* it, but we can't look directly at it and read it.

DAN: No.

NELL: Just like other people. Their experiences. We can't dig a borewell into them. Find their groundwater.

DAN: No.

NELL: I guess it's about process. Knowing Earth's qualities and tolerances, and processes.

DAN: That's it. (*He pauses. Nell just looks at him for a moment.*) Are your feet not cold?

NELL: I have no idea. I can't feel them.

DAN: They're cold, so.

NELL: Nope. I just can't feel them. Can't feel the rocks beneath them.

DAN: Jeefers. That doesn't sound good.

NELL: Probably not.

DAN: (*awash in fear of his ableism*) Now it might be harmless. What do I know?

NELL: Right. So not *good*, but it could be *neutral*. Like baldness? (*shrugs*) Neither here nor there?

DAN: (*still flushed*) Could be. Could be. (*Pause.*) I wouldn't think so.

Some time passes, neither of them making a move to end the silence. Then, pedaling through the gates on her bicycle, Olwen does a gymnastic vaulting-horse maneuver, swinging a leg back over and across the pannier bags, newly fat with provisions.

OLWEN: Dan of the no-helmet.

DAN: (*twists to look at her*) Howya.

OLWEN: You want to watch yourself with that one.

DAN: Is that right?

OLWEN: She walks on thin air, she swims for hours without coming up for a breath, and she asks personal questions for a living.

DAN: No harm done, so far.

OLWEN: So far! (*She removes her helmet and clips it around the handlebars.*)

DAN: And she hasn't asked me a thing yet.

OLWEN: Yet . . . I bet you told her something.

Dan looks nervous.

DAN: You never said you'd a sister.

OLWEN: Three of them.

DAN: Three!

OLWEN: They closed in on me today, along with them cumulonimbuses. (*looks to the clouds*) How's that for witchiness? And did she tell you about the black cat they slew on the way here?

DAN: (*to Nell*) She's always tearing strips off me, for being tuned in to my surrounds.

OLWEN: (*to Nell*) If he was on about the "good people," that means fairies.

DAN: I don't know what the difference is between the warnings you'd be giving me and my own superstitions. "Don't touch that jack of spades. Don't converse with the barefoot woman." So what if I tell you not to go under a ladder?

OLWEN: I don't judge who or what anybody prays to, in the sky or in the crannies of old houses. I myself used to have a rabbit friend I whispered to in the small hours, till his ears broke off and he'd to go in the recycling.

Nell lifts her chin to intervene, and both Dan and Olwen wait to hear her.

NELL: Do you know Schopenhauer? He talked about how both a Chihuahua and a St. Bernard are categorized as *dog*, to show how humor can come from suddenly noticing the incongruity between an abstract object—the concept, *dog*—and our perception of the same thing. Here, the incongruity between the fairies—who are no more or less mythical figures than Jesus, no less worthy of worship—and rampant rabbit vibrators. That little incongruity trick—it dispels reason, and it gives real thought and feeling no occasion to get going. See Olwen's mocking you there, Dan? Schopenhauer would have loved it. Taking the discrepancy between the concrete object—a rabbit you insert in your vagina and sing praise to—and the abstract conception of a spiritual creature, and using that to make you feel ridiculous. The overall purpose of such humor being to keep things flippant and meaningless. And to shield them from interrogation. (*Pause.*) I might use that in tomorrow's lecture. It's not personal. It's her tactic. She thinks it keeps other people safe. It's never worked, but she keeps at it.

OLWEN: (*suddenly steering her bike toward the shed*) Nevertheless, she gave up.

Olwen clocks Maeve approaching from the forest. Pushing her bike through the barn door, she calls out:

This one's worse. This one meddles. Just wait for it. She'll offer you a shiny apple.

Olwen pulls the door shut; inside, a barrel bolt scrapes closed. Maeve is carrying several large sticks and a wad of wood sorrel; she also has Leo strapped to her front, as if the baby is just another thing she's foraged. Dan looks behind him, wondering if he has the space to do a U-turn and head for the gate.

MAEVE: Hi! Hello?

DAN: (*already crabbing backward*) Nice meeting ye.

MAEVE: (*nodding back toward Olwen*) What did she say to him? (*to Dan, shouting over the bike*) Are you Olwen's neighbor?

DAN: I'm Dan.

MAEVE: Dan, where are you headed, and can I bum a lift? I just want to get cod, for this sorrel pesto.

DAN: (*glancing at the Tesla*) That's full electric, is it? Not a hybrid?

MAEVE: It's electric. Why?

She deposits Leo, still strapped into the carrier, onto Nell's lap.

DAN: I've to call into a few locals, make sure their phones are charged and they've batteries in the torch. (*Pause.*) There's Martin-Joe drives a cab. 856 9506.

MAEVE: Is the power out?

At Dan's nod, Maeve claps her hands gleefully.

NELL: (*to Leo on her lap*) I'm so sorry for your trauma . . . literally being dumped into a stranger's arms. (*She clips the waistband around her middle and slips her arms from her sleeves to enclose them both in it like wings.*)

DAN: If you want fresh fish . . . you're talking Manorhamilton. You'd cycle it on a dry day, but. Sorry now to be rude . . .

MAEVE: You're not a bit rude.

Dan looks at Nell, who's handling the baby like an antique globe she can't get her bearings on.

DAN: (*to Nell*) Tomorrow's meant to be clear. There's a lake fifteen, twenty minutes on a bicycle that way. Olwen said you're a swimmer. You might even catch a fish in it. The border goes right through the middle of the lake, mind. So cast out to the southern end. There's no fish to be had in the North, poor bastards.

MAEVE: Dan, we'll get fish tomorrow, and you'll come round for dinner.

Dan rubs the back of his neck, pausing, wary.

NELL: She's a chef.

Dan looks at Nell, half smothering the child in her coat, and inhales the brisk air with traces of tempest.

DAN: It's taboo to turn down hospitality. So you're cursing me here. Because I own a small pub, and I can't have the doors shut—

MAEVE: Ooooh! Where's the pub? Do you have a kitchen?

DAN: Kiltyclogher. We've only crisps.

MAEVE: You'll have a roaring trade tomorrow, Dan. I'll bring some appetizers to keep things peaceable.

NELL: (*to Maeve*) You think Ol would come?

MAEVE: Oh, come on! She's a regular.

Dan tries to offset his eye contact with Maeve, not wanting to betray Olwen.

We'd love to meet Olwen's friends.

Dan jerks his head in a way that looks like an invisible force has tried to break his neck. He revs his engine and descends the road, an arc of muddy rainwater flying out behind him.

Maeve gathers the sticks from the table and goes to the barn. She knocks. After some time, Olwen opens the door a sliver, as if to keep the light in. She's been setting the barn up to sleep there. Olwen finally lets Maeve in.

Nell, still seated, observes the sky and remembers this about Ireland: How the sky is lower down. How the heavens seem to be at close quarters, as heavy sheets on the line that graze the grass. She's glad, she realizes, that she and Maeve didn't make it to their childhood house. It's better to trick her sense of object permanence, to preserve the notion that home exists someplace.

Leo's eyelids flutter shut, and Nell closes one more button on her coat to tuck them in securely while he sleeps.

Inside, Rhona looks through the French doors at her sleeping sister, and her son taking an unscheduled nap in the silage-spiced air. So it's a day for interrupting cycles. Rhona regards Nell with admiration, despite the strange physical shutdown she seems to be accepting, at odds with her will. There's no shutting down or diminishment of her interests. So true is Nell to her discipline, to her ideals, that she has forfeited every capital advance, every political advantage, and nearly all real-world impact by refusing to play the game. Why? For reason? To protect reason itself, as . . . a methodology?

Alerts ping from several programs on Rhona's laptop, and her phone is going off. Her screen fills with unread emails from her assistant, twelve marked urgent. More than a hundred sit unsorted in her personal account. The consequence of half a day's distraction.

She's about to try Beatriz again when a new cluster of notifications stops her in her tracks. Pedro Da Rocha started following you. Pedro Da

Rocha liked your photo. Pedro Da Rocha wants to send you a message. *He's found another account. That red-haired portrait turning toward her from new corners, like some tormenting, repetitive cubist installation. Rhona's Instagram profile consists of five screenshot images of her journal articles. She only uses the app for Maeve and Nell's videos. She clicks the profile, finds the ellipsis, hits* Block.

She flinches again: another notification. A video message from Jim. She presses play.

JIM: Rhona, Rhona, Rhona, it has rained. Take a look at this for a carnival! (*He turns the camera to show the view out his kitchen window, zooming in on the beach-facing gardens below, including Rhona's.*) Can you see that? Sopping. The good news is, the swell wasn't as bad as last time, *but* . . . the construction work is paused. And I won't tell you how I feel about that, in case the big man's listening. The waves this morning would've cleaned the bloodstains from Hannibal Lecter's smock. They were that ravenous. For our houses. That's all. Wherever you are, stay put. And send me an update on the sibling situation. Oh, and if you need a shift covered at the college, say the word. I, too, have a Pretty Huge Degree.

Rhona checks her car's charging status, then makes two calls: one to the hotel confirming the suite, the second to book Tesla's roadside assistance for 9 p.m. at the hotel. The Tesla assistant laughs and says it's unusual to prebook emergency roadside assistance at a hotel . . . verging on not technically allowed. To which Rhona says: Thank you. See you then.

She goes outside with her day bag and finds both Nell and Leo asleep. She riffles through mini-shampoos and soaps to find a matchbook sewing kit. Withdrawing a needle, she hunkers at Nell's feet. The foot is cold and dusty in her hand. Since Nell seems totally unperturbed in her sleep, Rhona sticks the pin in her heel, rotates it until blood drips to the tile. Nothing. Rhona mops Nell's heel and the tile with a disinfectant wipe, then tries another, more sensitive spot, between the toes. Dismayed by her nonresponsiveness, Rhona's gaze falls from Nell's closed eyelids to Leo's open ones.

RHONA: (*whispers*) Oh hi, darling. I'm just . . . (*showing him the needle*) a hem . . . she had a fallen hem. All done.

She stands, slotting the needle back in its packet. She undoes a button of Nell's coat to free Leo from the thrift-store musk, but his face contorts at her touch and he whines.

Oh.

Rhona retracts her hands and holds them at her chest, waiting for her son's readiness. But as soon as she reaches for him again, he whines: a theremin played badly.

I'll give you a moment, then.

Slowly, through the French doors, she goes back inside.

Leo cranes his neck to inspect his yawning host. Nell stretches her eyes open, pulling faces, and blinks to clear her vision. She has no feeling in her lower body whatsoever, but she's fairly sure that's due to the deceptively heavy child.

NELL: Hiya.

LEO: Hi.

NELL: What?

Nell blinks rapidly, looks around for witnesses, but no one else is there.

Do you remember your birth, little man? Was it an experience of trauma?

LEO: Ya. (*Pause.*) Hiya.

Sensing a stink coming from the child—a scent with the power of hundred-year-old trapped chi—Nell tries to breathe through her mouth.

NELL: Is that a "ya" on both counts?

LEO: Hi.

NELL: Or maybe you mean hi as in Japanese for "ya"? (*Pause.*) Nihongo hanasemasu ka? No? I mean . . . don't get me wrong, Leo. There's profound debate over whether "ya" can ever be the right answer to a philosophical question. If you can simply answer "ya," then by definition it's a closed question, right? Ya?

LEO: Ya.

NELL: Ya. And that's . . . oh my god, sorry, buddy. That is . . . I mean, how are you not passing out? (*Twisting back toward the French doors, she shouts, for the first time in years.*) Rhona? Maeve? Olwen? Rhona?

SCENE FOUR

When Rhona sees the call from Beatriz finally coming in, rather than take it within earshot of her son, she escapes through the mudroom and hurries up the field behind the house, toward the polytunnel. "Give me thirty seconds," she says into the phone, jogging lightly so as not to sink the heels of her Givenchy boots into the erratic ground.

Though the polytunnel is sickly warm, at least the ground inside is firm and dry. The grass is matted yellow. The diffuse light seems brighter than being outside. There is nothing in here. Not even a planter box, or a packet of seeds, or a trowel. She closes the door, whose plastic sheath has been folded and staple-gunned sloppily into the wooden frame like eleventh-hour gift-wrapping. The tunnel is supported with four large metal pipe arches. It's the size of a squash court and just as sweaty.

RHONA: Beatriz! Sorry about that. How did it go?

BEATRIZ: Rhona!

RHONA: Is it over already?

BEATRIZ: Rhona, just listen to me.

Beatriz's voice comes though with an echo, like she's in a tunnel of her own. She's speaking with a horrible whispered urgency.

RHONA: Where are you?

BEATRIZ: In the toilet of the Parliament. And no! It's not over.

RHONA: Are you okay?

BEATRIZ: No.

Rhona cups the palm of her hand against her other ear to better hear her. Her quick breathing.

RHONA: I'm listening.

BEATRIZ: I had to stop, fifteen minutes into my presentation. I asked for a pause. I made some excuse. I don't even remember what I said. They were very surprised.

Rhona wants to ask what the turnout's like, how many MPs showed up, but she doesn't.

RHONA: I'm sure you're doing great. But I'm confused, Bea. Why did you stop?

BEATRIZ: The whole room was confused that I stopped. Except the corporation men. They knew why. The slides were *deleted*, Rhona! I was presenting, and everything was going fine until the slides jumped forward—five or six slides were missing that were there this morning! The whole section on electoral quotas and parity laws. On the reserve seats for Māori representatives in New Zealand. *Rhona!* They must have got my computer.

RHONA: Jesus. But *how*—

BEATRIZ: (*anger hardens her terrified tone*) The men from the hotel are *in the hall. In* Parliament! They have passes. And not only the two I told you about, but the man from the airport and this other woman—I didn't even think to suspect her, I thought she was just some woman having breakfast. After I called you. She was there with a laptop. That was why I didn't feel embarrassed to be on *my* laptop in that restaurant. Maybe she hacked my computer *then*, somehow. My Bluetooth was on—

RHONA: Are there security guards in the hall by the toilets, Bea?

BEATRIZ: Your friend, I didn't hear from him! I waited! I only went out once, to buy stockings, because it's freezing here. I was *ten minutes*! Then the driver arrived and I came straight here. To this horrible congress building. I thought maybe I could take a tour!

Beatriz is almost laughing with adrenaline. At least she's not in shock. She can act.

RHONA: I'll call the police.

BEATRIZ: The police! (*There are sounds of something being chewed.*) No. What would they do? Take my laptop for sure. And how would I know there was no bribe? No.

A moment passes, when Beatriz is out of breath, and Rhona can feel sweat break through her scalp.

RHONA: I'll get the next flight over.

BEATRIZ: And what?

RHONA: I'll make sure you're safe.

BEATRIZ: They already did what they set out to do. They hi-jacked the presentation. Censored the report. Undermined my . . . professionalism.

RHONA: But it's ridiculous! How do they—

BEATRIZ: It *is* ridiculous . . . to let that happen.

Rhona hears another call coming through. When she looks at her screen to see who it is, the phone is covered in condensation.

RHONA: Sergio's calling now. I'll send him straight there. I'll call you back?

BEATRIZ: No.

She says this in a loud volume now.

RHONA: What floor are you on? It's the Chamber of Deputies, right?

Rhona can hear her stand up and unlock the cubicle.

Bea . . . What are you doing?

BEATRIZ: I'm going back in.

RHONA: Beatriz! Go straight out to the driver. Stay on the phone the whole time. Forget the presentation. I'll fix it. It's not more important than your safety.

The second call has stopped ringing, so now there is no clicking to disguise the silence of Beatriz looking in the mirror at herself.

BEATRIZ: Don't call me. I want this on video.

RHONA: You want what on video? . . . Beatriz!

BEATRIZ: I know them by heart.

Pause.

RHONA: You know *what* by heart?

BEATRIZ: The slides. Don't call me. I'll call you.

Rhona looks at her phone, which has gone to the home screen. The call has been dropped. The space around her feels cling-filmed. Like somewhere a hostage might be kept. She takes off her blazer and untucks her blouse, pinches it from her chest and lower back to waft air in. It's some genius silk blend that doesn't darken when wet. I can call the embassy, she thinks. Paul something is the ambassador. He'd be in Santiago, but he'd send someone. Her phone vibrates in her hand before it makes a sound, and Rhona's heart grabs an extra beat.

RHONA: Sergio?

SERGIO: ¡Rhona! ¿Qué tal?

Rhona can see a shape skulking about outside the polytunnel. Is it a cow? From outside she must look like a restless shadow herself, like a bee cut off from its hive.

Can you hear me?

RHONA: Sergio. My colleague is being intimidated by some . . . corporation men who've been following her since she landed. They've broken into her laptop and deleted the recommendations in our report. They *deleted slides* from the report, which was commissioned by Servel. I did know about the men this morning, they turned up at her hotel—

SERGIO: ¡Mierda!

RHONA: —but I didn't appreciate the threat they posed until now. She just called me from Parliament. She's hiding in a toilet cubicle.

SERGIO: Wow wow holy cow.

Pause.

RHONA: Did you hear all that?

SERGIO: I'm in my car, but the line's clear.

RHONA: She's in Parliament right now, and so are those men.

Sergio takes a deep breath.

SERGIO: So you're not in the country?

RHONA: What? No. *Sergio.* My colleague is in peril! I'm calling for help. Are you able to help? Or . . . I just thought of a contact in the Ministry for Justice—

SERGIO: She's in Parliament?

Waits.

Your colleague?

RHONA: Yes.

Waits.

SERGIO: So she's fine.

RHONA: She's *not* fine!

SERGIO: Nothing's going to happen to her in Parliament. I promise you.

RHONA: Something *is* happening to her.

SERGIO: Don't worry, I'm going to make absolutely sure. But the Irish are untouchable in Chile.

RHONA: She's Peruvian.

SERGIO: Oh. (*Waits.*) Oh shit. I do have a Peruvian colleague who got chloroformed walking out of Parliament and woke up in his car over the border in the middle of the highway.

RHONA: Oh my god!

SERGIO: Not really. Just kidding.

RHONA: Jesus Christ, *Sergio!* This is not a joke! I'm hanging up!

SERGIO: Cálmate. I'm nearly there. I'm twenty minutes away. Less. I'm going to break speed limits for you, Rhona. Okay?

RHONA: You're nearly there? You're really on your way?

SERGIO: *And . . .* I actually don't *live* in Valparaíso. I'm at Adolfo Ibáñez University since two years. I'm associate professor now. (*Pause.*) Congratulation, me.

RHONA: You're seriously nearly there?

SERGIO: I jumped in my car as soon I heard your message earlier, after I got out of a meeting. I was giddy to see you, Rhona. But I'm glad you're not the one hiding in a toilet. Did I hear you have a kid?

Pause.

RHONA: I thought I was sending her to home turf.

Pause. Rhona's inner ears are throbbing, as if the phone is suddenly emitting the wrong wavelength.

SERGIO: What?

Rhona pushes open the door of the polytunnel for some air, and the wind grabs it and swings it outward. She has to take the phone from her ear to pull the door shut again, to close herself in. She twists a splintery piece of wood for a lock.

It's probably the same landowners and corporate interests who ran that disinformation campaign that flipped the constitutional referendum. Just your . . . vanilla baddies.

Pause.

RHONA: Baddies?

SERGIO: Mira, I'm gunna get there, and I'm gunna pull her out of the boat like Kevin Costner. The Secret Service are gunna try to recruit me. I'll call you later to tell you the whole story, vale? No one's getting stabbed with a poison umbrella in Parliament.

He waits for thanks, or some sign of relief. But instead he hears something like Rhona must have heard when Beatriz had called.

What's her name, for the intercom?

RHONA: Beatriz Mori.

SERGIO: Mori? Seriously?

Pause.

You're not kidding. No one's kidding. Send me her number. Send her my number. Everything will be okay.

By the time Rhona has come back to herself, it's nearly 6 p.m. and the spring sky is darkening with the second storm. Emerging from the polytunnel, she catches sight of Olwen and Maeve heading from the barn to the house with walking sticks, like weak-kneed pilgrims. Rhona ducks into the woods out of view. A plonk of water lands on the nape of her neck and she smacks it. She turns her blazer collar up. A few wrens that had been scrummaging the forest floor scatter. The whole place has the sheen of having been negotiated by slugs, and the smell is so thick—of beetroot and moss and mushroom and resin—that it will penetrate her hair and clothes, the way a lapse in judgment occasionally does. An urge to check her phone, but she's put it away and she doesn't want to look at it again until this episode has fast-forwarded. She'd made further phone calls. She'd done what she could.

Nell and Leo are alone in the kitchen. Nell has a notebook open, because Leo is sparking all sorts of ideas. She hasn't ever had the chance to hang out with a baby; the only kids she knows well are Ron's, and they were older when they entered his life. Leo is in a high chair clipped onto the table, reaching toward a packet of crackers he's flung across the room.

NELL: Really?

She and Leo both turn to see Rhona come in the front door. Leo makes glorious cooing sounds at the sight of his mum—even though he has to double-take her popped collar—and Rhona hurries to him.

Hey. How's your—

RHONA: Thank you for spending time with him.

NELL: Oh. No. My pleasure. He's a whole universe.

Rhona lifts Leo from the chair and takes him on her hip. She could cry, feeling his warmth and well-being. She follows his outstretched arm and holds him out to let him collect the cracker packet from the floor. Maeve and Olwen can be heard clattering through some box in the mudroom, whose door is slightly ajar.

RHONA: We have to go in five minutes. Time to say bye to your nephew.

MAEVE: No!

Maeve bullies Olwen through from the mudroom ahead of her. On top of her own clothes, Maeve is wearing one of Olwen's jumpers, a midnight blue Aran knit that's flecked in sawdust. With the look of someone woken up in the middle of a nap, Olwen heads to the corner, where a pair of crutches they'd fashioned from sticks leans against the back wall. Olwen takes one of them and begins wrapping bicycle handlebar tape around the hand rests.

RHONA: He's going to have his snack, and then we'll be off.

Rhona inserts Leo back into the high chair, to better concentrate on the crackers. Olwen, she notes, has consumed a quantity of alcohol, so her taping job has the same finesse as the polytunnel's stapled plastic sheath.

MAEVE: You *have* to stay for dinner. It's practically ready.

She rushes to the kitchen, where sorrel, pecorino, lemon, garlic, oil, and walnuts are already on the island, ready to be made into pesto. She starts collecting straps of fettuccine she'd hung out earlier. Leo is extremely torn between the strips of food Maeve is pulling off the furniture, the packet of crackers, and Olwen's spool of sticky black tape.

OLWEN: (*to Nell*) Would you give them a spin?

Olwen rests the crutches against the table, beside where Nell is sitting. Nell considers them. Olwen then goes to the kitchen island, where Maeve had set out a bottle of red wine for dinner.

MAEVE: She can try them in the morning. When we're sober, eh?

Olwen fills her gin tumbler with red. A bulge in her pocket knocks against the counter, and she pulls out an empty beer can, sets it on the floor, and stomps it to a disc. Leo squeals approvingly.

OLWEN: You like that, do you? You like crunchy, crackly pops? (*Olwen pops all the knuckles in her hands, and Leo pounds a fist to his tabletop as speaker of the house.*) Are you your mother's at all?

MAEVE: You're so good with kids!

Nell snorts at this, at how weird and appeasing Maeve is being. Nell doesn't know what pact Maeve has made with Olwen, but somehow the two of them have been granted permission to stay the night.

NELL: *Olwen*, good with kids?

OLWEN: (*defensive*) I didn't ruin ye, at least. (*Pause.*) Bringing ye up.

MAEVE: You did a great job, Ol. And with Cian and Tommy—

OLWEN: *She* tried to! (*Olwen thrusts her tumbler toward Rhona, roiling the wine.*) She put a match to yer childhoods.

Nell frowns at Olwen.

NELL: You threw me into the river Vartry. And not figuratively.

Rhona looks inquiringly at Nell, turning down her blazer collar. She'd never been told this fact. She would have used it.

OLWEN: How about when Rhona left ye in the middle of Dublin that time? Without the change for a bus, she left ye! Because ye were too noisy! (*Smiling at the flagrancy of it. Louder.*) Too noisy! They were wrecking my head, she said. What were ye, twelve? It's lucky the nuns didn't rob ye off me.

Rhona brings Leo's mug to the sink, next to where Maeve is shimmying walnuts in the pan.

MAEVE: Oh yeah! You told us to return the things we'd bought if we needed the bus fare home. I had that one-armed silver top, and I wouldn't bring it back. But you returned your blue mascara, Nell . . . You took it to the counter in sunglasses because you'd already put it on! You got the refund, but it wasn't enough for two tickets. So we bought ourselves KitKat Chunkys and traipsed around for hours, deciding who had to stick out their thumb.

OLWEN: Ye didn't hitchhike!

Rhona passes behind Maeve, saying mostly to herself:

RHONA: You *shoplifted* that top. I wasn't about to take any security guard's spittle on your behalf.

The nuts are smoking up the room a little.

OLWEN: What did ye do next? Ye phoned me. Ye phoned *me*.

Maeve comes to and turns off the induction hob. She watches Rhona return to the table.

MAEVE: You loved it, Ol. You were our knight in shining armor. We fell into your arms like fainting Victorians. How could anyone compete? Frankly, I don't know how I'm straight.

OLWEN: And how about you, Nellie? Have you any woman or man about the place?

NELL: No. Wait. We were talking about Olwen's responsibilities, and now we're talking sex lives?

OLWEN: Wasn't there some woman who got a bit obsessive, you were saying at your thirtieth? Avery, was it? She was throwing pebbles at your window and stalking your lectures, months after ye broke up?

MAEVE: Ava.

Nell gives Maeve a look of bafflement.

NELL: I'm not dating anymore.

OLWEN: Ava, that was it. Well, if you've cut out the men, you best let Dan down easy. Tell him—

NELL: I'm celibate.

OLWEN: —that you're convinced ye were siblings in a past life.

NELL: (*to Maeve*) I know you think it's just a fallow period. Or overwork. But it's not. It's a choice and a way of being. I don't need it. Relationships get in the way of what I need. Even if the sex is completely unattached, it's not *mentally* inconsequential. It creates a dizziness. And a fog.

OLWEN: You're not serious?

NELL: To a fault.

Nell notices that Maeve has a garlic casing stuck to her thumb. When she can't shake it off, she goes to the sink and washes it off. She splashes her face with water.

OLWEN: Well. I get you on the fog. I do. Love needs a fierce set of headlights. But . . . (*A moment passes in which all eyes are on Olwen,* *trying to anticipate if her weird, sudden agitation means she's about to share something.)* It's no wonder you don't need sex . . . if you can't feel your nethers.

MAEVE: Olwen. (*Maeve turns from the sink, her face glistening.*) Sober up.

Olwen crosses one arm and presses the tumbler hard against her mouth.

Returning to the table, Rhona checks her phone at last. A text from Sergio comes in just as she does so: In parliament w Beatriz. She got invited to another session. She pulled RANK!!! Her tía's CFO of the world's biggest lithium producer. Couple of corporation men out of a job today! Call you when we're out in 30/40. *Rhona reads the text twice and says, quietly: Well, blow me down.*

Besides Olwen's loud breathing and Maeve grating pecorino onto the oil and lemon juice, it's gone quiet enough to hear rain pop on the vaulted roof. Leo cranes his neck. Rhona gets up and collects the day bag and her laptop to take them to the car. She unplugs the car charger on the way. From outside, she retracts the plug through the bay window. When she comes back in a moment later, Maeve looks to be on a thirty-second countdown. She throws a pinch of salt into a pot of boiling water.

MAEVE: Like . . .

RHONA: All right, my darling. (*In an excited whisper*) We're going to a candlelit castle!

MAEVE: This is ready in *five* minutes! And it's baby-friendly—I looked it up. It makes no sense to leave now!

RHONA: It's his bedtime at eight. It's an hour's drive on these windy roads. He needs a bath. There's a lot to do before bed, Maeve. Sorry to disappoint you.

She smiles brilliantly at Leo, at the proximity of her favorite time of day with him. She considers asking Olwen to remove the high chair, to help Olwen contend with the fact that it's she who is turning them away.

MAEVE: You're seriously going to drive a barely charged car into a storm, into landslides, to a cold, unlit hotel, rather than spend the night with us?

NELL: It does seem . . . When he goes to bed, we'd be able to talk?

RHONA: When he goes to bed . . .

She stops herself from telling them her intentions: to get in a full working day from 8 p.m. to 1 a.m, then a round of Spanish lessons before bed. She tucks Leo farther up on her hip.

Does it really matter if I'm here, anyway?

NELL: It matters.

RHONA: You'll deride me either way.

MAEVE: Hey!

RHONA: (*to Nell, pointedly*) And she won't answer my questions.

MAEVE: It's been years since we've all been together!

NELL: (*to Rhona, quietly*) We need you for the blunt ones. They can take a while to get through, but when they do . . .

Pause.

RHONA: How long are you home for?

NELL: Home? I dunno.

OLWEN: Your man's had his bedtime story already anyway, from Nellie.

Rhona turns to Olwen, hoping to see her relent, to see her admit that her isolation was never going to work, because it had never been complete. She's stayed in touch with Maeve, for one thing. But Olwen is staring now at the spot in the ceiling where the leak had been, as if she finds it hard to look at Rhona and Leo together.

RHONA: (*to Leo*) Aunt Nell told you a story? Did it have a happy ending? Or no ending at all? And no moral.

A moment passes in which there are only the sounds of water boiling, rain encasing the house, and the low hum of the fridge and inverter. Rhona looks to Nell and speaks with a note of menace.

What was that phrase Auntie Kitty used to use, when she tired of your questions? "Sin an fáth."

That was it. "That's the why." To all your whys—your very deep questions—she'd say, "Sin an fáth."

Nell lifts her chin. Flecks of water hiss on the induction hob.

NELL: What made you think of that?

MAEVE: (*whisperingly*) Sin an fáth!

NELL: What did you make of it?

RHONA: It was a cop-out.

Nell makes a sound of recognition.

You wouldn't mind some placation, if she had no answer. But it wasn't even soothing.

MAEVE: And she lasted, what, a fortnight in the house?

NELL: Till we gave her the boot.

MAEVE: So sin an fucken fáth, Kitty. For a bedtime story.

RHONA: Don't you remember Mum's bedtime stories, though? They were no better. They had no morals or real-world meanings.

Just pointless, jumbled theories. The magic porridge pot was a perpetual motion machine. The Mad Hatter's tea party went on and on in a loop because the time parameter had been removed from its quaternion arithmetic. Green eggs and ham—

MAEVE: Whoa! Slow down! You *remember* Mum's stories?

RHONA: Her abstractions. They weren't stories. We were too young to know what a story should contain.

OLWEN: She was nurturing our brain elasticity.

This is so slurry that no one can make it out.

RHONA: At least in the folktales Leo and I have been reading, when arbitrary things happen, there's an embodied warning. Something left-field happens, something acausal, and it's a reminder and a warning about the fallacy of control, the disruption of order, the limits of causation. And there's *practical* advice, like: Don't go into the woods without mace, young women. If you're being fitted for the shoe of upward mobility, cut off your heel.

NELL: If I understand . . .

MAEVE: If we're talking folktales, how about a little reenactment of the Last Supper?

NELL: . . . your issue's not with what was *in* Mum's stories. But what *wasn't*.

MAEVE: Could someone set the scene with a bit of cutlery, by any chance?

NELL: And you feel the missing thing was a moral?

OLWEN: (*pouring Maeve a glass of red*) The cook needs fuel.

MAEVE: I'd go for white, actually, with this—

OLWEN: On your orders . . . (*goes to the fridge for a bottle of white*) we'll switch.

RHONA: Why on earth she had four children, I'll never know. (*She squints at Leo; she's practiced telling him this before.*) Your granny had plenty of time to act responsibly. Leave a note on the fridge: If I jump off a cliff, don't follow. Something simple like that? She had plenty of time, on her good days, to clip all the netting connecting her to her family. Could have done it with a bread knife. But she didn't see the netting. All she saw was holes. She saw absence. Everything was abstracted from everything else. Oh, I suppose there was a moral in her final story, at least from Dad's perspective: If someone's intent on jumping off the edge of the earth, reach out to them at your peril.

Rhona's gaze goes to Olwen, who's standing in the middle of the house like a fault line.

NELL: What?

The water is boiling over in the pot behind Maeve.

MAEVE: There's no way to know that, Rhona.

NELL: Sorry, what? What do you mean, "jumping"?

OLWEN: (*finally meeting Rhona's stare*) Oh, there's always a way to know. This one finds a way.

MAEVE: Wait—

NELL: (*to Rhona*) How?

OLWEN: She got permission for an autopsy. From Auntie Kitty— Mum's next of kin. (*coughs a sort of laugh, leans her elbow on the kitchen counter, like a barfly stocktaking her comrades in the wee hours*) Barely sixteen, and she did that behind my back.

NELL: An autopsy?

MAEVE: An autopsy can't show *intent*.

RHONA: Blood tests can. (*Breaking eye contact with Olwen to look at Maeve.*) She'd stopped her antimanic medication. Started taking benzos. For dissociation. (*to Nell*) Downers.

MAEVE: (*rigid*) We know how our own mother was.

OLWEN: Doctors!

RHONA: Don't know where she got them.

MAEVE: *Yes*, she'd go *dark*, she'd be manic, intense as fuck, but . . .

OLWEN: 'Twas her doctor told me. Dr. Brennan. I went in for a urinary tract infection and he started talking about suicidal ideation. Tact 101. Because she was dead, the confidentiality was lifted or something. Or was it that he thought, at eighteen, my own medical history needed furnishing? Ah, sure. (*Pause.*) Your makeup is your makeup. (*Pause.*) We're all loose units.

A silence follows. Olwen makes a diving motion with her hand, which Leo enjoys.

NELL: That's not a diagnosis.

Olwen drains her glass of red and starts in on the white. Rhona goes to extract Leo from the high chair. She puts her hand to her breast pocket, but her phone isn't ringing yet.

MAEVE: Is there anything we can do to make you stay?

Rhona looks at the crutches they've so caringly made Nell. She is struck with a nightmarish image: the four of them sitting on the cliff edge, powdering their mother's face before seeing her off.

RHONA: If Olwen has a cup of coffee . . . I will.

MAEVE: *That* we can do.

She chucks the whole pot of boiling water into the metal sink, which contracts with a loud thuck.

OLWEN: What did you do that for? It was boiled—we could have used it.

MAEVE: (*shaking her head*) It was salted. (*Leo is cheered by whatever is going on. Maeve's eyebrows shoot up as she collects Olwen's tumbler of wine from the counter and takes a sip from it.*) Salt water makes you go mad?

NELL: Ha!

OLWEN: And there's a kettle!

Thinking better of it, Maeve gulps the wine down and drops the tumbler into the sink. She refills the pot, then goes about searching for coffee things.

RHONA: Sin an fáth.

OLWEN: (*turning to Nell*) I don't blame Kitty, using that answer to get back at you. (*Pause.*) One time you asked me, Where does the wind go? (*Olwen wipes her mouth, then looks at her hand as if she's checking for blood after a blow to the jaw.*) Does it keep going round and round until it drops dead?

NELL: What did you tell me?

OLWEN: It peters out, I said.

Nell can tell that they wouldn't have left it at that—or at least that her younger self wouldn't have accepted that answer—so she waits for the rest.

Who is peter anyway? says you.

Pause.

No one knows him because he faded away.

After a moment, Rhona and Nell exchange a look, to say: The floor is open. Will you take it, or will I?

Olwen straightens up to make out Leo's crackers, which are—she notices— little animals.

NELL: What about your students? Don't you feel you owe them?

OLWEN: Owe them?

Olwen comes to the table and pulls out a chair. She sits down, plucks out one of Leo's crackers, and shows it to him. It seems to be a dodo.

Will we call this one Peter?

Then she eats it.

Peter's out. He was extinct anyways.

NELL: An explanation? Or . . . a handover? They'll all be wondering what happened to you—

OLWEN: They'll get their education all the same.

NELL: It won't be the same. Take it from your first student. (*Pause.*) I spoke with some people from your department. Your colleague Markus said there was a student screaming in the hall? The day you left? Classes in the building were dismissed. (*Pause.*) That sounds like a lot.

OLWEN: That was nothing. It made perfect sense to me. (*to Maeve*) I take it frothy, with two and a half sugars.

RHONA: Did you write them off as unteachable?

Olwen squints at Rhona. There's no such thing as a neutral question. The ask always says something of the asker.

Maeve feels herself to be above her body, looking down at herself looking into Olwen's cutlery drawer, where she finds—she cannot quite believe it—a frother.

Rhona has lifted Leo out onto her knee and is reaching below the table to unscrew the clip-on high chair.

RHONA: Or were you not up to leading them where we're headed?

OLWEN: Where they're headed? (*Pause.*) Your son will be fine.

Once she's detached the chair, Rhona pulls out the back of Leo's trousers to see if he needs a nappy change.

He'll be able to afford seawalls and private security.

MAEVE: (*quiet*) I bet Cian and Tommy would love to meet Leo. Their little ginger cousin.

Rhona carries Leo away, toward the study, leaving the chair by the front door.

Nell catches Olwen's attention as it roams about the cottage.

NELL: You say it made sense to you, that screaming on the floor? Is that why you came here, where no one would hear you?

MAEVE: I bet Jasper wouldn't mind . . . even if you weren't together, he'd be glad—

Olwen smacks the tabletop lightly with her palm, but it makes a loud crack.

OLWEN: You ask questions for a living, and these are the questions you're asking?

She turns her cheek to Nell before she'll be made to feed them the questions they really should be asking. To Maeve, she says:

I'm sorry your first boyfriend ghosted you. And I'm sorry your family made you think everyone you love will disappear. They won't. Simon was a thick. He was afraid of your free spirit. But that was years ago. It's your job to make sure he took none of it with him. But I'll have you know, I didn't ghost Jasper. I didn't leave him in a spin, at a loss about himself. That's not what happened. They know it.

The water is boiling once again. Olwen's face flushes suddenly.

I sawed myself off them like a cast.

Pause.

The steam from the water bends as it rises, revealing a draft. Olwen gets up to close the curtains, to keep out the night.

MAEVE: Where's Leo?

Headlights cast through the window, sending rain-mottled light across the back wall and across Olwen. The front door is off the latch. Rhona left, without anyone noticing.

Having watched much of the heat escape their meal, Maeve fills three plates with pasta and carefully garnishes each one. Olwen has gone into her room to strip her bed, then carried the sheets out to the barn, and hasn't returned.

Maeve looks around the suddenly still house, as at a restaurant that has just emptied out. Nell is looking over something she'd written in her note-pad, making edits. Now that there's nothing to rush for, Maeve crumbles a few candied lavender sprigs into the salad, slowly, as if doing it any faster would overpower the other flavors. Item by item, she takes things to the table. She wonders if the wood will be scarred by the heat, but she doesn't have it in her to search for place mats. If it stains, Olwen can fix it. It'll give her something to do. She places a tumbler of wine before Nell.

NELL: Sorry I was no help.

MAEVE: You're fine.

Maeve piles her side plate with salad.

NELL: It looks beautiful.

MAEVE: Does it?

Nell twists her fork through the pasta, looking at it. She can't eat just yet. Her digestive system is tied up.

What were you writing?

Nell inhales as if to wake herself, but she sounds irreversibly sleepy.

NELL: Some edits to tomorrow's seminar.

MAEVE: Oh yeah?

NELL: I haven't updated some of this course in a couple years. It just feels . . . inauthentic. I think I'm gunna go from scratch.

Maeve gets up for the bottle of white. Nell hasn't taken a bite.

MAEVE: What's it on?

NELL: The seminar? . . . Well. I just rewrote the title: "Self-Care, and Caring About Nazis."

MAEVE: (*bemused but flat*) And what inspired that?

Pause.

NELL: You've heard of Heidegger?

Maeve groans iffily.

NELL: Heidegger believed that care is what makes us human, what defines and delimits the species. We're borne of care, it's an intractable phenomenon of being, our central way of understanding the self. He described two types of care: anxious, burdensome care, stemming from fear and the struggle for survival. And solicitude, which is about lifting up others, being attentive, devotional. (*She searches her plate of food for the visual will to continue.*) So the first kind is *taking care of*, or Besorgen . . . and the second is *caring for*, or Fürsorge. With care-as-anxiety, you might just relieve someone's situational suffering. But with care-as-solicitude, you can enable that person to get out of their situation.

MAEVE: So you can care badly?

NELL: No, not *badly*. But, for example, right here. We can't tell if she needs saving . . . or supporting.

MAEVE: You can be shit at caring?

NELL: Well— (*She stops herself to think.*) I'd say—

MAEVE: You can ventilate the sweatshops, type thing?

NELL: (*sitting up straighter*) Lemme put it differently.

Pause. Nell seems quite hard at work suddenly.

Our capacity to *know* the world is always going to be greater than our capacity to *care* for it. No matter how caring a parent or sister or teacher or citizen or activist you are, the deficiency is in-built. But you can improve the *quality* of care . . . by orders of magnitude.

MAEVE: And . . . the guy preaching how to care efficiently . . . he's a Nazi?

Nell rolls out her lip, looking at her notepad. Lightly, she scratches out the page.

Do you mind if I open the curtain again?

Nell nods.

I know it's for heat conservation, but . . . I want to see where I am. I keep forgetting.

Nell makes a sound of recognition—but she doesn't feel disoriented. She looks to the kitchen counter, where Maeve has left out a plate in case Olwen returns. Like the whiskey and shortbread Maeve used to leave on the sill of their parents' bedroom, for months after. As if they might return to the house, smiling and sopping wet, wanting supper and nothing more. Maeve would be the first to forgive them, Nell thinks. The first to adapt to any new arrangement. The first to glorify their bid to disappear. Nell watches her sister eating ravenously, eating the moment for all it's worth. How to send her kindly away?

3.

No time seems to have passed before a new day smolders through the gable window into the mezzanine. The storm has died to embers. Whatever time sunrise is in May, it's too early to be awake. Maeve is hungover, watching dust motes flinch behind the ceiling beams. In the barge, she loves to lie in bed in the mornings watching reflections of sunlight on water quiver across the walls. The constant movement. Here, in the house, it's so still. The storm had concealed the remoteness of this place. The weather had seemed like a close community. Now, only her own reflections are here to trouble the walls. A spliff wouldn't go amiss. She'll cycle to town for supplies. But it's too early.

Sometimes she forgets that masturbation is an option. She gives it a go, trying to let the craving for a lemon and rosemary scone be subsumed by the craving for a tongue to her sternum while a hand has her as assuredly as a favorite bowling ball. She likes to be held in the balance, then thrown. She likes to be sampled in unoriginal ways. Throat. Nipple. Small of the neck. Back of the ear. Calf muscle. Cunt. The semeny appearance of the lemon glaze occurs to her and she comes. Hard to know which came first: the scone or the bite into it or the jizz confection. It's a terse, enunciated little orgasm—a pithy BBC *HARDtalk* dénouement—but she's hungover, so she cuts herself some slack. A conclusion is a conclusion, even if it was a scone she came to.

What the fuck? she hears herself saying. The flashbacks begin. The ceiling lowers a little, like a bus kneeling. Headspun, she's upright, throwing off the damp, cloying sheet.

An autopsy table. There'd been autopsies.

Had Nell known that? Had Maeve had been alone in her ignorance? She feels alone in it. Maybe Nell's decided to be alone because it's easier than admitting to so much baggage, issuing lovers with warnings: *Our mother had a condition. Hereditary, yes, in a huge percent of cases. No, it wasn't contagious, not strictly, but our father caught it in his fist. He was a drinker, so he fell easily to his doom, but he didn't want to; he was a social animal. Whereas our mother did. Our father cared profusely . . . but you can be shit at caring.*

It must have been Nell the others were protecting from that information. The youngest. The fact of one's mother taking herself out of the equation when you're eleven is heavy, to be fair. Perhaps Ol and Rhona decided to wait till she was sixteen . . . but then they'd all gone their separate ways, and the right time to tell her never struck. Perhaps they decided that Nell dealt better with doubt than with confirmation. And they kept it from Maeve just to protect Nell? After all, Maeve shared everything with Nell. Nearly everything.

And what difference would it have made to Maeve anyway?

To know a bitter fact that cannot be ripened, no matter what fruit you put it with?

To know that her own mother couldn't be fed or housed or remedied into a state of comfort? When she's in London, Maeve lies in bed most mornings, searching the reflections of light on the houseboat walls for the trouble of footfalls—for the sound of Halim on the deck. But he's always gone by the time she wakes. After prayer, he absents himself to some garden or pavement or parking space to perform. To make his discreet living, gesture by gesture. Why does she love so many people who want to be on their own?

In Bosnia, Halim told her, he'd spent months in a sleeping bag in a basement—blackouts lasted months during the war—inching a finger out every few minutes to turn the page of his torchlit book. He liked books with minuscule font, as it meant fewer page turns. He taught himself Russian because it's a highly inflected language. Maeve didn't ask what that meant. He tells her very little, but he tells her vastly more than most people do. Maeve's other Bosnian friend, Esma, a florist, once told her: "This Muslim you like, he is not Bosnian. There is no such thing as mute Bosnian. Except dead one. Laugh, Maeve. We choose cake, not death." But Halim, no. He is happy to live quietly; outside, without a trace.

Earlier this spring, they'd been moored on a spot on the Thames in a busy part of London. It must have suited Halim well, because she'd barely seen him that fortnight. He left at dawn and returned at dusk. He didn't touch the suppers she left out for him. She wondered if it would be worth lingering in the same spot—risking a fine for over-staying her mooring license—given how well he seemed to be doing there. One morning, she set an alarm to follow him. She just wanted to see him thriving, to know that he could. He walked straight to Bed-ford Square Garden, beside the British Museum, and set a beret down on the grass. She learned later that an instructor of great esteem from the Royal Academy of Dramatic Art had noticed Halim performing in the garden on a previous lunch break. From a distance, Maeve watched as the instructor of great esteem arrived with his "pure and expressive movement" first-years, sixteen strong, to observe this gifted mime artist. It was a fine day. The students with conspicuously good bone structure sat on the grass for nearly an hour, engaging their cores. When it was time to return to school for stage combat, Halim waved at the students as they left, and at the instructor of great esteem, who'd placed a ten-pound note in the beret. Then, with his back to Halim, the instructor felt around in his pocket for a coin, then flicked his thumb out of his fist to flip the imaginary coin so that it might land inside the beret, to weigh down the note. The instructor winced, as if he'd failed to hit his mark, and made a gesture to suggest that he was bad at all things coordination, but that he wasn't above having another go. He rooted around for another invisible pound and tried flipping that into the beret. (The students watched, with great esteem.) Again he missed, then looked to the sky, biting his tongue in self-rebuke. He swiped his hand in front of his face and made to collect the fake pounds from the grass surrounding the hat. He wasn't above picking up what he imagined he'd dropped. He made a fake basketball move to throw the fake coins in in an easier manner, but he hadn't actually let go of the fake coins—it had all been a trick.

Finally the instructor flashed the fake coin, still in his clutch, smiled, and bowed at Halim, then walked purposefully back to the school. Because it wasn't weighed down with anything, the ten-pound note was picked up by the breeze. It was all Halim could do to contrive a butterfly-catching net to capture it, but by the time he had mastered the net, the note had wafted beyond its reach. Only Maeve saw this performance.

That evening, when he returned early, Maeve did her best to seem casual when she said it was time to relocate upriver.

. . .

Descending from the mezzanine, Maeve sees that the ladder is another of Olwen's handiworks. She always knew Olwen had a sculptor in her, though she figured her medium would be clay. That said, there's so much wood lying about the place. And maybe Ol doesn't know you can make clay by boiling cornstarch, baking soda, and water. That old stove might even do for a kiln.

Maeve opens all the drawers and cupboards, taking an inventory to help her bring this kitchen up to a workable state. And to figure out what appetizers she can make for the pub in a microwave oven. In the fridge are five glasses of slow oats with almond butter, ginger-cinnamon apple compote, and maple syrup she'd forgot she made last night. She takes out the gin and vodka bottles and hides them in the mezzanine. Give Olwen a bit of dry counter space to work from. Maeve tries one of the oat mixtures as she surveys the kitchenware. Only one chopping board, no salad spoons—well, those are both things she can fashion. Outside the window, the dregs of showers are still hanging about the sky, like a party no one has cleaned up after. But it'll be dry enough to cycle to the shop by the time it's open. She'd spied another fridge out in the barn. She puts on a coat and heads out.

The old stone barn accommodated cattle when it snowed, but it had mostly been used for drying hay. It hasn't been insulated, and Maeve can still see her breath when she steps inside. She can see Olwen's, too, as she sleeps. A homely arena is set up in the middle of the barn, with a standing lamp, a space heater, and a settee—upon which Olwen is sleeping, as she had done when the house was being restored. Plastic boxes are arranged like a coffee table. The concrete floor could use a rug. Ol's birthday's coming up. Though it's hard to know what Maeve would be encouraging by making this place homelier. Who is this all for? Maeve is fighting the fact that none of this is what she thought it would be.

Which is her own fault; Olwen had never misled her. A month after leaving Jasper, Olwen finally replied to one of Maeve's hundred texts, warning her: Do not leave your own life to come after me. You're magnificent, but I don't want you for an understudy. Maeve had felt a flooding relief that Olwen was alive, but also an utter bewilderment as to what she was doing . . . still, there was something in her sister's untethering that Maeve was solemnly enthralled by, as if it were some kind of intrinsic tendency. Maeve was the only person she'd communicated with. It was like a voice from beyond the grave, and—like all voices from beyond all graves, Maeve knew—to breathe a word of it could make it fade away.

Olwen hasn't stirred. She's pulled a hat over her ears, and her sleeping bag is mummied around her. Maeve's head is tilted, watching, and she has to fight the urge to take a photo. She tiptoes over to turn on the space heater and clear a beer bottle. At the far end of the barn she notices two bikes, a lot of bicycle equipment, a lawn mower, variously bristled brushes, a clotheshorse, and a pulverized dartboard. The other side is stocked with chopped wood, towered paint tins, a cupboard, a trestle table covered in tools, and a barstool propping up a cardboard box. Saws, a rake, a shovel, and other handled implements hang from a coatrack on the wall with *Welcome Home* written in curly script. She must really have cut loose in the charity shop. Maeve leaves and returns before long with a tray full of frothy coffee, a Bluetooth speaker, a glass of slow oats, two waters, and a blister pack of Solpadeine. She sets it down on the plastic storage containers by Olwen and helps herself to a pill. Then, setting up on the trestle table and connecting the speaker to her phone, Maeve decides to make a chopping board. She props her phone on the table and calls up a YouTube video titled "How to Saw Straight." She chooses the smaller, D-shaped saw and takes a block of firewood just about wide enough for a small board.

Clamp, you need a clamp. Clearing some junk from the table, Maeve lucks upon a vise fixed to the edge, just like the one in the video.

She loves feeling her way around a new environment, getting to grips with new equipment, new office mates and startups, like the workstations she rents in London for catering jobs, for space, and for company. There are more and more of them—dark kitchens, ghost kitchens, cloud kitchens—where restaurants and online food companies operate from, without any dining area or storefront. She loves the serendipity of meeting whoever's cooking beside her. She thinks of these spaces as artists' studios, but of course they're far from it. Dark kitchens are about commerce and efficiency, not expression or purism. Maeve is part of the problem, availing herself of the mercurial neoliberal infrastructure that's making real restaurants disappear by the dozen. Not to mention the buzzkill of London's streets, the loss of permanent jobs. She is enlarging the ghost city . . . but it's a city she loves. It's where she lives. And if your colleagues are always temporary, there's no fear that they'll stop showing up.

The firewood is too thick to fit in the vise. She twists the rusty handle round and round to widen the opening, like some creepy organ grinder. The man in the video uses a ruler and pencil and a tidy piece of wood and sheds no blood. His workstation looks nothing like Maeve's, but what are a few new nicks to a pair of hands already so sliced and burned that masturbating feels like it involves ribbed condoms? Reluctantly, she accepts that she'll have to make a pencil marking if she wants a chopping board and not a cheese grater. For the sake of evenly cut, evenly cooked potatoes au gratin, she does as the instructor says.

Up in the corner of the YouTube screen, hundreds of notifications on her own channel beckon. She's been neglecting her community. The book deal has shuffled her priorities. Well, that's something she can do while she's here—while she has the real star of the channel: Nell.

No, Olwen says suddenly. It's not tomorrow.

Good morning! Maeve pauses the clip and frees the wood from the vise. I made you breakfast.

Olwen groans at the tray, tightens the sleeping bag hood around her face. No, she says. Tomorrow isn't yet.

And there's hangover pills. Will we have a dry Wednesday? Maeve goes to the fridge by the door and looks in, annoyed at herself for assuming such a light tone, which will only invite Olwen to parry any attempts at conversation again. While they were making the crutches yesterday, Maeve had barely got anything out of her. They talked renovations. They talked Rhona's overwork and how you can't see it in her face because she's probably had Botox. (That had been Maeve's trash talk, thanks to the afternoon gin.) They talked water supply and parching the soil beneath the polytunnel before she puts in planters, as leatherjackets—the larvae of daddy longlegs—travel up from the earth and devour vegetable roots. Maeve had ventured that last bit, hoping to impress Olwen back into society with the wonder of other people's knowledge.

You know me and Nell always knew Dad was a drinker? Maeve says

now. Just in case you thought we didn't know: we always knew. You
can't protect people from knowing things.

Besides the beer, wine, and gin, there's a massive tray of eggs in the
fridge that don't look store-bought, six jars of Vegenaise, a boxload of
squeezable tubes of vege-pate, two liters of peri peri sauce, and a huge
bunch of mucky carrots with their green tops stuffed in like Halloween wigs. Sautéed carrot greens are lovely. Good she didn't chuck
them.

You know it's hereditary? Too. Maeve closes the fridge, and the barn
darkens. In the gloom, she gazes at the strange sight of her big sister as
a swaddled babe. I found a keep cup full of red wine in the car once,
when Dad picked me up from the orthodontist. Dr. Shields had warned
me colorful drinks would stain the elastics. "Fanta gives you bright orange braces!" he said, which sounded like lies. I hated that kind of
babying—rather than just saying, Fizzy drinks give you manky teeth.
Anyway, I thought I'd test it with Dad's coffee, to see if they'd stain. I
pulled the mirror down to see my teeth and took a swig from his keep
cup. When Dad realized what I was doing, he went up on a curb. We
had to reattach the hubcap. I don't even remember what he said. I just
remember the *energy* that went into it. And the hazard lights. That button that'd been there all along but had never been pushed. All I'm saying is, we should just . . . be aware of our dispositions. Something like
fifty percent of alcoholism's genetic. So. Maeve feels a wave of nausea
as she flashes back to how she'd learned that information. Late last
night, squinting at her phone, googling. What else had she googled?
She watches the sleeping bag swell and ebb. The breathing she hears is
so thick, Olwen could be asleep again.

You're the one booked a family outing to the pub, Olwen says.

Oh . . . oh yeah. Sorry. Maeve gives Olwen time to say more, but
she seems to have tightened the cocoon around her. A sniffle emerges.
A blast of adrenaline eases Maeve's headache, but when Olwen says
nothing more, the headache returns in a rush of consequence. Distance. More distance between them.

He seems nice, the barkeep. Nice to have someone looking out for you.

When Olwen speaks, it's hard to make her out: He did what it said on the tin.

Maeve tries to parse this. Sorry?

Dad did what he said on the tin. He was a school dropout who traveled the world, tiki bar by tiki bar . . . only to return twice as old and half as grown-up and still *optimistically* thirsty. Came home to an unrecognizably rich country, where loans were available for small-town wineshops called "Vino Allot." He never pretended to be anything other than what he was. A sociable idiot whose love could be deadly. He wanted things. A big, chatty family. A gorgeous life. A wife whose mind was a tourist attraction he'd gawp at every day. His grasp of himself was as loose as that plank you have in the vise . . . A man who was reliable for a party piece, if not for sound advice or taxi money. Olwen lifts her chin, tamping down the fabric, and aims her eyes directly at Maeve. His *condition* was fool romanticism. And not fifty percent heredity in that, it seems . . . only twenty-five, at least in our sample.

The sun is being reeled up into the sky. It glints now directly through the low barn windows, illuming the steam rising from Olwen's coffee on the table, and the thin silver cooking scars on Maeve's hand, held to her chest.

One in four, Olwen adds.

Maeve tries to say something, but Olwen rustles her nylon bag like so much wrapping paper, freeing her arms to get to the coffee before the froth has flattened.

Maeve repositions the wood in the vise, thinking: When did Ol become such a fatalist?

You didn't have to sleep out here, Maeve says. Nell slept in the study. I slept in the mezzanine. When Olwen says nothing, Maeve takes up the saw and starts going at the wood ferociously. Without stopping to be heard, she adds: But maybe you wanted to drink in private.

I like it out here, Olwen announces, now wide awake. The outside noises remind me of . . . being outdoors, she says, stopping herself from uttering something truthful. It's nice, she says. One better than a sleep machine.

A couple of Christmases ago, Maeve had come over from London and spent the holiday with Olwen and Jasper and the boys. When Jasper complained of insomnia, Maeve made him a malt, almond, and melatonin shake. When he'd thanked her the next morning, he said that Olwen had bought a sound machine to help him sleep, but, if anything, it kept him up. The frogs-and-crickets nature soundtrack had the pulse of drum and bass! But that Olwen seemed to sleep better with it, which was great.

So when Olwen admitted she was sleeping out here to be reminded of something, was she thinking of Jasper?

Olwen tries the oat mixture, gingerly. You've the wrong saw for whatever you're making, she says. How did Nellie take the crutches, by the way? Did she reject them?

Sorry? Maeve has picked up her phone to text Jasper, to tell him they've found her, but she sees she'd texted him last night—sent him the Eircode at 1 a.m., and he'd replied with a question mark. An hour later, she'd followed up: This is where she is. She's okay. We're with her now. Call anytime you want.

Anyway, Olwen says, I'll skip the pub. Ye can go without me. She coughs and guzzles the water.

Sorry? Maeve's cheeks are flushed when she finally looks up from her phone. It turns out she'd sent other messages last night too. Including the draft email to her publisher.

I repeat, Olwen says loudly. Ye may go without me. And then . . . ye may *go*. As in leave.

To the pub? Maeve has put down her phone, is now sawing furiously.

Olwen grimaces at her technique. Lightly, for god's sake! Let the blade do the work.

What?

You'll buck the teeth of my saw.

I'm sorry, Olwen. Maeve flops the saw dangerously down at her side, overcome with a weird undirected stress. Her hands are shaky. How is she so unsure of everything?

I'm just making a chopping board!

Fine. But it's not an Olympic sport—

How can you manage with only one chopping board?

Fine, I said. I'm not against it. In fact I'm *for* it. Chopping boards. The smaller you cut it, the quicker it cooks. Says you, aged fourteen. I was convinced then, I'm still convinced. Less power. Olwen is sitting up now. The sleeping bag is unzipped to her waist, revealing yesterday's clothes.

Okay, Maeve says. Thank you.

Olwen watches her brush the blade free of sawdust with her palm and set it back on the hook. Maeve returns to the table and focuses on the wood in the vise.

That's . . . That's not going to work, Maeve.

It'll do for garlic and onions?

No. Not even that, Olwen says. It's pine. Too soft. Olwen hoovers in dusty air through her nostrils and stands up. Inching one foot out of the bag, she winces at the frigid concrete floor. She searches about and finds her Boston slippers under the settee. Behind you there, she says. To the left, slotted in by the bench. Yeah. That, no, that's the one. Maple, beech, walnut. Them fellas are hardy.

This? But this is only . . . three inches wide.

Three and three glued together makes what? Olwen steps over and takes the wood from Maeve. I thought you'd know your way around a plank of wood. Who keeps your boat intact?

A boat repairman, Maeve says. Called Steve. Has twenty years of experience.

Olwen hums at this, opening a cupboard to take out the circular saw. If he says so.

Not everybody needs to be able to do everything, Ol.

No. Indeed. If I needed a root canal, I'd hire a fella. Olwen tongues one of her molars.

That's what community's for, Maeve says. It's how we survive—

Day two and you're talking communes. Olwen puts on plastic goggles and plugs the circular saw into an extension cable. You were daddy's girl all right. Olwen looks through the other off-cuts and planks. Will we go a bit artistic and do a mahogany strip down the middle . . . or is that a bit porny?

Where are all those eggs from?

Hah? Olwen turns back to the workstation with a darker plank in hand.

It's a good thing! Maeve says. It's vital, really. That you're not . . . That there's a community. Looking out for—

What are you on about, *looking after*? Looking *out for*? Olwen is close enough for Maeve to have to step back from her funk. What *looking after* do I need, tell me? We're not geriatric, sister. Unless one of us finds herself pregnant.

I'm just saying, it's good that you've got a community. You've *people*.

Is that what I have?

And I think . . . I think that's really what tips the balance, of a life like this. I think it's sort of . . . what it all boils down to.

To Maeve, Olwen had always had the large, harboring presence of a captain of an icebreaker, who'd take delivery of a sandwich straight into her fist because she was in the middle of something. If you were lucky, and the business wasn't too serious, she might return you a wink. Now her focus is still on the looming horizon, but the ice is all broken up, and she's surveying it with a lost appetite.

If a fella on a quad bike checking for a power outage in an off-the-grid house counts as community, Olwen says, I find it hard to accept that that's . . . what it *all boils down to*. Behind her, morning sun gleams dully off suspended steel. You're overrating the invincibility of community, she adds, placing the hardwood over the table edge, clamping down with her bare hand. She stalls in the gesture, and her tone changes: You, of all people. I had you wrong. I'd have guessed that, to you, it all boils down to family—as the only point of anchorage. I'm glad if you've freed yourself from that notion.

She leans over the tool, already resigned to what it can accomplish. I'd recommend you move your mug. Unless cappuccino with wood shavings is the new fad.

. . .

Riding into town, Maeve has to dismount the bike to haul branches off the road. Her mind is spinning in horrible, tractionless circles. It's easy to identify *after the fact* what could have been done to prevent so much damage, which trees might have been preventively felled. Much harder to know, when things are creaking exuberantly in the wind, which one is about to come crashing through the rafters. In the whole of Maeve's life, Rhona is the only person she's ever known who had the foresight to make such a call, early enough and with enough brutal clarity to take action.

For instance, when she sold their childhood home out from under them.

Rhona had been in her second year of university. Maeve was putting in a year's work in a Dublin restaurant before starting a diploma in culinary arts, but she spent Mondays and Tuesdays back in Wicklow with Nell, who had just turned seventeen and was still living in their family home. Olwen, who was already doing her master's in Galway, came back on Fridays for long weekends, so that Nell was alone just one night a week.

In February of that year, though—2007—Rhona had called a family meeting. She drove to Wicklow, gathered them in the front room, and announced that they'd received an offer to purchase the family house. She'd put it on the market without telling anyone. An identical folio in the same estate had sold for €215,000 three years prior. For the €310K on offer, she said, they'd be idiots not to sell. After the mortgage left on the property, transaction fees, and taxes, they'd get around €65K each. She could handle the paperwork. Nell, she said, you have two sisters an hour's bus ride away who'll host you on our couches till May, till you finish school.

At this, Olwen started moving in like Nell's bouncer—standing broad, making some hosting suggestions of her own—until Rhona did something uncharacteristic: she laid her plans bare. I'll use my share as a deposit for a studio on the docks, she said, though I might hold off for a few months till the bubble bursts. It's a toss-up, as far as I can tell: lock in a rock-bottom interest rate now, if I'm willing to hold the property for at least a decade, or buy it for peanuts in a year's time, if I'm up for putting in a lot more money up front, as the rates will have sky-rocketed, and the banks will be making everyone stand on their heads for mortgages. You'll have the same dilemma—she said to Olwen—if you want to buy in Galway. City-center property will hold its value better. Either way, I've a trader I trust, and I'll be giving him twenty thousand to start with. I suspect he'll be doing a lot of shorting. Maeve, if you wanted to consider going in on a larger property together, since we're both in Dublin, I'd consider it. We could use it as a renter down the line.

Maeve gasped and said, How did you know it was my childhood dream to become a landlord?

I presume your childhood dream was to fly, like everyone else's. But this way, you'd be spared a lot of lab experiments.

You think *I'm* the one with boring dreams? Maeve had shouted. And she'd said something further that has been redacted from her own memory. She can only recall a flash of Rhona's face in response. It was an injury there was no coming back from.

Nell parted her lips—just to breathe, as it happened, but since every-one turned to her, she said out loud: Consider the lobster. This was the title of an essay collection she'd taken out of the library, and which Maeve had picked up, excited that Nell was starting to care about food.

Now she's said it *herself*, Olwen piped up. *Consider* the exquisite, learned lobster. And here's you talking about throwing her out into the boiling water of the world, alive—

I don't want anyone waiting for me, Nell said. Then she turned to Olwen. It's weird, anyway, in this house with all these empty rooms. It's a waste.

Olwen had been taken aback by Nell's conscientiousness. Even if that wasn't quite how Nell had meant it. But they were all distracted enough by the talk of lobsters and waterfront studios that Rhona felt able to take their gobsmacked silence as a quiet consensus.

Forever after, Maeve blamed Rhona for sending Nell away. She was only just beginning to recover from the homesick feeling of being parentless when her house key no longer fit its lock. She didn't even have a city: Wicklow had no universities. If you have no point of origin drawing you back, there's nothing left but to drift apart. Isn't that what the universe is doing? Maeve asked Olwen sometime later.

No, you've that mixed up, Olwen said. Yes, the *universe* is expanding, but most of the galaxies within it are moving along as units. Like the Milky Way. We're a stubborn little pack, us rocks. The force keeping the moon there, and ourselves tucked up to the sun here, is a stronger force than the universe's expansion. Ah for flip's sake, Maeve. The look on your face. You think that's romantic?

Maeve spent some of her inheritance on a backpacking trip to Patagonia with her boyfriend, Simon, in an attempt to let go of resentments and the overwhelming sense of loss. Of what? Of their dinner table so ring-stained that future archaeologists would consider it primitive art; of their mother's wristwatch in the hallway drawer, with no hour hand and time passing nonetheless; of what they had in common. The rest of the money she'd spent on two years' rent, and cash during the recession, when she couldn't get enough restaurant shifts to make ends meet.

Rhona was right, Maeve thinks now, about selling the house.

Rhona is right, too, about the book contract. She should grin and bear it.

It isn't the *right* thing to do. But it's what Maeve should do. Already 50 percent of her family are barely on sure footing. What would it cost her, really, to write the book they want, get it done, fulfill the contract, preserve her bank balance? *Then* she can make the book and the admirable content, the communal meals and political points she wants to make. Given the instability in every direction—which, in many ways, she cherishes and calls into play—she can't afford to be so obstinate. One anodyne book isn't a big price to pay.

From the side of the road, with the bicycle resting on its stand, Maeve emails her editor to apologize for last night's email and to retract it. She'd been in the midst of a family crisis, she says, and she sent the note ~~rashly,~~ in a state of ~~hotheadedness~~ ~~conflictedness~~ apprehension. The third book is obviously hugely important to her, and she's very grateful for the ~~advance~~ ~~belief~~ teamwork. She is confident that they can find a version of this manuscript that ~~all parties~~ everyone can ~~be proud of~~ take pride in.

All the recipes she's been working on—improvising based on a food bank pantry of canned vegetables, pulses, and legumes—she puts out of her mind, as she remounts the bike and takes a country road no wider than a towpath running parallel to the main route to Manorhamilton. All around, the wholesome green romps on and on, hurdling stone walls and clambering hills, having gulped down yesterday's foul weather like a good sport.

· · ·

Nell is in the middle of her online seminar when Maeve returns in the afternoon, having taken a tour of Manorhamilton Castle, befriended the arborists of Leitrim county council, and returned via a different route, which made for different dogs to hit it off with. She'd so loaded her bike cart with groceries and wares that it took her almost an hour to cycle the ten kilometers back uphill.

Nell, in headphones, is delivering her phenomenology seminar at the dining table. Maeve tiptoes around in the kitchen, now and then carrying a particularly noisy bit of packaging into the study to open. If they're going to the pub at five or six, she needs to start making pastry for the carrot-top and shallot mini-quiches. Once she's laid out the ingredients for the dough and filling, she changes into an organic bamboo linen boilersuit (made by a designer friend she'll tag), then sets up her phone and an additional camera to record the process. She positions the microphone to pick up Nell, whose lecture will be part of the audio track. In the silences, when Nell is listening to her students, Maeve will bump up the music to fill the gap. Cooking instructions and quantities can be a text overlay. Into a large bowl, she drops flour, salt, baking powder, spoons in oil and water . . .

Nell sounds more American than yesterday:

Our presence in the world, according to Heidegger, is intrinsically a state of care. It's impossible to be in the world, devoid of care. Our being comes about in the womb: from the ovule, from the organ, genital, parental outset, we are cared for systemically, inextricably. We are homed in the world of the body, whatever the state of the womb. However challenged the body, we are in many states of caring. We inhabit the world by caring for it. Not only the sweet kind, the moral, sentimental, chicken soup kind; to hate is also to care. To slide a knife across a chicken's throat is to care, too. To mute Nazis is to care about Nazis.

As embryos, we don't choose existence. Existence is intractable from being. Being is embodiment. Being is caring. Anxiety is a consequence of embodiment, of being, of caring. We are thrown into the world. Thrust into existence, experience—involuntarily, but *not* indifferently. Indifference is the opposite of being. Being is subject to aspects of the world, forces like gravity. Being is a mode of falling away. For example, falling away from our deepest potentiality. Our unique, *own* power and possibility for existence. Our *own-most* possibility for existence. We rarely achieve this, says Heidegger, because of our fallenness. We fall away from our own possibility in every moment of conformity or obedience or concession or tiredness: You're listening to me because of your fallenness. It's inauthentic. You're falling away from yourself by listening. Possibly. *Unless* . . . unless you're listening to me—possibly with this Microsoft Teams window minimized to make room for horoscopes, or CNN.com, or a draft email demanding an assignment extension for a dramatic reason. Unless, of course, your presence, in *this moment*, is your *own-most* potentiality; your most authentic, powerful state. Even then, that moment is likely over now. You are already falling from it. You are closer now to the default state.

The third element of Heidegger's care structure is *existentiality*, which is the opposite of fallenness, the default state. It is your purest authenticity. You *choose* yourself, as opposed to just being. You live toward your deepest possibility for existence. You might achieve this for just a moment—a moment in which you enact the best, most profound, beautiful, unique, nuanced, harmonious, curious, big-spirited, phenomenal subset of your potentialities. And, understand, this isn't about sincerity or honesty. That's not what Heidegger means by authenticity. He means an authenticity borne of existentiality, which is about choice; about acknowledging *facticity*—our thrownness, our givenness—while resisting *fallenness* and inauthenticity. Those are the three elements of the care structure: *facticity, fallenness, existentiality*.

That's structure. How about content? What is at the heart? Care. Being-there. In German: sorge. How does it manifest? How does care express itself? Nathaniel?

Maeve finishes kneading the dough. She peels the price sticker from the rolling pin, then scatters flour on the pin and on the stone surface of the kitchen island. She sits the pastry dough onto the floured surface, like a hunk of clay onto a wheel, and rolls it slate-flat. Yes, there is something of the default state in her doing this, recording it . . . but it feels bona fide, big-spirited, harmonious, beautiful, unrepeatable, living *toward* . . .

Not quite, Nathaniel. You're taking Bethanne Vyse's humanistic psych class, am I right? Well, you're certainly onto something with self-actualization, but which do you think came first? Maslow's hierarchy of needs or Heidegger's care structure? And how might that matter?

Denuding a stick of butter, Maeve readies a new tart tray she's just picked up. Then she presses the pastry into the nooks and pricks each base with a fork. Carrot tops are meanwhile on the boil. She preheats the microwave oven and sets aside the tray as she prepares the filling—draining the carrot greens, chopping shallots, grating cheddar. Sour cream, eggs, seasoning . . .

Oh. (Nell's tone changes.) That's your prerogative, Jeff. Just . . . for my own learning, you're struggling to hear the *ideas* independent of the politics of their originator? . . . May I ask which of the concepts specifically? . . . Just the fact of . . . Right. So it's not that the concepts are triggering? . . . No, I'm asking in case I should introduce a content warning, for example, in the future . . . I hear you, Jeff. And that's your prerogative. Let's see. What would you think of approaching these ideas from an absolutist stance, which would hold that reality—these concepts included—exists independent of our knowledge of it? Care exists without you and me, and without Nazis . . . Of course, it *will* hinder your understanding of the historical context of continental philosophy, from the progression of phenomenology straight through to the political philosophy of Holocaust survivor Hannah Arendt, who I know you— . . . Uh-huh . . . Still, from Nathaniel's astute comment earlier, you can see that Heidegger's influence stretches across disciplines, all the way to environmentalism today? . . . Right. Okay. I wonder, would you go so far as to doing the reading? . . . But you could torrent it, right, so it's not like you're paying into his estate.

Maeve's phone pings: an email from the publishers. Fuck.

She stops mixing, knowing she'll have to edit out this part of the video. The ASMR of egg yolks marbling sour cream. Damn. Just as well she'd decided against Instagram Live. It's a shame, because live is better and more beautiful. The stakes are higher. Fucking fallenness, she says. Nell clears her throat at Maeve's cursing. Fuck, Maeve says,

and covers her mouth with her hands to promise silence. But she cannot
hold this promise, because now she opens the email from her publisher.

Oh *fuck*, Maeve whispers. She goes into the study and shuts the
door. The email isn't from her editor. It's from the editorial director.

Dear Maeve,

This letter relates to your three-book contract of 12 June 2017,
and subsequent correspondence regarding the third contracted
book—the manuscript for which was due for delivery in
November 2022 (to publish in Sept 2023) and which is six
months overdue—and your written request (of 2.02 a.m.,
17 May 2023) to cancel the publication of this book.

This request has been discussed by the Publisher and your
editor, Claire Aldringham. While you subsequently emailed to
revoke that cancellation request, we are in accordance with your
initial email with regard to it being in the Publisher's best
interests to cancel publication. We acknowledge your
statement that the cancellation is in your own interests too. You
felt disappointed that the draft submitted in November was not
met with enthusiasm and you felt surprised by the extent of
changes suggested in your editorial letter as of December 2022.
However, if you revisit the book pitched in the editorial meeting
for this three-book series and outlined in the contract, you will
see that it bears little resemblance to the draft manuscript
submitted in November. The title alone, *Feasting on Scarcity*,
is a cause of dispute and controversy. As indicated, your
objectives have diverged from its original vision: a book that
the whole editorial team, along with marketing and publicity,
was dedicated to publishing with care, energy, excellence,
and ambition.

Despite the losses the Publisher will suffer by being unable to collateralize the back catalogue with a third book, individual accounting for each book will make the cancellation relatively straightforward. This will involve a repayment of one-third of the original advance, and a new contract will be drawn up to clarify commitments for the promotion and media engagement surrounding the first two books, already in print, henceforth. Our legal team will reach out with next steps, and to coordinate the return of the advance on royalties.

We wish you the very best with your future endeavours.

Sincerely,
Victoria Staines

Maeve looks around for a swivel chair. Where is she? The study of Olwen's cold house. Not her mother's study. There's only a wooden chair and a rheumatic-looking futon. She doesn't want rigid furniture. Growing up, she'd spin on her mum's swivel chair until whatever was bothering her had moved out of her body and whirled away like stains from clothes in the wash. As she spun, she'd feel the best part of herself being held in place, as all the frustrations and grudges and anger flung outward and off. One evening she'd been spinning and spinning—to shake off the memory of a wittering man who'd matched her pace walking home from school—when her mum came into the study, cradling a huge stack of copybooks and all her cumbersome demons. Maeve said sorry, but she needed another hundred spins at least before the chair would be free. Her mother responded: Only if you can tell me the equation behind the force at play? As was often the case with Leonora Flattery, her words were in good faith—she was aiming for a teachable moment—but there was no force behind them. She would have pointed at a truck spinning in front of them across a motorway with the same inquiry. Maeve dragged her heel on the carpet to come to a stop and said, I dunno, Mum. Leonora drooped like a top-heavy sunflower.

Sorry, Maeve said. I mean . . . E equals M C squared is always, like . . . at play? (If her mother laughed, it was concealed by the smack of copybooks on the desk.) *But* I'm the only daughter who'll tell you to your face: you look like a soggy Weetabix. You need some time in the chair. Come on. Maeve patted the seat. A solid week of spinning should do the job. I'll write you a sick note.

A swivel chair might be tricky to make, Maeve concedes. A rocking chair, she could manage. The wooden chair in the study can be mounted on curved sticks. That will be tomorrow's project. If she hasn't ruined it by throwing it across the study just now. She decides she'll keep this book stuff from Nell. And from Olwen. She wants Nell to think she's flush. She wants Olwen to . . . believe that she is what she says on the tin, and her tin makes grand claims. Or to protect whatever seedbank of optimism might be left in the vaults of Olwen's psyche.

She forwards the email to Rhona with the message:

> Well that's that then.
> Have to admit this is galling.
>
> Thanks for your advice yesterday. I'd actually taken it believe it or not. In my own time. Victoria Staines ffs. M

Within sixty seconds of Maeve hitting send, a WhatsApp message from Rhona:

> Utter tripe. There's ample legal recourse to get around this. Just tell me what you want Maeve. We'll make it happen. Do you want to publish book 3 with them, if so on what terms? Or do you want out? Without returning the advance. Just define what you want.

Maeve looks at this message for a long time—Nell is wrapping up her lecture in the living room—surprised to discover that tears have welled in her eyes.

A new message from Rhona now: Oscar Delahunty, lawyer friend in London. He won't charge if it's just a reply to stains & co on legal paper. Which you should do even if you're just rolling over w this one. He'll ensure you're free to write the excoriating op-eds you're so eager to write.

Maeve is rereading that last bit, to figure out if that last phrase is a bit of passive-aggression or Rhona's earnest attempt at sisterhood, when a shared contact pings on her screen. And a last message from Rhona: I'll give him a heads-up.

Maeve tries to imagine Rhona standing in the window of her castle hotel, waiting for the words *Maeve is typing*. She tries to imagine her older sister—the only mother among them—having such a *hint* of need, of vulnerability, however temporary. But it's hard to see it . . . even for Maeve, who has belief in abundance. How to believe a woman who has a lawyer in every capital? Who orders autopsies on her parents? Who won't say who she votes for? Who lives in a community gated by seawalls?

Fifteen minutes the quiches will need in the oven before she'll sprinkle the rest of the cheddar on top and throw them in for another ten. Pity it's not mushroom season. She could've collected a few magic mushrooms with Leo yesterday and bucked up the bar snacks. Maybe lure Rhona out of her coconut crab shell, hale and lustrous as she is in it.

Just in case Maeve has it all wrong, and parenthood has changed Rhona more than any of them can know, instead of sending the reply she'd intended to—Thanks R, but I don't want to legally threaten my book into publication—she sends this:

Come to the pub in an hour and we'll talk?

act two

A pair of men an anthropologist couldn't carbon-date are established on the barstools of the Spa Sláinte. The extent of their movement since Maeve and Nell arrived has been to glance an acknowledgment toward new bodies in the room before returning their focus to the heads of their pints, like the white line on the road of a foggy night. Dan lays down the line before them, steady as you like, leading them surely into the dark hours.

When Maeve arrived, an hour ago, she'd approached them with her loaded snack platters, but they just side-eyed the food in bewilderment and puffed out their cheeks. One said they were just in from a carvery dinner at Quinn's of Tullytrasna, and after that they couldn't manage the wafer of Christ if it was their last rite. There'd be good aytin in that place, the other confirmed, cocking his head. Maeve repeated the name of the place to them, much to their approval, and she left them in peace. Since then, they've barely spoken among themselves, as though transfixed by each other's dramatic pauses. At the sight of the boys turning down hospitality—that being taboo—Dan shuffles beer mats with the solemnity of tarot cards. He might drive them home in their own cars later.

The pub looks as though it's been set up for a wake. Arranged on a vacant table is Maeve's untouched banquet: platters of mini quiches; goat's cheese and herb-stuffed tomatoes; soda bread with black-olive-anchovy-brandy-smoked paprika tapenade; devilled eggs; breaded asparagus with a lemony hollandaise dipping sauce; stacks of cocktail napkins. Maeve had wrung every second out of the hour between four and five, before Rhona picked them up. (Rhona, right now, is out in the car, on a call. Olwen is home, babysitting.) The only dent in the platters so far has been to the stuffed tomatoes, which Dan throws into his mouth every time he passes.

DAN: When you beat this, you've it all done.

He's wearing a figure-hugging black T-shirt for the occasion, as opposed to his usual comedy T-shirt, and he did extra sets on the barbell today before opening up. When he collects Nell's empty, his tricep is somehow enlisted.

MAEVE: Are you a vegetarian, Dan? Like Nell?

DAN: I'm not, no. But I'd like to be.

Nell is at the table. Dan keeps checking to see that she's there all the same.

MAEVE: Yeah?

DAN: Listen here. If I could cook like you, I'd be the Leitrim vegan. I'd be Gwyneth Paltrow drinking goop.

Maeve laughs. Nell's outer-space stare happens to have fixed on Dan's chest, and Dan feels his own torso turned into a black hole—sucking in all her intelligence, giving her nothing back. Holy fuck, he'd treat her delicate.

MAEVE: I'd say there's loads of vegans in Leitrim. (*Pause.*) Isn't it the hippie capital?

DAN: No. That's West Cork.

MAEVE: Oh.

Dan climbs various branches of conversation in his mind, in search of the most philosophical fruits. But he's not fast enough. There aren't enough people in his pub to buy him time.

DAN: It's never guaranteed, a crowd on a Wednesday. I should've said.

MAEVE: It's lovely.

Pause.

DAN: I suppose they've morgues, too, in New England?

Maeve looks around, eyes a guitar hung on the wall. Dan realizes he's been rude to her.

In London, it's a rugby scrum to get into a pub at all? Any day of the week?

Pause.

MAEVE: Can you play?

DAN: (*simultaneous*) Sorry you did all that.

MAEVE: Not at all, Dan. It's my pleasure.

DAN: Ye should eat up, yourselves.

MAEVE: It's early.

Dan steps backward with the glasses pinched in one hand.

DAN: I'll fix these.

He doesn't glance back at Nell. He doesn't collect a tomato.

Maeve observes her sister for a while. Enough time passes in silence for the fresh-poured Guinnesses at the bar to settle. It's sort of amusing how bad Nell is at small talk. If she had a boat, her unwillingness to talk weather and cuppas and bilge pumps with every other passing boater would have her excommunicated.

MAEVE: Are you thinking about Mum?

Nell glances at Maeve, just for a moment, then smiles in Dan's wake, just as he's turned after laying down a new round of half Guinnesses. She's a moment in lag, and she seems genuinely not to have heard Maeve's question.

MAEVE: He's a bit of all right.

NELL: (*laughs*) I haven't heard that in years!

MAEVE: Is it a red flag, though—

NELL: "A bit of all right!"

MAEVE: —the way he put away those tomatoes? I'd say the last vegetable to pass that bloke's lips was the iceberg lettuce in a club sandwich.

Nell looks wistfully at the tomatoes. Maeve gets up and transfers half of them onto the other platters, then takes the stuffed tomato platter with a half-dozen eggs, asparagus spears, and tapenade toast to their table. Maeve watches Nell eat one of each, besides the anchovy tapenade, and awaits the verdict.

NELL: It's all fire. But the tomatoes are . . .

MAEVE: (*pulls a face*) Not in season. I cheated. (*She bites one down the middle to see the cross-section.*)

NELL: Tomatoey—

MAEVE: Hey, Nellie?

NELL: —which would make them unaffordable back home.

MAEVE: I know you're *always* serious . . . but you're not fully serious about the celibacy thing? Like, it's . . . a palate cleanser, for now? Not some enlightenment philosophy end-goal?

NELL: (*frowns*) Maeve. I'm processing a lot today. I'd appreciate it if you let me. (*She lifts her chin so that Maeve can read her eyes beneath her fringe. Maeve's shoulders slump a little in concession.*) How about you?

MAEVE: Am I seeing anyone?

NELL: Sure.

MAEVE: Well, you know the highlights. The great abstention of 2020. Then the rebound. That events guy, what was his name? Scaffolding rigger-upper. Oh, and Tristan, from Patagonia back in the day, messaged me on Instagram, saying: "Lucky me to have known you when you were rating empanadas on a scale of one to ten." Then he got very specific in his compliments and I was like, Fine but just for a minute, and then he's like . . . in my fucking *boat*, and I'm like, No I won't sign your rubber spatula . . . but okay I'll use it. (*Nell is rolling her head in loath enjoyment.*) So he turns up, all gorgeously filled out from flapjacks, the tanned abs nowhere to be seen, the hairy ass cheeks going strong. 'Member I sent you the one of him tying his laces, looking up at me with his dimples and the flash glinting in his eye? In his camper van with a novel manuscript in the glove compartment? I mean, it fit in his glove compartment 'cause it was thirty-one pages long.

NELL: Don't tell me about how it fit, please, it's still my workday—

MAEVE: Like a leather glove that got soaked in the rain and you can't peel it off, you have to—

NELL: Oh my god.

MAEVE: —cut it off with scissors.

NELL: (*jokingly*) You about done?

MAEVE: You know it all anyway! (*Pause.*) Just . . . puddles everywhere.

NELL: I'm storming out of the pub.

MAEVE: (*bottling a smile*) Leaks all over the boat.

NELL: And slamming the door.

MAEVE: Yeah. (*Pause.*) Ha! (*Pause.*) Nah. (*Pause.*) No. Not really. Nothing lately. Lots of fun. No one I miss in the morning, if they don't stay. (*She sniffs to conceal the uncertainty in this last statement.*) It's good. To feel complete enough. I mean, you know me, Nell. I crave people . . . Their spartan conversation! Their egg breath. And just fucking . . . skin! Touch! The body! (*Maeve leans over to sniff Nell's scalp. Groans. Nell bats her off.*) And obviously I get lonely as fuck, on and off. But that's what art's for. And friends. That's when I go to a marina, or a dark kitchen. I was lonelier when I was with Simon than I am now.

NELL: No surprise there. That guy was a manchild.

MAEVE: I think I've just . . .

NELL: But that was a long time ago.

MAEVE: . . . totally separated lust from love. And I know a lot of people worry they're not going to be lustworthy in ten or twenty years, but fuck that. Too grim. I don't want to host that fear. Anyway, you can have companionship in other ways—

NELL: Sure. Loneliness isn't the opposite of coupledom.

Her body lifts and resettles, as if resetting the needle on the vinyl after a scratch. They are both put in mind of their father—his passion for company and chaos, his overspill of love, his need for a teeming house, loud with chatter. It was his idea, surely, to treat postpartum with more children. To treat aloneness with company.

Anyway, you can't live without loneliness. It's the ultimate lover. The self is the one relationship you can't escape. . . . Take Mum's self: her selfhood. I could never access it. And she couldn't access mine, even if she wanted to. Not even as a guest. That's a condition of being. It can't be negated. And shouldn't be. Solitude coexists with accompaniment. We are all in the social world, sure . . . (*Nell follows Maeve's gaze to the bar, where Dan is inspecting a pint glass.*)

Have at the social part all you like, but it doesn't cancel out the lone-liness. They coexist.

MAEVE: (*rendered a little lonely by all this*) Yes, miss.

NELL: Sorry.

MAEVE: (*lightly mocking*) Just don't start on about the mind-body separateness of a pint of Guinness.

NELL: Promise.

MAEVE: Unless it's somehow tantric.

NELL: It's still my work hours, so I'm . . . in a mode.

Nell unbuttons her jacket. She's wearing an extremely faded top that Maeve gifted her a few years ago, with a Katsushika Hokusai print of the Amida Waterfall on Kisokaidō Road in Japan. In the woodblock print, three figures are picnicking on a precipice facing the celestial waterfall. Maeve melts at the sight of it, until the spell is botched by Nell's turmeric corduroy trousers, which belong to a totally different aesthetic, not to mention a different season.

By the way, I didn't mean your wanting a kid has anything to do with any of that. I know it's not to fill some void.

MAEVE: I have been wondering if it's private land making every-one lonely. I can see so clearly from the water the wilderness it creates . . . We've all just internalized the Do Not Trespass sign.

NELL: How? (*Pause.*) You think we've made ourselves inaccessible to one another? With the walls between our gardens?

Maeve looks to be zoning out. Nell looks at her lap, trying to remember something, and misses the pint that Dan's pulling overflowing into the tray.

I dwell in Possibility—

A fairer House than Prose—

More numerous of Windows—

Superior—for Doors—

Of Chambers as the Cedars—

Impregnable of eye—

And for an everlasting Roof

The Gambrels of the Sky—

Of Visitors—the fairest—

For Occupation—This—

The spreading wide my narrow Hands

To gather Paradise—

When Nell looks up, she sees that Maeve's line of thinking has been cast into a different body of water—she hasn't heard a word—yet Nell doesn't mind.

I'm not big on poems about poems, but Dickinson lets you co-opt it. To me it's about solitude and philosophy and . . . how the very best land is private, but it's not owned. Anyway, it's a poem. Turns out I'm interdisciplinary. Ron would be so proud.

MAEVE: (*nervous*) You know Halim?

NELL: My dean.

MAEVE: Halim, I said.

NELL: Huh? Halim, yeah. Your roommate. The mime.

Waits.

I was gunna say I like the sound of that guy . . . but I guess he doesn't sound . . . of much.

Maeve doesn't laugh. Nell languidly cheerses the air.

MAEVE: I'm thinking of asking him to be my sperm donor.

NELL: Oh?

Nell takes a moment.

MAEVE: It's not sexual. It's not that I want to be in a relationship with him. We already have this strange, floating companionship, and even if that ends . . . He's just such a beautiful, unassuming person, somebody who puts goodness out into the world and takes absolutely nothing. I can see him being amazed, just by the idea of it, and even if it's a no, I'd love to pay him the compliment of suggesting it. Not as a favor asked, but as a propo— As a suggestion. He's not the sort of person to be weirded out by something like that. And I don't even mind if he doesn't really consider it, but if he *does* . . . I mean, it would be so much more beautiful than an anonymous donor. The whole idea of catalog shopping . . . He could be involved as little or as much as he'd want. He knows I'm not alone, that I can manage. I'd thrive. He's seen the communities I have. Whereas for him? He won't have a kid any other way. He has no family, no address. I've never seen him so much as touch anyone. I mean, *I've* touched him. We've hugged and horsed around, and . . . (*breaks into nervous laughter*) He fell into the canal once, accidentally, just fell in, and he couldn't swim. Which was a shock. And of course I'd have jumped in after him, but I was stunned. I just sort of . . . stood there. He was only a meter from the hull. I threw in the life ring, and he didn't even try to get it. It was like it wasn't there, an arm's length from him. The water was putrid, but I was about to jump when I saw his whitened face glaring at me, and the black diamonds around his eyes elongating, and I realized that if I threw my body in, he might not take it. So I mimed throwing him a life ring . . . and he caught that and leaned on it, like this. (*She does the gesture.*) His legs must have been spinning below. Or maybe they were touching the ground? I grabbed the paddle from my little canoe and he grabbed it with one hand, the invisible life ring in the other, and I pulled him in. He could've caught a disease from that water. He has no health insurance. (*Maeve looks squarely at Nell, as if to scold her sister for being in the same boat. But Nell isn't in the same boat exactly. She isn't a deserted citizen, but an adjunct one: a brutal institutional contingency.*) He's undocumented, you know, so he's not on the NHS. And that's the other thing . . . I know he wouldn't take it, and I won't say this when I first bring it up . . . but if I had a child in England, they'd be a British citizen, which would give Halim a strong case for a Right to Remain. As it is, he's petrified of the police. Plus . . . with a mime for a dad, the baby might not cry!

NELL: You'd want a silent baby?

Rhona has just walked into the pub. She nods a greeting to the barman, and, hearing this last exchange, goes straight to the toilet. Maeve remains fixed on Nell, eager for her reaction.

Where's Halim now?

MAEVE: He's on the boat. He's minding it for me. Why?

NELL: I'm just thinking. (*Pause.*) So, to separate the questions: I fully support your decision to have a kid . . . in an elective way. Sorta solo, sorta commune, et cetera.

MAEVE: (*guardedly*) Et cetera.

Maeve starts eating the asparagus spears, one after another like breadsticks.

NELL: Even if it means you'll be panning my mind daily for a quick TikTok buck.

Maeve chews.

Halim sounds like somebody I'd get along with. And it seems like he's been in your life for, what, a year and a bit now? Two years? The thing is, though: from everything you've said about him, I had the impression he's a person who wants to leave no trace. Someone who's tiptoeing through this earth, trying to avoid land mines.

Pause.

I've never seen him, but I wouldn't be shocked if his ears are full of cotton. And are you sure all that makeup isn't concealing some kind of . . . defacement?

Maeve's eyes have welled with tears. With a mouthful of food and a one-shouldered shrug:

MAEVE: He's really handsome.

Nell smiles to ease Maeve's sudden sorrow.

NELL: Is he a bit of all right?

Maeve smiles; when she nods, tears land on the table.

MAEVE: He's really thin, but he won't . . .

NELL: Do you have a picture?

MAEVE: (*shakes her head*) Doesn't like pictures. (*Pause. Hearing what this might imply*) He has this fear of police and identification and . . . records.

NELL: (*calmly*) Maeve. You clearly love Halim. I've haven't met the guy, and *I* sort of love him. It just seems to me like the last thing he'd want is to create a body in the world. Not to mention, out of his own body. To manifest physicality in that way. Send new footprints across the world that might trample . . . might *travel* the world very differently. When you have a kid, eventually, what you have is an adult. The majority of its existence will be as an adult.

Rhona arrives with a fizzy water, pulls out a stool between them.

All I'm saying is, if someone's leaning toward . . . *disappearance*, it might not be right to suggest they have children.

Maeve feels Rhona's cool hand on her back and looks to her. Nell can almost see it: the new door Maeve opens up to Rhona.

MAEVE: I'm fine. I'm just . . . Nellie's just helping me realize I had a bad idea. An *unfair* idea. I wanted to ask my friend Halim—you know, Halim?

RHONA: (*searches Nell for a clue*) I—

MAEVE: The mime artist who stays on my boat?

RHONA: Oh, yeah, of course. Your tenant. The refugee.

Maeve looks to Nell for courage after hearing him described in such terms, but Nell is far away.

MAEVE: I was going to ask him to be a sperm donor, for me.

Rhona immediately sees past the sociologically sticky bit and onto the outcome.

RHONA: Maeve, that's wonderful! I didn't know you were decided. On parenthood.

MAEVE: (*shrugs again*) As much as we ever get to decide. My body might have a different idea. (*She tries not to dwell on the word* parenthood, *as if it's a condition and not an act. She nudges the platter toward Rhona, who takes a tapenade toast obediently and holds it on her palm . . . the napkins being on the other table, and this being her Brunello Cucinelli pantsuit.*) I really don't want to do the anonymous-donor thing, you know. It seems so cold. The detachment of it. Thawed-out sperm just doing some medical task . . . the fake control of it, what and who you decide against. (*Remembering what Rhona's told her about Leo, she swallows the rest of her diatribe.*) Sorry. I forgot you . . . I'm just someone who wants to know the greengrocer's name. You're just better than me at . . . seeing stuff intellectually. 'Member, my degree's honorary. (*She smiles a little.*) Anyway, I'm probably wrong. Maybe that's not how it feels at all? Is it? How was it for you?

Rhona has ample time to consider opening up to her sister.

NELL: Wasn't there a kid called Halim at school with us, briefly? A Bosnian refugee, right?

If the man at the bar hadn't been wheezing just then, they would all have heard the gasp Rhona let out when whatever had been in her throat—hesitant to come out—had to be sucked back in. She bites into the tapenade toast.

RHONA: (*cautiously*) Mmm.

NELL: (*to Maeve*) A little boy?

Maeve frowns. She feels like puking. Might she be pregnant already?

MAEVE: That wasn't his name. It can't have been.

NELL: No? God, though, that's weird. (*Pause. Her tone is measured.*) When you totally forget a person and then they suddenly . . . refract back onto your memory . . . in weird detail, like a childhood holiday. It was Rhona using that word—*refugee*—that brought him back. Wasn't he put in fourth class when he should've been in sixth? (*Maeve shifts uncomfortably. Nell turns her attention to Rhona.*)

RHONA: It's more likely he was from Kosovo. A few hundred Bosnians were let in, but at least a thousand Kosovars. I remember when they were all sent back in 2000. The year before Mum and Dad died. It was callous. They were given tiny repatriation grants to rebuild their lives, from razed homes and unemployment. As if we couldn't possibly absorb those numbers. And Moldova welcoming half of Ukraine with open arms in the space of a month last year!

A sound from behind the bar snaps Rhona round on her seat. Dan is tuning the Spanish guitar that was hanging on the wall. The minute she hears feet start to tap, Rhona will exit this county.

DAN: Ladies. If ye hear a bloodcurdling scream, it's not a banshee. Ye're not cursed. There'll not be an imminent death in the family.

The men at the bar are puffing in anticipation of this. One says, "There'll be murdurin, for a fact." While Dan tunes the instrument, Nell reaches for her crutches.

NELL: I meant to ask, is everything okay with your colleague?

Rhona doesn't follow. Maeve is so unnerved by now that she is briefly angry.

MAEVE: Your au pair, she means. The postdoc.

RHONA: Beatriz is fine, thanks. She had to deal with a bit of gangsterism. It was a little harrowing. But par for the course.

Maeve grunts at this, and Nell deems the situation stable enough to leave the table and go to the toilet. Rhona and Maeve watch as she uses the crutches awkwardly to stand.

(*to Maeve*) She's done now. She's visiting family in Peru. I've told her to stay while they're building the seawall on our street. At least while everything's being brought in. But now there's delays because of that damn storm.

NELL: (*standing behind Rhona, on her crutches*) Do you know if it hit England, Maeve? Maybe there's . . . someone who could check on your boat? And Halim?

Not subtle, she thinks. But it had to be done. How had it not occurred to her before that Maeve has a companion who makes no sound, whose thoughts are inaccessible, who barely consumes anything and lives so nimbly as to leave no footprint? Of course: it would be impossible to be abandoned by such a friend.

*Dan—fearing Nell's departure—launches into "A Case of You" by Joni Mitchell in exactly the pitch and key signature Joni sings it in. "If you want me I'll be in the bar," he sings, following the line with a wink. Nell can't help but snort out a little laughter when he jumps an octave as she passes—"Oh Canada*ᵃᵃᵃᵃᵃᵃᵃᵃᵃ*"—levering her way to the restroom. One of the men at the bar lifts his dry pint glass, protesting, "My glass is busht."*

Rhona had turned around, ostensibly to watch Dan's recital, secretly to watch Nell's movement across the pub. Still twisted, she speaks to Maeve:

RHONA: I don't know much about Freud, but I know he'd have a field day with our sisters. Their radical resignation.

Maeve blows air out her lips. Rhona twists back around to Maeve.

MAEVE: Come the fuck off it.

RHONA: What?

MAEVE: You've *written* about Freud.

RHONA: No, I haven't.

MAEVE: Yeah, you wrote a thing about the superego in political discourse, or something.

RHONA: That's something to take up with a therapist. (*Maeve's expression withers again.*) By the way, how did you get on with Oscar? My solicitor.

Maeve did not *imagine that article. She* read *that article. Just as Halim was* not *that schoolboy's name. She takes out her phone.*

MAEVE: I need to make a call. Is it rude to make it in front of you here? (*Rhona has taken out her own phone, like one yawn sparked by another.*) I just don't feel like being alone when I make it. It's important.

Rhona looks up and sees this strange shakiness in Maeve again. She returns her phone to her handbag.

RHONA: Of course. I can take one ear if you need a witness? Or a second opinion?

The phone rings. Maeve glances over toward the bar, where Nell is in quiet conversation with Dan.

MAEVE: Mrs. Charles? (*"Speaking."*) It's Maeve Flattery. (*Pause.*) The Irish chef— (*"How lovely to hear from you. Do you know, I was on the brink of opening the phone book. You left a rather large pot here, and I wondered when you might miss it. There's simply no place to put it."*) Oh, that's the lobster pot, Mrs. Charles. That's not mine. That was already in the kitchen. (*Pause. "Was it really?" Pause. "I'm so sorry, Maeve, it's all quite chaotic here today. We have a chap in to fix various things, and the dogs are disgruntled. But I'm . . . delighted you called." Pause. "Was there something else?"*)

Maeve has the sudden sense that what she was going to say isn't the right approach. She looks at Rhona, trying to channel her sangfroid sister—to imagine herself in that relaxed-fit designer suit of a Wednesday evening in charming rural Ireland.

I just called to thank you for the flowers that were sent to the publisher, and to apologize for being *so* late in sending my thanks. I was away, and I did see an email from the publisher about the most beautiful flowers that had arrived, but I didn't think anything of it, because gifts often turn up from followers and fans and things, and I usually just tell my editor or her assistant to take them home and enjoy them, but when they said it was a giant bouquet of hollyhocks— there was no note with them—you jumped to mind. You must have remembered me admiring the hollyhocks in your kitchen. There was really no need whatsoever, Mrs. Charles. It was my pleasure feeding your party, and it's too generous—on top of the mooring in the North Wessex Downs, which, by the way, is so peaceful. It's such gorgeous countryside. Really . . . quintessentially British. Have you spotted the boat, by any chance?

Rhona is pulling a sommelier's face at this gushing gratitude, to pick out hints of feculence.

Oh, but spring is the best time of year— . . . Well, that's— . . . I couldn't agree more, Mrs. Charles. That's great. Oh just, while we're on, did you say you had the phone book handy? Do you have a number I could reach Edmund de Ramsey on, by any chance? Baron de Ramsey. We'd had a really meaningful conversation at your party about the new book—he knew all about it, which was a surprise to me; of course I knew he was on the board, but I didn't know he'd be so engaged with the day-to-day publishing business—and his advice has been so influential as I've been redrafting, I wanted to thank him and to get his seal of approval before I submit it. Since he'd shown such interest, that is. If you have a number for him, that would be perfect. I have a pen.

Maeve gestures to Rhona, who takes out her phone and opens the Notes app. Maeve waits as Mrs. Charles fusses through her internal etiquette handbook in advance of opening the phone book. To grant access to the baron? But requested so agreeably, with such sunny character . . . Which impropriety would be the grosser? A quandary.

. . . 0605. Perfect. Thanks again and take care, Mrs. Charles.

Rhona is regarding Maeve with what might be an arched brow if her brow could arch.

RHONA: If you ever tire of mincing garlic, a career in cultural diplomacy—

MAEVE: (*Staring at her phone, she holds up a finger.*) Here's Jasper writing back. I sent him the Eircode last night.

She reads it aloud:

I didn't know you were still looking for her but good you found her. I won't be coming. It wasn't easy for her to leave and it's taken me time to accept, but I trust her decision. She was too smart for me to fully know or second guess her, so I won't. It's pretty late for her to get around to taking her own pulse instead of everyone else's. Better late than not at all. The truth is I was bleak af when we met. The boys were wrecks. And Olwen must have buried all her own stuff to help us. I can see that now. The boys were confused and hurt when she left, but she taught them how weather systems work and that it's okay to have a storm. So they let a few cyclones rip. But they're doing great now. I can't mess with that. Cian calls her Rock Mamba. The superhero who moved in for a while and they got to ride around on bikes with, but whose power it is to knock you out with her rock force and when you wake up she's vanished. I'm paraphrasing. You know, Tommy makes the pasta bake from your book on Wednesdays. He's in the kitchen now. He changes it up. He put parsnip in once and I took a bite and absolutely lost it. Be well Maeve. J.

Maeve rereads the message, feeling differently about it each time. Finally Rhona takes the phone to read it herself, lingering over the image of Rock Mamba.

MAEVE: I always loved Jasper. But . . .

RHONA: You should be more sparing with your love. Clearly Jasper is. Olwen up and walks out of their lives, and he just . . . lets her.

MAEVE: I know, but . . . *not* letting her would be worse?

Rhona considers this.

RHONA: Conceding is a sad way to love.

Pause.

I should head off—

MAEVE: Please don't. Please stay.

RHONA: I need to get Leo.

MAEVE: But I have to phone this baron, and I need your—

RHONA: Maeve . . . You should come with me to Northern Ireland. If you need inspiration, and you want to talk through your options. Properly. Since you don't seem to want to play dancing monkey.

Nell returns, sits down.

I'm going tomorrow, after a few meetings in the morning. I could drop by for you at eleven.

MAEVE: No, it's too soon. I just got here. My head is spinning . . . and no one will sit down!

NELL: (*emphatic*) We're all sitting down. Right here.

Maeve's mind dashes: from her womb to the manuscript to her bank balance to Halim's deliberation to Olwen's unbuilt pantry and her sleeping bag tautened around the fumes of her head; to their mother's body . . . no; to their father being secondary to their mother, his story told by way of Leonora's, as if he'd never been centered in his own life. The last thing the four of them need, now, is distance.

MAEVE: But we've gotten nowhere with Olwen? We can't even rule out a psychotic break! And I don't know what we *should* be doing, but I know we shouldn't be parting ways. We're nowhere *near* ready. There's too much uncertainty.

RHONA: Yes, there is. And if your call with this baron is to convince him you *are* willing to publish the book as they want it, so he'll get the team back onside—

MAEVE: (*to Nell*) How the fuck did she know that?

RHONA: . . . then that's all the more reason to come with me. For your next book. To see what crops are likeliest to fail.

MAEVE: I'm grateful for the invite. I mean it. I know how sparing you are with your time. (*Pause.*) That sounded bitchy—I didn't mean it to. I'm just saying, that's a big gesture, after one get-together a year for the past . . . twenty? But we can't go anywhere right now.

Rhona inhales at length through her nose.

RHONA: Onto something we *can* do right now . . . Nell: Why do I have a feeling you're squeamish?

NELL: (*askance*) About . . . get-togethers?

RHONA: About blood.

NELL: I wouldn't, you know . . . watch an autopsy. If that makes me squeamish?

RHONA: Or is it not about blood, it's just that you won't touch meat?

NELL: I don't eat meat. But if this is a sex joke, I'm—

RHONA: It isn't. I ordered you some tests. Let's see what we can rule out. (*She collects eight chocolate box–size blood-test kits from her handbag, stacking them on the table.*) You can do them at Olwen's. I'll collect them in the morning when I swing by for Maeve. This is just preliminary, process-of-elimination stuff. To save time.

Nell picks up one of the boxes and looks at it sideways, as if it can only be seen in her peripheral vision: it's too absurd to see straight-on.

This is FIT for colorectal cancer . . . unlikely. Some more useful ones: CMP. CBC. TSH. Gout. Fat chance, with all your snorkeling and facsimile burgers. *This* one I'm very interested to see: Lyme disease. That whole part of the country is crawling with ticks. Though often it won't show up after . . . To be fair, this next one's a waste of money—a whole range of sexual diseases, it covers, and since, well . . . Que será. I think I missed one or two of your birthdays, so happy birthday. Christmas. Hannukah. What is it philosophers celebrate?

NELL: (*reading the waste-of-money box*) God. I don't know. Hopefully an unsyphilitic Thursday?

Maeve snorts tapenade toast into her nasal passage and has to run to the loo for tissue.

RHONA: Well, as one last gift, so that you might *have* a next birthday . . . The best consultant neurologist in the country owed me a favor, so I'm waiting for his secretary to confirm a slot in early June. His wait list is normally six months, and you'd need a referral. My guess is, he'd get you in for an MRI if he suspects neural entrapment or to rule out benign spinal tumors. He'll check autoimmune stuff, multifocal motor neuropathy. I have my own theories, based on some reading. But you don't need to hear them.

NELL: No, go on. I'm fascinated.

Rhona tries to read Nell in every way she knows how to read a person, but she cannot resolve her. She's too exactly herself. So she resorts to a partial, physical reading.

RHONA: I really like the idea of it being environmental. Because you can extricate yourself from that. You've been snorkeling in Long Island Sound? I assume you're not using a private beach? I'd first thought, if you're entering through farmland, it could be pesticide or phosphate exposure, but then—Nell, isn't there a huge naval base just across the Thames River from your campus?

NELL: Yeah. It's not ideal.

RHONA: With an active nuclear submarine!

NELL: I try to imagine it's a walrus—

RHONA: I'll grant you, topical exposure's a long shot, but that water's bound to be military-grade nasty. In the same vein, I'd considered hemlock poisoning.

Nell cracks a smile.

NELL: Because my colleague Socrates died by hemlock?

RHONA: I wouldn't put it past a vengeful student with a lab pass who likes the idea of a progressive centripetal paralysis for their philosophy professor.

NELL: You what now?

Maeve arrives back, shoving tissues in her pocket before sitting down.

RHONA: I'm offering you my couch, Nell. (*pulls her bag over her shoulder*) In Dublin. For the month of June, until the MRI. (*Pause.*) As long as you wear nasal strips for your snoring.

MAEVE: (*with widened eyes*) That's massive.

NELL: Rhona. The time you've spent thinking about my body is the sexiest thing that's happened to it since Dan diagnosed me with Stoneman disease, where your tissue turns to bone. According to him, you can get that by walking over a burial site.

MAEVE: What?

Maeve snaps round to beckon Dan to join their table.

RHONA: Not a chance. Your feet are horribly callused, but they're supple, so it's not Stoneman. Or Munchmeyer, I think they call it. But *good on Dan* for—

MAEVE: How do you know her feet are supple?

NELL: Point is, I can't. You've got to be ordinarily resident here for at least a year to get health care covered. I don't pay tax here. More important, I'm teaching summer school at UConn. On campus. And there's a colloquium thing, and my books are there. And summer's *it* if I want to do any writing.

Rhona stands and brushes the crumbs from her suit. Logistics trump life, then, Rhona wants to say. But why keep pushing them? They don't want to do the calculations. They like *beholding the wall of logistics before them and describing sections of it, as if to lend their impediments museum worthiness.*

RHONA: I'll see you tomorrow. For the blood.

Pause.

And I'll put a rehab voucher in a birthday card for Olwen.

On her way out, the door is held open for Rhona by Feidhlim and Sheila, newly arriving at the pub.

Sheila is a short woman whose ill-fitting hospital cleaning scrubs are visible beneath her knee-length beige padded coat, which she keeps on, along with her soft, apologetic smile. Her neat, curlered hair is only slightly flattened from the scrub cap. Feidhlim keeps his green raincoat on too; beneath it is a collared shirt and navy V-neck jumper. Their usual table, where you can fit a few people for the cards, is taken, so he tips his flat cap in their direction, in peace, and they head toward familiar company at the bar.

Dan had been waiting for Rhona to depart the general area—an embodied Sovereignty if ever he saw one—lest he trespass her personal space. Now that the coast is clear, he finally responds to Maeve's beckon. En route he catches Sheila by the elbow and céilí dances herself and Feidhlim through the social gauntlet.

DAN: Feidhlim. Sheila. Come here and meet Nell and Maeve Flattery. They're Olwen's sisters. So was the dark-haired one ye held the door for. (*to Feidhlim*) They're her guests in the old farmhouse. (*to Nell and Maeve*) Which belonged to *his* grandparents. (*to Feidhlim and Sheila*) Maeve is an important chef who spent her day cooking us munchies. And I'll tell you what, but they put my Tayto Rancheros to shame.

MAEVE: (*laughs*) Can I put that on the cover of my next book?

DAN: (*looking boldly at Nell, who meets his gaze*) And Nell . . .

A moment passes in which Dan can't summate her. Feidhlim inspects his cap in his two hands, then fixes his squinty eyes on the crutches against the wall. Sheila is holding her smile and makes a sound of veneration at the platters. With her hands buried in her pockets, she rocks in polite refusal. Dan drags over extra stools to the table, asking Maeve and Nell:

Will we blend?

NELL: Huh?

DAN: We'll join ye.

Feidhlim puts the cap back on for embarrassment. Dan goads Sheila gently by the shoulder. Sheila has a double set of dimples in one cheek and none in the other, which gives her an unbroken expression of cordial acceptance. Often the information she's accepting is troublesome, but she handles it with an easy attention.

SHEILA: Dan, leave these women in their peace—

NELL: Oh, no, you're welcome.

MAEVE: *Please* join us.

NELL: Lemme clear away these boxes. (*She stacks the test kits into a tote bag and slips it under her chair.*)

DAN: Look at that. She couldn't be making the place any more scenic if she tried. (*He collects the empties.*) Settle in there and give me two secs.

He goes to the bar to fix drinks.

MAEVE: (*laughs with more relaxation than she feels*) He's a hard man to refuse.

NELL: He shouldn't set foot on an American campus.

MAEVE: (*to Feidhlim*) He was serenading my poor sister a minute ago.

SHEILA: Stop.

FEIDHLIM: (*abashed*) Oh.

DAN: (*shouts from the bar*) 'Twas only John and Diarmuid at the bar I was serenading. Didn't they deserve it?

John and Diarmuid, too cozied in to respond on cue, shimmy a bit and wag an arm.

JOHN: We were only sat here, lawful.

DIARMUID: We saw nathin.

Dan puts in some time with the men so they know they have more than one friend in the world. But with everything going on, they're quiet as penance.

Dan gets a vision of later in the evening. Of Nell and Maeve taking a lift with Feidhlim and Sheila. Of being left here alone. No, not alone. With John and Diarmuid and the spirits. He feels the weight of coins in his hand for the cigarette machine. He feels the weight of himself stood in the middle of his pub, smoking, searching the place for what had sent everyone away. Is it a warning there's something lurking that needs smoking out? Some demon. Some creature of habit. How to cleanse the place? He looks around for a portal he might have accidentally opened up. And then it strikes him: There's no portal to his pub. No weatherhead. Not even a chimney. He'd made sure of it. To seal it off from forces he can't control. (Weather, he can handle. A fella off his gourd, too.) But that could have been his fuckup. It could be he needs to let spirits pass in and out of his life, as they will, and the same with romances. To accept that passage, noncommittal, that might have to do with the other person's overflow and not his own deficiency. To accept that a woman unsteady on her feet may not collapse into his arms, much as they are open. But he would have to make these quarters into a site of transition, willingly . . .

At the table:

MAEVE: (*to Feidhlim and Sheila*) So you all know Olwen?

She looks from one to the other, refusing to take nods for an answer.

FEIDHLIM: I was delighted to sell her the old house.

SHEILA: You were, that.

MAEVE: Are you good friends?

Trying to catch their eyes is like playing Whac-A-Mole.

Dan and her seem to be real friends.

Waits.

I'd just love to know if she's made friends.

SHEILA: (*gentle*) Why wouldn't she.

MAEVE: Is she here a lot?

FEIDHLIM: Sound woman.

He says this with the closing cadence of "Amen."

MAEVE: (*to Sheila*) Do you know, like . . . why *here*? Why she picked . . . Leitrim?

Sheila looks to Feidhlim.

I mean it's gorgeous and everything, it's just that—

SHEILA: The weather's been desperate for ye.

FEIDHLIM: Cúpla lá lofa, cinnte.

SHEILA: For the month of May anyway. It's unusual. Well, the new usual.

Feidhlim nods.

MAEVE: Is this where ye met her? She just showed up in the pub?

Having already observed that the local language has no questions, in the way that Mandarin has no future tense, Nell tries to kick Maeve under the table, but perhaps she misses. Silent, Feidhlim squints at the air as if racking his memory.

We just . . . it's not like we came here as kids. I've never been to Leitrim in my life.

Sheila looks up from her padded lap to her husband, speaking softly.

SHEILA: Nárbh í an chaora í?

FEIDHLIM: That's it. (*He runs his knuckle down the philtrum of his moustache.*) There was a sheep shtuck. (*Pause. He makes a little "heh" sound at the memory.*) A lost sheep.

Sheila draws her hands declaratively from her pockets, now that Dan is arriving with their tray of drinks. Feidhlim looks at Maeve, candid. He'd told her something. She couldn't make head nor tail of it, please God.

MAEVE: Did she really sleep in that barn while she was doing up the house? For months?

DAN: Sleeping in haysheds . . . conthraband drugs. Come on, Feidhlim. Out with that one, for the girls.

FEIDHLIM: Oh no, I'm no use telling tales.

DAN: (*to Maeve*) Sorry now, this story's not about your sister in a barn, but trust me you want to hear it.

SHEILA: No, no, Dan.

Dan has set a Bulmers cider before her.

DAN: Go on, tell it. (*He sets full Guinnesses before himself, Nell, and Maeve.*)

MAEVE: Ah feck, Dan. I'm still rough from last night.

DAN: (*with concern*) Did ye have a bad pint last night? They're like oysters. You can have fifteen good ones, then one bad one . . . and it panels ya.

Sheila clicks her tongue, having heard this line from Dan before, but without the affected accent.

MAEVE: Ha.

Dan sets a pint of Ribena water before Feidhlim and sits down. He eyes up their jackets, still on, and Feidhlim's reluctance.

DAN: Take off yer tags and tell us the story, Feidhlim. (*to Nell*) I want you to hear this.

NELL: So why don't you tell it?

DAN: I haven't the flair by half.

NELL: You seem pretty flair-y.

DAN: No. I can only bring it out in people; the best, or the worst. Nothing midway. It's a dicey trade.

SHEILA: Now, Dan. You must be back on the fags, if you're bullying stories out of people.

Offended, Dan lifts the sleeve of his shirt to show the nicotine patch on his shoulder. Feidhlim chuckles.

Agh.

DAN: (*to Feidhlim*) For the visitors?

At last, Feidhlim nods.

Good man.

Sheila thinks of how to lay down the odd stepping stone for Feidhlim, so he can jump through the telling quicker. Feidhlim catches Sheila's hand as it goes for her glass, and she wonders if he might flee the place, but he takes her hand to his mouth and kisses the back of it. His umbrellaed moustache keeps his lips soft and unweathered. With her other hand, Sheila takes a drink of cold cider to quench something flaming in her chest.

FEIDHLIM: Well. Now. It's a fact daily teshtified by the weather-man that a dull night has never crossed this neck of the country. (*Dan calls "hup!"*) Nor a dull blade. (*Dan scans Nell for signs of beguile-ment.*) Ye glimpsed it yerselves, and yer luggage not even unbuckled. If it's not wild shkies, it's politics or divilment or worse. We had our own version of a Berlin Wall here, not three mile from my house. Not between the east and the west but between the north and the rest, a border wall put up by the British Army. 'Twas only knocked down in ninety-one. I won't ask were ye born then or not. (*Sheila's smile is back, because this is not really the story: he's making himself comfortable.*) You might have a cousin lives half a mile away from you, but you'd to drive thirty miles to reach her, with that blockade between you. 'Twas common sense to take it down. That's why I was shtood up on the concrete wall, holding steady the fella with the jackhammer. We were braced against the Fermanagh elements. The guards and the priest were arranged around the place, watching. Pulling the wall down was illegal, but the law wasn't against it. That's how it was, and it's a fact. Shocking for that to need stating, thirty-two years on. Myself, I'd a been . . . twenty-two year old then.

Maeve is distracted, doing her slow maths to confirm that Feidhlim cannot possibly be only fifty-four now.

By the end of that year, that road had joined the island's smuggling network. An unapproved route with no customs huts. Truth be told, smuggling was almost its own industry then. A lot of goods were way cheaper in the north—you're talking teabags, you're talking cattle—and a few bob could be made. During the height of the Troubles, it was more than that. It was arms. It was different. (*Pause.*) I was aware of all that carry-on, but I stayed well away from it. In ninety-one, I was new married and only two years in our house. A farm takes longer than two years to set up, and a lot longer to come viable.

DAN: How much longer for this story to come viable?

FEIDHLIM: (*unruffled*) 'Twas a very dark winter night that was in it . . . with the moon left in the cold as ourselves, and a quilt of clouds trasna na réaltaí.

Nell mouths the words "trasna na réaltaí" in case a muscle memory might kick in . . . She remembers "trasna" as "across," but mistakes "na réaltaí" for "reality" instead of "the stars." Seeing her knotted brow, Feidhlim resolves to leave out the Irish.

It was *that* dark, I'd have seen Dan lighting his fag out the back of this place from my front door in Larganhugh.

DAN: (*rolls his eyes*) You would in your hole. You're talking to doctors, here.

FEIDHLIM: Oh jays.

SHEILA: You either want a story, Dan, or you want a fact.

NELL: Doctors who can't cure constipation.

MAEVE: My degree's honorary.

FEIDHLIM: For a *fact*, then . . . That night, getting on to midnight, I heard a car nearing. You could've seen the headlights of a car from that border crossing at Rossinver, three mile from my door. But what use are facts if a truck has its lights off when it hares along the Glenaniff River and swings right up your road? I heard tomorrow's potholes being plowed out of the gravel driveway, with the speed he came up it. If it's robbers, I thought, they'll come away with a wealth of blue willow china, the wedding present, and that'd be the height of it. I told Carmel, my late wife, to lock herself in the toilet if there was any commotion and she was practiced at that, God rest her soul.

Feidhlim touches the rim of his cap, takes a moment to remember Carmel, who had suffered at the hands of an abusive partner before him and had

never overcome it. Lest he be unable to continue at all, he continues in
a rush.

I had a shotgun, but I didn't take it when I went out to the lad. I
opened the door to him and his spiel. He gave his full name and
named the Kerry village he was from. He was in a spot of bother and
could I help him out? He wanted to be honest with me: the customs
were after him. He had a few car parts in the truck, and he was in a
tight spot financially, and he was only trying to make it through the
tight spot he'd got himself stuck in. Now . . . he had the "car parts"
bit nice and wide, like a Kerryman. But I've never known a Kerryman to say "spot of bother" in my life. It wouldn't work, because the
T and the O . . . it can't be said. I sympathized with the lad on the
financials. The very same thing as keeps a lot of us wakeful. We
were similar aged. He was someone's younger brother. Ah, I had
that hay barn nearly empty, you see, and he wanted to park his truck
in it, and he'd be gone first thing in the morning.

Ten years earlier, now, the customs our side would've been hid in the
bush with a rifle and he could have had his tires shot, and lost his
life, for the price of them car parts. *If* car parts is what he had. Have
you anything like drugs or guns? I asked him. Definitely not, he
said. I'm sure they'll be down the road in a short while, he said. But
he didn't look away from me. And maybe that's all it was. I gave him
a little nod, and like that he drove the truck round the back and slept
in there too. Sure enough, I saw the lights of the customs officer
coming from miles off. And I lay down anyways and took what rest
I could, for the time it took him to check the other houses and get to
my own. No, I haven't seen this man, I haven't been disturbed by
this vehicle, I said. Off they went. I got into the bed again, still
stuck on that accent. Was it the O in "bother" itself? Too closed? No
more than the stars that night, I didn't catch a wink.

MAEVE: You thought it was weapons? That he was a para-
military?

FEIDHLIM: 'T'wouldn't have been a quantum leap.

MAEVE: And you worried—sorry—you worried he was . . . what?

NELL: (*whispers*) Don't say Protestant.

MAEVE: On the loyalist side? Because of his accent?

DAN: They're catching on.

FEIDHLIM: I'll be perfectly honest with you. Growing up on a farm, you learn the feet sometimes come out first, and weapons kill all animals no matter the shape of them. The Troubles came out of particular historical conditions, but the threat of violence was in the air long before and long after. There were gossuns lighting new fires out of embers that might have cooled off, had there been an alternative distraction. Had there been more investment in their futures. Them in the North, I mean to say. So 'twasn't about sides or creeds perturbed me with the accent. It was about barefaced lies, since it was the lad's hardship that made me take that risk on his behalf. On good faith. But true to his word, the fella and truck were gone in the morning, and he'd left the flask of tea I'd brung him. 'Twas a frosty night.

DAN: Was there milk in it, was there? (*to Nell*) Are you sick of the weather yet, being back?

SHEILA: (*soberly*) If a long winter night gets into your bones only once, Dan . . . you'd run in circles to spare it getting into anyone else's.

There is a pause in which Sheila realizes everyone's looking at her. She goes for her pint, to cool her baking cheeks, but the glass is drained. Before Dan pushes another round, she turns to Feidhlim and speaks low in Irish: We'll go in a minute. She'd learned Irish when she met Feidhlim. Feidhlim bows his head and lines up the next happenings efficient as row crops.

FEIDHLIM: The June after—'t would've been a Sunday, because I had the papers bought. I only noticed because it took up the front page of the sports section: photographs of the top ten placements at the Donegal International Rally, color-printed. And there is your man, unmistakable. I wouldn't forget a face read under the light of my own front door. He was not a Kerryman, it turns out, but a wee fella from Newtownards County Down by the name of Sammy Crawford. (*Pause*.) The article said he was on a scholarship from Shell. It had him destined for a career in the Formula One racing.

MAEVE: And Newtownards is . . . ?

NELL: (*whispers*) Don't say—

Dan bucks with a silent laugh at Nell.

FEIDHLIM: Well indeed.

MAEVE: (*gasps*) So he *was* doing an accent?

FEIDHLIM: He was.

MAEVE: The cheek of him!

FEIDHLIM: Oh, I'll tell you. I don't know was he a grandson of Frederick H. Crawford, but you wouldn't know. He was a British Army officer and gunrunner for the UVF back in the day. I never looked it up, and I have no interest. Sammy wasn't running guns through my haybarn.

NELL: Right, it was a *car* rally. So . . . it *wasn't* a lie, with the car parts.

FEIDHLIM: Oh, that was a lie, all right. He had a rally car in the back of that truck. He told me himself, whether he meant to tell me or was it out of awkwardness. Mind you, in them days, a Ford Escort rally car cost seventy percent more south of the border than north. And he tried to let on that profit made all the difference to him, as if it was a one-off thing! It was a side racket. Private sponsorship on top of the corporate. And if he was caught at a crossing, he'd have been handy driving blind at speeds a garda car couldn't touch.

DAN: And *can you believe* that this man didn't sell his story to the paper when Sammy turned jet-setting Formula Three racer!

SHEILA: Sell his story! (*shaking her head*) Have you met the man?

FEIDHLIM: Out of the blue, Sammy tears up the drive of the same house twelve years later—

DAN: (*interrupting, spreading his arms wide*) He's back! For fucken nostalgia!

FEIDHLIM: No.

SHEILA: (*with a frown*) Dan! You weren't there.

FEIDHLIM: 'Twas to . . . express gratitude he came back.

DAN: (*to Nell*) So *here's* the chance to at least *threaten* the tabloids. You tell me, girls. Was Feidhlim not duty-bound to his parish to at least *spook* the shite out of Sammy the chancer Crawford?

Sheila hasn't seen Dan like this before, commanding the atmosphere by way of a leash. Making his customers do tricks. He normally lets an exchange go where it will.

MAEVE: (*clutching her belly*) Okay . . . this is where I'm hoping this story has a happy ending, that Sammy came with a thank-you card and the keys to his Ferrari. But I feel like I've already been *in* a rally car, so—

FEIDHLIM: I'll put ye out of your misery: he came to deliver me an autographed portrait of himself leaning on his single-seater Italian vehicle.

Dan stands up and gestures toward a picture on the wall, with the flourish of a 1980s gameshow glamour woman.

MAEVE: No!

FEIDHLIM: Yes.

NELL: He genuinely thought you'd be pumped to have . . . his signed promo shot?

Sheila glances at Feidhlim and sees that he's injured, in some small internal way. He has no will to give the thing a coup de grâce, nor should he.

SHEILA: He handed it over like a Jehovah's Witness brochure. Convinced it would answer our prayers.

Amid laughter, Feidhlim swallows down the rest of his purple Ribena and readies his posture for departure.

NELL: Oh wow. So he . . . he confessed about the car? To, what, cleanse his conscience?

FEIDHLIM: He didn't mean to. It just shlipped out in his blethering. He was being awkward after . . . he ran over one of me hens.

Nell's eyes widen. Maeve presses a napkin into her eyes, wheezing. They won't mind an embellishment. Feidhlim smiles slyly through his moustache and ad-libs:

Clucky.

Maeve clutches Nell's arm.

NELL: Look at the dead hen!

Maeve laughs so hard at this that even Nell starts up. And Feidhlim knows from this that they're laughing at something else, from their own lives, and that is grand.

Fearing the end of their time together, the four of them, Maeve jumps at the offer of a lift from Sheila and Feidhlim. She loads the remaining food onto a single tin platter—Olwen would have her head if she binned them—and runs back inside for her coat. Dan and Nell are at the wall. He's showing her the photograph.

MAEVE: Come on, love.

The two men at the bar are waiting wondrously patiently for their next drink; aware that a forlorn pub owner might pour a liberal measure, if they wait his blue devils out and switch to spirits. Dan notices a tenner tucked under Nell's pint glass. He collects the note and—as Nell's crutches are in the way of her jacket pockets—slots it into Maeve's tote bag.

DAN: You don't tip the barman in Leitrim. You let him beat you at cards.

He raises his brows at Nell, in yet another plea to stay.

NELL: It's for the musician. Not the barman.

Maeve lands her arm across Nell's shoulders, and they make for the exit. On their way to the car, Nell halts on her crutches. It's impossibly quiet, besides the engine of Feidhlim's car. Dark is falling quickly, with no cars passing to disguise it as an earlier time of day.

MAEVE: What's wrong?

NELL: You should go to Northern Ireland with Rhona. (*Maeve inhales to reply impulsively.*) For one thing, this could be a once-in-a-lifetime gesture from Rhona. And I think it'd be a mistake to reject it. Besides, you can hang with the kid and see what that's all about.

MAEVE: Let's get back and talk—

NELL: And the truth is . . . I need to be alone with Olwen.

Without offering any further explanation, in the brightness of Feidhlim's headlights, Nell stills her quiet, gray eyes upon her sister's, evoking that old rationale from their grieving youth, without having to say it. Sin an fáth. *"That's the why." Then Nell levers herself forward and repeats, encouragingly:*

You should go.

She opens the door.

As the car pulls away and the taillights lower into the understory, in the window of An Spa Sláinte, a match is lit.

4.

Back at the house, Olwen has been wrangling the baby into a sort of padded wagon in lieu of a pram. Unable to manage the straps of the baby carrier, she hustles Leo into the sleeping bag and pushes him around in a wheelbarrow, for a tour of her rainwater harvesting system. Shortly after arriving, she'd rigged up two twenty-five-thousand-liter IPC totes—great containers fed by underground pipes running downhill from a homemade catchment device beyond the woods—and in the wake of the storm she needed to check them for dislodged joins and clogged funnels.

The month previous, a waterman had appeared at the house, insisting she'd have to pay for her water unless she could prove she wasn't siphoning off from the public mains. She'd made short work of him. For small talk—she tells Leo—I gave him chemical weathering. Rainwater is a chemical agent of geologic processes, you see, and the important clay minerals—calcium, magnesium, sodium, potassium from the bananas you're mad on—simply cannot be acquired from rainwater that's so *negative* on the level of the *ion*. Negative . . . on the level . . . of the ion, I told your man. Nonsense, you know. The soil mineral balance beneath our very feet is quaking, I said, and it's a vicious cycle when the clay changes the ions that are emitted in drainage water in the first place. Because where does *that* water go, but up and back down again? Isn't it only *sane* for me to have my own supply to ionize, when the officials are busy gaffer-taping leaks in rusty pipes and sending toll collectors out in SUVs to the remote houses of single women? Olwen clicks her fingers loudly. Oh, he reversed handy as Sammy of Newtownards.

Olwen is pleased with how the babysitting is going, but she's thirsty, and it would have been better had Leo fallen asleep from the gentle juddering of the wheelbarrow. Instead, the mention of bananas has him all riled up. His mother had instructed Olwen not to feed him for the first hour, except in an emergency, and Olwen had instructed herself not to hydrate for the first hour, except in an emergency. The both of us are on the wagon, she says, as she looks around for wholesome outdoor activities to occupy another wee while as she carts the child downhill. Maeve had bought her some seeds in town: aubergine and Romanesco courgettes, with a lovely nutty flavor, she'd enthused, and they make big yellow flowers, perfect for stuffing with tofu cream cheese and frying in tempura batter! They would sow the seeds together on her birthday, Maeve had declared before they'd taken off for the pub, inviting herself to stay for the foreseeable. Apparently she's decided Olwen's fortieth will be a day for literalism. New roots laid down. Olwen had been too sore-headed to suggest that Maeve make herself a mood chart, to better see the gourd-seed-rooting imagery for what it was, and to take herself to a naturist colony or a disco or a convent with her edible flowers, for the love of Lilith.

Come on so, till I get us some hoes, she tells Leo, now caterpillared in the green sleeping bag. She collects him from the barrow and sits him on her hip as they collect plastic pots, seed sachets, kneepads, and implements from the barn. They make another trip to the wood perimeter to fill a bucket with compost. Various heaps of it have been cooking for about eight weeks, aided by worms, but the storm has quenched the compositing process, and she'd had to add new green matter and sawdust from yesterday's carpentry to get them going again.

The polytunnel is mostly empty, so they both crouch down on their hands and knees on the sleeping bag, with the bucket of soil-compost and a plastic tray loaded with mini planting pots. Leo is shaking the aubergine packet, delighted at its maraca rattle. Olwen is showing him how to sit the seeds vertically in a container two-thirds full of soil. Then, she says, you take a fistful of compost and scatter it over loosely. In a fortnight I'll think about moving them to a raised bed. Which I'd have to make. Or else . . . I'll do nothing of the sort. She becomes absorbed picking out un-broken-down pistachio shells from the compost already in the pots. Salted roasted pistachios and a pint of Connacht Guinness—that would do for a last meal. The trouble is . . . it would have to be canned Guinness. And that's Leinster water goes into the canned stuff. The province of her youth. The water her parents drank by the lungful.

The trouble is, it was suggested by Rhona only well after lunchtime that Olwen might mind her baby, if she wouldn't come to the pub. That had been her olive branch, and her challenge. But all morning Olwen had been projecting the conversations she knew would take place at the pub. The many details the sisters would exchange, with Dan and the others, about who she was, what she'd learned, what she'd done, what she is capable of. Speculation as to why she'd given it all up. Those details would spoil the precious ease she'd found here. It had given her relief, these past months, not to be asked the things she'd come to be asked unremittingly—by her own peers more than the youth—all of which boiled down to one desperate question: Do you have hope?

And now her sisters are here, where she hadn't invited them, their mouths making those same onerous shapes. This refuge from expectations—from what she was expected to say, and what she expected herself to be able to say—had *almost* made the place seem livable. Not beautiful. There's still the stink of ammonia in the air. But livable. In the unexpected, bleary relief of it, she'd even moved a few materials around. Used her hands, to touch the bedrock: to feel that it was still cool. It still holds the story she'd chosen to read to herself once upon a time . . .

It is not enough—and the guilt is tremendous—but she is deranged from it. From caring for; caring to answer, to excavate positive proof. From entertaining. From commandeering. From supervising so much promise that her wards feel rich with leeway. She *wants* the young to be rich. She wishes for their curiosity to branch out and up magnificent as an ancient oak . . . and, later, for the water-saturated sediment that's coming to subsume and petrify those intrepid branches, so that whatever new society survives might find those fossilized trees and admire some exquisite, tender, knotted filament of their gilded ancestors. Two gin miniatures were had with her sandwich and, though that was hours ago, it might account, now, for her zoning out a little, as she sits quietly by her pile of new earth and picks out the undecomposed pistachio shells.

It's a sort of cough that finally calls her attention to Leo, who has packed a black fistload of compost into his mouth, with a worm curling in it like a tongue.

Olwen hears nothing through the adrenaline of the next minute. She scrambles, pawing out the soil from his tiny mouth, checking the fast pulse of nostrils for signs of breathing. The black pile is, soon, a terrifying emission at his lap. When she has run her finger along his gums and palate until she feels no more dirt, she wants to tell him to spit—he has so many teeth for it to lurk. His little hand grasps again for the upchucked worm as she picks him up, and he whines when she jogs him in through the back door of the house to the kitchen. She thinks of blocking his mouth with her hand so he won't breathe through it, but if he cries, he will surely inhale whatever remains. Legionnaires' disease, she thinks—that's the one you get from inhaling soil. That little cough! He watches her with the fixed attention of a security camera as she washes her free hand, wets a cloth, and approaches his mouth with it. He turns his face away. Leo, Leo, pet, I have to. I'm sorry. It was mostly compost . . . so *Legionella* can't be in it. She had *made* it, after all. She knew everything that had gone into it, all the food scraps and wood chippings and such. It was earth she made! Earth she made! Jesus Christ . . . a rodent might have pissed on it. A terrible ache inches up Olwen's gullet, but she is still pulling silly faces at Leo, making goofy sounds to stop him crying. Should she make him vomit? Should she call Rhona . . . ?

But Leo isn't upset. The child is inconceivably perfect. Rhona will have antibiotics in her handbag. She will give the child's mother all the information. All the information. Rhona has always been better equipped to carry it.

Hot water fills the basin in the kitchen sink as she carries Leo to the bathroom for a towel and a toothbrush, making singsongy noises to keep his self-awareness at bay. He's resisting her hold a little, and she can feel sweat trickling down her cleavage, carrying him back to the kitchen sink and removing his tiny down jacket. She is so grateful to discover what Maeve has purchased—this box of no-allergen, no-active-agent pure lye soap and a fancy sponge—that she'll let her stay a month if she wants to. She passes the sponge to Leo, reading out selling points from the box as the child acquaints himself with this new puffy, amber-colored friend: *unbleached honeycomb natural sea sponge.* It's biodegradable, Leo, but no eating it. Okay? Have we a deal? He holds the sponge with quickly learned lordliness as she removes his socks, then lifts him by his waist, slipping the jeans and soggy nappy off him in one go. He doesn't enjoy being bare-bottomed all of a sudden, and he wrestles her, so Olwen finds even more whispery astonishment in her vocal range for the sake of his compliance. Harvested *sustainably,* Leo! From the Greek Aegean Sea! Lads above! She tests the water temperature and sets Leo into the basin before his shirt is even off. She gasps amazement at him, shimmies the water for bubbles, then peels the shirt off and scoops the warm soapy water over his shoulders. Showing him how to load the sponge with water, she squeezes it out from on high, a sensation for which even Leo is willing to come off the fence.

What you hold in your hands there now, she says, is your daddy! And that's not a slay. That's not me throwing shade. It's a matter of fact. We evolved from sponges, Leo! No, I'm not. I'm *not* codding you! The students gave me the same fishy look when I told them, and I'd to phone up a pal in human biology and put her on speakerphone till they were persuaded. Like clients, they are, wanting second fecken doctors' opinions. Two point five billion years ago, we were sponges. Take it or leave it. She prods the sponge gently, then Leo's belly. Her sleeves are saturated. This was you . . . when you were basic. Sponges were the first animals. *And* the first to reproduce sexually. Go like this: Ahh-hhh! She sticks out her tongue demonstratively and tries to brush Leo's tongue and teeth with the toothbrush, but he purses his mouth invincibly against it and pushes out a bit of spittle. She wipes the spittle off with her thumb and inspects it. It's clear, so she goes back to helping him use the sponge to wash himself. To calm the pair of them. Her voice still sounds weird to her. She is not convinced by it. How's that for a collagen skeleton against your cheek? she says. Is it nice?

Would you believe it, Leo . . . that skeleton is *also* a *brain*. What? Isn't that savage? In a way, we were better like this. Don't you think? We were less complex. But don't you worry, we'll collapse back to a simpler form, sooner or later. So no harm in seeing the upside. Your liver, for example, is the size of my thumbprint, and it has to process whatever poisons we've imbibed. In these fellas—she jiggles the sponge—there's no special organ assigned to the job: *every* cell works to pump it out. We humans need separate bits for separate functions. Bones and blood and loins and giblets. That makes us dependent. And contingent. Put a sponge through a sieve, though, and all those cells will still know they're from the same animal. They'll collect together and make thousands of baby sponges. Imagine that hardiness. Put me through a sieve and you'd get . . . a bloody Mary. So you would. She tickles him a little on the side and gets a clean, pink smile. There are teeth in it, and it is glorious.

The ache in Olwen's gullet comes out now in a wet wail, which she tries to smile through. He'll think she is singing. He seems to be okay. If he isn't, there are still antibiotics that work, despite the growing resistance. Everything is sharp and precarious. The business of enter-tainment, of keeping another human being diverted, is exhausting. She had almost forgotten just how exhausting, forgotten why she'd left.

A faint brown streak dripping down Leo's forehead brings her to. Her first horrible impression is that the soil is seeping through his pores. That the hungry microorganisms in the compost are working rapidly through the carbon-nitrogen cocktail of his body—but no. Soil in his hair, is all. It had got everywhere. His tiny nails host dark moons. She cleans them with the toothbrush. Then she washes his hair. I thought it looked brighter in the photos, she tells herself. Do you know, Leo . . . it's been an hour, roughly. Roughly. I'd say we could mash a few carrots to rebrighten you. Do you think? She chuckles. That haughty look on you . . . if you hadn't that look, and the pinned-back ears, I might suspect your mammy hired a surrogate.

Leo squints and winces at the clean water fountaining down his forehead, which Olwen is cupping from the tap and dropping over him.

Okay, we'll towel off, she says. Though she doesn't want to. She wants to prolong the moment in which they are calm and accommo-dating together. In which he doesn't understand and nothing needs to be explainable. The age in which he is bare and washable as a sponge. Taking what nutrients he wants. Absorbing things good and bad, then easily sicking them up. Forgetting them.

When he is dry, he yawns hugely, and Olwen cowers at the tiny bits of soil still tucked in the creases of his teeth like cavities. Like rot. Even if she manages to brush it all loose, how do you make a baby spit? A soldier of white bread might do it, if she pulls it out as soon as he bites down. When he cries, she can give him a banana. She looks for somewhere to sit him to put his clothes on . . . She has him by the un-derarms, but he isn't so inclined to stand up. A sleepy, serene look has come over him. It is unperformed. He might just let her lay him on his back.

There, on the counter by the bread, is the lovely striped chopping board she'd helped Maeve desplinter with an electric sander. She had coated it in tungseed oil herself, even enjoyed the process. Had she? Had it been meditative? Blankening? Certainly, she'd enjoyed a beverage as she did it. She lays the child gently down on the board.

Headlights swing across the room, with the crucifix shadows of window beams racing toward them. No sound from outside but the crunch and scatter of gravel. It's the Tesla. Then a shadow much larger than a crucifix: Rhona standing at the window, staring at her naked baby on a chopping board. Her sister standing over him, drenched, like a storm. Like a system ready to tip.

Of course . . .

Olwen's eyes blind suddenly, and she troubles her wrist. When she blinks, it comes clear as a windowpane. What Rhona had long ago discerned, from a safe distance, to be true. That Olwen isn't really a danger to herself.

part three

1.

Crossing the border has the pregnant feel of a New Year's Eve, with all the dread of resolutions owing. A strip of red tarmac across the road and a sign reading speed limit in miles per hour marks the moment of their crossing. Maeve is reading all the signs and symbols out the car window with great concentration. "Post Office" instead of "An Post." Yellow registration plates instead of white. A kilo of oranges for £1.50 instead of €2.50. Better hairstyles. She'd been to Northern Ireland only twice before—for a hen-do in Belfast and a catering gig at Carrickfergus Castle—and this was something she'd noticed.

Is it okay to say "the North"? Maeve asks. And "down south"? People hardly say the Republic, do they? That sounds . . . sort of drastic.

Rhona adjusts her rearview mirror to check on Leo, who is occupied with a squeezy bag full of sparkly water and gel goldfish, attached to his car seat. She admires his perseverance, attempting to grip the elusive fish. At some point in the future, he will wrestle the toy off its attachments and spill open the ocean with his teeth.

Just don't say "southern Ireland" and you'll be fine, Rhona says. Just stick with naming cities—that's a fail-safe. London, Wicklow, Dublin. Except for Derry, she says. Don't say Derry.

What?!

Tonight's town hall meeting is in Coleraine, which is the second-largest city in the county Lon—

Don't say Londonderry! Maeve shouts.

Rhona winces from the noise. *Do* say Londonderry, out of courtesy for the municipality. Only ten percent of Coleraine ticked "Irish" in the last census.

No way. Maeve shakes her head. *Londonderry Girls* would've been a shit TV show.

They fall quiet again. Rhona decides to let that comment slide, knowing that whatever had caused Maeve to change her mind and be ready with her bag packed this morning—before Nell and Olwen were out of bed—wasn't anything triumphant. It wasn't Maeve's decision, but something she'd resigned to go along with. This two-hundred-kilometer drive will be the longest time they've spent alone together since they were teens. Despite all they have in common—entrepreneurial qualities, unpaying tenants, parental pursuits—their frequent silences suggest they have little to say to each other. Rhona keeps glancing at Leo in the mirror to ensure he's not paying them any heed. She doesn't want his barometer to pick up on the frontal boundary between his mother and his auntie. She is trying to let go of an ancient feeling that Maeve's opinion of her was sculpted in brass in their youth and can never be changed beyond the inevitable tarnishing or a quick polish. Surprising even herself, Rhona is distressed by the silence. Such that she blurts out:

Why did you hide the fact you'd heard from Olwen? When you knew she was okay?

Maeve rests her elbow on the window ledge and presses her knuckles to her mouth. She tries to think of why exactly she'd done that, but it's so overwhelming to contemplate that her mind just fogs over, like when warm air crosses frigid canal waters. Into her fist, she asks:

Do you think she *is* okay?

Rhona fills her lungs, and holds the breath in for a moment, before saying: I think that if she wants to believe in the future, the last place she should be is all alone.

I told her that! I agree with that!

But she's chosen not to, Rhona continues. She's entered a phase of willful decline, which she's experiencing as a kind of capitulation to the mean. And that—

That's not what she's doing! Maeve turns toward Rhona, and then to Leo, wearing the sort of smile that Leo knows not to mirror back to its wearer. She just needed to get closer to *nature*!

Did that look like a nature retreat to you? Rhona glances at Maeve, but they're passing over a bridge and Maeve's attention splits.

No, but . . .

Her *job* was a nature retreat, Rhona says, and she left it.

Out Rhona's window, the river branches apart, with an island of trees in the middle. Maeve tries to pin down the strange beauty of this little town, despite all the low gray buildings. Maybe it's just that the buildings are different, the aesthetic unpredictable. Maybe it's just the river, which is so calm she could take her barge on it. Faintly, she says: So maybe I don't know what she's doing.

Did you ask her?

Maeve reaches round to stare at Leo working his bag of fish, which keep evading him. Remember with Dad, she says. How hard he made it to confront him on anything? Even if you'd want to ask him just . . . if it was a busy week at the shop, he'd send out this pulse that stopped the questions even forming in your mouth.

Because the stock was depleted, Rhona says. And the till was light.

And then he'd give you all this good energy once you got onto some safe topic, so you'd feel rewarded. It was a sort of dark magic, Maeve says. It's like it has a brain of its own, addiction. Its own intelligence that works on the host's behalf, coming up with all these ways of shaping the person's life around it and keeping threats at bay.

She's mistaking a symptom for the disease, Rhona thinks. Like their father, however, Maeve responds best to positive reinforcements. Not quite able to muster one up, Rhona moves on:

I'm running a workshop at the Ulster University at four, then the town hall event's at seven. I'll be taking Leo to both. If you want to come you're welcome. I can make some introductions. It's up to you.

Or I can put you on my car insurance, and you can visit the Giant's Causeway.

Maeve, who has been watching Leo corner a fish, turns back to the front. Sorry, what's the town hall thing again?

She asks this quickly, flushing at the prospect of driving. She does still *have* her license after writing off her van, but if she so much as speeds, she'll lose it. It had been a twenty-three-thousand-pound write-off, plus a fine. Luckily, she'd only taken out a trailer mobile warning sign for road works . . . in a school zone.

I'm going to come along, she says, but what's it all about? A United Ireland?

No. Rhona spritzes her windscreen and sets the wipers going to clear it of that topic. You've heard of citizens' assemblies?

Yeah. I listened to a podcast you were on.

Really?

Maeve nods.

Rhona takes her notification-manic phone off its holder for a moment. What did you learn?

Don't check your phone while driving.

Sorry, Rhona says. Thank you. She turns the phone upside down.

Maeve frowns, almost motion-sick from this new dynamic between them.

I won't grade you, Rhona says, but it would be very helpful for me to get a sense of what the people of Coleraine might know tonight.

Maeve had actually listened to the podcast twice. Once at double-speed, expecting it to be boring. The second time, at normal speed, because it wasn't. She reaches inside her collar and pulls at the strap of her bra, so that it snaps more comfortably onto her skin, like a high diver buying herself time.

It's where . . . you have a bunch of randomly selected citizens who get invited to give up a couple of weekends to talk about a social issue affecting the country or region, like drug use or transport or climate change, stuff the government's been crap at. And the people debate among themselves as to what the problems are and what could be done about them, and they have people guiding them to make sure there's no catfights, and they have experts come in and do presentations and Q and As, they do some reading and listening and learning and accidental bonding—and in the end they agree on some policy suggestions. Which are usually at least *heard out* in Parliament, if not implemented. Depends on the country. How seriously they take it. No prize for guessing Westminster doesn't give a toss—

You've got it, Rhona says. That's effectively it.

Maeve glances with widened eyes at Leo, and whispers: Does she ever give out gold stars?

For Ireland's first assemblies, there were ninety-nine citizens involved. And a retired judge chairing them. Do you know how the citizens are selected?

Can't remember what it's called—

Sortition.

But I know it's not *random* random. It's controlled random. The idea is for the citizens to be properly representative, 'cause politicians obviously aren't. But isn't this kind of a sudden pivot? The other day you were onto your colleague in Chile, covering for you, so you could come to . . . Londonderry *out of courtesy?* Is it not a bit . . . parochial? It just seems a surprising choice. For you.

Political history in the making is hardly a surprising choice for a political scientist, Rhona says, casting a libelous look Maeve's way. Brexit pales in comparison; it's just a descension story. Man eats the horse he rode in on, then eats himself. Whereas citizens' assemblies in Northern Ireland could set a global precedent, a shift in power—for the first time—to its people. It's supposed to be a democracy, but the Northern Irish Executive hasn't been in session for over a third of its life span. There needs to be a *massive* effort to explore viable alternatives, before any plan for the future can get enacted. And I don't believe that work is best done by career politicians with vested interests, or by a dysfunctional assembly with no transparency. It needs a diverse array of people coming together in a room, with the authority to set an agenda, to hear evidence, to determine priorities for new policy, within a time frame. It has to start small, in a room or a town hall. Then once we prove we're still capable of reaching some kind of civic consensus, the results will be the opposite of parochial. I believe our future hangs on our willingness to get together in a room and agree on what progress looks like.

Maeve makes a faint droning sound. You weren't even willing to talk things out in a room with your own sisters, she thinks but doesn't say.

Rhona is caffeinated by all she has to add, but right now, they're approaching Omagh. Thirty-one mirrors on poles reflect patches of sky at the Omagh bombing memorial. Rhona spots a car park behind them . . . No, she'll park at a charging station while they have lunch.

Just as she's about to tease Rhona, Maeve is hit with a twang of envy. And then culture shock, as the car is suddenly surrounded by flags: Union Jacks, orange flags, red-and-white flags there's not enough wind to unfurl. The charger they're navigating toward comes up with an out-of-order alert. Rhona clicks her tongue. Half the chargers in Northern Ireland.

The Catholic half, or . . .

In the rearview mirror, Rhona tells Leo: Your aunties are hoots.

So you're taking Leo to the university? And to the town hall? Maeve says. By choice? When Rhona only nods, Maeve adds: I guess it keeps you in touch with the People. Having to bring your kid to work.

Excuse me?

Come on, Rho. Don't tell me it's not a *wee bit* strategic to bring your incredibly well-behaved, adorable toddler to some tricky community meeting. To soften the interaction.

Rhona signals, which masks the *tsk* that escapes her mouth. My child isn't some *hobby* I attend to after clocking out intellectually. He's not the nonwork part of my life. I don't want to dedicate my days to something Leo isn't part of. A baby is serious intellectual work, Maeve. Not the enemy of scholarship or promise.

Maeve leans her chair back and looks up at the tinted glass ceiling, taking it in. She half believes it. She believes that Rhona means it. Yeah, she says. Fuck me.

That's it. Consider yourself permanently stricken off the babysitter list.

Sorry! Maeve says. I forgot! Sorry, Leo. Hi!

Tentatively, Leo replies: Hi-ya.

Rhona gasps and hastily pulls into a driveway, unclips her seat belt to twist back to him. So that his first word might be for his mother. If it's the same word, it's the same first word, it will have been for her. Hiya! Rhona says, and she waits with test center expectation.

After a long, bright-eyed assessment, Leo repeats: Hi-ya.

Rhona's eyes flood as she repeats the words at him and looks to Maeve to see she heard it. A tear falls from her cheekbone. Tell me there's a Michelin star in Omagh? My son's first word is a full sentence! We're going to need reinforcements.

. . .

Coleraine Town Hall would be at home in Whitehall. The edifice is hulking enough to have hosted an early stock exchange. A Union Jack flag is at full mast on the entrance end. Inside, a red velvet curtain hangs closed in front of a stage. The panel, four strong, are seated at audience level. Rhona has Leo on her lap, since the long table was a bit flimsy to hold his clip-on chair. He's wearing a herringbone paddy cap and a tan cable-knit jumper with suede elbow patches, an outfit all agree is *too* adorable. During setup, when she was told for a third time that he looked like something out of a catalog, Rhona replied: He is. Now he's entertaining an audience a hundred strong, playing with an abacus-style toy made of rods and sliding rubberwood beads, designed to make only soft noises.

The front-row members are dressed formally. There are business-people, NGO workers, lobbyists, people from activist groups. The

mayor of the Causeway Coast and Glens is in the front row, though
he's not wearing his livery collar, as he's also a councilor and is attend-
ing in that capacity. In the third row, beside Maeve, a journalist is taking notes. On the way in, she'd seen a pair of police officers circling
the building, and there's a stocky man stood by the entrance in an
army green shirt and a radio holster.

The vice chancellor of Ulster University, Professor Graham Coade,
is chairing the panel, titled *Direct Democracy and Northern Ireland's Future*. Besides Rhona, the speakers include a twentysomething called
Ben Wilks-Harding from the research group UK in a Changing Europe, and a board member of the cross-party campaign Best for Britain.
Seeing that Ben still has three pages of notes to go, the vice chancellor
nudges him to a conclusion—first through body language, then by
shuffling papers, finally by standing up.

We've heard from Mr. Wilks-Harding, he says, arguing that the
House of Lords needs to be abolished. Now Professor Rhona Flattery,
one of the world's leading scholars on deliberative democracy, and professor of political science at Trinity College Dublin— Here the VC
halts and stiffens at some banter from the hall. Questions from the
floor will be taken later, he says. From the floor? says the heckler,
brushing down her clothes as if they're filthy. Rhona takes a guess that
this particular disdain relates to the university strikes, covered in all
the local papers, listing UK vice chancellors' salaries as half a million
pounds, when teaching staff—even those with PhDs—are hired course
by course, for sixteen pounds an hour.

Thank you, Professor Coade. Rhona speaks firmly, then waits for
him to sit. She stays seated with her hands around Leo on her lap.
People prefer not to be talked down to.

It's very inspiring to see this turnout, she says. Especially when
22.6 million voters who turned out for the last general election may as
well have eaten their ballots, thanks to the system we know as First
Past the Post: a voting system less sophisticated than my son's abacus.

In the UK, a member of Parliament is voted in if they get the most votes in a constituency. Fair enough. But the idea that the other votes count for naught—that the values, the politics, the vision for the country of all the other voters mean nothing—is a recipe for disaster. It's not democracy when a party can win power with 43.6 percent of the votes.

Besides the UK and Belarus, European countries primarily elect their politicians proportionally: If the Dutch Tories get 43.6 percent of the votes, they get 43.6 percent of the politicians. And if no one wants to get into bed with the Dutch Tories to make a majority, Greens and Labour can pool their 15 and 35 percent to govern in a coalition. And the parties that aren't part of the majority still get to be in Parliament, as the opposition, representing the voters who put them there. Be they Nazis, be they the far more reasonable Looney Raving Monster Party. Proportional representation means more power-sharing and compromise, instead of regressive years of scribbling out red policy and writing blue, followed by years of scribbling out blue policy and writing red. It reflects the actual politics of the country. Labour and the Tories don't represent all British voters. There should be a Blairite or Bidenesque centrist left in Parliament, alongside a Corbynite or Sanders-style socialist left. That's how the people get a voice. Voting can seem pointless when the parties we vote for don't end up in Parliament. People become disenfranchised. The frustration with majoritarianism fueled Brexit. You see the same dismay in the US. Thankfully, since the only major party holding out on proportional representation is the Tories, it's likely to transpire sooner or later.

But more *immediately*, more urgently . . . it should matter that you're here, now. While your government building's empty. The Northern Ireland Assembly's been suspended for more than a third of its life span. It's too much for them to work it out. And I know what it's like to grow up without adults in the room. You go gray standing by the door, waiting for them to lead you through it. You should defend the right to govern yourselves *effectively*—

Steady on there, Professor, calls a fiftysomething, short-haired woman in a "street pastor" sweater. It's not from sitting on our hands we've gone gray! A few other things contributed.

Rhona nods. No crowd likes to be told how to act, so she moves swiftly through her points: that engaged citizens like them, who are willing to gather in community halls like this and organize to further their own progress, are proof that Northern Ireland can ignite a new history of democracy. One that nations around the world will study, and take their lead from.

Dubious expressions crinkle in the hall. That's something a bit different for you! a lady in her nineties declares, in a tone that Rhona can only interpret as saucy.

A woman calls from the back: She's Professor *Flattery*! Catch on!

There's a bit of laughter. As the crowd's energy settles, Rhona takes the opportunity to unlock her phone and open a voice memo she'd covertly recorded in her car, which had also miraculously captured her son's first word. She holds it up to the mic and says:

Here's a layperson, who happens to be my sister, explaining citizens' assemblies better than I can.

Then she plays thirty seconds of the recording, and the crowd is stilled.

As it plays, Maeve looks like a whole table has just sent their meals back to the kitchen. Rhona gives her a thumbs-up—a show of approval, not a request for consent—but Maeve has to respond to the people around her jostling her with *Was that you?*s and, *Too right, the government's shifting the blame! Them'uns don't give a puff! We're just the country cousins in the group photo.*

When I first started studying citizens' assemblies fifteen years ago, Rhona says, nobody'd heard of them. Now they're blossoming the world over. There's a region of Belgium that has a *permanent*, randomly selected body called a citizens' council that sits alongside their elected chamber, to bring the wishes and judgments of citizens into the political process. They hear evidence from Parliament, from civil society groups and citizens, about issues they think a citizens' assembly should take up. Paris City Council just set up a permanent citizens' council, too. The population of Paris is 2.2 million. What are we here, 2 million?

When someone in the front row calls out 1.9, Rhona *hmms*.

The Republic of Ireland was the global game-changer for citizens' assemblies. Opening up political space among the establishment class to accept that this could be a sensible thing to do—not to mention a handy way to break political deadlocks, and forge ahead on issues that political parties won't touch. Reproductive autonomy. Marriage rights. Biodiversity loss. The list goes on. Rhona takes the toy Leo is handing her, done with it. Does anyone know if any citizens' assemblies have been held here?

Aye.

Rhona searches the crowd for who'd spoken, but pockets of talk around the hall obscure its source. From the front row, a member of a charity called Involve projects her voice: In 2018, there was one on the future of social care for older people that was *very* successful. The woman is itching to offer more specifics, but Rhona powers on:

"The future of social care for older people." That's an important topic. Rhona squints a little, bracketing her own claim. Intergenerational activities, she says. Holistic approaches to care, and so on? But is it the most *urgent* problem hurting the region? It's barely a political issue, really. As opposed to, say, "the future of healthcare." And there hasn't been another citizens' assembly here since. As if there's some consensus that Northern Ireland is too risky a place, too awkward and complex and polarized a place, for a progressive, participatory democracy. That you don't have the right, or ability, to govern yourselves effectively.

There's risk in it! says an older man who'd caught Rhona's eye for the fury of his expression. He's mumbling something now that she can't make out, but it's causing a stir around him. Professor Coade makes to intervene, but Rhona signals him silently: Keep back.

If you can, Rhona says, do stand so we can hear you.

The man, in his seventies, quickly gets to his feet. He is wearing a brown wool suit, with three pins in the lapel. The pulled seams of his face suggest he took all his holiday leave in pay, no more than Rhona.

It is a risky activity, he says, going round community halls, telling locals they're not being heard.

Rhona lowers her head for a moment, to take this in. The last thing anyone needs are populist demagogues stirring up grievances, she says. I'm not asking for you to put your faith in me. You'll see there's a table by the door where you'll find—

Would you ever just stop and think? the man says. You don't get it. You're legitimizing a form of political *will* that some will interpret as insurrection. He is swaying subtly now, like a disused rocking chair by a drafty window.

I know there's a sense of existential threat—

I'm not talking about identities! the man snaps.

Nor am I, Rhona says. I'm talking about disenfranchisement. Which can result in violence. When there's a crisis of trust in your core institutions. In the constitutional government. Petrol bombs being thrown at police vans. Rhona waits for a moment to see if the man wants to say something, but he seems to prefer the track she's now on. The last community hall I was in, Rhona says, in East Belfast, I spoke with a man who was concerned for his children's future. His kids were nearing voting age, but he'd stopped voting after Brexit. He said to me: "They're all just fancying up the question: *What are the terms of our surrender?*"

The man facing down Rhona lifts his clean-shaven chin and purses his lips to reject whatever connection this was supposed to have to what he'd said. Rhona doesn't break eye contact with him, even though Leo is squirming. I don't want that to be your question, she says.

It isn't, he says brusquely. It's thon other man's. His face is flushed now. His accent has a staccato tempo, with pauses for many of the consonants.

There's every reason why you should ask a different question, Rhona says. One of your own devising. And, collectively, provide the answers. The point you raise about the challenge to peace, sir, is vital. And it's the reason direct democracy can't just be a small-scale experiment in the North. Tentative steps in one privileged part of a borough. The defunct government here makes Northern Ireland the *ideal* place for a permanent Citizens' Senate, like that Belgian example, but effectively . . . on a national scale. For the first time, anywhere in the world. Northern Ireland can set a precedent for civic participation. Where could it be more justified, more effective, and more meaningful?

Rhona is still addressing the man, who is still standing.

Unmoved, he says: You'd have us do their jobs for them, on our weekends?

Leo has stolen the vice chancellor's fountain pen from the table and Rhona helps him to uncap it. The previous speaker, Ben, takes the only page in his stack that isn't printed double-sided and slides it toward Leo for something to draw on. Rhona bides her time. There is something this man hasn't yet said.

They're elected represen'atives, he says. They're paid professionals. Not just in Stormont. In Westminster.

They're entrenched in party politics, she says. They don't represent you. You show up, for one thing. Rhona hopes he might get some light relief from this. Don't you think extraordinary times call for extraordinary measures? she presses. As long as they're democratic.

Where's the money come from?

The money's a detail, Rhona says, then she catches sight of Maeve pressing her fingertips into her forehead. She hurriedly adds: There's no point sourcing the money if there isn't the will.

The vice chancellor has found a Biro and is trying to exchange it with Leo for his Mont Blanc. Rhona sees this and slips the pen out of Leo's grip while he's distracted, riveted by this standing man. A few people smile at Leo, looking out at them with such openness (*lovely wean*, someone says), and Rhona smiles, too, seeing Leo learn what it's like to be addressed by a town hall full of people.

A brand-new body is easy to sell, the man says. But it's just as soon corrupted.

The audience would love to have something to applaud, because the man has been standing for too long, but his bruising wisdom is difficult to celebrate. His stick is hanging off the back of the chair in front of him, and everybody knows he needs it. He has been arguing procedure for too much of his life—far longer than this young woman and her money-is-a-detail.

A sneeze seizes the man before he has a chance to reach for a hankie—but just as well, as it frees his hands to catch his glass eye as it pops out. The skin around his eye slackens something dreadful. He needs the eye refitted—or a face-lift, his wife used to joke. People who'd been looking at him now look away. Allergies, he says—lest anyone think it's Covid. The woman beside him puts a tissue in his other hand, eager to pull him down to his seat.

But then, in the same moment, Leo starts to laugh. He's seen the eye popping out. How it's in the man's hand, and his eye-place is empty. The man resists the kind tug at his sleeve. It's rotten, the tension. The restraint. For a long time, he's been trying to break it. He feels heat rush up the side of his nose, toward the duct there, but he can't stop it. He looks at the child.

Me and your mammy, he says . . . we weren't seeing eye to eye.

A few people in the crowd can't help but laugh, and there is a second of deathly silence until everyone joins in. The mayor in the front row half twists around and—though he doesn't look directly at the man—raises his hands to show that he's clapping. The hall's pressure releases like a parachute safely landed.

• • •

After, Rhona hands Leo off to Maeve, then heads for the media corner. At one point she tries to break away to catch the man in the audience, but someone tells her, "Billy's away out." The only way she'd get to shake his hand would be to show up for another congregation.

The town hall rumbles with chatter and movement. Maeve has Leo by his two hands, following him wherever he wants to walk. He makes a beeline for the busts of King Edward VII and Queen Alexandra, at which he screams until Maeve picks him up to face them, straitjacketing his arms since he seems to want to slap the monarchs.

Who is this person she's holding? Maeve wonders. His mouth is just like Rhona's, bending up at one side and down at the other, like the tilde in *niño*. None of her sisters shares that trait.

Hi, darling, Rhona says, appearing out of nowhere to rescue Leo from Maeve's haze. Did I see a yawn? Have we noticed it's bedtime? Or is there *far* too much excitement to think of sleep? Hmm?

Maeve's now trawling her mind for what she'd wanted to share with Rhona, a thing Olwen had told her once upon a time: that the north and south of Ireland were once parts of two different continents separated by a vast ocean. The northwest was on the continent that became North America. The southeast was on the ancient supercontinent . . . Gondwana? And later it rose up from a warm, tropical sea. The south was soft mud for millions of years, until it evolved and baked into tough, fine-grained limestone and fossil-filled shale. The sands became quartzites. She can't recall the names, but she remembers the tactile details. She remembers that the soil in their hometown graveyard drains into the sea. The soil in the whole southeast drains better than the northwest, which explains the bogs of the northwest, with their knack for preservation, and why Olwen likes it there. There's a scar somewhere in the landscape, where the two converged, she remembers. Maybe they could drive to it?

She hasn't said this aloud; she's in some sort of shock.

Rhona is peering across the hall, to the exit. The woman by the stained glass window there . . . I want to introduce you. The Black woman in the dogtooth jacket.

Oh yeah? Maeve says, without looking around; her back is to the hall and the shrinking crowd.

That's Dr. Adeline Trainor, Rhona says. She's a member of the legislative assembly. I'd put money on her to be elected to British Parliament soon. And my god but it's imperative to have Irish people of color in the midst of it. I'll introduce you, and you should suggest a lunch date, not only because she's a foodie, but she's a crusader for the food and agriculture transition.

Rhona. Maeve looks at the floor between them and shakes her head. I have to say it: How could you do that and think it's okay? She feels that her cheeks are hot, but she's cold without Leo in her arms.

What, the recording? Rhona asks. I didn't have time to ask permission, sorry. But they wouldn't have heard it *half* as well if I'd explained it.

Maeve takes Leo's outstretched chubby hand and cups it. I was really nervous about hanging out with you, she tells Rhona, and it made me ashamed, to be that nervous. I cried all last night. Have you seen the bags on my eyes? But then I felt so relieved when Leo spoke and we were able to just . . . go from there. She smiles at Leo with glossy eyes and squeezes his hand. But then you do something like that, Rhona . . . and you wonder why we can't trust you're ever being sincere. You used a vulnerable moment between us for your professional advantage. It's like . . . you weren't even *there*, where I was. Were you? Tears now skip down Maeve's cheeks, and she lets them. Is there anyone really there, where I see the people I love?

Maybe it's everyone putting their coats on, maybe it's the accents, but the hall sounds to Rhona of static. Stained glass windows, added during some renovation, conform all times of day to the same churchy hour. It's dry in here. Her throat is dry. Leo must be thirsty too. But he isn't complaining. He is such a self-possessed child. He's teaching her so much. Many responses occur to Rhona. She has no idea how such an innocent recording could have hurt Maeve. Is she afraid of sounding stupid? Because she hadn't, and she isn't.

I wasn't there, Rhona says, to her own surprise. She is concentrating on relaxing her face. On not wincing in any way. After all, she is here in a professional capacity.

What? Maeve rubs the cushion of her thumb across her jawline.

I wasn't there, in whatever childhood you all had, Rhona says. Whatever we're supposed to have gone through together. We couldn't all be intoxicated by that atmosphere. Now Rhona looks to Leo: I'll admit, it felt exciting—accepting I had to be the one to sneak ahead, to lay down tracks, since the ones we had led off a cliff. Anyone could see. It felt like sophisticated work. More interesting and meaningful than the work Olwen was doing. I thought that, *then*. Rhona props Leo higher on her hip and looks at Maeve again. It *was* lonely. But I did think I'd be loved in the end for it. I had to take the long view. That's the angle you see me working. It's a bit of a scar I have. I try not to think of it as ugly.

Behind Maeve's shoulder, a new agenda is closing in. Two students. Perhaps postgrads. Not ones Rhona recognizes from earlier. She goes to the day bag on a bench a few meters away to get a drink for Leo.

It *is* her! A smoker's voice wheezes toward them. I told you! Maeve turns to see two highly made-up twentysomething students, clutching phones. After pushing back the curtain of a fuchsia blow-wave, one of them says: Sorry tee interrupt . . .

It's Meals and Meditations! the first one says.

Are you Maeve Flattery?

You're Meals and Meditations! the first one repeats. On Insta!

It feels impossible to smile, so Maeve says, I like your hair.

Thank you, I had it done the-day, the girl replies without hesitation. We didn't know yous were sisters? She looks toward Rhona for the resemblance.

That's not the one in the videos, the grainy-voiced one says.

You wouldn't know, Jan, the fuchsia-haired one says, surveying Rhona with new generosity. It's just her voice in the videos, not her face.

It's not her, Kathy. The accent's totally wrong.

Would you mind if we took a photo? Kathy asks Maeve.

Your baby's wile cute, Jan calls over to Rhona, as if letting her off this once on a technicality.

Rhona busies herself, keeping Leo well away from the Instagram selfie requests. Maeve obliges, as second nature, even though she must look a wreck.

We saw you on the *Good Food* show with Nadiya Hussain . . . it was actually heart-stopping, the food shortage stuff. I sent that link to everyone I know—

She did, Jan confirms. My granny was raging, because Digestive biscuits are half the size now, and she has to eat twice as many to keep her regular.

Maeve has to moderate her laugh, lest it turn into a wail.

Kathy says: It's brilliant what you were saying about how we need to wise up. I'm in my final year of business and food science, and Jan does nursing.

Aye, Jan confirms, busy zooming in on the photo of the three of them as if it's a very worrying pie chart.

My dissertation's on food security and decentralization in the—

I've no top lip in this picture, Jan says. Can we take it again?

Kathy powers through: I actually got data from that Best for Britain crowd, she says, pointing at the seat where its board member had been sitting, and from the charity Feeding Britain. I look at what can get produced locally if the national net zero targets are met, transforming the whole food-water-land-energy system in one go. Which means an absolute refit tee agriculture in Northern Ireland, and that'll need more decentralized power to do that, and I think the citizens' assemblies like your sister was saying could be brilliant for it. I'd never heard of it. But it'll definitely get a mention now.

Stunned, Maeve just nods, repeating Kathy's language of conviction: "Absolutely."

You know, seven percent of households don't buy fruit and veg 'cause they're too dear, she says.

Seven? Maeve says. She is amazed by their self-absorption and their aplomb. And rubbish food gets subsidized, Maeve hears herself saying—as some knee-jerk reflex to feeling like a fraud.

Aye. It's totally shameful. But that's what I love about your cookbooks, Kathy says—they make people *think*. And not to be superficial, but you're very pretty and cool.

Speaking of shameful, Jan intrudes wheezily . . .

What are you working on now? Kathy says, recovering.

She'd be a brilliant researcher for you, Jan tells Maeve. If you were ever lookin'. Maeve frowns suddenly at this, which Jan reads as a boundary newly set. And *I'm* a bigger ride than that picture lets on. We'll have another go. Jan extends her phone in front of them.

Taking another won't give you a top lip, Kathy says. You need fillers.

I could do a piercing and just let it get infected? Jan says.

Kathy cackles.

Maeve is only vaguely aware of being given a filter for better definition, of being lent a caption. How can she hope to understand their captions, their dissertations, if she's never had a thesis of her own? The baron was right. Of course a cookbook has a thesis. A *text message* has a thesis. Jasper's had, to her sorrow and amazement—and a romantic one at that. Nell's seminar probably had one, if Maeve could clear her head enough to understand it. And not just words. Take Halim. He spends all day signing his into the weather, spelling it out to each and every stranger and ghost. She had mistaken it as her responsibility to translate it. Not into a book, but into a relationship, however untouching. A body. A moving form. A naturalized citizen. But Halim has no trouble with articulation.

She has long Covid, Kathy tells Maeve to explain Jan's coughing. Her tone is warier now that the celebrity chef seems to have tuned them out.

Maeve's eyes focus suddenly. Do either of you have a pen and paper?

No, Kathy says. We've only phones.

We've to go, Jan says.

Em . . . Kathy? Sorry, Maeve says. She passes Kathy her phone with
Instagram open. Type in your handle.

Oh. Kathy takes the phone. That's me there.

When she hands it back, Maeve clicks Follow. You've just given me
an idea, Maeve says. Both of you. I don't know what we're doing, but if
we're still here tomorrow, I'll give you a shout. But now I'm just . . .
going to find a quiet corner . . . Maeve searches the wooden floor for a
wastepaper basket. If I could find a pen and paper, she says . . . Sorry
to be rude, I—

I'll sort ye! Jan says, riffling madly through her bag, finding liquid
eyeliner and a receipt.

Kathy doesn't say a word, knowing from experience that mental
clarity muddies easily.

When Jan hands over the eyeliner, she says: You keep that. It's pure
shite.

Maeve smiles as thanks.

I'm starving, Jan says, pulling Kathy by the elbow. The pair of them
shriek enough on the way out that the security guard clutches his radio.

. . .

The hall has nearly emptied out. Rhona and Leo are by the stage chatting with the mayor and a handful of people. Maeve is sitting alone,
far enough away to have tuned them out. It's twilight, and her tummy
is rumbling by the time she's stopped writing. Writing on her arm—
the receipt was too small and felt too provisional—she has written in
veiny script on her inner wrist, where she'd once seen her mother trace
a knife, to test herself for readiness. She didn't know that Maeve was
standing in the kitchen doorway, but she didn't drop it when Maeve
approached. Maeve took the knife from her mother's shaking hand
and began to cut onions and celery for soup, and to blame them for
their tears. She could take almost anything on, in the moment.

Ever since she'd learned to test a knife for sharpness in culinary school, Maeve wondered what might have happened had she prized the knife from her mother's grip in that moment and said something more decisive, less forgiving: *It's not baby's milk. You don't test it on your skin.*

. . .

While Rhona wraps up her conversations, Maeve takes Leo for a walking tour and he falls asleep in the pram. When they return to the town hall, Rhona tells Maeve that she should head back to the hotel, that the vice chancellor wants to have a word with her privately. Maeve offers to take Leo back and put him to bed, but Rhona wants to have him with her. She has the feeling she'll need him in her line of sight for whatever conversation is about to take place. So Maeve delightedly takes up an invite to the pub the students had DMed her. It's so instinctive to Maeve, Rhona thinks, to love strangers, and to be loved.

Rhona, her sleeping son, the vice chancellor, and a caretaker are the last people inside the hall.

What would a job description have to include to entice you, Rhona?

Professor Graham Coade is a stylish man, in a navy polo-neck and a dark blue suit, on the baggy side due to two stone he'd lost during lockdown and somehow kept off. His round eyes are unobscured by the reading glasses on the end of his nose. This has the effect of making whoever he's speaking to feel flood-lit.

You'd be a great addition to Ulster University.

That means a lot, Rhona says. Thank you.

Full professor, of course.

Rhona reconsiders his tone and looks askance. This isn't just flattery. I'm already full professor at Trinity, she says.

I am aware, Graham says. I am aware we're comparing apples with oranges.

He smiles. He hasn't yet delivered his pitch. First, he wants Rhona to feel that she can speak her pragmatic mind. Trinity is one hundredth on the world rankings to Ulster University's six hundredth.

Their conversation has to bridge that gap. It won't happen one step at a time. It needs a run up to it and then a leap.

With a furrowed brow, Rhona admits: I do have my frustrations, it's true. The faculty's behavioralist fetish, for example. But I've been re-arranging things so that grad students and colleagues have room to move into . . . the big-picture stuff, once they've outgrown their quant focus. Less doctrinaire, with more historical context. I'm proud of what we've done so far. And besides the *research* . . . my consultancy work is built into my time. And I have a standing invitation for the annual trimester at the Kennedy School, which I hoped to take up again once my son has . . . established his Irish accent! So, to be frank, what I've got at Trinity is a wonderful setup.

Graham knits his fingers and bows his head. It is indeed, he says to the floor. Harvard. Trinity. It's very comfortable, there among the an-cients. But is it a place where history is being made today? Keeping his head bowed, he directs his gaze up to Rhona. You can be cozy in a redbrick, or you can be at the cusp of historical change. He tucks his head back, as if to take in a very large map. If you hope to be at the forefront of a pivotal moment, to drive revolutionary change . . . you can't hope to do it from Trinity.

I wouldn't have the same resources, Graham. I'd lose so much momentum, retraining PhDs and postdocs . . . other members of staff—

You'd have *ample* resources.

What's ample, in your world? I know the salary's not commensu-rate, and that's not my only concern. But several of my grants are tied to various research groups.

Let me come at it another way. Graham looks around the empty hall before saying: On the quiet, Rhona . . . We've come into substan-tial funding for a new cross-university research unit on participatory democracy. It's across Queen's, the University of Glasgow, and our-selves, with support from NGOs and access to all the legal and judicial institutes. Plugged into the state apparatus, let's say. And I'd like to put you down for chairing it. You'd have a task force, there'd be sponsors in place when it comes time. This is exactly what you're intellectually invested in, he says. But if it's *only* in theory, a document held at arm's length, from another *country*, then people here? They won't buy it. Here's the way to bear it out. To ensure you have an impact. Graham glances at Leo now, twitching in his sleep. He could bring a Coleraine accent to Harvard later, he says. Lend the place some cosmopolitanism.

Rhona sighs, smiling. What about a visiting professorship? And Queen's might be easier—

Graham clicks his tongue and squints. The chair will be based here. And a year wouldn't do us, Rhona. I can't see anything less than five. To see it through. Otherwise, there's no glory! He smiles now, having given his final offer.

Rhona looks at her sleeping son. His hat has fallen behind his neck; one glimpse of his red hair and she thinks of the new university email account Pedro Da Rocha would have access to. Then again, if she's in the UK instead of the EU, he might be less likely to turn up in person. Before too long, he might need a visa.

I'll give it some thought? Rhona says in the doubtful tone of someone bidding on an antique they can't afford. Graham lifts the glasses off to rub the end of his nose.

Rhona punches him on the forearm. He looks confounded.

Sorry, she says. My sister always did that when my nose was itchy, because it means you're about to have a fight. It's to try and get it out of the way.

Oh, Graham says, in a high-pitched voice, entirely unsure of this dynamic. Does it work?

Rhona huffs. No.

Graham frowns and returns his glasses to his nose. I'll take four years back to the powers that be for discussion, he says. No guarantees. It's a permanent post, but . . .

The upward inflection of this accent is accusatory.

All of a sudden, Rhona is a bit flushed. He's making it sound like she's *asking* for the chance to spend years in a place without a single Tesla charger. And with a recent history of pipe bombs! To center her life in a city smaller than the Dublin suburb of Swords. What of all she's done to ensure that her son won't be an outsider? Won't be distrusted, as she'd been? Soon Leo will be entering the preoperational stage of development; he'll be starting to think at a symbolic level. Marching bands and bonfires and the red hand of Ulster are just some of the symbols he'd absorb, embedding in him a language she would never truly master.

Now Graham is bowing to Leo, in deep sleep. Rhona has the uncanny feeling that they're negotiating for his soul. He's saying that there comes a time when even the most promising of people are tempted to press cruise control and stay where they're comfortable, lower the stakes of their ambition.

He isn't bargaining. He's asking her to put her life where her intellect goes. To follow through. Yes, it would give her a sense of integrity. She'd truly be acting for the ends that she's declaring. But does she really need to prove that, after all? At such an expense? Her concern has always been for outcomes. For what's *effective*. But by that argument . . .

Leo is sleeping all the same, on new ground. Heavily storied ground, it is. Foreign symbols clapping in the sea breeze. It is another coastal town, so there's that familiarity. It faces not the Irish Sea, but the Atlantic Ocean. Against which there is no possible seawall.

Rising from somewhere in her breastbone, or her jawbone, a sharp electric whine sounds. Like someone attempting to tune in to a new frequency, but never locating it; never finding her. It is tinnitus, she will later find out. A square wave, five kilohertz. All of Leo's first words will be underscored by it. His first inflected sentences. No matter how many gadgets Jim sends her to quiet it, no matter how many MRIs she has to endure, that square wave refuses to break.

2.

It put Olwen in a good mood to have a project, as long as new materials weren't required. So a few days into her stay, when Nell requested a chalkboard or whiteboard for her lectures, Olwen mixed some black latex paint (left over from the rafters) with a bit of unsanded tile grout and painted a large rectangle on the back wall for a blackboard. One or the other of them used it daily until, one night, it was streaked with green chalk residue, and Olwen commented that it was a window onto the northern lights. Nell hasn't used it since. Olwen hasn't asked Nell when she is leaving. They are framed by night, at all hours.

Every morning, Nell sits in the study, reading. She waits for Olwen to get up. She lets Olwen be with herself in her own house at the beginning of each new day—at the end of the beginning. The first sound she hears is the kitchen tap running: Olwen's hangover being treated. Her palms unsticking from various windowsills after looking out each of them—for what, Nell attempts to discover. After some time, Olwen makes the expedition to the barn for a pair of eggs. By the time she arrives back in with them, it can no longer be called breakfast. Whatever thoughts had besieged her in the barn the night prior, she finds their embers and stokes them. By noon, when she comes back inside, Nell is working at the dining table, always. She meets Olwen's gaze, if ever it's directed at her. She is always listening. They have gone through various phases of silence and moans, talk and conversation.

What are we doing here? Nell asked one day as Olwen passed through the house with a glass badly concealed in her hand and a purposeful look she'd long cultivated.

Nell looked up from the couch, where she was winding gauze tightly around her big toe. The whole nail was a blood blister where she must have stubbed it.

Olwen leaned on the kitchen counter in a way that Nell recognized all too well. After a long pause, during which Olwen retrieved the answer to the question *What are we doing here?* from the murk of her mind, she said: I'm freeing myself from the restraints of conformity. I'm giving myself back to my nature.

Nell frowned at this. Thanks for reading my undergrad essays? she said. But if this is Brook Farm, then you're—

No. 'Twas the Philosophy of Peaceful Protest lecture you gave.

What?

On Henry David Thoreau and Martin Luther King and them fellas. Olwen smirked with pride that she'd pronounced all of that so well.

How did you manage to watch that lecture?

It's on YouTube, Olwen said. The sound quality's very poor, though. I wouldn't put up with it if I were you.

They're filming me! The punks.

Olwen swallowed a hiccup, horribly. And there's a student in the front row, she said, picking scabs off their scalp the whole time.

So much for IP. Nell made a noise of injury and rummaged the first aid kit for scissors.

But I got a kick out of it.

Well *good*, 'cause that's my audition for any tenure-track spitballing I may have going on. She tears the gauze.

"Avoid conformity and false consistency," Olwen hauls up from memory. "Cultivate self-reliance. No revelations, no external tuition, only personal intuition." Olwen didn't so much as glance at Nell to register her surprise—she gave herself all the kudos she deserved for her fabulous memory.

Doesn't *gin* count as false consistency? Nell said. But Olwen talked over her:

Apart from the civil disobedience bit, which was very *American*, it was worth the watch—

Don't tell me *I* inspired you to walk out of your life? Nell said loudly.

No, Olwen said.

If she'd been lying, Nell would have known.

Olwen placed her tumbler on the counter. I looked him up, the Walden fellow. He was just as bad—

Thoreau. Walden's the name of the woods he lived in—

His pond has the highest urine concentration of any pond in the state, Olwen said.

Nell tucked the end of the gauze into the dressing. Right, she said. It can't all have been his.

Olwen went to the freezer to pour herself a new measure of gin on top of the soggy rhubarb in the glass. She extended the glass to Nell for a cheers: To giving ourselves back to our nature.

. . .

Olwen's birthday began in the same way. The tap ran. The windowsills were frisked. Olwen made her way out to the barn. Rhona had arranged for the delivery of an over-the-top (but secondhand, on Nell and Maeve's insistence) telescope. Rhona told Nell to add a note reading "From your sisters," even though she wouldn't take their financial contributions. Nell contributed one euro fifty for the wrapping paper and stretched the note to read: "From your sisters, who look up to you." It lay on the dining table ready for Olwen's return from the barn that noon.

I made you birthday pancakes, I think? Nell said from the kitchen, holding a bowl full of stodge, when Olwen came in from the barn.

Olwen gave her a sweet, coy rub on the back as she passed. But her eye caught the package on the dining table and she stopped.

It could be English muffin batter, Nell said, or kind of . . . cake. It's got potatoes in it. It's called Boxty. Maeve sent a link. But I cut some steps outta the recipe, to keep it realistic. Will I fire up the pan and find out?

With her back to Nell, Olwen began unwrapping the telescope. Her rounded shoulders concealed her reaction. Nell melted a bit of vegan butter in the pan.

We figured . . . if you're finding close-up rocks a bit real, you might like some faraway rocks?

Olwen's shoulders started to tremble. It could just as easily have been laughter. So that it might become laughter, Nell said: Rhona wanted to buy you a week in rehab. But we sold her on the fact a telescope was equally passive-aggressive. To make you feel small in the scheme of things.

Nell could hear Olwen gasping for breath, crying. Nell unplugged the hot plate and put on her coat. Come on, let's get some fresh air. Can you pass me my crutches? I fancy a walk down the road before the rain comes, if you don't mind the risk of having to carry me home.

. . .

Nell had agreed to make every other dinner. One night, when it was Olwen's turn, it was nearly 9 p.m. before Olwen realized that she'd have to make something herself if she wanted to eat. She emptied two cans of three-bean chili into a pot, but she was too boozed to remember to stir it. At the table, while Nell waited for this bowl of piping-hot congealed goop to cool, she mentioned that she'd found an Intro to Mechanics textbook in one of the ottomans. Olwen dug into her chili, silently, heedlessly. She wouldn't feel the extent of the blisters on her palate until the next morning. Nell spooned up beans and let them plop back into the bowl.

And I saw there's more where this came from, she said. You're prepping.

I'm not prepping.

I live in America. I know a prepper when I see one. They have this whole—Nell drew a circle in the air toward Olwen with her spoon—*learned misanthropy* thing going on.

Olwen spread her arms into a crucifix pose. Search me for a gun.

I didn't say you're prepping *well*. You have a nail gun.

I'd be a better bicycle repair woman than a stripteaser, Olwen said with drunken fluency. Nell rolled her eyes at this seeming non sequitur.

I did a number on my own derailleur, Olwen said, and I was *quite impressed* with the satisfaction I got . . . from fixing that. And then Dan's nephew had a bucked wheel. Olwen twitched her nose like a rabbit, then scratched it. There was a pause while she thought about slapping Nell to get the fight out of the way . . . but she was losing track of her story. The bike wheel. That was trickier, she said, but I managed to get it nearly true. And your manno, I told him to take out life insurance just in case. But then . . . being a bicycle repairwoman who can't manage electric bikes is like being a piano tuner who can't manage baby grands.

What are you talking about, Olwen?

For making money, Nellie. I'll run out of money, in a few years anyways. So I'll fix bikes.

I don't get it, Nell said. If you're prepping, why aren't you doing it properly?

In Olwen's drunken swiping of her own puffy face—the hand slipping down off it too quickly, as if wiping off soapy water—she knew there was some answer to be given but couldn't quite . . . where was it? Something to do with Mum, was it? By the time the truth arrived to her tongue, Nell was gone. She'd filled her glass at the sink, watered the windowsill plants with it, then refilled it and taken it to the study. It was the sound of the door shutting that made Olwen realize she was alone.

• • •

This morning was bad, but at least it was different. Nell didn't wait for Olwen to get up. She filled her a mug of coffee from a cafetière at the dining table as soon as Olwen emerged from her room. It was eleven. Olwen's usual path to the barn wasn't clear. A chair at the dining table had been pulled out for her, obstructing the way. She sat down in it, directly across from Nell.

Are we nearly there yet? Nell asked.

My dearest, Olwen said, releasing her first words of the day like fracked gas. If you mean rock bottom, let me ask: What's below the rock?

The oat milk in Nell's coffee had separated, and she didn't have a spoon to stir it. The curdled milk looked like a coral reef. What's below rock bottom? Nell thought to herself, then made a little grunt of sudden recall. A west-of-Ireland cottage, she said—at least according to Wittgenstein. You know Wittgenstein?

Olwen steered her bloodshot eyes to Nell.

He spent a lot of time in the west, Nell went on. Way out on the Connemara coast. He found the countryside crazy beautiful. He couldn't get enough of the colors . . . but the *houses*? The "primitive" way people lived here? He thought he'd struck rock bottom in Poland, he said. But no.

Olwen shifted her head to take in the cottage, to come to its defense . . . but she didn't quite manage it, as the room had started throbbing toward her. I like it, she said sullenly. I'd been wanting to make it nicer . . .

Do you want to go, Nell said, to visit Wittgenstein's coast? "The last pool of darkness in Europe." The one place left where we might think.

You go, Olwen said. I'm not going to Galway.

Ah, of course—Jasper and the boys. No, okay, Nell said. Sure. I get it.

Olwen hoovered in air through her nose suddenly. I'm afraid you do. I'm afraid you always did, Nellie.

Is that it? You're afraid, and you hate having to hide it? Nell asked, and waited. Or hate it that you can't hide it? Again, she waited. Or . . . is it just all the information you have, you feel you *should* be afraid?

Ah, no.

No?

There's no *should*, Olwen said. There's no . . . reasoned distance. Between me and fear.

Nell made a gentle sound of recognition. Olwen lowered her head to nod, perhaps—Nell thought—but she didn't lift it up again. She couldn't.

So what are your options? Hole up here and never snap out of it, and live a lonely, quiet life in mental desperation, in the last pool of darkness? . . . Free from the pain of being in society, sure, and unburdened by having to show a brave face to young people. Or turn around and fight the dying of the light.

What light?

Because Olwen wasn't looking at her, Nell glanced over at Olwen's makeshift blackboard, but the chalk wasn't there to draw a big yellow moon. Instead, she reached across the table and tapped the crown of Olwen's head. This one.

Cute, Olwen said, and then she bit at the inner flesh of her cheek. But we're a faulty batch, my love.

So go stand near someone else! Nell said. Hog other people's light! Hog my light. Nell could see that her sister was chewing on her own tender flesh, breaking herself down. Be a freeloader, for a change! she said. You never had the chance, bringing us up. You never got a minute to coast. To cower a bit, make mistakes. Even before Mum and Dad died. I almost knew that back then. Now I see it clearly. You shouldn't have to moderate your disturbance for anyone, Ol. Or keep your pain to a palatable level. Is that what it was? With the boys?

The blood vessels on Olwen's face all pulsed brightly at once, and she shook. There was a nod. And the undergraduates, she managed to say. And Jasper. And Maeve.

Nell nodded. It's not easy.

And the woman down the hill who keeps bringing eggs.

Nell let out a little laugh, loath to let her away from the subject. I *thought* you didn't eat eggs.

Olwen shook her head. If I tell her I don't eat them, the innocent question *why* could follow; or maybe she's looked me up, and saw Earth Science; and then it can be as little as one move to the question *Do you have hope?* . . . And then you've to calibrate how long they have to listen, what they know, how much you're willing to poison them.

Olwen.

Once I knew the boys were grand, Olwen said. That they were okay, finally. That was a—she made a lift-off gesture with her hand— a recovery they'd made. Now they're off on a journey of their own. Like each of ye. And I just held my breath, Olwen said. Tried not to . . . She sucked in a quivery breath and held it.

You should be proud, Nell said. What you did for them.

When you think they're finally safe, and you think it's safe for you to look somewhere else? Olwen looked at Nell with a desperation Nell recognized but had never seen on her sister's face. There's nowhere to look. There's—

Yeah, Nell said, and added so that Olwen wouldn't have to: It's like algae. No light makes it through to the pond.

Olwen had to breathe with her mouth open because there wasn't enough strength in her lips to press them shut. There's a lot of suffering, you know? To be getting on with. One of her eyebrows cocked a bit in repugnance, as at her own reflection. And it could've been avoided.

Okay, Nell said. She watched Olwen, knowing she needed water. You can go dark for a bit, she said. Okay? You can feel gravity. But only for a while. Like . . . one of those really thin bands of time. Too brief to make it onto the most anal geological scale. You and I will know it happened. That part of you got no light at all. Nell saw that Olwen was watching the steam from her mug, seeming to shiver. How about you take a hot shower and we start today a little different?

If you didn't rob my hot water, Olwen said, every day . . .

A huff of laughter from Nell dispersed the coffee's steam. Sorry, Nell said. I miss water.

We haven't seen the sun in a week, to charge up.

Okay. Nell smiled. I won't shower today.

And tomorrow? Olwen's eyes widened a little.

Instead of looking out a window, Nell turned to the blackboard, with the smear of green chalk as mineral evidence of this meeting point.

Here's the thing, Ol . . . I don't know if I can wait it out. Your microscopic dark age. I have things I want to get back to. But maybe you don't need me? To wait it out?

Olwen looked suddenly addled. Me? What do *you* need? Maybe I need you to be needy.

I'm good, Nell said.

Are you?

Well, maybe *good* isn't a word I should throw around—

Why did you run off to America and never come back?

Nell lifted her chin so that her fringe fell open.

Because I couldn't stand being worried about, she finally said. All the concern—it was suffocating. I'd take a nap and there'd be a thermometer under my tongue. That social worker smile everywhere. I couldn't move for crashmats. I couldn't think. I couldn't be curious. Like, inconspicuously curious. Even just . . . being bi: I didn't want a family meeting about it! I just wanted to email home and be like: Cassandra gave me herpes. Lemme tell you: I am ridiculously grateful to you, and to Maeve. *And* Rhona. But just, *then*, I needed time *not* to be interpreted. It was more that I didn't need anything. And you kept giving.

Olwen took up her mug finally, trying not to feel guilty. The coffee looked to have paper shreds within it, like potting soil packed into a baby's mouth.

You don't even need the ground to be solid under your feet, Olwen said, with awe.

For a while, Nell considered this. She imagined iron filaments constantly dispersing and collecting wherever her next footfall would be.

You don't even need the ground to be solid under your feet, Olwen said again, with alarm.

Nell said: I am constantly confronting the fact that it is.

· · ·

That was this morning. Now, well after midnight, Nell can't get back to sleep after waking to pee. She's normally a good sleeper. If she ever struggles, it's usually because she needs to write something down. But here, it's not what's on her mind keeping her awake. It's something in her body. Not her feet. She tries to identify it, and the more she does, the more she feels physically ill at ease, like she's too far away from the spring whose mineral waters she relies on. Her absent books are a phantom limb. The Long Island Sound is where she cools off on a humid night. She can't just lie there.

Briefly, she turns on roaming on her phone to download a map. There are two lakes nearby, nine and ten kilometers away: one small, one big. Dan mentioned a lake that's half in the Republic, half in the North, but both of these lakes straddle the border. The smaller one will be warmer. Less likely to be rippled by anglers at dawn. Those roads will be quieter. Sunup is just after five, so the way will be bright, and she can hitchhike back along a busier route. As quietly as possible— knowing that Olwen's sleep is easily troubled, even though she's gone easy on the gin since their talk—Nell rolls her two suitcases out the back door to the inverter room, where she gets changed. She packs a waxed canvas messenger bag with an extra set of thermals, a book, crackers, a banana, cereal bars, and a flask she'll stuff with the fresh mint growing outside. She steals the kettle out to the barn to boil water.

Overhead is a quarter-moon, mostly obscured by clouds, but the faint glow is enough to light her way. It's a cool night with a tender breeze. There are no streetlights and almost no houses on the small road descending Sliabh Dúch, as far as she can tell. Sometimes she sees an opening that looks like a driveway; a chunk of black might be a water tank or a derelict shed or a trough. The bluish slate of a roof comes briefly visible, a brushmark that quickly dissolves into wet black paint beneath. A couple of times, the darkness becomes taller and the familiar air-freshener smell of pine betrays the towering shadows as forested fields. They explain why she can't see lights farther down the valley.

Descending, she slows herself with the crutches. Her footfall registers in the knees and hips with a slight delay, so she could easily tumble forward and keep tumbling through the darkness. There's so much overgrowth on the sides of the road and along the middle that it would be a soft landing. She hears the slosh of the mint tea in her flask, the rush of spring water too. Only one bird seems to be awake, despite its best efforts to keep the street rowdy. It bleats persistently, like the elderly scholar in the reading room who's always using her digital camera to photograph entire books, page by page. Would you like me to show you how to mute the shutter sound effect? Nell once whisperingly offered, but the woman replied at full volume: Then how will I know if I got it?

Once she'd confronted it, Nell found the sound reassuring.

This makes her think of a text Rhona'd sent a couple of weeks back, a sudden offer for Nell to housesit her soundproofed home "for a year . . . or two." Take a sabbatical, she'd said. Hatch a landmark philosophy. Nell had phoned her back—to turn the offer down, and to find out why Rhona was leaving her house empty—but after a few minutes their chat was cut short. "Beatriz just landed," Rhona said. "The way it goes now . . . When she calls, I drop everything but my baby."

The road turns back on itself now, so the bird solo is still within earshot. Nell is tempted to take her phone off airplane mode to locate herself, but she'll need the phone later, for a torch. There might be wetlands to navigate to reach the water. It had been a mistake to sell her waterproof headtorch in the yard sale. She'll be broke when she gets home, and she won't be able to rebuy those things. But Ron, the dean, has a lead on a 350-square-foot studio sublet for eleven hundred in New Haven—he's pressing her to move to New Haven so they can carpool to Quinnipiac. She's going to need to show her face at more admin meetings if she wants to succeed with this tenure track bid—he emailed her from his personal account—and she'd have time to do all that stuff if she could just roll out of bed to her Southern Connecticut classes . . . *Plus* the sublet doesn't require a deposit, because it belongs to a colleague taking a Fulbright for six months in Perugia. That's Umbria, land of truffle and Seneca the Younger. Remember the Stoics?

Nell wrote back: Notice how there's a Ron in Stronzo? As his friend, it's Nell's duty to derange Ron's managerial streak, just as it's Ron's duty to trick Nell into playing the game, into academic-capitalist compliance. Nell smiles in the dark, thinking of Olwen spouting her own transcendentalist lore: "Avoid conformity and false consistency." She laughs out loud, thinking of the kick Ron will get out of this story. She can't wait to get back.

The town can't be far now. Kiltyclogher. The last town south of the border. Home to the Spa Sláinte, home to Dan in his tight black T-shirt, with the way information bends as it gets near him. Nell grips her crutch handles. Her palms would be blistered now but for the bike tape wrapped around the handles—the thoughtfulness. Pushing through the second hour of the walk, Dan keeps stepping out of the dark toward her, and her thigh tickles where her fish knife ought to be holstered when making for water in the dead of night. She sees Dan leaning against electricity poles, emerging from the Rorschach splotches of trees.

· · ·

And, finally, Dan does step out of the dark toward her. She doesn't hear or see him coming, because her eyes are closed and her ears are submerged in the water. A large bird has been beating its wings since she got in—its wing flap heavy as a wet towel. Perhaps a great cormorant. All sounds are muted with her ears full of water, so the dominant sensation is one of feeling. The occasional nip of a small roach fish on her legs. Maybe there's pike too . . . maybe wild trout. Hardly salmon? Sleek tentacles of kelp. Is that the slightest trace of sensation in her feet? It's . . . It's hard to float in the fresh water. She has to kick gently to keep her legs buoyant. She makes lazy motions with her arms.

All at once, a spotlight scanning her body makes the cold tighten her chest. She tips upright and opens her eyes, scanning the lake's limestone banks for car headlights. First she looks to what the light is illuminating, then to its source.

Nell? Is that you?

It's Dan's voice. What she's seeing is the headlight of his quad bike, shaking as he tries to position it on its stand with the engine still running. He's wrestling off his leather jacket and his belt.

Shhhhhhh, she says. She can hear the wildlife fleeing from his shouts. Turn it off! she hisses in a stage whisper. She shields her eyes from the light, then—when she sees he's down to his T-shirt, socks, and boxers, about to pull a lifesaver dive into the water—she swims quickly toward him from a hundred meters across the lake. Her first feeling is anger at being disturbed. Then, suddenly worried—has Olwen done something awful?—she stops swimming and calls out: What is it? What's wrong?

Dan has his boots off by the time she's close enough for him to see that she doesn't need rescuing. The headlight illuminates the smoke of his breath.

Cut the engine!

Are you well?

I'm swimming!

Are you . . .

Dan! What are you doing here?

Looking for *you*, he says. Will I get in?

Is Olwen okay?

Olwen? She's out cycling the county searching for you.

What? Cut the engine, I can't hear you.

She phoned me up. She said you packed a bag and walked out in the middle of the night. I'm your search party.

Nell swims in a circle a couple of times, scanning the lake's perimeter, then looking up to a tiny patch of sky where stars are visible. She sees them as the torch beams of a distant search party, sure to give up before they're even close. Dan powers down his bike, and now she can hear him, panting.

I remembered you wanted to swim, he said. You don't seem like a runaway.

You should call her? Tell her go back to sleep. I'm fine. I'm just . . . finding my balance.

I will, yeah, Dan says. Jesus, he says. But he doesn't make a move for his phone. He's stunned.

Call her, will you? It's not safe, if she's out there cycling . . . still drunk.

I'll send her a text, Dan says. He goes about it. After, once his phone has darkened, the calm makes itself available again. The darkness swells. Nell is in two worlds, and she passes between them easily.

Dan wonders if she's reluctant to come out of the water while he's looking. Maybe she has nothing on. It's too dark to see her well, but he'll turn around just in case. Will I give you some privacy?

Am I making you uncomfortable? Nell asks.

No, he says quickly, before the question has time to confound him. No. Am I?

No.

His feet must have been in the water, as Nell can hear him lifting them out. She does a few turns in the water and sighs. It's really nice.

A momentary gap in the clouds reveals Dan standing among pale yellow water reeds that look windswept in the still night. The reeds swoon in the memory of the wind that shaped them. Now, there isn't so much disturbance as a thread being pulled in the water's silken surface.

Dan is putting back on his vintage biker's jacket. Nell sees the tan leather stripes on the arms, like motion lines as he moves. His good legs.

She sighs again, running her hands along the gooseflesh of her stomach, knowing that it's all over if he comes in. Something's wrong with her body, and maybe Rhona was right: it's environmental. Something in her surroundings. She'll be fine again once he leaves. Once she gets back home. She'll walk on air. She'll think deeply.

You should come in.

Dan is bent down to retrieve his jeans, and he catches her watching his legs. The clouds close over his expression, but Nell had seen enough of it to know it had been one of wariness.

It doesn't take much to be braver than me, Dan says, but still. You're ballsy, Dr. Flattery.

You can't know that. Nell paddles backward, a little farther out. You're going to have to come in, she says.

To be in that water? he says.

What? Is it haunted?

At first Dan doesn't respond. He doesn't know if he's only a fool to her . . . or if she likes him. Or if he actually is a fool. Or if he could be one for her, if that's what she wants.

Is it intoxicating? she asks. He doesn't reply. Come fill me in on the local history, she says.

Dan takes a deep breath, but he doesn't move to take off his jacket. He is scared of her power to make him forget who and where he is . . . even if he likes the fugue state. Lír, he announces. You know Lír, the god of the sea? (Nell has no response. For some reason swans come to mind, but she doesn't know why.) Lír's granddaughter was called Síonnan. Nowadays we call her the river Shannon. One night she came to a lake in these parts—just like you have. She went in for the Salmon of Knowledge. The great salmon was here, right enough, swimming around her. She need only have brushed a knuckle to its scales to have all the wisdom in the world. And like you, maybe, that's what she wanted. More than leisure and riches. More than marriage and children or an easy life? I'm only guessing. But the salmon angered at the sight of this maiden, and the fact of the knowledge she was after. So the salmon made the pool overflow until it drowned her. And that's how she became a river.

Nell looks at the dark shape where Dan is. Can't you swim?

I can swim, Dan says, just about. They invented the butterfly stroke by watching me.

She hears the soft slap of his leather jacket on the ground.

Nell says: I promise I won't let you drown.

You might, Dan says. And there's the plush of his shins moving through the shallow waters. You have me half turned to stone.

Nell feels something swim up her back, and she runs her hands around herself to check she isn't tangled in kelp. But she isn't. There is nothing latching her to this place. To this circling set of thoughts. I've got a condition, she says.

I know. With your feet. Do you need me to carry you?

No, Dan. (She can hear him halt, still in the shallows. Still with his feet on the ground.) Not that kind of condition. It's to do with after.

After what?

After we fuck. I'm going home.

Dan is quiet for a while. A car passes across the lake, and they are briefly outlined. Nell, I was a twat in the pub a few weeks ago, with your sister. I don't know what I was at. I was freaking out over you.

That's fine, Dan. I want you to freak out all over me. I want you to lift me over your head like in *Dirty Dancing*, but without letting me go until you've sung the whole soundtrack into my body.

Fuck.

Then we'll duet, Nell says.

Holy fuck.

I know you can reach the notes, Dan. You're Joni Mitchell.

Dan moves through the water, but pauses when she says:

But that's my condition: it's one time only. Then I'm going home to the States. And I don't want anything after. Nothing. Not even something casual. I'm incapable of casual. I find this . . . very all-consuming, mentally. And I used to come to resent it. But now I don't do it. And a lot of people would find this disappointing and frustrating, unacceptable even. And if that's the case, that's perfectly fine, Dan. I'm gunna swim away, far into the lake.

Dan breathes heavily. She can see him steam. She can see his hands on his hips, then crossed high on his chest.

Do you consent? she asks.

Dan clasps his hands behind his head now and turns like a cockerel weather vane. He feels like crying. Nell, I can't even look at you to say this. But I'll try to be honest, since you were. Even though you put that *Dirty Dancing* image in my head, and I swear to fuck—I'd consent to anything you asked me to. I'd say anything. But would I mean it? I wouldn't, Nell. He tucks his hands now into his armpits. He's shivering. It's like with selkies, he says. They shed their skin when they come on land . . . and we humans who fall in love with them, we hide their tails so they can't return to the water. I'd hide your tail, if I found it. Or worse, I'd try to put it on.

Nell can't be sure if her feet are touching the ground now, but she thinks they are. She thinks she can feel a new pressure. The chill air on her bare chest travels down her neck and sternum as she walks toward him. I'm not a myth, Dan. I'm just atoms and void, getting closer and getting farther apart.

Dan tries not to stare at the smooth rise of her breasts, dunes that can never be adequately taken in, close up or from far away. If it's just once, he thinks, he could never settle on how he'd want to see her. He's thirsty. She isn't flesh. If he clutches her, she'll pour through his fingers and collect back into perfect formation. If he lets her pass through him, she'll be gone before he got any map of her. Before he knows what story he'd been part of. She said so. She knows her mind. Though . . . that *is* what he'd committed to allowing for, that night in the pub: to accept the coming and going; not to seal himself off from journeying spirits. But what does it mean to commit to something? What's his commitment worth? His word? A nicotine patch has slipped off his shoulder. It's rafting toward her.

I'll drive a few laps of the lake, he says with his gaze fixed on his litter. Until you're ready. Then I'll take you home, so you can swim back across the Atlantic.

He plunges forward to grab the patch at the same moment as Nell dives under and twists like kelp. There is that chain-mail-heavy wing flap: a whooper swan, lifting up out of the water.

. . .

Olwen loitered around the quarry. She pushed her bicycle along the fenced perimeter, scoping out quarriers on smoke breaks. One of them eventually moseyed over, with the suspicion a prisoner reserves for the woman beckoning him at the gate.

Are you lost?

I've my eye on your shale.

I thought you had.

I'll tell you why, Olwen said. I need twenty-two tons in crushed shale or limestone, anything five to ten millimeters. And I won't complain if it's dusty.

You and half the country. He threw an unamused look at the horizon, as if the clouds stacked there were a stubborn bluff he had yet to cut into. His frown traveled the brute horizon to land upon her. Have I seen you in the Spa Sláinte?

That depends, Olwen said. Was I behaved?

You didn't let me win, he said.

Ah, that was ungenerous.

I'll tell you that much, he said.

Ah. Olwen nodded at the ground, as if they were standing over an open grave, summarizing the life of the departed. But come here to me for generosity, she said. Take a look at them coordinates. Through the wire fence, Olwen passed the man five hundred euro wrapped in a piece of paper with a map scrawled on it. There's the location of the trench I'd need the stones for. It's not far from the pub at all. (In fact, it was well outside their free delivery radius and when she'd phoned earlier she'd been told there was a four-month wait list.) Will five hundred do now? You can come with a triaxle, *whenever* it suits you. Friday, Saturday, Sunday. Any time. I'm not churchy.

This was how she'd come into the hoard of silvery stone out in the field behind her house. The quarrier had only been able to deliver it the very same night or not at all—some business to do with the trucks—which was very inconvenient for Olwen as she hadn't yet completed her excavation. So she built some shuttering above the site, a sort of wall built from bits of timber and plywood, supported by strong beams, to hold the stone—so she could just push it in, when the site was excavated. She'd told your man it was all for a trench, but when he saw the site marked out in the late-summer sun, he said: Is it a bunker you're building, or what?

It's a cash pit, Olwen had stated loudly, inviting no further interrogation.

She has hired a lovely yellow digger and is making quick work of the excavation, because the forecast is dry for six days running, which might not happen again till next summer. Tomorrow she'll start work on the drainage before pushing those stones for the base. In three days' time, the cement mixer is coming with the insulated concrete forms: two bundles of straights and two bundles of corners. She'll have two locals to help—folks she knows and trusts, who'd helped her do up the house. They'll set the forms and pour the foundations; they'll lay out and stack the blocks, then carry the base onto the cement foundation before it's solidified; they'll set the rebar, then stack the blocks on, setting the rebar along the way; they'll prepare and form the concrete lid. Dan might even show up to flex his triceps, revving his engine, the dosser.

The ridiculous mood Dan's in at the minute, Hosanna in the highest. He's an advertisement for what a mutually satisfactory hump can do to a person's life span. He'd driven Nell up to Donegal, to Killybegs marina. Nell had managed to book herself free passage on a seven-night transatlantic cruise ship in a shared four-berth cabin, in exchange for agreeing to deliver a series of pop philosophy lectures to the passengers. She opened her brief description of the course with a Bertrand Russell teaser: "Is consciousness a permanent part of the universe, giving hope of indefinite growth in wisdom, or is it a transitory accident on a small planet on which life must ultimately become impossible?" followed by: "Come to the Harmony Conference Centre on Deck 11 to find out!" Dan had seen her off, threatening to fulfill his longtime dream of doing a motorcycle tour of the States. Nell told him she'd only saddle up with him if he'd let Olwen watch the pub while he's gone. It would be good for Olwen to implicate herself in the community, she'd said, with Olwen in earshot. If she's going to keep doing what she's doing, Nell and Maeve have been insisting, she's going to need friends. And networks. They had a whole WhatsApp family forum on the matter:

I really like bicycle repairwoman for you, Maeve said.

Nell agreed: I can see you with a store selling polytunnel produce and rear derailleurs.

And a rack of recycled Lycra, Maeve added. Maybe even a shelf of crystals to keep Dan at bay!

In response, Nell sent some utterly confounding emojis, then finally added some English:

Ol: Be careful Maeve doesn't turn you into a tourist attraction. You wanna be stealth for the apocalypse.

To all this, Rhona replied with a photo of Leo on a balance bike, with a helmet on. She didn't risk lowering her historic approval rating by adding accompanying text.

It was all a bit much, so Olwen turned off her notifications. But she didn't turn off her phone. Which is a step to have taken.

Maeve phones less these days, now that she's busy with her team, developing their documentary series, *Shortbread & Food Nationalism*. She has leaned into her collaborative impulse, such that she knows ITV's every staff member, down to their affairs and their allergies. Good on her, Olwen thinks. Anything to muffle the biological clock. And Halim had surprisingly agreed to a photo, once Maeve told him her sisters feared he was an imaginary friend. Nell seemed to be relieved by that more than Olwen had been. But however one gets one's relief.

This morning—well, it's lunchtime, but she's been drinking less and getting up with greater purpose, so it's only fair to call it morning— Olwen is in her mini-digger, moving mountains. She's doubling down on the earth, is what she's doing. On being here. She's following through, working to free herself of the implication of her project by just forging ahead with it. As mindlessly as is possible, at this hour. She has to admit to feeling a bit of excitement at the sheer, shameless power of a diesel engine. Revving it, up on her open-air throne, joysticks in hand, she glories in its destructive clout—its impunity, like a dumb meteorite. She scoops up the earth and dumps it into two skips: one for the topsoil, which has been removed across the whole pit, and another for the subsoil. The whole width isn't excavated evenly, as she wants to see how deep the subsoil goes, and it's handy to have an incline into the pit for the digger to travel, so that one end is much deeper than the other. She knows the soil well; she knows there's no risk of it caving in. This part of the construction process is the most beautiful and the most tragic: the raw materials are pure and reassuring in a way that cannot be replicated and won't be restored for eons. She feels about cement the way she feels about a painting of a sunset: It's cheesy and it's basic. Even though the Romans used it and their buildings are still standing. As she's thinking this, a dental chink hits the bucket of the digger. Olwen raises the arm out of the way and hops out to inspect the situation. She takes a piece of rebar to push into the soil around the deepest excavation, to see if it's a lone rock or if they're down to the parent material.

She is feeding the metal bar into the ground when a little click announces that one of the long sticks supporting the shuttering holding back the stones up above has been knocked out of place and—it happens in a single second—the shutter collapses and crushed stone pours into the pit like frigid water, burying her up to her chest.

Olwen tries to gasp at the fact of it, as at something impressive—an enthusiastic physics demonstration?—but her lower ribs won't accommodate the gasp, and her belly has no appetite for it either. Her stone-corseted bosom heaves so that the shale around her shoulders shifts and slides, her breasts seeming buoyant. Her cleavage is gray with stone. And still: there is a higher pack of it in front of her, ready to slip down—to sink her up to her neck—if she so much as twists to extract herself. So she goes completely still, ossifies, inside the chalk dust vaunting all around. Instead, a rush of activity inside her: a pulsing in her body . . . a rapid scramble through her memory, that catchment basin of regrets . . . though she realizes soon that nothing feels broken or dislocated. It was incredible, really, the smack of it. The weight. What did it? The long timbers hadn't snapped. She hadn't heard any snapping. Only a little *tick*. But nothing in her structure was so perilously balanced that a small creature could disturb it. She listens for one such thing—for any presence—but all she can hear is a mean robin having an entitled conversation with itself in the warm air above, on a sally tree or an alder branch, broadcasting its radio play, and now she is obliged to hear it, and must try to act devout, to lend it meaning.

What's so special about you? she finds herself asking, belligerent.

She is still breathing. The whole thing is interesting. But stupid also.

She looks up to the bank of the pit and feels herself put in Nellie's position—the place where Olwen had put her, back in the day, when she'd thrown her over the side, trying to prepare her for the certainty of flash flooding. But Nell had a bag full of books on her back. She was as prepared as she would ever be. Is Olwen so ready?

Nell would like this. Well, she'd see the profanity in it, anyways.

The treachery of rock! Our elders. The opulence of it. Ah! Look! Stones! Stones! She really wants to laugh. She *wants* to. Equally, though, she has the equal and opposite impetus: She is sober. She had done everything right and soberly. She had even uprooted the wild rhubarb bush. She was planning to throw it in the compost, just to avoid temptation. Jesus. Was that a hare . . . with a wand of it in its mouth? What?

Hello? Olwen asks. Her voice isn't her own. It has no boom to it. She tries again. Hello?

She tries for a good while.

As the afternoon turns into happy hour. Happy hour somewhere.

Oh, she says, with a bit of a croak. She wonders if it'll be a hot night or a cold one. If the stones might contract, and what way that cookie will crumble. Ah, here. Rhona would take one look at her and have a solution. Where's the pen and paper to do the maths? Where's the wall painted with blackboard talc, with that clay mineral upon which everything centers and settles and resolves? What would Maeve prepare for a last meal while Olwen's working out the equations?

If she doesn't, she can last the three days, surely, until the cement delivery crew turns up. Those nice people she knows, who wouldn't jilt her. Even if she misses their calls and doesn't open the gate or send confirming texts. It's dark already and the sunrise will come in a wink. In this lovely weather, it will look diabolic. It will look kitsch. She closes her eyes to it, and thinks of sponge.

It is very early in the sky's pinkening when she realizes that her phone is not lost in the rubble—that she'd left it resting on the digger. She'd charged it recently. It's not on airplane mode. And there you have it. It's up there and she's down here, the way the techno-optimists would have it. Just as well. Probably. Go on. If it was in her pocket, there'd be incalculable risk in trying to retrieve it. It would be a dilemma. It would kill an hour, though. To *think* about it as an option. The Russian roulette of it. But she wasn't Russian—

Not Russian, she thinks, but Norwegian. Wait. What on Earth was that woman's name? Jesus Christ. The beautiful woman who leads you to victory. Not Karen.

Siri! Siri!

There is a bleep, maybe. Olwen has become the sheep, all tangled up in briar, out of her mind with loneliness.

Siri! Call . . . Who?

. . . Feidhlim.

There is no sound. Barely a glow in the scant twilight. Olwen thinks of the spelling of Feidhlim's name, and cries at it. Such a name was beyond Siri. She'll have to find the breath to try again—to go for Dan this time, and then to put up with him telling the story for the rest of his life, taking a picture for his pub's wall of fame.

But then there's a sound. A voice. Ah, it could be all in her head. But there does seem to be a glow over that way, the light of someone else. Of someone who knows her.

Sheila?

Sheila . . . I can't hear you, she does her best to shout. Sheila. If you can hear me . . . can you come here? Sheila?

She swallows—and maybe the glow was only wishful thinking, because she cannot see a thing.

As the fella says, Sheila . . . I'm in a spot of bother—

Acknowledgments

With huge thanks to . . .

My publishing family: Bill Clegg, Calvert Morgan, Rebecca Saletan, Catalina Trigo, Claire McGinnis, Kitanna Hiromasa, Michelle Waters, Lauren Peters-Collaer (for the boss cover), Alexis Farabaugh, Nicole Celli, Andrea Monagle, Juliet Mabey, Anna Webber, Marion Duvert, Seren Adams, and everyone else at Riverhead and Oneworld, at the Clegg Agency, United Agents, and WME. You're a hell of a clan. Bill, you encouraged me to write this when I didn't think I could. Cal, you prompted Nell's revelation about the quality of care by being such an outstanding exemplar. Cal, Juliet, Becky: You made it *inestimably* better. What an utter privilege to work with you.

Friends and writers who supported this book and my last (with unforgivable omissions): Hernan Diaz, Rumaan Alam, Joseph O'Neill, David Fleming, Mary Cregan, Sarah Perry, Kevin Barry, Chris O'Dowd, John Crowley, Tessa Ross, Anthony Doerr, Bette Adriaanse, James Shapiro, Doireann Ní Ghríofa, Eoin McNamee, Roddy Doyle, Fatima Bhutto, Jan Carson, Max Porter, Olivia Sudjic, Rick O'Shea, Colin Barrett, David Nicholls, Elnathan John, Patrick deWitt, Kimberly King Parsons, Meakin Armstrong, Danielle McLaughlin, A. L. Kennedy, Sebastian Barry, Ann Marie Wilson, Laura Bertens, Crispin Simon, Mona Awad, Diane Cook, Ian Baxter-Crawford, Stephen Baxter-Crawford, Bri Lee.

Experts who chimed in: Christopher Jackson, Fintan O'Toole, Daniela Vicherat Mattar, John Hayes, David Farrell, Kai Hebbel, Ed Frettingham, Louise Kennedy, and Helen Gordon, whose *Notes from Deep Time* was an inspiration.

I wrote part of this novel at the Yaddo artists' retreat, where I was (figuratively) defibrillated by fellow artists: Marcia Walker, Caroline Van Hemert, Jeff Hiller, Molly Zuckerman-Hartung, Alexis Okeowo, Miriam Horn, Jonathan Santlofer, Lisa Warren, Dona Ann McAdams, Tirtza Even (and her son, Nino). I did the copyedits a couple of years later while at MacDowell, flooded with luck and gratitude. At some point in between, I spent a fortnight as writer-in-residence at Gladstone's Library in Wales, where I communed with books that fortified this one. And a few days at The River Mill were precious. I wrote the last four pages of *The Alternatives* in an ice cream shop in Magherafelt (once the library'd shut) the day after an event at Seamus Heaney HomePlace. Something to be said for a mint-chocolate chip.

The writers, booksellers, festival folk, librarians, and readers who supported my previous novels: you made this one possible. *Industry* is a misnomer when it comes to books. In my experience, the book world is made up of people: some of the very best ones.

My sisters! and brothers and parents: I'm so grateful for your love, and for your brilliance.

With thanks to the Bertrand Russell Peace Foundation Ltd. for permission to quote Russell, and to Tony Simpson for the lovely exchange. Likewise, to Martina at the Leitrim Tourist Office.

Thanks to the Arts Council of Ireland for a Literature Bursary Award for this novel. In 2020 and 2021, it made *all* the difference. I'm grateful also for the Writing Fellowship at Trinity College Dublin, and to the many inspiring students and colleagues I got to work with there.

Paul Behrens: wonder, champion, anomaly, reformist, high bar in my life, bit of all right.